THE LOVERS OF
ALGERIA

Anouar Benmalek

THE LOVERS OF ALGERIA

Translated from the French by
Joanna Kilmartin

THE HARVILL PRESS
LONDON

First published in France by Éditions Calmann-Lévy, Paris
with the title *Les Amants Désunis* in 1998

First published in 2001 by
The Harvill Press
2 Aztec Row, Berners Road
London N1 0PW

www.harvill.com

1 3 5 7 9 8 6 4 2

The publishers would like to express their gratitude to
Dr Laïla Ibnlfassi of London Guildhall University for her
help with the translation of the Arabic or Algerian terms
to be found in the glossary at the end of this book

A CIP catalogue for this book is
available from the British Library

This book is supported by the French Ministry for Foreign Affairs,
as part of the Burgess programme headed for the French Embassy
in London by the Institut Français du Royaume

ÍÍ institut français

ISBN 1 86046 868 3

Designed and typeset in Minion by Libanus Press, Marlborough
Printed and bound by Butler and Tanner Ltd
at Selwood Printing, Burgess Hill

To my maternal grandmother, Marcelle Wagneres, a circus artist, who was driven by the blows and hazards of fortune from her native canton of Vaud, in Switzerland, to the turbulent shores of North Africa.

To my mother who, throughout her life, has had to wrestle with exile, her own first of all, then, more recently, that of her children.

To Nora, Nejma and Samy.

To all those in Algeria who no longer have a voice.

There are not five or six wonders of the world, but one alone: love.
JACQUES PREVERT

PROLOGUE

Aurès, 1955

The day is hot, and yet, in the bus, everybody is shivering with fear. From time to time, a nervous cough, a resigned sigh, breaks the silence. Outside, spring is exploding in splendour. The yellow of mimosa is everywhere. A myriad poppies and wild roses dot the hillsides, lending an air of gaiety to the austere landscape beyond the vehicle's dusty windows. But no-one has the heart to notice. The passengers have just caught sight of the massive roadblock ahead. "Good God, there's even a chopper!" someone exclaims. A long-bodied, twin-rotor helicopter is surrounded by army lorries, jeeps and large groups of soldiers, a mixture of infantry and Red Berets. Sentries stand, rifles cocked, behind walls of sandbags. Anna shrugs and tightens her grip on her bag. It contains all the essential documents. In the eyes of the world, whether people like it or not, the man sitting on her right is now her husband. To Arabs and French alike she would be seen, at best, as a naïve girl who has taken leave of her senses; at worst, as a slut who has managed to find a husband, but at what price! She repeats the word husband to herself, comparing it to lover, unable to decide which she prefers. She would like to have talked it over with Rina. Or with her real mother. Both are dead and gone, long since reduced to small piles of bones . . . Her companion, dark-skinned, moustached, "a typical Arab", as she sometimes tells him, looks at her fondly. He guesses that she is thinking of their official papers from the town hall, and forces himself to smile at her. Yet again, he pats the inside pocket of his jacket with the flat of his hand. His fingers crack with anger. Yet again, he curses himself for having agreed to carry this damned letter. What's more, he doesn't even know whom it's for: they had told him that somebody would introduce himself once they arrived

1

at his mother's house. The roadblock is coming within earshot. He steels himself to mask a sudden onset of panic, for he has just caught sight of the figure lurking on the fringe of the first group of soldiers, slightly stooped, the head shrouded in the loathsome black hood of an informer . . .

The previous day had been horrendous. The rickety Algiers bus had had to stop overnight in the last Arab village before the mountain *douars.*[*] A major offensive was in progress a few kilometres away, and from what they could gather there had been heavy losses on both sides. The road was choked by half-tracks and GMC lorries carrying, aloft, soldiers on the alert, tense, heavily laden, their faces lined with fatigue. T6s and P28s flew over the Arab village, launching rockets and bombs at the crests barring the horizon. The army herded the terrified villagers on to the main square, outside the mosque. Beside himself with fury, a sergeant screamed at the bus passengers, who didn't seem to think that the assembly order applied to them. When he noticed a woman aged about 30 or 35, modestly attired, staring at him apprehensively, the soldier took her for a compatriot. Giving her a conspiratorial wink, he growled that, naturally, the order didn't apply to the French and she could stay on the bus. As he left his seat, Nassreddine discreetly patted his wife's hand. This raised her spirits. But her anxiety returned when she saw him roughly handled by an infantryman. Dry-mouthed, she watched as, one by one, the passengers dismounted, helped along by an occasional kick. The interminable waiting had begun.

Her husband Nassreddine had insisted on leaving their two children with his mother. With all the formalities to be completed in Algiers before they could regularize their situation, it was better not to drag the kids along. He had flashed his infectious grin: "Can you see us turning up at the town hall and asking some civil servant to marry us with our two children as witnesses! It wouldn't exactly ensure us a warm welcome . . ." He had kissed her tenderly. "You'll see, Anna, everything will be fine. My mother can certainly be temperamental, as you well know, but she is a person you can trust."

* A Glossary of Arab or Algerian terms appears on p.279

It was true that their visit to Nassreddine's mother had turned out well in the end. It was equally true that she had dreaded the meeting with her mother-in-law in that remote, impoverished *douar* perched on a hostile outcrop of rock. Nassreddine had described his mother to her as a matriarch who, since her husband's death, had run what remained of the family farm with a rod of iron. A matriarch who could hold her own with any man in the district, resorting if need be to a vocabulary so crude that Nassreddine would blush with embarrassment lest some gnarled peasant should complain, sobbing with rage, that she had called him "a useless billy-goat with the balls of a frog!"

Nassreddine's mother had received them coolly. She was not pleased to meet her grandchildren for the first time several years after their birth. Matters were not improved by Nassreddine's sheepish, confused explanations. The irascible old lady observed sourly that the *gaouria* must possess a great many charms if she could prevent her poor boy from visiting his decrepit old mother for so long. Nassreddine tried to calm his mother down, doing his best not to laugh at Anna's anxious face. The grumbling lasted no more than a day, for the grandmother was completely disarmed by the twins, a boy and girl as dissimilar as cat and dog, whose sole intention was to climb on her back, or to strip her nearly bare by tugging at her skirts. Zehra declared that the boisterous, short-legged boy took after his grandfather, her husband, while she and the little girl, with her almond-shaped eyes perpetually widened in wonder, were as alike as two drops of water. From then on, the grand-mother treated her daughter-in-law with gruff good humour. Anna, in her heart of hearts, was impressed by the bearing and fortitude of this solitary woman well into her fifties, with her frail body and tattooed face, fiercely independent, who rose before dawn, doing everything from the ploughing to the marketing, standing up to the men, never once bewailing her fate (one or two ripe curses apart), passing from gaiety to anger like mountain weather, who was essentially free, despite her penury, despite the war.

At first, communication was far from easy, the Arabic of Algiers which Anna had acquired proving of little use in this part of the Aurès. But Zehra, who spoke nothing but her native *Chaouï*, rapidly learnt to make herself understood by gesturing forcefully in dumb-show. At a pinch, she would call on her son to translate, only to berate him like a small boy if he stumbled over a word: "Bah, runt of my litter! Are you not ashamed to join in women's chatter? Out with you, be off, see if the sheep will talk to you!" At first, she nicknamed Anna the *Chetaha*, the Dancer, a far from flattering term in her vocabulary. Then, little by little, grudgingly accepting that her son's wife had her good points, opted instead for the *Meddaha de Santa Aissa*, Troubadour to Our Lord Jesus Christ. Notwithstanding Nassreddine's amused explanations of the difference between a circus artiste who performs beneath a great tent known as a big top, and a *meddah* who journeys from market to market recounting, amid the fruit and vegetables, the stories and legends of olden times, she stuck to her guns. Both were applauded by people sitting in a circle; whether on the ground or on chairs, what difference did it make?

A few days later, as the two women were squatting on sheepskins in the little courtyard, peaceably sipping the bitterest of green teas, Zehra confessed to being curious about what went on beneath the famous big top. It took Anna some time to understand her mother-in-law's question. In the end, she called her husband to the rescue. The translation effected, the old lady, blushing, banished Nassreddine outside. He tiptoed back to watch the scene: the twins chasing one another round the courtyard, squawking like excited chickens and Anna, in the middle, dressed in an Aurésian robe gay with yellow and ochre fringes, juggling with one, two, three, four, five, six potatoes. At first, her mother-in-law adopted the bored expression of somebody who has seen it all before. But with the fifth potato (especially as this daughter-in-law of hers was also trying out a few dance steps . . .), Zehra came to life, screwing up her eyes in disbelief. Nassreddine saw astonishment, then wonder, rejuvenate the worn features of this woman who had given him life. This woman who was grunting hoarsely: "Well, look at you, my *meddaha*! Well, well! Where did that son of mine dig you up? Look at her jump, the hussy! May God protect her!" Anna, her skirts hitched up to her waist, was giving a veritable performance, leaping, whirling, turning cartwheels. Flushed with pride, she threw herself into it heart and soul for the sake of this crotchety, highland-bred woman who had never seen a circus in her life, and probably never would. "Stop, stop, Anna! You're a *mahboula*, a madwoman!", screeched her mother-in-law, drumming on a saucepan

4

with her hands. Crouched behind the door, Nassreddine contemplated the four people he loved most in the world, moved to the core of his being. Although unaccustomed to receiving gifts, he had the impression, beneath these harsh, unforgiving Aurésian skies, of being taken back 20 years, to the time when the entire neighbourhood would praise and curse the beauty, the virtue, the fiery temperament of this wonderful mother of his. A thistle with a rose at its heart, his father would grumble. Ah, his poor father, so gentle and irresolute, who had passed on to him all his weakness and formidable capacity for indecision . . . And Aldjia, almost forgotten, his second mother, his father's first wife, who had died when he was still a little boy! Her features had dimmed, but his memory of her, indelible, tender, survived in the form of a bouquet of scents: of barley galettes fresh from the griddle, fat pieces of which she would secretly break off for him, burning hot and filled with crushed tomatoes and pimentos – which, to this day, had the power to whet his appetite – and of the orange-flower water which she knew how to distil better than anybody in the village, a more delicate scent, whose capricious, almost feminine texture had inexplicably troubled the lad he was then . . . A fierce, bitter nostalgia abruptly overcame him at the thought of this life which flashes by so fast, too fast, while doling out parsimonious moments of happiness, grist to this damnable mill in its fabrication of its sorrows.

As he was to explain to his wife when they left the town hall after some civil servant, surly in the extreme and barely able to conceal his contempt for this "abnormal" couple, had married them: that scene had reconciled him to himself, to his life, to his humiliated country, had made amends for the disdain of the colonists, the cruelty of their soldiers, the arrogance and brutality of the *maquisards*, his own spinelessness . . . They emerged on to the Place du Gouvernement, where the equestrian statue of the Duc d'Orléans turns its iron backside on the Djemaa Djedid mosque. At the town hall, Anna had overheard an employee say to a colleague, in a whisper, but loud enough to ensure that she heard every word: "She must fancy being fucked by wogs . . ." She said nothing to Nassreddine, trying to master her feelings on her own, not wanting to spoil his pleasure in the day. But all the same, Nassreddine guessed that something had upset her. Awkwardly, he put an arm round her shoulders, saying under his breath that he loved her, loved her, loved her. Then they leant on the balustrade along the front. For a long while, they gazed at the sea together, hand in hand, feeling their rings touch, trying to console one another, until Anna kissed him on the cheek, saying in a voice that trembled slightly: "Come, my dear poet, it's high time that we went home to the kids. They must be driving your mother crazy . . ."

Now they are almost at the barrier, close enough to see the chains strung taut across the road. Infantrymen and paratroopers, some of them at the ready, rifles cocked, behind their half-tracks, watch with displeasure as the vehicle grinds to a halt with loud groans from its worn axles. Anna, her stomach knotted in an onrush of anxiety, sees that her husband is doubled up, as if needing to be sick. Even though he has turned away from her, towards the window, she has caught sight of the gleam of sweat on the Algerian's tense face.

A heady scent rises from the landscape which, in all its glory, is utterly contemptuous of soldiers, of their quarry, to the sordid ugliness of their combined fear and rage. An occasional breeze wafts over the roadblock, like drifts of perfumed mist with complex associations of wisteria, lavender and wild roses.

The passengers are lined up, hands on head. Anna watches, white-faced, standing a little apart. A soldier examines her Swiss passport and her brand-new family dossier from the town hall. He spits on the ground in disgust: "Madame, you are a traitor to your race!" At that moment, Anna hates everybody: she hates these military men with blood on their hands and a crushing contempt for anyone who doesn't bear arms; she hates these cringing Arabs literally shaking with fear; she hates her husband, who can only stand there, his hands on his head like the rest, and allow her to be insulted. To calm herself ("My God, my God, what am I doing in this damned country?"), she closes her eyes and, under her breath, calls on her children, her beloved children . . . The hooded man limps forward, breathing loudly behind the cloth. Evidently, each step is an effort. Nassreddine guesses that he has been beaten up. The informer has just pointed a finger at two people, a man of about 40 dressed in a white *gandoura* and *cheche*, and a terrified adolescent who is sobbing like a child. Two Red Berets drag them roughly out of the line and, with a kick in the buttocks, direct them to one of the lorries. The man, who has the air of a rich cattle-dealer with his stout walking-stick, turns round to protest. A paratrooper grabs the stick and hits him across the face. There is an unmistakable sound of breaking bone. Blood spurts out almost immediately, spotting the immaculate *gandoura*. The man, grim-faced, pulls out a large checked handkerchief, calmly wipes his face, then climbs of his own accord into the lorry indicated by the soldiers. Whimpering, the adolescent follows him docile as a puppy.

The informer is now within a few steps of Nassreddine. The sergeant in charge of the checkpoint waits, visibly impatient, for him to pick out someone else. As if regretfully, the hunched figure points a finger at the man next in line to Nassreddine. The toothless peasant, half paralysed by stupefaction and terror, sees the Red Beret with the walking-stick approach and makes a run for the lorry.

Now the hooded man is staring at Nassreddine. Something in his attitude has changed. Nassreddine feels his tongue grow wooden and scrape against his palate like a foreign object in his mouth. He sees the dark eye-holes light up as the informer abruptly raises his head then quickly turns away. It is as though Nassreddine's heart had been seized in flight by the talons of an animal: he knows those eyes, despite not having seen them for years! Astounded, he hears himself say: "Is it you, Hadj Slimane?"

Eagerly, the sergeant grunts: "How about him?" The informer shakes his head and moves on swiftly to the next man. The sergeant grabs him by the sleeve, barking: "Don't play games with me, you stinking jackal's arse, why didn't you point out that man there? One of yours, is he?"

So they arrest him. At that moment, in spite of the blows, he doesn't have time to feel real fear because his wife is screaming at the top of her voice: "Stop it, he's my husband, it's our wedding day, stop it!" And the louder her screams, the greater the soldiers' pleasure in beating him. One, indeed, giggles: "Talk about a bitch on heat. That wog must have one hell of a prick!"

A woman, yelping and sobbing: "Leave him alone, he's done nothing wrong, I tell you!", earning herself a slap in the face when she adds: "Bunch of thugs, stop hitting him like that, you're hurting him!" Such is his last image of his wife before the flap of the tarpaulin on the Dodge comes down.

Fear, true fear, doesn't come at once. True, the kicks have left their mark, and he seats himself gingerly on the wooden bench in the lorry. But he is too dazed to take in the fact that he is in the hands of an active French army commando, that he has been mistaken for a genuine FLN *moudjahid*. The soldiers have found the letter, but surely a piece of paper wasn't enough! He would explain, they were certain to understand! He has managed, throughout this stage of the war, to keep his involvement to the minimum, thinking only of his wife, of his children ("my dear little ones"), and how best to provide for them. Like many Algerians, he would have liked to see rather more justice in his country as well as rather more dignity and, why not, independence, should that turn out to be the only means of achieving the one and the other. But he considered himself too ordinary, too timid, too much of a coward, in fact, to put it bluntly, to take to the hills and bear arms. And then, to set explosives, to kill and be killed or die from hunger and cold on the run in the *djebels*, he knew quite well he could never face that. True, he has done the "brothers" small favours from time to time, but only in order to avoid reprisals, that's all. A form of insurance, not too risky, in case the nationalists should win the war. Call it opportunism, but how else was one to survive in this country of madmen? Sometimes, Anna would tease him: "The *gomina* for your hair worries you more than the state of the world." And he would merely whisper, pushing her gently towards the bed: "Untrue, star of my dreams, my *gomina* is the least of my concerns, as you have reason to know . . ."

The torture begins as soon as they arrive at the barracks. The officers are thrilled to think that they are holding an important member of the local FLN network. Imagine: he even has a European wife! They want to know everything: leaders' names, the regional network of *katibas*, his own role in it all . . . Over and over again, the sad-faced sergeant who whips him day in day out with a bull's pizzle says tenderly: "You'll talk sooner or later, my fancy wog. So why not now? What will it gain you, my little cock-sparrow, to wait till you're completely broken?"

That evening, they bring his uncle to see him, Hadj Slimane. All his life, he has heard this uncle who used to dandle him on his knee inveigh against the humiliations of French colonisation. The old boy had long worked for the Front, although this subject was never mentioned at

8

home. Wordlessly, he contemplates his nephew, bloodstained, choked by mucus, saliva and the pain of flesh reduced to raw, swollen meat. He suppresses a sob: "You are my beloved sister's child, you are my own flesh and blood and I love you like a son. And yet I'm powerless to help you. I can't even give you good advice. You can see the state I'm in for yourself. Nowadays, I'm so terrified of being tortured again that I'm lower than a hyena ..." Dully, his uncle mutters that he had held out for two long weeks but had finally yielded: "Not even God in all His Glory could have withstood such pain." His mother's brother adds with a tired smile that he is confined to barracks from now on: "you see, my son, at the roadblock, you revealed my identity to one and all. My brothers in the partisans" (much to Nassreddine's surprise, he pronounces the word "brothers" with something like warmth) "wouldn't hesitate to kidnap me and slit my throat!"

That day, rather than be like his uncle, poor Nassreddine refuses to talk. In the poky recess which serves as a cell, he weighs up the pros and cons. To talk would be so easy, so tempting, and it would earn him a moment's respite from this hell. The army had lost many men in the region. They were angry, and if he told them nothing they would end up by killing him without even troubling to find some excuse to cover up his murder. This place was a long way from civilisation ... The *moudjahidine*, on the other hand, would disembowel him at the slightest hint of disloyalty. At the *douar*, he had heard of a peasant from a nearby *mechta* who was kidnapped on suspicion of spying for the French; when found, his body was horribly mutilated: his penis impaled on a reed and the whole inserted into the traitor's anus. The partisans had then forced his wife and children to spit on the corpse. He thinks of his own wife and children, buttressing his feeble powers of resistance by telling himself that it would be intolerable for them to have an informer as husband and father. Ah! His wife, at once gentle and fierce, who dyes her hair with henna to please him, who makes him weep with laughter when she sings in Arabic, with her comical Swiss accent, the song he has taught her: "*Assafi ala madina fi Diar el Andalous*" "Great is my longing for our past in Andalusia", and who, when he goes too far, throws a pan of chick-peas at his head. "Andalusian, Andalusian, don't ruin such looks as I have left," (here he beats a retreat, catching her round the waist, stroking

9

her long black hair and kissing the nape of her neck) "my mother suffered torments to make me a passable face!" As he endeavours to tame the grief and terror hammering in his breast like a gigantic second heart, he relives in his mind, down to the last detail, a farcical episode at the start of their life together, after Anna left the circus to live with him, when they had bought a flock of cocks and hens on credit. At first sight, to people like them who hadn't a penny in the world and were completely ignorant about chickens, the prospects seemed excellent. But they had no sooner rented a stall in an Algiers market than it became apparent that the flock was diseased. So he and Anna had had the idea of waxing the feathers and painting the cockscombs bright red, thus restoring their moribund flock to its former glory. Several buyers were fooled. The first time, Anna had laughed so uproariously that the customer had almost rumbled them. Passionately, desperately, with every claw in his soul, Nassreddine clings to the memory of that laugh.

So they use electricity on him, then the bottle up the anus, then the rag soaked in urine and disinfectant. Everything seems to proceed according to some well-established, rather tedious routine, so much so that there is one functionary for the whip, another for the electricity and a specialist for the bath and the rag: the whole purpose being to avoid the cardinal blunder of killing the prisoner before he sings!

On the third day, inevitably, Nassreddine sings, his courage having deserted him from one moment to the next like a gigantic cliff splitting off from a glacier. He tells them everything he knows, which isn't much. They torture him some more, to make sure. He starts to blurt out the names of Algiers acquaintances, first those people whom he vaguely suspects of being Front supporters, then, for no other reason than to stop the appalling pain, neighbours, whose names he picks at random, according to the vagaries of his memory and the intensity of the whip.

The officer realises this and stops the treatment in disgust. The prisoner is, at best, a mere stooge. The commandos bring a few of those whom he has named to the barracks nevertheless, and all turn out to be partisans, some of them important. One, as he is being dragged down the corridor, teeth broken, hair plastered to his forehead with blood, spits out contemptuously: "Filthy traitor, look out for your throat when you get out of here!"

10

A lieutenant in the intelligence service suggests to him that, since his cover is blown, and he can't return to the *douar* in any case, he might as well join the army. For over a month, Nassreddine is kept under lock and key, prey to a nameless horror which renders him dumb and stupid. Then, perceiving the threat represented by the *fellagha* to be as good a jailer as any, they allow this mute, dull-eyed detainee with the heavy tread the freedom of the barracks, giving him a good kicking whenever he is too slow at cleaning the latrines or, once a week, hosing down the captain's private car.

He escapes easily for, after a while, nobody pays attention to his movements. His heart bursting with anxiety, he makes straight for the *douar* where, to avoid meeting people, he approaches his mother's house via the *oued* path which bypasses the village. At the end of the cactus hedge lining the path, he halts, struck by the silence. For a few merciful seconds, he thinks he has lost his way.

He wants to howl when he recognises, scattered over the vegetable patch among the cardoons and artichokes, several of his children's toys and items of his mother's clothing. No sound emerges from his mouth. He pushes open the door to the courtyard with his foot. In the centre, there is an upturned *kanoun*. Other things lie here and there, thrown about in the utmost confusion. He picks up a little vest, then a pair of boy's underpants. Curiously, he remembers arguing with Anna at the time of their purchase at the little Clos Salembier shop in Algiers. He had wanted to take the larger sizes because they would last longer. "You mean thing! You buy yourself underpants fit for a maharajah, and those trousers you're so proud of, and me a dress and a slip, and the kids must dress for free till they're grown up!" The shopkeeper had been highly amused and, without too much bargaining, agreed to give them a considerable discount . . .

Nassreddine puts a hand to his chest. He can't breathe. "Yemma!" he murmurs, half reassured for, as usual, the air is fragrant with the scents of violet and jasmine, the two flowers which his mother adores and calls the "bringers of happiness".

The door to the main room, the room in which they live and sleep, stands wide open. He enters. He would have chosen to die under the lash rather than to see the great carpet which covers the earth floor stained with a huge pool of congealed blood.

By the time he has managed to get to his feet, it is almost dark. The vest and underpants still crumpled in his fist, he goes next door to the house belonging to the midwife. Concealed beneath his blue cotton jacket, his other fist holds a kitchen knife which he has picked up in the courtyard. When the woman opens her door to this skeletal, wild-eyed tramp with a crew cut who is shaking a bundle of rags in her face, she trembles with fear. The same age as Zehra, she often drops in for a glass of tea. Then the midwife's gaze clouds over. She covers her eyes with her hands, murmuring: "My poor boy, my poor boy . . ." Nassreddine, grim-faced, shows her the underclothes.

"The *moudjahidine* said that that you were a traitor, my son . . . Forgive me, my son, I'm only repeating what they told us. They also said that because of you a *mechta* was flattened by the infidel planes: men, women, children, almost all were killed."

Examining him greedily, the woman intones: "May God be your saviour, may God grant you forbearance, my poor Nassreddine . . ." A trickle of saliva runs down the man's chin:

"And after that?"

"They said that you too must pay . . . You and your family . . . That it wasn't right that your family should go unpunished, it would be unjust to the others, those whose kids were blown to bits by the bombs. And that it would serve as a warning to anyone who thinks that the walls of the enemies' barracks will protect him. So they came after sunset and they cut their throats, your mother's and the children's . . . Your mother Zehra protected the children as far as she could. She even took an axe and split the skull of one of her attackers. But she was no match for the other three, and in no time . . ."

The man gives a savage groan, as if to interrupt her:

"And did no-one do anything?"

"No-one, my son. What can anybody do when such things happen?"

Unable to bear the man's stony face any longer, the old woman breaks into sobs:

"We buried them next morning. Everyone wept, my son, the men as well as the women. It broke your heart to see those three bodies lying side by side! The village will never be the same again . . ."

Still brandishing the vest and underpants, Nassreddine gulps. He says:

"And my wife?"

"She was here, the day after the burial. She couldn't come before because the soldiers had held her for questioning. It was just as well, or she would have died with them. She was like a madwoman, pulling out her hair in handfuls, the poor thing . . ."

The midwife wrings her hands:

"And then those curs who do the bidding of France came back, and they dragged her away with them. She didn't even have time to prostrate herself on her children's graves . . ."

So that was that. Nassreddine put the vest and underpants into separate pockets and set out for the pass. He walked all night. The paths were steep, and more than once he stumbled on a loose stone or a thorny scrub. At dawn, exhausted, he stops, takes out the vest and underpants and kisses them. "My little ones, my dear little ones." Unable to cry, he falls asleep where he lies, the sobs caught in his throat.

A kick awakens him: men in combat uniform, speaking Arabic, are examining him with curiosity. FLN soldiers, they carry a strange assortment of weapons: Mauser pistols, Berettas and Stati repeating rifles. One man, armed with an ordinary shotgun, shakes him roughly:

"Hey, idiot! What do you mean by wandering about in a forbidden zone? These lazy bastards would happily have taken a shot at you."

One man grumbles:

"As long as he's not working for them . . ."

An older man, apparently the leader, interrupts:

"We can't hang about here, we're too conspicuous on this ridge. The paras are sure to be on our track. What's more, that plane has been circling around all morning. We make a perfect target. Ali, you try and find out what this fool is up to. And then rejoin us, at the double!"

The *djoundi* with the fat red moustache grunts:

"You heard, shepherd: what are you doing here?"

The group quickly disappears behind a rocky outcrop. The *djoundi*, impatient, pushes Nassreddine, who gets to his feet.

"Are you dumb, or what? Those rags you're hiding in your hand, what are they?"

Wordlessly, Nassreddine shoves vest and pants under the *djoundi*'s nose. Then, as the man steps back to take a better look, he pulls out his knife and lunges with outstretched arm at his interrogator's chest.

He cries out, for the partisan has twisted his arm brutally. Furious, the man throws him to the ground and sits astride him. Holding Nassreddine's knife, he bellows, mad with rage:

"Son of a hyena, I'll cut you to pieces! What made you pull a knife, answer me!"

He follows up his question with a punch. Nassreddine moans. The blow has caught him on the nose, almost cancelling out the pain from his twisted, probably broken arm. He stares at the kitchen knife as it nears his throat. Is this the end, then, some fellow scowling with incomprehension and stinking of sweat and billy-goat? Is this what all the song and dance is about? . . . He exhales, suddenly at peace. It's nothing, really, to be murdered!

"Get on with it, please."

The smile, the tone of voice, disconcerts the partisan:

"You really are crazy. Do you want to die?"

Nassreddine gestures towards the garments on the ground. The man examines the vest and underpants. His voice has grown hoarse:

"Children . . . Your children, eh? Are they . . . dead?"

Nassreddine doesn't reply. The voice is colourless, unexpected:

"I've got children too. Three, for your information."

Nassreddine shrugs, but the movement is painful.

"I'm a traitor, my friend, and my family paid instead of me."

Exasperated, he adds:

"Get a move on, *djoundi*, your cut-throat pals are waiting."

He closes his eyes. For a few seconds, his facial muscles tense in anticipation of the fatal blow. Then his body is relieved of its burden. The man has got to his feet. Haggard, he flings the knife some distance away.

"I'm no executioner, you fool. I fight to free my country. Hear that gunfire in the valley? Do you know what they're doing, those soldiers: they are exercising the latest guns on the *mechtas* and their flocks. And our people, displaced, die of hunger in the camps. I miss my own children

14

with all my heart, and for all I know they too may be dead."

His features taut with emotion, he gazes intently at Nassreddine:

"I'm not responsible for the death of your children. You can believe me when I say that I've never so much as touched a child. And I never would, no matter what."

Nassreddine is still prostrate. He has earth in his mouth. His eyes beseech the partisan. The *djoundi* averts his gaze and spits on the ground:

"Death would be too easy, after what you've done. No, you must live. It will be your punishment, traitor."

I

(1997 . . .)

1

The elderly lady is wandering through the cemetery. She is white-haired and wears a blue dress patterned with little white flowers. She has left her raincoat at the hotel, for it is hot and sunny in Algiers today. She pauses to caress a tombstone bearing the forename Mehdi. So many of the inscriptions, even though Muslim, are still in French: *né le . . . décédé le . . .* (curiously abbreviated to DCD). Soon, she will continue her search, this time for a tombstone with the forename Meriem. A faint smile lights up her face: fortunately, both are common names in Muslim countries. So far, she has been in luck: in every single Muslim cemetery, even back home, in her canton near Geneva – yes, there is one, albeit minute! – she has succeeded in finding tombstones bearing at least one of the two names. And then Meriem has the added advantage of being the same as Marie in French. At the worst, she can always fall back on Christian cemeteries, where she will be able to unearth Maries galore. She catches her breath, thinking of the expression which she has just employed: to unearth.

The cemetery is cramped, squeezed between dilapidated blocks of flats and the mouldering walls of a tobacco factory. High up, to the south, one can see the tiny barred windows of a prison. Where the path ends, on a sort of waste ground, the elderly visitor meets a group of veiled women walking up and down between the dozens of rudimentary graves. In serried ranks, often overlapping, the little mounds of earth are covered in crude wooden planks upon which some careless brush has scrawled a name and number in letters dripping with paint. Sometimes the name is missing. A few mounds, the most recent (to judge by the dark colour of the earth), have no inscription at all. The women move slowly from grave to grave, holding pieces of paper, distraught. They run their hands over the wooden planks, consult their lists, then resume their despairing lamentations. "Like sheep, yes, slaughtered like sheep," wails one. Another takes up the refrain: "Pigs, you mean, they killed our lions like pigs . . . and as if we haven't enough to grieve over, they don't even tell us where they are buried. Straight from prison cell to grave . . . My God, that such injustice should be permitted!"

The elderly lady walks through the wailing group, unnoticed. The women make her think of tall black storks, wings drooping beneath the weight of tears. Only one, an old woman bent over a cane, her face deeply wrinkled, stares at her with a mixture of affliction and sympathy. She quavers: "What are you doing in this unhappy place, my cousin? You should be at home, preparing the meal. The master of the house will be displeased . . ." The white-haired woman halts, embarrassed, and smiles at her interlocutor. A young woman, her face hidden by a black veil, her hands also gloved in black despite the heat, comes up and angrily grips the old crone with the cane by the arm:

"Silly old fool, fancy taking a foreigner, a *gaouria* without a veil, for your cousin!"

Penitent, the bent old lady joins the group. The young woman in black flings a look brimming with hate and tears at the foreigner. The elderly European, raising her arms in a gesture of incomprehension, opens her mouth to protest – "Sisters, I am one of you, I too am watching over my dead" – and then, leaving arms (and words) dangling, decides to walk on and continue her examination of tombstones elsewhere.

For hours, she wanders from tomb to tomb, stooping to peer at the stones. Her eyes are tired. Her total is satisfactory: several "Mehdis" and two "Meriems". She has avoided looking at the dates of birth and death. The third forename has never formed part of her search, perhaps because she has been told that it is rare. It would seem like tempting fate. She has always drawn a blank when it came to obtaining news of him. He may still be alive. My God, how long ago it was! "It" had happened nearly 40 years ago, after all. She is reminded of the dictum "When God created Time, He created enough and to spare". She wants to object: no, for the living there is never enough time. Only for those who no longer need it. The dead, in other words. And yet, given all the nonsense that she has heard tell of the Beyond, she cannot be entirely sure.

She prays a little. Not to the Saviour of her childhood. Nor to anybody else. But she prays all the same, seriously, methodically, as only a Protestant can. It is discipline that God needs, not faith! An old folk song, gay, insistent, echoes in her head: "We shan't be going to the woods any more, the branches on the bay trees have been lopped/ Here is the fair lady who will go to gather them up . . ." That part of her brain which she calls her clown's bump of intelligence chimes in mercilessly: "Pray all you like, poor fool, as if putting your hands together will change anything! The Other, the weary Patron reclining on His cloud, is having a good laugh at your expense, if you only knew."

Once again, this desire to weep which has been haunting her for the past three days has her old heart in its grip. Her eyes don't care, they refuse to pour out more tears. So her heart seeks another way to weep. And finds none. And this makes her suffer all the more. What use are tears against something which is neither good nor bad but merely Time and its years of stone, no less impassable and secure than a prison within a prison?

Three days ago, this elderly woman, an ordinary citizen of a country evoking little except perhaps snow-covered mountains, chocolate, spotted cows, excellent pastures and, of course, prosperous and rather louche banks, had been in Switzerland. Hans, her 25-year-old son, had done everything in his power to prevent her leaving. For she was too old, too frail after her heart attack, to take herself off to Africa just like that, with no plans, without even the help of a travel agency, and to an Arab country at that.

"They don't have much respect for women over there, you know, Mother."

She shrugged, "You exaggerate, son," her eyes as calm and grey as a millpond. She smiled, thinking: "They may not respect women, but when they love them . . ." Inside her head, that mountain morning smile, luminous but cold, grew broader: "Ah, my poor Hans, if you only knew . . ." But she had already decided, a long, long time ago, that he should never know.

She lied to him methodically, stating with an air of the utmost inno-cence that she was going to Egypt, to gaze upon those famous pyramids

21

and the mysterious Sphinx, a project she had cherished since her child-
hood, and that there was no time like the present because she was afraid
of becoming a total invalid. She even went so far as to buy guide books to
Egypt, studying them ostentatiously and commenting on the country
to the irritation of her son. And all this time she was gripped by a feeling
of perpetual terror, like a chronic stomach ache, lest she should die of
a heart attack having failed to join up, at least once in her lifetime, both
parts of her existence abominably split in two: before, after. Before the
death of her Algerian children, after the death of her Algerian children. If
the worst came to the worst, she promised herself, she would return to
Switzerland via Egypt. She made inquiries: yes, notwithstanding terrorist
threats, there was a flight from Algiers to Cairo. Just as Air Algeria
continued to operate its Paris–Algiers flight . . . She would go to France
and fly on to Algeria from there. Now that she was approaching the final
stage of her life, surely she had a right to squander some of that damned
money which had been so lacking in the old days!

Hans even suggested coming with her to Egypt:

"But there's your job," (he was a vet) "and I wish to go alone, have a
rest, see something of the country . . ."

Hardly able to believe his ears he stared at his mother, with her face
like an old wrinkled apple and her meticulously arranged white hair.

"But why just now, when you're not yet fully recovered? If only Papa
were alive; you would have listened to him."

He sighed, bewildered. His mother had always seemed to him utterly
transparent, devoid of secrets. Rather dull, in fact.

"But what on earth will you do over there?"

She changed the subject without replying. Giving up the struggle, he
asked her:

"Do you have a visa? Ah, good. And your reservations? Don't forget to
confirm your return ticket! And your medicines?"

"Yes, don't fuss so, Hans."

She stroked his head as she had when he was a child. Suddenly, she
thought how alike they were, father and son: the same freckles, the
same rather soft blond hair, and that insistence on leaving nothing to
chance. She thought of the father, her husband Johann, who had died
a painless death a year ago, in free fall, a stone dropping down a deep

well, relinquishing life as unobtrusively as he had lived it. She closed her eyes, suddenly moved, for dull though he was, she had come to love him, her Johann.

And yet she was being unfair: no sooner had he begun to decline than he had developed a sense of humour.

"Don't worry," he would say to her, taking her tenderly by the hands, "we all end up in the grave; it's the one thing we can be certain of. But we'll have the last laugh afterwards, when we rise from the dead."

He had added with a broad grin, between terrible fits of dry coughing:

"That is . . . if we rise from the dead. At last I'll know whether those innumerable masses I've paid for are the real thing or so much hot air. Listen to me, talking like a banker. In any case, it's a bit late to change my mind now. If I've been cheated, nobody is going to reimburse me . . ."

And it was so surprising to hear him talk like that, this husband of hers whom she had thought such a bigot, that she, the virtual agnostic, was left speechless. He had laughed at her stunned expression:

"What's up, surely you're not going to reproach me for trying to be more like you!"

Hans questioned her again about her travel arrangements. Seized by remorse, she kissed her son on the cheek. A little roughly. Asking his forgiveness from the bottom of her heart for his father's sake.

From the cemetery, Anna contemplates the Casbah, the old town terraced into the hillside, its little white houses decaying beneath the Mediterranean sun. From time to time, the sound of a siren breaks the silence. Straining her ears, she thinks she can hear muffled gunfire in the distance. But she can't be sure. Last night, the sounds of gunfire near the hotel were much more distinct, coming closer, then receding. She had awoken with a start, her heart beating like an over-tight drum, and put her ear to the door. There was no undue commotion. Nevertheless, laboriously, conscious of the absurdity of her gesture, she pushed a table up against the door before going back to bed. Angry: if she gave in to fear the very first night, how was she going to see this thing through? Cursing, she had dragged the table back to its place and then, with a sense of relief, quickly drifted off to sleep.

She examines her right hand with its two wedding rings. Two gold circles on the same finger, side by side for the first time. When she left Geneva, she had been wearing only one, that given her by Johann 27 years earlier, on their wedding day. A lavish ceremony, far beyond anything she could have expected in those times of austerity. In Algiers, in the luxurious hotel beneath the arcades, a few steps from the Law Courts and the Ministry of the Interior, she had carefully unpacked her things. The little box lay at the bottom of the suitcase. She hesitated for a moment before opening it and placing the second ring on her finger, as if she were about to impose a presence on her husband. Johann had disliked foreigners, and Arabs, for him, were more foreign than others. Be that as it may, she had never told him anything. He wouldn't have accepted it. He might even have decided not to marry her.

Finally, with difficulty, for her finger had swollen, she put on the ring. She lay down on the anonymous double bed. Drained of all feeling. Then she realised that what she felt, like a white noise drowning out all emotion, was an immense fatigue, far greater than could be accounted for by the journey or, at Algiers airport, the jostling queues going through the formalities, followed by a succession of barriers manned by soldiers or traffic police, scowling, on edge, an insult ever ready on their lips. One young policeman, visibly exhausted by the need to be perpetually on his guard, gave a start when she handed him her passport. He examined the document closely, unable to credit the sight of a foreign woman alone and unescorted in a taxi.

"What the hell are you doing in this country of madmen? Do you want to get yourself butchered?"

Taking down the name of the hotel and the licence number of the taxi, he threatened the driver in Arabic:

"Take her straight to the hotel! No question of going out of the way, if you get my meaning . . ."

To her astonishment, she realised that she still knew a little Arabic. She felt a disagreeable pang of apprehension. So, it was done, she was truly back. In the unimaginable: the past, her past. With all its attendant baggage: the language, the suffocating heat, the leprous walls, the cacophony of children shouting to one another in the street, and this raw, merciless light which, as a young woman oppressed by cold and fog, she had found so welcome! Suffering from shock, and also from the pain of returning memory, she closed her eyes. Dizziness caused her to utter an involuntary groan. The driver inquired if she was ill. She muttered something unintelligible in reply. Once in her hotel room she slept a heavy, dreamless sleep for a good hour.

At the desk, she asked the receptionist for directions to the cemetery.

"What cemetery?"

"It doesn't matter which," she replied.

The man specified:

"Christian, naturally?"

"No, Muslim, naturally."

"You are Muslim, then?"

"No, Christian, naturally."

The receptionist coughed with embarrassment. She persisted, using all her wiles as a rich, elderly tourist. In the end, he drew her a map of the route to the nearest cemetery on a scrap of paper. Full of misgivings, he caught her on the way out and urged her to change her mind. The cemetery was in a "rough" district, a dangerous area where street battles were an everyday occurrence. Even the police refused to go there without an escort, afraid that they would be swatted like flies. Why, only last week, two Spanish nuns had been murdered there more or less in view of an army post. When the receptionist saw that the elderly lady with the embarrassed smile was determined to have her own way ("But I assure you, Madame, their stab wounds were truly hideous!"), he begged her at least to cover her head with a scarf and to go everywhere by taxi. To please him – and also to get rid of him – she took a scarf from her handbag and waited patiently while he called a taxi. Dry-mouthed, her lips trembling a little, she thought to herself, looking through the glass doors of the hotel, that it was definitely too glorious a morning on which to die.

She is walking in the cemetery. Hardly anybody about. A few heads turn in surprise at her passage. In a place where somebody has just watered geraniums planted in the newly turned earth, two frogs stand sentinel, patiently awaiting a juicy insect. According to an old wives' tale in her part of Switzerland, a frog's cry of pain resembles an infant's, so that it is inadvisable to kill one, frogs being the souls of dead children. She looks into the amphibians' unblinking eyes. And, for a moment, into the eyes of her two Algerian children.

Weeping parsimonious, painful tears, she is aware of a watcher, a tall man, wearing a white burnous despite the heat. He seems to be smiling at her. An inscrutable, kindly smile, which she acknowledges with a nod.

What was it he said, her first husband, whose ring she is once again wearing after so long an interval? He spoke of a mythical character, El Khidir, the immortal guide to souls in the Koran, said to have been the companion of Gilgamesh and the prophet Moses, and to have witnessed the crucifixion of Jesus. He swore that he existed, this personage, you only had to call his name for him to be present, enveloping you as the skin envelops the muscles, and retaining thereafter, for all eternity, the memory of the soul who had summoned him.

Through the mists of time, she recalls asking if he truly believed in the story of El Khidir who, according to him, was the "Pole of Time", a symbol of "the rhythm which governs all things". Mildly irritated, he retorted that it took little for a belief to become a reality, at least to oneself ("Take the Heavenly Father, for example: if you believe in Him, He exists, you are ready to die for Him, even to make war in His name. But if not . . . pouff! There will be nothing left except one more lousy confidence trick. In any case, one ought to believe in such things. What is the good of being too lucid, eh, my beloved, tell me that? Undiluted reason is worse than acid, believe me!") And kissing her on the mouth to prevent her from replying, he began to chant, laughing: ". . . for better or for worse, in sickness and in health . . ."

That was long before they had children. In those carefree days, they took things as they came . . . Life had yet to take on its definitive colour and, "Pole of Time" or not, her love for the man who was to give her this ring had been straightforward and unquestioning. Which was to account, in part, for her misfortune. For he had given her happiness, that simplest of things which can so easily vanish.

The old man in the cemetery salutes her, Arab fashion, placing his hand on his heart and returning her nod. Of course it must be El Khidir, she had thought as much the minute she saw him. The idea makes her laugh. The man in the burnous quickly walks away, exchanging a smile with her as though they were old acquaintances. Her laughter dies on her lips. Ought she to have questioned him? Even though he didn't look the part, he might have known Moses, and Jesus, and all the rest of it. Above all, he might have known the man who had shut her up with a tender kiss on the lips.

There is nobody left in the cemetery. The elderly lady sighs: "Oh my madcap husband, you and your weird tales that wouldn't deceive a child, see what ideas you put in my head!" She stands transfixed, one finger on the second of the two rings, realising that she has just addressed her first husband as if he were at her side, here and now, in this tiny cemetery, instead of separated from her by at least four and half decades, over there beyond the ocean of the past.

". . . For better or for worse, in sickness and in health . . ." With a poignant joy that is like a stab of pain, she reminds herself that before she knew this husband of hers, this person who may no longer exist and whose bones may even have crumbled to dust, she was a circus acrobat. So, in this cemetery where frogs are left to croak in peace, Anna vows that, henceforth, she will believe unreservedly in his story of the Prophet of Time, sending the trapeze-bar winging back to him, over and above the memories and the remorse, to signify her consent.

2

Nassreddine is uneasy. To be more exact: in addition to the perennial layer of anxiety, so familiar that he has come to wonder whether he has ever known a day free from this tension in his stomach muscles, he feels an anxiety of a different kind. He wants to laugh and to cry. To laugh bloody laughter, to weep bloody tears. And both simultaneously. Now what, he asks himself, I hope I'm not losing my mind, on top of everything else . . .

It is past six o'clock. A fine morning. Not for a long time has there been so splendid a light. From the window he looks out over the city. There is nobody about, although the curfew ended more than an hour ago. He feels well enough, that is, nothing hurts: his sciatica isn't paining him, nor is his ulcer. Whistling, he spoons coffee into his Italian cafetière. Good coffee is hard to come by, and he knows that he ought not to be so extravagant. But this morning he can drink coffee to his heart's content, for he has decided to kill himself. The notion suddenly came to him as he was contemplating the balconies on the flats opposite: all the shutters were closed! Those mute balconies seemed to him to have the right idea: to close the shutters, conscientiously, firmly, to take your leave after having consigned your carcass to the scrap heap, to be free henceforth from terror, from the daily butchery, above all, from your life, in his case such a total disaster that he cannot understand how he has endured it for so long. Oh, the word suicide never passes his lips! Too grandiloquent, it implies a degree of self-esteem: you don't commit suicide unless you think so highly of yourself that you are prepared to sacrifice your life on the altar of what you imagine to be your true nature. No, for him, suicide is as it were an imperative dictated by common sense: he must cease to temporize, since time procures him nothing but one dreadful blow after another! It was the obvious thing to do, like clearing the table after a meal. He has lost his appetite, literally lost it, and it only remains for him, as a conscientious housekeeper, to sweep the crumbs from his breakfast off the tablecloth. He removes his pyjamas and dons his best suit. For such an occasion, the jacket needs to be better pressed, he notes, vaguely annoyed. He struggles to unhook the light fixture on the ceiling, cross with himself ("She was right, I'll never make a handyman") because he has dislodged flakes of plaster and they have fallen to the floor. He manages to attach a length of cord to the bare hook and, having climbed on to a chair, places it around his neck. The cord, thinner than the wrinkles in his neck, has a tendency to disappear into their folds. He is almost happy (let us say rather: content), for he is about to do something sensible and, above all, practical. The smell of hot coffee rises to greet him. He feels strongly that it would be indecent to leave without turning off the gas. Moreover – and this, by contrast, irritates him profoundly – he has an urgent desire to urinate. He pauses, unsure whether a hanged man is capable of controlling his bladder. He doesn't fancy himself as a corpse stinking of urine. He can't bear to think of his neighbours stooping over his dead body, holding their noses in disgust. So he dismounts from the chair. He turns off the gas on the cooker, then does his best to urinate. In vain. Even when he presses on his bladder he cannot squeeze out a single drop. Yet the painful need is still there. His old body is disagreeing with him, playing him tricks. He pours himself another cup of coffee, good and hot, then a third, and no longer has the courage to remount the chair.

He lies down on the settee, dismayed at the thought of having to replace the ceiling-light. He is scarcely able to disguise from himself the pleasure he feels at being still alive. And the longer he stays curled up on the settee, the greater becomes his astonishing, absurd contentment at not having inflicted the supreme penalty on his decrepit body. He looks down at his freckled hands with their complicated, fragile network of veins, his heart thumping with emotion ("Well, well, my Andalusian, if you could only see this!"). If he didn't restrain himself, he would be dancing across the room with joy . . .

A strange howling awakens him with a start nearly an hour later. He rushes to the balcony: four storeys below, in front of the entrance, a neighbour from his landing, *couffin* in hand, is clawing at her face and howling with all her might. The old man strains to hear: at first he thinks that Lalla Yamina is calling for help, but the dreadful sound has become unintelligible. All the same, he understands that she is bewailing a death. Horrified, he runs downstairs as fast as he can. He is very fond of this particular neighbour who is always ready to do him a service. Every morning, she offers to pick up his daily carton of milk, thus sparing him the fatigue of the crush around the milk cart. When he tries to thank her, she protests in her good-humoured peasant fashion: "Saving your grace, El Hadj" (she is convinced that he has made the pilgrimage to Mecca and only hides the fact out of modesty), "but I wasn't brought up soft, like you. What are four storeys without a lift to me? I used to take the goats to pasture up and down the mountains! In any case, I have to buy that nasty factory milk for myself . . ." And she loves it when he addresses her, an overworked cleaner employed by the council, by the deferential term "Lalla" (the ceremonious form of Madame). Clumsily, she tries to disguise her pleasure by chuckling: "Stop it, El Hadj, no-one else talks to me like that! You make me blush like a girl, me, a grand-mother four times over!" And he would go one better, eyeing her wasted body with a lustful air: "Ah, Lalla, if I wasn't so afraid of your husband, I'd have carried you off long ago!" And she would run off, laughing: "To the devil with you, El Hadj, fancy you still saying things like that at your age!"

Already, a crowd has gathered round the woman. Locked into a definitive solitude, her face a mass of bleeding scratches, she is howling with unbelievable force. She is kneeling beside a tray that holds two coffee cups and, surmounted by kepis, two round objects resembling footballs. Despite his sleep-befuddled brain, he instantly recognises one of the "footballs" as the head of his neighbour's eldest son. Bizarrely, the hand-some face wears a sulky expression, as if displeased by his mother's lack of restraint. The second head appears to be merely dozing. The clean cut at the base of each neck is bloodless: the executioners had taken especial care with the presentation of their abominable still life. A boy aged six or seven, barefoot, clinging to the arm of an adult, gazes at the scene, wide-eyed, teeth chattering non-stop. A piece of cardboard placed on the ground proclaims, in ballpoint pen: "For those who serve Pharaoh, this is their breakfast!"

He is overcome by an immense sympathy for the poor peasant woman. A few weeks ago, she had confided her fears to him when her son received his call-up papers. The armed groups had warned that they would kill anybody reporting for duty at the barracks. The military treated deserters as terrorist sympathisers, hunting them down without mercy. She had grumbled with a rueful smile: "Ah, my God, You know that I'm a good Muslim, and yet You do nothing to smooth my path in life!"

A sort of stupefied horror paralyses the circle of onlookers around the woman. He overhears someone in the crowd whisper fearfully: "The other one is a pal of Hassan's. They were due on leave yesterday. They must have been picked up on the bus." His neighbour adds: "Nothing escapes them, they know everything, that's for sure! Look at that coffee, it wouldn't surprise me if it was still hot . . ." Then, with a furtive glance, the pair hurriedly duck as if afraid of having said too much. You never knew who might be spying for the Islamicists or the security forces, that friendly neighbour, perhaps, who was staring at you so insistently a few seconds ago. The old man can taste the bile in his mouth. He wants to put his arm around his neighbour's shoulders and console her, but he lacks the courage. Pursued by cries like those of a wounded animal, he goes back upstairs to his apartment, and paces back and forth, sick with shame and impotence. A quarter of an hour later the city echoes to the sounds of sirens, of rifles being fired into the air to disperse onlookers, of barked orders and the curses of the police and the security forces. There is a violent hammering at his door. Hooded Ninjas burst in, push him roughly aside and point their automatic rifles at him. They tour the apartment at the double, as if searching for some-body. The one who appears to be in command growls: "Seen anything, Granddad? No? The same as everyone else, eh! Bastards! Two poor kids decapitated under their noses and nobody has seen a thing, as usual . . ."

On the way out, one of the Ninjas points to the cord hanging from the hook on the ceiling. He laughs drily, for the benefit of his companions:

"Maybe that's the best solution for Algeria!"

Nobody joins in his laughter. From behind the closed door, the man follows the progress of the cavalcade of policemen from floor to floor: their shouted questions, the forced doors, the supplications of those arrested. By the time he can bring himself to peer over the balcony again, street police are loading ten or so young men, heads bowed, handcuffed, into 4 × 4s. So what's new, he thinks, resigned: it's the usual thing, whenever the police and the security forces arrive at the scene of an outrage they take their revenge for people's terrorised silence by turning on the local young unemployed. Having rounded up as many as they can lay their hands on, they beat them up, either at the police station or at the barracks, in the hope of unearthing a terrorist or recruiting a potential informer. Occasionally, one or two will fail to return to man the walls of their council estate, their corpses being found at dawn, flung down on a cracked pavement, or their names cited on a long list in a victory communiqué issued by the State police.

His hands are trembling so much that he gives up trying to smoke. He ought to have looked after his neighbour, he knows it, and can't forgive himself: "My sister, my sister in misery, pardon my cowardice, but I just couldn't . . ." The despair with which he is only too familiar has returned, driven by a fever that grips his chest, his stomach, his guts. He knows that, sooner or later, he must leave his apartment, his city, Algiers, the dirty, cruel capital which, in lieu of family, he has learned to love so dearly. Perhaps the time has come for him to return to the *douar*, to look after the family house and the graves of his mother and children, to live out the rest of his life there, trying not to let his thoughts dwell – for he finds it too painful, even now! – on that train of events which left him, an eternity ago, with three deaths on his conscience?

The old man has found a postcard in his letter-box and is hurrying on his way to a hotel, to meet a friend. Somebody he hasn't seen for three years. No, four. Jaourden, his Targui friend. And how long has he known him – 20, 30 years? Since Independence, he has worked off and on as a travel guide for an agency in Tamanrasset. He probably still does, though he must be getting on a bit. What else could he do, after all, that old goat of a Targui who always grumbled that he could never manage to save so much as a sou?

He hurries on, but limping, for his corn is playing him up. Just now, in the overcrowded bus, somebody trod on his foot. He hasn't taken his old car because it has broken down yet again and he can't find spare parts at a price he can afford. True, they are to be found on the black market, but his entire monthly pension wouldn't cover it. Shit! he curses, and yet, his despair notwithstanding, he is happy because he is on his way to meet a friend. Nobody has real friends any more in this cursed town, he rages. He thinks of the two heads on the breakfast tray and then, because the image of the two cups set before the supplicants' lips quickly becomes unbearable, turns his thoughts to what happened yesterday, that business about money and the man who insulted him. But he refuses to dwell on it. He pats the 100 dinar notes in his pocket. The sum represents a considerable part of his pension. He knows that tomorrow or the next day he will regret it bitterly. But today is today: after what he has witnessed this morning, he needs friendship like a drowning man needs mouth-to-mouth resuscitation. A vision floats briefly into his head: fancy kissing that smelly old wreck of a Targui, ugh! He smiles ruefully, a little alarmed by his need for friendship. Also rather annoyed that he should have this craving. Good God, has he sunk as low as that? He rubs his right hand, for the black spot is bothering him. He has never known where it came from. It calls attention to itself now and then by a vague discomfort, not painful but unpleasant. He rubs it again, more out of habit than necessity.

They have arranged to meet in the Hotel Beau Séjour, in the Bab El Oued area. Jaourden hasn't changed much, slightly shrunken with age, perhaps, though still as lean as ever. His jacket is clean, but threadbare. Without his desert robes and, above all, his impressive *cheche*, he cuts a sorry figure. Indeed, he is not out of place in this seedy hotel lounge.

"You might have picked somewhere better," Nassreddine cannot help saying.

"Look here, the other places were expensive, this was all I could afford!" Jaourden replies, rather put out.

The meeting is a little frigid. Nassreddine is aware that the fault is his. Whatever had induced him to begin with a criticism?

"Have you eaten?"

The Targui nods.

"How about going for a drink?"

The two men examine one another, careful not to spoil their reunion.

"All right, I'll just go and tell my wife that I'll be out for a while."

Nassreddine smiles:

"Ah, so she is with you?"

The man with the lined face and almost negroid features doesn't reply. He seems weary:

"I won't be long."

Now they are seated at a table in a grimy, smoke-filled bar. The shutter over the street door is down and, through a gap, a man is surveying the pavement. Bars have been attacked with Kalashnikovs, and there have been deaths. Not even good deaths, say the habitués, for you are slandered at your funeral: "Ha, ha, a drunkard gunned down with a glass in his hand? At a time like this? He was really asking for it, wasn't he?" The customers have to raise their voices over the rackety music. They order several beers at a time. Not enough beer and too many customers. "No more beer" is what they all dread to hear. Now, what was the point of drinking, if not to get drunk? There is always water, if you're thirsty. Only the rich drink for pleasure. And how many rich people do you see in this place? . . . The proprietor excepted, of course, they say knowingly, resentful and envious. And some, intent on achieving that laggardly drunkenness, give a hard, belligerent laugh.

Jaourden doesn't drink beer, nor wine, for that matter. He doesn't like either. He prefers whisky. For a very odd reason, one which he unfailingly repeats whenever he and Nassreddine are drinking together.

"Back home, in the Hoggar, I never learned to drink wine or beer because there was almost none to be had. It was the foreign tourists who, at night in the bivouacs, introduced me to whisky. It's a foul tasting drink, but you only need a couple of glasses to appreciate its good points. To get the same result with wine, you have to put up with the taste of rot for nearly a whole bottle. And don't talk to me about beer! It turns you into your own piss pot!"

Normally, he adds, chuckling, that while the Koran forbids wine, it makes no mention of whisky. But today, Jaourden downs his first whisky, then his second, almost without a word. He is in gloomy mood. He holds the glass tentatively, with both hands, as if the contents were boiling hot. Furthermore, the Targui is making a sucking noise with his lips as though he is drinking tea. Nassreddine contemplates him: worn, crumpled, weighed down by some unknown burden. This was not what he had hoped to see. Finally, feeling cheated of his expectations, he grows impatient:

"We're friends, no? Well, I'm not buying you whisky at this price to have you to sit there glowering at me. What's the matter?"

The Targui fingers his glass. He raises his head, the eyes sunk in their orbits:

"I'm old, so is my wife, and she is seriously ill. What more do you want?"

He goes on, in his rough speech, a mixture of Tamachak and poorly assimilated Arabic:

"What does it profit a man to live, to be young and vigorous, to believe in the impossible, to see the sun all day long if it's only to grow old, die, and rot in his grave?"

His lips tremble:

"You see, I love her, I love my wife. Maybe to you she is ugly, wrinkled, too dark-skinned, a proper sack of potatoes. But there you are, she's my wife."

He looks like nothing so much as a despairing old vulture; he rages:

"I'm an arsehole, do you know what I nearly said: that I loved her! . . ."

He lets fly a foul oath in Arabic, impossibly obscene. A nearby customer turns round and repeats it, amused by its grossness. The Targui shuts his eyes. Nassreddine too shuts his eyes, abashed by his friend's grief but also wishing not to be being engulfed by it. Each is closeted with his own thoughts. Not even friendship can bridge the gap between their respective dreams. Each sinks into his own ooze, alone, slowly losing his foothold in his memories.

A lullaby comes into old Jaourden's already tipsy head; it is one that his mother, long buried beneath the stony desert, used to sing to him: "O hare, won't you bring sleep to soothe this wakeful child . . ." Jaourden squeezes his eyes tight, for the nostalgia evoked by this lullaby is truly unbearable. His poor head swims to think of the sweetness of his mother's milk. Suddenly, the whisky on his lips tastes of disinfectant.

Each man is an ensemble of deaths: the death of childhood, of

35

adolescence, of first love, of maturity and much else besides. For Jaourden, at this precise moment, it is his long-dead childhood that cries out: "Please, O please! I beg thee. Give me thy word that I may go on breathing a little while longer, just a second, just a minute . . ."

3

Jallal sells peanuts and single cigarettes from an upturned cardboard box. He is nearly ten years old, but looks older. He is dozing, seated on a makeshift stool, his back against a tree. The Place des Martyrs swarms with people, but Jallal's little business is slow. He is not stupid, he knows that peanuts make you thirsty, and that there is definitely no future in selling them in this heat. But anything else would require funds which he doesn't possess. Unless (now there's an idea!) he were to steal from that old European woman who bought a bag of peanuts from him this morning ... He smiles disdainfully: she had spoken French. He was disappointed, having thought she was more foreign than that, someone seriously rich, an American, maybe, or a German ... Grumbling to himself in Arabic, he had handed her the bag:

"Here you are, old nanny-goat, chew on that, it'll make you younger!"

She had appeared startled. He had added, in French this time:

"Five dinars, Madame, for only five dinars you can fill your belly!"

Gravely, looking him in the eye, she had handed over the five dinars. He had thanked her in Arabic, wagging his head, confident that she couldn't understand:

"That's right, old widow's arse, five dinars won't make a hole in your purse at today's exchange rate."

The elderly lady had walked off, scarlet in the face, but Jallal put that down to the lobster-effect of the Algerian sun on Europeans' skins. In retrospect, her presence here surprises him. She had a nerve, walking around Algiers like that when foreigners were being killed as casually as dung-flies. Or perhaps it was just senility that made her so bold? For once, to be a *gaouria* was not an advantage ...

Now Jallal is dreaming in the sun, still smiling: he has succeeded in improving on his favourite daydream, the one where he becomes immensely rich and takes his revenge. After cars and properties, he has collected swimming-pools from all over town. The muezzin at the Ketchaoua mosque is braying his call to prayer. He is out of tune, each unfortunate sharp disastrously amplified by the loud-speakers. People hurry to prayer, appalled, mentally blocking their ears.

Jallal takes no notice. He hears the unpleasant voice, but is now so rich that he has engaged a second muezzin for the Ketchaoua mosque. Then he decides for no other reason than that, irresistibly sweet, of doing as he pleases, to buy the mosque and send the two muezzins packing together with the faithful come to pray. Nevertheless, he knows instinctively that he mustn't go too far in his laboriously constructed fantasy for fear of losing his belief in it, dream or not. Having reopened the mosque, he acquires his favourite football stadiums, Bologhine and Annassers. Now he turns to vengeance. He quivers with nervous concentration: he shuts down the Bab El Oued barracks and the State police headquarters opposite the Lycée Abdelkader. Then he drives before him, under the lash of whip and insult, like terror-stricken ants, the officers of army and police, among whom is always – my God, where would the miracle of dream and revenge be without him! – the silver-haired colonel, that ignorant, vain president who, even if no good on television, commanded universal admiration for his ability to ruin and despoil his country. It's true – and the boy cannot get round this weakness in his scenario – that since the start of the butchery, "Tête Blanche" has been succeeded by other presidents, but the boy's hatred cannot focus on them, for they come and go too fast: first there was "Le Maigre", a bricklayer by trade, so thin-lipped that that you could cut yourself on his smile and who, six months later, ended up assassinated by his own bodyguards; then came "Le Gros", the one with the fat moustache of a pastry-cook whose real name he has since forgotten; and now, dragged from some obscure retreat, there is this surly general who cannot read a speech in classical Arabic without stumbling. So the boy decided, once and for all, that the president in his daydream, the butt of his execration, should be "Tête Blanche" and nobody else! This passage in the dream is tricky, for if Jallal digs too deeply he invariably finds himself back in the earthquake with the soldiers, and at that moment anger usually awakens him.

So he abandons vengeance. He ponders his dream: it now resembles a delicious sweetmeat into which Jallal bites with care, fearful of breaking his teeth on a stone. Above all, he must stay quite still, take short, shallow breaths and keep his eyes shut, regardless of what is going on around him.

A wasted effort. Soon, he gives up, discouraged: his dream won't "take". Jallal isn't drowsy enough to let himself "go under". The air is stiflingly hot, its humidity presses down on him like a tepid cowpat. He opens his eyes, surveys his pitiful stall and looks away towards the port and the blue of the sea, as superb as ever, as heartbreaking as ever. He can't know that at this moment, from her hotel window, the elderly lady whom he had vexed is contemplating the same imperceptible ripples while in the throes of a despair which, when compared to his, is rather more comprehensive. Nor that the elderly lady, who still understands a little Arabic, was wounded, perhaps more deeply than she need have been, by that "widow's arse". She turns her gaze towards the concrete blocks of the Admiralty buildings, trying to clear her head of this irritation which nags at her like a bout of nostalgia. Then she decides to laugh it off: "Perhaps underneath the old girl is still a bit of a flirt!" Nevertheless, the insult has hit home. While Jallal scratches his nose out of boredom, she thinks again of what she has done this morning. An icy cold penetrates her in spite of the heat. The contrast between the goose-pimples and the drops of sweat on her skin makes her feel sick. She tells herself that she is a fool, a crazy necrophile who scrabbles in the earth around tombstones, but the turmoil in her breast starts up afresh. Suddenly, she makes the same gesture as Jallal: she scratches her nose. She mustn't give way to the feverish agitation, part superstitious fear, part insane hope, which had so nearly caused her to faint this morning: she had sent a telegram to her first husband at his *douar*. It read: "AM AT HOTEL ALETTI UNTIL 20TH WILL THEN GO TO YOUR MOTHER'S HOUSE IF YOU ARE STILL ALIVE COME TO ME ANNA." Address: "NASSREDDINE B. DOUAR HASNIA NEAR BATNA." She had queued for a quarter of an hour in the hall of the main post office, her heart beating wildly. The clerk, objecting to the vague address, would have refused to send the telegram had she not brandished her yellowing family dossier, blurting out, on the verge of tears: "You can't stop me sending a telegram to my own husband!" A man who had observed the scene approached the counter and crisply admonished the clerk in Arabic: "Stop this, you're driving us nuts with your row! We've got enough on our plate as it is. You can see that she's only a crazy old woman. Send her telegram. What do you care if it doesn't arrive?" Sulkily, the employee bent his head to his task. Outside the post office, the man caught up with her. He wore the shabby jacket of an underpaid civil servant, fully buttoned, but showing the tell-tale bulge of a pistol in the left-hand pocket. Lowering his voice, he addressed her in French, patronising her as if she were a child: "Madame, I take it that you can read, so you must have seen the newspapers. You would be well advised to return to your hotel at once! Unfortunately, our towns are not very friendly to foreigners these days." He stank of tobacco, sweat and fear. Looking from left and right, on his guard, he repeated his warning with gathering menace: "Believe me, certain ill-disposed people might have designs on your . . . well . . . on your safety, and it will be said afterwards that we couldn't protect you!" Coming after her attempt to stir up the past, this policeman's offensive scolding left her feeling so ill that, half suffocating, she dived into the nearest café, oblivious to the astonished expression on the faces of customers doubly disconcerted at seeing a woman, for women don't go into cafés in Algiers, and a European at that. She ordered a glass of water, too dizzy to notice the ordinary-looking young man with a crew cut and trainers who hurriedly slipped out of the building.

It was definitely not going to be one of his good days. That will teach me, Jallal thinks, resigned. In his longing to go on repeating this dream, he is ruining his chances of believing in it a little and burying himself in its delights. The first time – it was just after the earthquake! – it had worked wonders: after a dreadful week of wishing he were dead, he had dozed off beneath a tree, dizzy with self-loathing. The dream had taken him by the hand and given him back the joy and dignity of vengeance. It lasted no longer than the time it took for a refreshing siesta in the meagre shade of an olive tree, but Jallal urinated with pleasure in his sleep. To hide the smell, he waded up to his middle in an *oued*. A remedy worse than the ill, for the stink of stagnant water overpowered that of the urine.

For him it remained, like an unbearable truth, the perfect dream, the dream of dreams which, through its very perfection, had the power to work miracles! Jallal was convinced of one thing: if through sheer will-power he could recreate reality in every detail, then one of these days his daydream would become confused with that reality and, at least once, the derisory and ineffectual punishment to which he regularly condemned his sister's executioners would be transmuted into vengeance, their flesh lacerated in reality . . .

Jallal spits on the ground. Not that he particularly wants to, but he can't think what else to do in this vast square, by now almost deserted. Anyhow, it annoys his neighbour, the man with a club-foot who sells parsley and aromatic herbs. This cripple spits as much as the rest of the locals put together, but nothing enrages him more than other people's dirty habits, notably those to whom he refers, day in, day out, as the spoilt brats of the filthy rich:

"With any luck, the brothers will clean it all up with their knives and machine-guns: a head here, a head there, and there'll be enough blood to wash away the muck. You'll see, they'll laugh on the other side of their faces when their heads are cut off, all those godless sons and daughters of nobodies who lounge about while the likes of us slave all day!"

The cripple roars with laughter, pleased with his wit, but his good humour rapidly evaporates when he sees that the boy is unimpressed:

"Clear off, son of a police spy!"

Saïd has warned him: unless be brings back more than the few miserable sous he earned yesterday, he can look for somewhere else to rest his idle bones. Jallal knows that he isn't joking. Saïd is a strange fellow, given to mood swings from the most disconcerting kindness to the vilest of rages, capable of killing you on the spot if you thought of defying him. Jallal chooses to stay with him, taking the rough with the smooth. He hasn't forgotten — he won't forget in a hurry — all that Saïd had done for him after his arrival in Algiers.

His heart bursting with pain and rage, he had run away from his native village in the Chenoua. He had just enough money to buy bread for two days. He set out to beg, but all the best pitches were taken, and people gave so little, more often than not accompanying their alms with a disparaging remark such as: "You know, you wouldn't be holding out your hand if your mother had brought you up properly . . ." One elderly man, wearing the handsome *djellaba* of a pilgrim, had even propositioned him, stroking his hand. His manner being affable and fatherly, Jallal hadn't caught on immediately. The boy took to his heels, calling the venerable gentleman a pig and the progeny of a pederast. The fellow made off, raising his arms to heaven and loudly denouncing these runts from a bitch's litter who came tumbling down from their hills to foul the streets of Algiers. Passers-by turned round, nodding their heads in approval. On his fourth day in Algiers, Jallal was badly beaten up by a policeman, apparently the boss of the beggars working the Rue Didouche-Mourad.

But the nights were the worst. Every evening, the nightmare began anew: he had to find a safe place for his cardboard box so that he could get a little sleep. Safe from the deranged, for a start: one should never fall asleep without a razor-blade handy in case of attack. Safe from the curfew, above all, and soldiers who fire at the least suspicious movement. His first nights were filled with terror. Once, for instance, hiding behind his flimsy cardboard box, he heard somebody running down the steps of a nearby apartment block. The soldiers spotted him and ordered him to raise his hands. Whoever it was – the boy could hear his whistling breath – refused to comply, shouting: "*Allah Ou Akbar*, sons of bitches!", answering them with a long burst of gunfire and raging: "Fuck your mothers and sisters!" before being caught in the beam of one of his pursuers' torches and instantly gunned down. His cardboard box upturned over his head, the boy heard the clumping of army boots approach his hiding-place, then retreat. A vehicle pulled up, and he heard somebody cry: "Serve him bloody well right! Now the bastard can explain himself to Abassi and Belhadj", and then give a nervous laugh. The boy's teeth had chattered for the remainder of the night.

Then a boy of his own age had tipped him off about the Oued Smar rubbish dump near the airport. He talked of it like some kind of El Dorado where you had only to bend down to find treasures. "Algiers is full of rich people, wait and see!" With a dubious look at Jallal's thin, dirty face, the boy added:

"Anyhow, when you're down and out in Algiers, you're not exactly spoilt for choice: either you beg and steal, or you open your legs and play the whore. To steal, you need a lot of courage and a lot of luck. To be a whore, you need to be young and handsome. If you want my opinion, you're neither brave nor handsome. So there's nothing for it but the rubbish dump . . ."

He took himself off there, starving and full of hope. There, too, he faced disappointment. The dump, cut in two by the motorway, stretched as far as the eye could see; cars glinting in the sun crossed it at high speed, all with their windows shut. The stench was so appalling, and the flies and rats so numerous, that he had spent the morning wandering around the periphery, not daring to join the gang of grimy boys who rushed to cling on to the back of each arriving truck and leap into its tip, heedless of the danger and the driver's weary shouts.

Inhaling this evil blend of pestilential odours and the fumes from partially incinerated objects, Jallal sensed confusedly that the last remaining scraps of his childhood were dropping off him, like shreds of flesh from a corpse. Naturally, as was inevitable, hunger won the day.

By evening, he had earned no more than a few dinars. He was sickened by the taste of the sweat running down from his forehead to the corners of his lips. He was exhausted, as much by the constant need to keep watch on his finds as by the incessant race for the trucks. Thefts, and the ensuing violent disputes, exacerbated the tension among the feverish little army of pickers who toiled ceaselessly to amass small piles of plastic jerry-cans, empty scent bottles, old saucepans and, if they were lucky, odds and ends of copper, lead and other metals.

Several times, slipping in the countless puddles, Jallal had fallen over. Seeing his disgusted expression, somebody let fly with a sarcasm:

"Watch out, fathead, you think you're all cinnamon and roses, but cut yourself badly and you'll be one big abscess from head to toe!"

His heart full, Jallal choked back his tears. If he allowed himself to cry in front of the others they would call him names for sure: little sissy, pansy! And then he would have to stand up for himself, and he didn't feel strong enough to take on the entire world all the time. He had felt weak, so very weak, since he had had to fend for himself! Struggling to control his tightening jaws, the precursor to sobs, he noted with grim humour that he couldn't even wipe his eyes on his sleeve, it looked so like a floor cloth in a public toilet. Furthermore, something told him that he must on no account allow tears to escape his body, for these would become contaminated on contact with the pollutants in the atmosphere, poisoning his eyes and skull. He might be hungry, and smell worse than a dog's turd, but there was no need to go mad into the bargain!

The buyer examined his meagre pile of plastic odds and ends with a thin smile. The boy was too quick to accept his derisory price. The rag-and-bone salesman jerked his chin at the basin containing Jallal's offering:

"You mean to say that you collect your stuff in this old thing . . . First time, eh? You're a real country bumpkin, you are . . ."

Jallal tried to brazen it out, but the man looked at him with such contempt that he lowered his eyes without answering back. The wizened old fellow, who had some fingers missing from his right hand, produced a motorbike and sidecar, an ancient Lambretta. The sidecar was overflowing with discarded objects bought from the waste-pickers. He lit a cigarette which he held pinched between the remaining joints of his fourth and fifth fingers. Jallal, fascinated, expected it to fall out at any minute. Before leaving, the man said casually:

"I have a hut on the far side of the dump. If you have nowhere to sleep, come and see me. I might have a proposition for you."

His neighbour in the market sneered:

"A proposition? My eye! It's your ass he's after, old Saïd, believe me!"

Jallal gritted his teeth, pretending he hadn't heard. The youth – nicknamed "Old Fatima" because of the way his lips were drawn back over his missing front teeth – rubbed it in, sneering:

"Anyhow, if that's what you fancy, see that you grease your arsehole well. I bet he has a big one, the old bastard!"

It was Jallal's first experience of a brawl. Unfortunately, his adversary rapidly gained the upper hand. Squeezing the boy's head under his right armpit, he gave him a violent shove. Caught off balance, Jallal fell to the ground. More in sorrow than anger, "Fatima" grumbled:

"Look here, my lad, if you flare up like that every time someone cracks a joke, you're in for a hard time around here! I'm sorry for you, brother. Believe me, you ignorant highland brat, dirty job for dirty job,

I'd rather be stuffed up my backside than go on wading through shit. At least it doesn't tire you out. But who would look at an old scarecrow like me, unless he was blind?"

He made off, cackling, with his fellow pickers, all doubled up with laughter:

"Is there a blind man among you lot, well and truly blind? Come on, you Muslim bastards, do your good deed for the day!"

It was dusk when Jallal finally found the hut with the ramshackle Lambretta parked in front. Smarting from the comments of his fellow pickers, he had hesitated for a long time, but the chance to spend the hours of curfew sleeping under a real roof, even a corrugated iron one, made him choke with longing. He salivated with desire at the thought: a roof, with walls, just like the old days, just like home ... Saïd caught him lurking behind a pile of rusting iron. The boy, embarrassed, didn't like to refuse the rag-and-bone man's mocking invitation. Set on a makeshift table was some sort of sardine dish which they ate together with bread, taking it in turns to dip the crusts in a pan of sauce. Jallal took the precaution of seating himself near the door, so as to be able to flee at the least sign of impropriety. Saïd talked little, smoking throughout the meal. With his second cigarette, he pushed away his plate, complaining that the smell given off by Jallal was making his stomach heave, so the boy had better go and clean himself up a bit, always supposing that he knew what was meant by a good wash.

"Here, shepherd boy, take this bucket and give your bottom a good scrub ..."

Jallal scrambled to his feet, humiliated. He stammered something in the way of thanks. A kick up the backside made him stagger with pain. For the second time, trying to fight back, he found himself flat on the floor. Stunned by the fall, he was slow to take in what Saïd, leaning over him glaring, was saying:

"Little shit-picker, I don't know what they've been saying about me, but I'm not one of them if that's what you want to know. Do you understand? And even if I was, have you ever looked at yourself in the mirror?"

He pursed his lips, adding ironically:

"As for your backside, I've just given it the only thing it deserves!"

The man's voice softened:

45

"Here is what I propose: you can sleep here, but in exchange you fetch the water in the mornings. The tap is a good kilometre from here, and you have to queue for at least an hour to fill one can. With all this curfew business, I don't have time to do it myself. What you do after that is your business. We share the cost of food, of course. Nothing comes free, brat, as you have doubtless discovered. If the idea suits you, take this bucket and give yourself a wash. If not, you can clear off, quick sharp . . ."

Jallal clambered painfully to his feet, reflecting that he seemed to be making a habit of kissing the ground in this rubbish dump. He was hardly able to stand for the pain from the kick, but still couldn't help feeling immense gratitude to this cantankerous individual who had offered him hospitality.

Saïd turns out to be difficult to get along with, silent for evenings on end, brusque and often spiteful in his rare exchanges with Jallal. Several times, the boy is on the point of quitting, determined never to set foot in this damned dump again. But a combination of fatigue and terror, the hard days spent sorting rubbish, piece by piece, the terror, novel and irrepressible, of living alone, discourage him. So, lips compressed in disgust, he always returns to the hut with the decrepit motorbike parked outside.

This evening, Saïd is gloomier than usual. He has returned, after an hour's absence, with a crate of beer. He had gone to bed very early without food, woken with a start and taken off on the Lambretta. He is knocking back the beer, frowning, as if he has a deadline to meet. Jallal, mute, observes him from the corner of his eye, watchful for the first signs of anger.

Saïd bursts out laughing – a genuine laugh, loud and jovial:

"Come here, monkey face. I won't eat you. Try this!"

He hands the frightened boy a bottle of beer and then, rummaging through a box under his bed, produces a strip of white pills:

"Take it from me, peasant, there's nothing like a dozen beers and an Artane pill to clean out your skull and your heart. When you've had enough of this world and of your own dirt, take them, and for the time being you find that you can stand anything."

He jerks his chin emphatically:

". . . You can even stand yourself."

He gives a bitter laugh:

"And when it really works, when you've taken a good swig of the mixture, you even come to like yourself again, to like the son of a bitch you've allowed yourself to become. But that doesn't often happen."

He swallows a pill with a click of the tongue. "Drink up," he urges Jallal, yet without offering him the Artane pills. It is the first time in his life that Jallal has drunk alcohol. His throat tightens at the idea of the blasphemy he is about to commit. He thinks of his sister – she would furiously disown him! – then chases her from his mind. Under Saïd's amused gaze, the boy puts the bottle to his lips and drains it. At first, nauseated by the bitter taste, his gorge rises. But such is his desire to prolong Saïd's unaccustomed good mood, he finishes the bottle without vomiting. Saïd hums a tune by El Anka. His gestures grow broader, he drinks more slowly, smiling continuously. He voice takes on a silky tone:

"Do you know . . . who taught me that song?"

In a rambling speech, he talks of his former occupation – he had been a coppersmith – and of his quarrels with the proprietor of his workshop. In the end, his boss sacked him and Saïd had become a dustman ("Believe it or not, they said I was lucky to get the stinking job!"). At the time, he was engaged to be married to a distant cousin with whom he was madly in love.

"You know, Jallal, when I thought of her . . ."

The boy is in seventh heaven, because, for the first time since he has known him, Saïd is speaking to him kindly.

". . . my heart overflowed with joy. And when I thought that one day I would hold her in my arms, my prick rose and fought like a lion against the zip of my trousers. Ah, how I could have loved her, the bitch! They choke me to this day, these stupid things from the past. Memories play dirty tricks . . ."

He closes his eyes and drains another bottle. Then sighs, shallowly, as if it hurts to breathe:

"The bitch . . . As soon as she knew I had become a dustman, she sent someone to tell me that all was over between us, she wanted a respectable man for a husband, not someone who would be the laughing stock of every kid in the neighbourhood from morning to night: 'Do you smell worse from the arse or the mouth, Uncle Dustbin?' . . . That same evening, I had a round in the Casbah. There, the streets are so narrow that one has to use donkeys to pick up the rubbish. Nobody wants the job, the old timers prefer the lorries. So naturally it's left to the newcomers. I was still in shock from the message. One donkey, having hurt itself badly during the round, kept braying while I was filling the *couffins!*"

Saïd slaps his thighs. His laughter comes in jerks:

"You should have heard it bray! It brayed and brayed, that grey donkey, with incredible force for such a small beast. And all the time my head was ringing from the blow dealt me by that tart of mine! Eventually, I could stand it no longer. I had a pitchfork, and I used it to beat that stupid donkey, about the head, about the belly. It tried to defend itself, kicking like a mad thing, but it had the loaded *couffins* on its back. I had gone crazy myself. The other dustmen were scared of me when they saw the bloodshed. The police arrived. I struggled violently, they wrestled me to the ground and gave me a dreadful beating. I refused to be locked up in a cell, and clung on to the door. They slammed it on me all the same, that iron door . . ."

Grimacing, he holds up the hand with the missing fingers:

"It hurt like hell at the time!"

He uncaps another bottle:

"What with one thing and another, I was charged with resisting arrest and destroying State property. That donkey could hardly have known that it was so highly prized by the powers that be. I got six months' hard labour. Inside, they called me 'donkey killer' and whenever they saw me go by, they brayed."

Saïd chuckled:

"But I dare say it served me right. The wretched creature had done me no harm. Poor beast, but there you are . . ."

The candlelight plays weakly on the boy. Saïd has finished the last of the beers, surprised at having got through them so quickly. He breaks into drunken laughter:

"Now brother dustman has the wherewithal to avenge himself!"

With his forefinger, he mimes pulling a trigger:

"Bang, bang . . . A puff of smoke and it's over. Simple, isn't it?"

Somewhat alarmed by the direction the conversation is taking, Jallal manages a meaningless smile. His host's pupils are impressively enlarged, no doubt as a result of the Artane. Prompted by the boy's deceptively calm gaze, he raises his voice:

"Now you were probably born to be fucked up by life till the day you die. If you accept that, nobody can help you. Take it from me though, there is something more powerful than money, or the police, or contempt. And that's bang, bang . . ."

And, once more, he pulls an imaginary trigger:

"One doesn't need more than one finger for that!"

He yawns, lies down on the bed, fully dressed, and turns his face to the wall:

"You'll understand everything soon enough. Blow out the candle and don't breathe a word about what I've told you. Otherwise you'll pay for it, fathead!"

This threat, and the pointless insult, breaks the spell. Jallal would have liked to tell Saïd all about his despair, and the shame which has gnawed at him since the earthquake and tainted his every feeling. The boy is left with his burden. He has only a nagging desire to vomit and a sense of disappointment equal to the immense affection he had been ready to lavish upon this human being who is now snoring his head off. Biting his lips to keep from crying, he lies down on his foam mattress then, defeated, gets up again and spends a long time throwing up the contents of his stomach behind the heap of scrap iron.

Jallal tells himself that it's time to pack it in, it's too late, he won't earn any more this afternoon on this cursed Place des Martyrs. True, he could sell his wares in the bars, the Pasteur or the Didouche-Mourad, except that to carry them he would need a rucksack rather than this huge cardboard box. Bar owners object to their customers being pestered and are free with their kicks. If he has time, Jallal promises himself that he will return from the dump with something more discreet in which to carry his cigarettes and peanuts.

After a 15-minute walk, Jallal arrives at the dump feeling rather pleased with himself; thanks to the barging to get on the bus, he had managed to sneak a free ride under the nose of the wiliest conductor on the route. With his black eye-patch, unkempt beard and breath smelling perpetually of garlic, this conductor had no equal when it came to picking out the passenger who, despite the attributes of a respectable traveller, an immaculate *gandoura*, or a jacket and tie, was no better than a common fare-dodger. Jallal has already experienced the merciless grip of One Eye, as he was known to the waste-pickers at the dump: having stopped the bus, he plucked you from your seat, professing his pity for the deformed vagina which had had the misfortune to bring you into the world, and, to the delight of the passengers at this improvised show, literally threw you on to the tarmac, drenching you in his spittle. Today, admittedly, Jallal's exploit was of minor importance, as One Eye was occupied in telling a passenger about the car-bomb which had caused a dozen deaths that very morning at Blida. He had apparently been impressed most of all by the crater in the road: "A real abyss! By the Prophet, it might have been the mouth of Hell! And the strips of flesh, you should have seen them . . ." Jallal had laughed scornfully at the squeamishness of the man in the peaked cap. True, at first he too had been shocked by those stories of women raped by the GIA, then beheaded and jettisoned on the motorway, of journalists dismembered and returned to their families in a body-bag, of policemen's wives burnt alive. These days, having repeatedly heard this type of story, he has come to the conclusion that none of it concerns him and that it's best ignored. Because there is absolutely nothing he can do about it. Because he suspects that to maintain otherwise would be to call down the worst horrors upon himself. Because, when all is said and done, he has his own life to lead, perpetually demanding, perpetually hard: pity for others, whether he felt it or not, would do nothing to ease the burden of his private anguish, of water-duty, with its hour-long wait at the tap, feet in the mud, or the recurring rows at the baker's, when those who could afford it would buy up to 100 loaves at a time in order to sell them to you an hour later at double the price. In any case, everybody, child or adult, had his share of misfortune in this world. Jallal – who has learnt this the hard way up till now – has decided once and for all that the God of whom his sister talked to him in the old days and whom he had held so dear, is terrifying and unpredictable, tyrannising whom He pleases, when He pleases, without anybody – least of all a starving kid from the rubbish dumps of Algiers – being in a position to ask Him for an explanation. So while he's still alive he might as well have a good laugh when a third of the passengers took

50

advantage of the situation to travel at the government's expense on a bus fit only for the scrap heap. He must be sure to tell "Fatima" (with whom he is now on good terms) about the terrified expression on the conductor's face as the latter, usually so quick to spot the fare-dodgers, handed out change to right and left, saying over and over again: "O My God, what a blessing! A few minutes later and I would have had it! My brothers, I can't believe it: I might have been a goner too!" Someone in the crowd had muttered: "A man with too many blessings had better keep a close watch on his wife!" Between the laughter of some passengers and the scandalised exclamations of others, the conductor had choked with rage.

Jallal is apprehensive, for his earnings are well below Saïd's demands. But the little peanut-seller is so tired he just shrugs. Let Saïd say what he likes, surely he won't go so far as to chuck him out! Perhaps he wouldn't even be there tonight, as has often been the case recently? Perhaps the cagey fellow has taken up again with that famous girl of his who had a taste for the good life? The cardboard box is growing heavy. Jallal starts to dream of stealing a day off tomorrow, at Bordj El Kiffan or Alger-Plage, with some pals from the rubbish dump. Nothing like a day spent rolling around in the waves for cleansing one's skin, nails and nostrils of the grime from the capital's garbage! They could also earn a bit of money by keeping an eye on a luxury car or two . . . Anyone turning up his nose at the offer of surveillance had better beware: nothing is easier than to scratch the proudly gleaming bodywork of a big, brand-new Mercedes!

Jallal is still engaged in these joyous reflections when he enters the hut to put away his goods and collect the two cans for water-duty: the large 20-litre one and the small 5-litre one. He had better hurry, for the taps would soon be turned off and wouldn't come on again until 6.00 in the morning. If there wasn't enough water to wash in when he wanted it, Saïd wouldn't hesitate to have his guts out. Especially as, if that were possible, he has become even stranger and more irritable these last few days . . .

Before Jallal's eyes have had time to get accustomed to the dim light of the hut, a violent kick from behind sends him sprawling on the earthen floor. He scrambles to his feet, but a second blow, from a rifle-butt, knocks him flat. The boy's urge is to cry out, his lungs inflating themselves to bellow with all their force. But the figures confronting him are so terrifying with their masks and huge rifles that Jallal knows instantly that he will be killed, purely and simply, should he think of letting out so much as a squawk.

So he swallows his cry. But he can't prevent his teeth from chattering uncontrollably when a gun-barrel is pressed roughly against his temple.

4

"You his whore or what? What the hell are you doing here? Talk!"

A slap stings the face of the little peanut-seller on the brink of flight. The hooded man staring at him appears exasperated and embarrassed. He turns to his six companions, each masked and wearing the blue uniform of the special forces of the Ministry of the Interior.

"Shit! What are we to do with the kid? We can't let him go, he might try and warn the others!"

The boy, huddled against Saïd's bed, tries to regain his breath. He is so stunned by the slap that his sight is blurred by tears. But panic is stronger than the pain, and no words emerge from his mouth. The man shakes him, a little less roughly:

"The dustman, Saïd, is he a relation of yours?"

The boy shakes his head, unable to suppress a sob of relief as he realises that they are not about to kill him on the spot. He replies with a trembling voice:

"No, but he's my friend . . . I've been living here for two months."

One of the policemen makes an obscene gesture with his Kalashnikov.

"To pay the rent, you let him fuck you . . . is that it?"

The boy hangs his head. Choked with indignation, he holds back his protests. Now that his eyes have become accustomed to the gloom, he can see that the intruders are heavily armed and, above all, dangerously excitable. The place has evidently been searched from top to bottom, and holes up to 30 centimetres deep have been dug here and there. Prudently, he holds his tongue. The policemen seem to have forgotten his presence in any case. They are arguing bitterly among themselves, careful to keep their voices down, as if trying to come to a decision. One turns to Jallal. His tone is bullying:

"What time does he usually get back, your chum?"

"It all depends, Uncle. He hasn't been sleeping here for the past few days."

The man taps him with his rifle-butt:

"I'm not your uncle, you little turd. What does he do with himself all day, this Saïd?"

"He has a little business. He buys and sells the stuff collected by the waste-pickers. It doesn't go far, Unc . . ."

He receives a blow on the side of the head.

"Are you deaf or something, arsehole? I'm not your uncle."

Jallal puts a hand to his forehead, smiling weakly in acknowledgement. Dry-mouthed, he replies to several more questions, doing his best to appear co-operative. But as all his answers are negative, he senses mounting irritation and suspicion in his questioners. An attitude of defiance, a wariness, an itching of the fingers on the triggers of their automatic rifles . . . In his heart of hearts, Jallal doesn't believe that they would kill him, the police don't do such things, he has done nothing wrong. All the same, he is not reassured; the boys at the dump have told him too many stories of summary executions, of bodies found in rubbish bins after house-to-house searches by the Ninjas . . . One refuse-picker had insisted that the police were a lot of old women who would never succeed in capturing the *moudjahidine* because they were the true defenders of Islam and God protected his servants. So the police in their fury turned on the weak and killed those who had neither the weapons nor the strength to hit back. "Insult me all you like, but please don't kill me," Jallal thinks. Perhaps this business was only a misunderstanding and these damned police, having asked their questions, would soon go away?

"Do people ever spend the night here?"

"No, never. Saïd doesn't like visitors."

"Where does he sleep when he's not in this slum?"

"I don't know . . . honestly, I don't, I swear it. Saïd never tells me anything."

An infuriated kick.

"So you know nothing, eh? Like everybody else in this bloody country. Do you want to know what he's been up so, your sodding pal? This morning, in El Harrach, he and three of his accomplices shot and killed three policemen who were having a quiet meal in a pizzeria. Didn't know that, did you, little whore?"

He kicks him in the flank. Jallal overbalances with the violence of the blow, then crawls to safety behind the bed like a wounded puppy. He utters little gasps of pain. One of the policemen interrupts:

"Take it easy, Ali, he's only a kid."

The other flares up:

"A kid? And what about the kid who tailed Abdelkader and informed his assassins? And he was a neighbour what's more, that little terrorists' nark. The runt was barely 12 years old, still wetting his pants. And Abdelkader and his entire family, his wife and two youngest children, his mother and father, all died with their throats cut, like sheep. His daughter, poor girl, only 15, was dragged off into the hills, and no-one has seen her since! If she hasn't been tortured, decapitated and buried somewhere, she is probably a tart and slave to some bunch of madmen who swear daily that gang-rape is authorised by the Koran . . ."

The voice of the man in the hated uniform is beginning to crack:

"And all because poor Abdelkader was a policeman! Not even a high-ranking policeman! No, an ordinary traffic cop, trying to make ends meet and living with his parents in three tiny rooms on a crumbling housing estate. And to cap it all, as a mark of gratitude for protecting his country, those dogs pinned his ID card to his cheek, right through the flesh. He was our friend! Remember, Driss?"

He splutters with rage:

"And you're not allowed to carry a service weapon, even if you live in a danger area. Government orders: guns mustn't be allowed to fall into terrorist hands, but when it comes to you, Driss, your life, your family's lives, your rotten wages, your fear, nobody gives a damn!"

He stares at the boy, more terrifying than ever, his face invisible except for two glaring eyes, red-rimmed with fatigue.

"In this benighted country, when it comes to war, there's no age limit. You can't even trust a bunch of children playing marbles. How do you know that this kid you're so sorry for won't be the very one who'll tail you so that some nutter can blow your brains out, eh?"

"Shut up!" The man at the door takes an anxious look outside. "You can moan later if the other side gives you the chance. It's getting dark. Driss, Ali, take cover behind the scrap heap. Belkacem, guard the entrance to the path. The rest of you . . ."

Dazed, Jallal has almost forgotten his pain. They have handcuffed him to the bedpost. The unthinkable begins to surface in his terrified mind: Saïd has shot and killed three men, Saïd is no longer the Saïd he knows, the crotchety dustman, the drunk, good at heart really, who has taken him in and makes a little money from objects salvaged from the dump, but a killer, a terrorist who murders policemen!

"No, it's impossible, I tell you! He can't be a terrorist!" Jallal wants to shout, outraged by the policeman's accusation. "He doesn't give a damn for religion, I've never seen him pray, he has never even mentioned that sort of thing . . . And he doesn't have a beard!" But faced with these terrifying, trigger-happy men, Jallal realises that such arguments are futile. "It's true that he doesn't like the police much, and he has a terrible temper, but he would never gun down three policemen in cold blood while they were eating their pizzas, not Saïd! Anyhow, it's ridiculous, people don't get killed in pizzerias! No . . ."

Darkness descends swiftly. The atmosphere in the hut is eerie. Now nobody is paying attention to the boy chained to the bed. The men, on edge, exchange disjointed phrases in the dark. A few have taken off their hoods because of the heat. They stretch now and then, to ward off drowsiness. Somebody hands round chewing-gum. A voice remarks in tones of deep disgust:

"What with the stink from this dump, I might as well be chewing on a mint turd instead of your gum!"

His neighbour retorts that he had better keep his big mouth shut then, it stinks enough as it is! Meanwhile, the hungry boy nods off, only to wake with a start when the handcuff tugs at his wrist. Overwhelmed by a sickening terror rather like a fever, he has stopped trying to understand. Around him, the policemen exchange bitter comments on life in the force. One complains that although his unit is below strength, they are often sent out at a moment's notice, straight after an exhausting patrol, to help colleagues in trouble.

"You just have time to swallow some revolting soup right there in the station, your *kalash* in your lap, when all hell breaks loose! Luckily there are such things as pills, or you would drop off in the middle of a shoot-out!"

Then the whispered conversation, punctuated by slaps on the cheek to squash the persistent mosquitoes, returns more calmly to the subject of their respective families.

At around one o'clock in the morning, long after curfew, things start happening fast. The walkie-talkie crackles and gives out curt orders. A policeman claps his hand over Jallal's mouth and breathes:

"One word out of you, my boy, and you're dead!"

Petrified, Jallal gathers that there is about to be a gunfight and that he will be caught in the middle, facing the door to the hut. Warning shouts break the silence, followed by bursts of fire from pistols and automatic rifles. Someone yells from outside:

"Watch out, there are two of them!"

For 30 seconds there is quiet, then a furious voice is heard, one which Jallal immediately recognises:

"Jallal, are you there? Answer if you're alive! Answer me, damn it!"

Immediately the shooting begins again. Bullets smash into the ceiling. Jallal whimpers with fear. The exchange of fire is brief, lasting two or three minutes at most, but the boy's heart is beating so fast that at first he doesn't realise when it's over . . .

A member of the commandos appears in the doorway, lit by the beam of his companion's torch. He cries out:

"Both terrorists out of action, sir. One dead, one wounded in the guts."

"Which one is still alive?"

"Don't know yet, but it'll be a right pleasure to get his name out of him, the son of a bitch!"

The men in the hut rush outside, except for their commander who is speaking into his walkie-talkie. To Jallal, half buried under the bed, his dissatisfaction is clearly audible, the annoyance in his voice interrupted by the crackling of the distant reply:

"What do you expect us to do about it here at the station . . . return to base . . . do you understand? . . . over . . ."

The commander breathes "message understood" and walks unhurriedly out of the hut. A few seconds later another shot, the final one, puts an end to the night's horrifying suspense, and to that of Jallal.

"This is not a place worth living in!"

He leaves the police station famished and in a state of utter despair. The Ninjas had taken him to a station in El Harrach. The police didn't beat him, just pushed him around a little. They soon decided that he knew nothing. He spent the remainder of the night in a cell with other prisoners, some as petrified as he was. One man, still in his pyjamas, his face marked by blows, was trembling from head to foot. He had cursed his son:

"They say that I must stay in prison till my youngest son gives himself up. I ask you, is that fair, at my age? He takes to the hills and his family takes the blame. But he has no heart, my son, I know him. He'll never give himself up!"

There was a row when another prisoner – little stubby beard and livid complexion – turned on the pyjama-clad father:

"What are you afraid of, you senile old fool? So they'll kill you? So what? They'll kill me too. God's reward will more than make up for our sufferings. Your son is a hero!"

Around midday, an inspector took him to his office and gave him a lecture. In short, he explained to the boy that, for his own good, he had better not breathe a word about anything he might have seen the previous night. On the other hand, should he ever hear of trouble brewing among the waste-pickers, he would be well advised to come and inform of it personally. Otherwise, nothing would be easier than to send him to prison or a reformatory "and we won't lack for excuses: such as the fact that you ran away from God knows where, or that you were your ex-landlord's whore!" The boy's vehement denial was met with a rap over the head with a ruler.

"Quiet! You don't raise your voice to a policeman."

He added with a contemptuous smile:

"We're not interested in your arsehole, little tart. We'll look the other way, on condition that you occasionally bring us a tid-bit about those bearded bastards or their supporters . . ."

The little peanut-seller didn't even have a chance to find out if Saïd were really dead. There had been two bodies covered by a blanket in the back of the 4×4 taking him to the police station. The feet were hanging out, and every time the vehicle swerved they bounced up and down. It was too dark to identify the corpses. The only sound was the dull thud of their shoes knocking against the bodywork.

"This place is not worth living in!"

He makes his way through the crowds along the main street of El Harrach. He seethes with an impotent rage which, curiously, is making him cough. Tears – which have ceased to flow – have been replaced by dry expectorations: he coughs and coughs, but whatever it is that has been tearing at his chest since Saïd's death and is now suffocating him in full sunlight, refuses to come up. His head is in a whirl: Saïd kills and is killed, the police kill and have their throats cut, and he himself, who has never done anybody any harm, is accused of prostitution ... Abruptly, and as unbearable as a toothache, the memory of ordinary mornings when only the usual, trifling irritations disturbed the pattern of everyday life, overwhelms him, and he feels as if he will faint. "O my God, give me back an ordinary life. I don't even mean the old days, such happiness is too much to ask for; no, just the recent past, when I sold peanuts and Saïd, my friend, was still alive. And, O God, don't let him have been a terrorist. And above all, don't let him have killed anybody. Bring him back to life, O Thou who can do anything, back to the times when he too was happy and wished nobody any harm . . ."

Jallal passes the next day and night in a state of total dejection. Fifty or so metres from the hut, he almost steps in two large brown patches covered in flies: dried blood from the corpses of the two terrorists. It occurs to him to look for the place where Saïd and his companion were surprised by the commandos. He finds it easily: a dozen spent cartridges spilled on the ground and bloodstains in the dust. His only food is a meagre sandwich, unfinished, for the seller had sprinkled the bread with *harissa* to disguise the taste of rotting meat. He stays awake all night, fearful lest the police return.

Next morning he hasn't the heart to go back to the Place des Martyrs to sell the last of the peanuts and cigarettes. He wanders round the outskirts of the dump in search of somebody to whom he can pour out his grief. Running into "Fatima" towards evening, he attempts to start up a conversation with a well-worn joke ("Still not made enough dough to

59

buy some gold teeth and get yourself a wife?"), but the other, unable to conceal his discomfort, interrupts:

"Drop it, Jallal. Go and bend someone else's ear."

The youth, dragging a plastic sack bulging with his pathetic finds, turns his back on Jallal and hurries off. Flabbergasted by "Fatima's" reaction, the boy grabs him by the shoulder:

"Hey, what's up with you? Have you got a plane to catch?"

"Fatima" shakes him off roughly:

"Don't make trouble for me, Jallal. It's hard enough earning a crust as it is . . . So far, I've got away with my skin. I've managed to avoid taking sides, do you see! And that's no mean feat in this crazy world, for either side would rub me out without a second thought. I'm nothing, worth less in most people's eyes than a scrap of orange peel. Who would care if I got my throat cut? You, I don't think so! So bugger off and leave me alone!"

Seeing Jallal stare at him, wide-eyed, the youth whistles through the gap in his teeth:

"There's a rumour that you're a paid informer for the cops!"

"But that's not true . . . it's impossible . . . it's a lie!"

"You were seen leaving El Harrach police station. Apparently you were cool as a cucumber even though they had just got Saïd the dustman and that chum of his, a fellow by the name of Hicham, from the Eucalyptus housing estate."

"Listen, 'Fatima' . . ."

Irritably, the youth shrugs off the hand touching him.

"Get away from me! If I'm seen with you, I'll be taken for one of your spies."

The boy drops his hand dismayed. "Fatima" looks at him uneasily:

"Listen, chum, I don't want to get mixed up in this, and I'm almost sure you're OK. But how is one to know? At the dump, they say you've just fixed it all up so that you could keep the hut and the Lambretta for yourself. So you'd better make yourself scarce as soon as possible . . ."

"Run away, you mean? . . . From the dump? But why? Anyhow, where would I go?"

The youth bends down to tie the laces on his filthy shoes and lowers his voice:

"There's also a rumour that tonight or tomorrow some GIA types, or

AIS for all I know, will come and take their revenge for your treachery. And they'll find you, all right, that lot."

"Fatima" passes his index finger across his throat. Seeing the boy's panic-stricken expression, he can't resist patting him on the shoulder. Then, pushing him away with the flat of his hand, he clears his throat to disguise his compassion:

"Maybe it's not true, maybe people started the rumour because they wanted to lay their hands on your slum, and all that goes with it ... Anything is possible in this sodding country. People would kill their father and mother for a roof over their heads, however rotten, especially if some other lunatic is prepared to do the job for them for nothing."

He wags his sad clown's head. As he talks, he examines his companion, thin, grubby, dressed in clothes almost identical to his – T-shirt and crumpled trousers – younger than himself, of course, but promising to be a similar down-and-out. They could so easily have become friends ... Repressing a sigh, he pushes the dazed boy away with more determination:

"But if you ask me it's too risky for you to stick around here. Clear off, little brother, and don't tell anyone that I warned you!"

Anna is vexed, but refuses to admit that her vexation is tinged with anxiety. Majid, the hotel telephonist with whom she has made friends – to the extent that they are on first name terms – has just told her that, earlier in the afternoon, the police arrested a youth who was asking about a hotel guest, a European woman. Aged about 18 or 19, wearing a pouch on his belt, a ring in one ear and a pony-tail, he aroused the suspicions of the Aletti's security guards. Unable to state the woman's nationality, despite his claim to know her, he drew a gun, and his arrest nearly ended in disaster. Once surrounded, he struggled violently. He tried to shoot, drawing a pistol from his belt-pouch, but the police were too quick for him and wounded him in the shoulder.

"Do you think he was after me?"

Majid nods. Apart from the elderly woman, the hotel lounge is deserted. Lolling back in one of the imposing armchairs, he absentmindedly rubs a finger over its faded tapestry. Before him, limitless, stretches the extraordinary vista of the port of Algiers at night. On the horizon, the lights of some 20 ships flicker like candles set into the surface of the sea.

"No doubt about it, Anna. You're the only European staying in the hotel."

He sighs:

"To think that, in the old days, this room swarmed with tourists and diplomats from every country in the world! Businessmen, writers, journalists, all more or less the worse for drink, and claiming, between whiskies, to be privy to the latest secret deliberately leaked by the Intelligence Services. There were gossips, liars, drunks galore among them, not to mention the occasional outright villain, but that was the life! . . . Even the tarts, excuse me for saying so, were good-looking, and if not overjoyed by it, at least they did their job with style! Those were the days, I can tell you; I spent hours watching the comings and goings, seated at my switchboard, sometimes having a good laugh to myself. These days, what a waste: our women look like crows in that damn silly *chador*. Our young men let their beards grow and massacre anyone who doesn't conform. There is misery, ugliness, barbarity . . . Take those ships, for instance: not one has dared stay long in Algiers since an Islamicist commando boarded a tanker and cut the throats of six wretched Italian sailors in their sleep. Now they all have at least a dozen armed men on guard every night, for fear of another attack!"

He offers her a cup of tea. She accepts, finding the green tea excellent in spite of its bitter taste. He smiles:

"One doesn't have to be a genius to observe that you have certainly chosen a strange time to visit Algeria!"

She smiles back at him, sipping her tea. She realises that she has become very fond of this affable, rather diffident man who has never tried to get her to say more than she wished him to know. From the way he looks at her, she can tell that he is dying to hear the real reasons for her visit to this city in the grip of madness – one doesn't take a holiday in a place where the colour of your skin is enough to get your throat cut purely for the pleasure of sightseeing! – but equally she senses that he makes it a point of honour to be discreet. She changes the subject:

"You love your country very much, Majid."

"Don't you believe it. In fact, I detest it! With a cordial detestation, as you might say. As one detests a favourite child: one calls it every name

62

under the sun, spits on it, betrays it at every opportunity, yet one is ready to die for it! That's the drama for us Algerians. We dream of one thing only: to quit this hell, to live in a normal country, among normal people, but we no sooner cross the Mediterranean sea than we pine away from nostalgia and guilt . . ."

Majid sees that he has spoken too passionately. He takes his cup in both hands and sips the scalding tea with a self-conscious air:

"I speak from experience: for three years, I lived in Amsterdam. I managed to find a job in the hotel business, not very well paid but acceptable. Then, just as everything was beginning to go well, I realised that I was unhappy. Outwardly, Anna, all was well, but inwardly I was no longer able to breathe, no longer alive. I was empty, like a shiny new plastic bag. It was as stupid as that! I came home, duly penitent, one hand outstretched, the other behind my back. Since when, of course, every time I cringe at the sound of a hail of bullets, or a strange noise in the night, I'm so furious that I could kill myself."

His chubby face recovers its habitual good humour:

"Speaking of killing, let's keep our fingers crossed, for these days one can pull the devil by his . . . er . . . his beard, once too often."

He gets to his feet, explaining that his tea-break is at an end. He chews on his moustache, suddenly grave:

"I would take the business with that young man very seriously if I were you. Be more careful. You've become very popular with the staff in the week you've been staying in the hotel, you draw them out in conversation, you take an interest in what they say and, unlike the average tourist, you don't ram your opinions down their throats. And, surprisingly, you seem to have a genuine liking for our poor country. So it's natural that the staff should be concerned for you. It would be a great pity, Anna," he smiles to soften the gravity of his warning, "if anything should happen to prevent our continuing this conversation . . ."

She goes up to her room, a little depressed, tired out from wandering aimlessly around Algiers while awaiting the miracle of a reply to her telegram. Moreover, she is alarmed by the business of the young man. How much longer can she stay in Algiers without endangering her life? But the moment she envisages the possibility of her departure, something snaps within her, turns into a desire for self-abasement, as though she were resigning herself to a life of shame for having failed to accomplish, just once in her life, what her two murdered children had been demanding of her for 30 years or more. She puts through a telephone call to her son Hans, only to become hopelessly embroiled when he asks her how she is enjoying herself. She answers that the sea has never looked so beautiful, and Hans interrupts, disbelieving:

"What sea, aren't you in Cairo? Do you mean the Nile, Mother?"

She hangs up abruptly, pretending that she has run out of change for the telephone. The call has further lowered her morale. She goes down to the hotel restaurant, but can eat nothing.

Around ten o'clock that evening – she is already in her nightdress – there is a knock at the door. Two embarrassed men in plain clothes explain that the hotel bodyguards are in a serious dilemma, being required by the highest authority to ensure her safety at all costs.

"You see, Madame, so far no Swiss citizen has been the victim of a terrorist attack in Algiers. Our superiors are most anxious to keep it that way. Yet you don't make it easy for us. You wander through the most notorious streets in Algiers, taking no precautions whatsoever. Yesterday, you even went to the Casbah! For any little terrorist group seeking cheap publicity by attacking a foreigner, you make an ideal target. Today you were lucky that we managed to intercept an individual who almost certainly intended to harm you. If you continue to behave in this way, we may be unable to intervene a second time . . ."

The elderly lady in the dressing-gown gives a deceptively innocent smile ("Ah, I see, you even know where I went yesterday"), at which the younger of the two officers flushes angrily. His tone becomes markedly hostile, his delivery staccato as if, unused to being defied, he is forcibly restraining himself from grabbing the woman by the neck.

"You may find it amusing, Madame, but for us policemen it's no joke. We have families, our wives and children mean a lot to us, as we do to them, believe it or not. When we leave home in the morning, we can't promise them that our day's work won't end in the morgue. We two" (he gestures towards the other officer, a gloomy individual with a paunch and curling grey hair, who is inspecting Anna with small, suspicious eyes) "are still alive, but many of our colleagues are not so lucky."

He waits expectantly for a sign of approval from his fellow officer, who murmurs in Arabic:

"You're a bloody bore, with your lecturing. Tell this madwoman what we came to tell her and basta! The rest is nothing to do with her."

The first man pales, but he ignores the pot-bellied man's remark. He is trying to see from the foreigner's eyes whether she has understood the reprimand. He continues, but with less assurance, having the impression that the "madwoman" is regarding him with a certain irony:

"Hmm . . . What's more, we don't feel like risking our insignificant lives for the sake of somebody who doesn't give a damn. So either you agree to abide by the rules, keeping your outings to a minimum and avoiding the city centre unless accompanied by a hotel bodyguard, or, if you are determined to commit suicide, you go home to Switzerland and do it there. Speaking of which, by the way, we must ask you to give us your passport and plane ticket."

Suddenly, Anna loses her temper:

"You have no right! I have a valid tourist visa. I shall complain to my consulate and . . ."

The second officer interrupts, his pitying tone mixed with irritation. He speaks French with a slight Kabyle accent:

"But Madame, where on earth have you been? Your consulate moved to Tunis years ago! As for tourism, there's a war on here, in case you haven't noticed! Your diplomats? They would agree with every word we've said. Naturally you are under surveillance! Do you think we keep open house? Besides, you should be grateful to us. If we have to save you from yourself, well, we shall have no hesitation in doing so. Unless your motives for wanting to remain under any circumstances are a good deal less innocent than you would have us believe with your pretence of tourism . . ."

Suddenly, seeing the elderly tourist glaring at him, he softens. He thinks to himself that this frail old bird has one hell of a temper, her husband must have a hard time of it at home! More amiably this time, he insists:

"Madame, kindly hand over your passport and ticket. The request doesn't come from us, you know. It's an order from our superiors . . ."

A woman dressed in a white *haik* makes her way hesitantly along the seafront. Reaching the National Assembly, she takes the precaution of crossing the road to avoid the police on guard duty. Wearing riot gear with visored helmets, they carry automatic pistols. One senses that they are nervous, ready to fire at the slightest provocation. Big blocks of cement are placed to divert the traffic, and as a protection against booby-trapped vehicles. Other buildings, such as the newspaper offices of *El Moudjahid* and the headquarters of the Central Bank, are surrounded by barbed wire. Her face half hidden beneath the small, triangular silk veil, her body enveloped by the long, uncomfortable surplice worn by the women of Algiers, the woman has the bizarre impression of existing in the world unseen by others or rather, worse still, of having no existence whatsoever, bar that of an observer, in cunning disguise, of the crowd flowing around her; it is as though, plodding along, she were peering through a keyhole. Is she under the protection of this *haik* or its prisoner? she asks herself, irritated by the folds of white cloth flapping against her legs.

It is true that in this man's country where a woman without a veil is considered to be little more than a potential tart, fair game for lewd stares and catcalls, Anna feels safe enough in her protective envelope. But lacking both face and shape, other than the vague, somewhat grotesque form of a sack, she cannot avoid a feeling of degradation. With hopeless sadness, she watches the throng of veiled women brandishing their *couffins* in front of the barred windows of the Bab Azoun State shop: fussing, noisy, ugly and, inevitably, as anonymous as a flock of ungainly birds. To be a part of a flock of female animals without identity or independent will, to be pushed along by dim-witted herdsmen whose sole pride and joy is the little tadpole hanging between their testicles, that, Anna thinks to herself, is a humiliation which must wound her veiled sisters of the Muslim world to the core, always supposing that they ever indulge in the dangerous exercise of questioning the status quo.

Anna rapidly becomes breathless, for the interminable length of cloth that wraps her from head to foot is difficult to wear. With its tendency to slip, she has to hitch it up over her forehead and shoulders, and it is hot beneath this pitiless sun. Moreover, to make matters worse, when she breathes in the veil is sucked into her mouth and becomes wet with saliva. She almost feels like accosting one of the veiled women in the crowd, to seek some sisterly advice on how to wear this damned *haik*, but fears the woman's noisy astonishment on discovering a European beneath the traditional dress of a grandmother from Algiers . . .

She smiles at the memory of Majid's face when, the night before, following the visit of the two policemen, she had asked him to buy her a *haik*. It was becoming too risky, she argued, for her to walk about the streets of Algiers. He burst out laughing and admitted that it wasn't a bad idea. He refused to take her money, explaining that his mother, who possessed at least six or seven *haiks*, would be only too happy to lend her one. True to his word, the next morning he brought her a superb *haik* which, according to his mother, had cost a fortune 20 years ago.

Now she has reached the vast Place des Martyrs. In mutinous mood, she decides to try out her disguise on the little brat who had called her "widow's arse". Ah, there he is, still sitting on his stool beside his eternal cardboard box! She passes the Palais des Princesses, retraces her steps, crosses the road, and deliberately walks up and down in front of him. The boy, a faraway look in his eyes, absorbed in his own thoughts, fails to notice her. Slightly annoyed, she goes up to him and, in Arabic, asks for a bag of peanuts. The boy's eyes widen in surprise, for his customer's accent is barely comprehensible. Anna, gloating behind her veil, snaps:

"It's 'Old Widow's Arse', back for more peanuts!"

Jallal is so flabbergasted that he hands over the bag without a word. Feeling rather uncomfortable at having produced such an effect on the little peanut-seller, Anna takes the bag and adds:

"Have you lost your tongue, wise guy?"

The boy looks away, adopting his previous fixed expression. Anna, disappointed, upbraids him teasingly:

"What, no more laughs, brat? Anyone would think that you had just come from a funeral."

Again, the effect is like magic. The brown face turns towards her. Gradually, as if in slow motion, a tear wells up in the corner of each stupefied eye. Anna watches as the two drops swell and prepare to roll down his cheeks. But all of a sudden the little peanut-seller buries his face in his arms. He is doubled up, his head on his knees. He weeps without a sound. His body is shaken by sobs, but so lightly that anyone giving him a passing glance would have thought he was sleeping. Anna, taken by surprise, is dumbfounded. She can see perfectly well that he is crying, but feels at a complete loss, not knowing what to do. The boy, curled up in a ball, is black with dirt. His cardboard box displays a few meagre wares: two or three bags of peanuts and an open packet of maize-coloured cigarettes. She leans over and rests a hand on his curly hair:

"Why are you crying, young man?"

Without raising his head, the boy whimpers:

"Leave me alone! I can cry if I want. It's none of your business!"

He repeats, louder, in Arabic: "Go away, go away!", his voice broken by sobs. People look round. Anna, crimson with embarrassment, hastily moves away. She has a lump in her throat. She is also furious at being obliged to flee. Then, 50 metres on, she turns back: the boy is still in the same position. The moment he looks up she hurries on, as if caught out.

She spends a miserable morning in the Aletti, having forgone her walk on account of the child's inexplicable grief. Naturally, no letters await her at the reception desk. The two policemen (whom she has privately nicknamed Laurel and Hardy) have returned her passport and ticket. Her stay has been curtailed by two thirds: her visa is now valid for three more days only, and the administration has graciously included a reservation for the Air Algeria flight to Lyon on the day it expires!

The 65-year-old Anna is desperate. She cannot leave without having prayed over her children's grave. She has convinced herself that the key to the meaning of her life – the worth of her life! – is to be found in that mountain cemetery. Should she flinch from visiting the patch of earth that has swallowed up her son and daughter, she knows that she will despise herself for the rest of her days. Therefore she makes up her mind to go, come what may. "This very afternoon!" she decides, in a sort of fever. She is mad, she knows it, but she also knows that for her, in her predicament, it is the only way of remaining sane. Batna, the first stage of her journey, is some 400 kilometres from Algiers, and from there she will still have to take the mountain track to Nassreddine's *douar*. To fly is out of the question, for she would be asked for identity papers which, with the few days left to her, might alert some zealous official! But after all, she calculates, two days should be enough for the return journey by road. She will take the bus as far as Batna, then hire a taxi. A tip, if sufficiently generous, should persuade even the most reluctant taxi driver to wear out his tyres on the mountain tracks . . .

But the hardest part is this: she can't travel alone! Protective *haik* or not, she will still have to buy tickets, give her destination, ask directions. Her knowledge of Arabic, extremely rudimentary after years of disuse, and above all her appalling accent, will give her away at once. She would be gambling with her very life! The morning paper she has just bought at the hotel kiosk reminds her that this is no mere hypothesis: the day before, at Bouira, a Belgian couple had been shot dead. According to the newspaper report, they had lived in the town for at least ten years and were much respected by their Algerian neighbours. Perhaps this same respect had spared them the greater horror of the butcher's knife? . . .

To help herself think more calmly, Anna takes a shower. She soaps her worn body and then, with a vigour to match her rising fear, scrubs herself unsparingly for several minutes.

"Damn, the water has been cut off!"

The incident puts her in a good mood. She gets out of the shower, still covered in soap. Meticulously, she wipes her knotted legs, her pubis with its tuft of wiry hair, her flaccid breasts, castigating herself: "How much longer before this old machine wears out?" Then she rubs her hair, cleans her ears and, piece by piece, constructs her plan. It is now almost complete . . .

Her bags packed, she asks for the bill and goes to see Majid. His expression, normally so pleasant, is grim. He tells his Swiss friend that, barely an hour ago, he had witnessed a man's death. He was on his way to lunch in the Rue de la Lyre. Two armed men who hadn't even bothered to put on masks brought out a youth, his hands tied behind his back. One man tripped the poor wretch up with his foot.

"And they cut his throat there and then, in broad daylight, in the middle of the street! Casually, as one would a chicken's! There was blood everywhere. I was standing in front of the restaurant. I panicked, like everybody else. Some women screamed, others fainted. The two murderers just slipped away quietly, as if nothing had happened. It was dreadful: the body went on twitching for what seemed like an eternity! The most terrible thing was . . ."

He passes his tongue over his dry lips:

". . . the young man wasn't gagged, yet he didn't cry for help!"

His eyes blank, he swears under his breath:

"I didn't hang about there myself. I was still trembling when I got back to the hotel . . ."

And, on a sinister note:

"Take good care of yourself, Anna. The devil has entered our country, and his hoofprints are everywhere. No atrocity is too horrible for these madmen to contemplate. They're quite capable of cutting up their fathers and mothers while sipping their morning coffee. So a foreign woman . . ."

Anna nods. But her heart is beating so wildly that she has to lean on his desk. She struggles to recover her breath:

"My dear Majid, I'm going to take a trip to Tipasa, to see those famous Roman ruins. I'll be spending the night at the hotel in the tourist complex. Can I leave my luggage with you till I get back?"

The telephonist hasn't noticed Anna's dizzy spell. Frowning, he says absently: "Yes, I'll take care of it," resentful in spite of himself: he is shocked by Anna's over-bright tone, her apparent indifference. He puts it down to foolishness, old age and the cold heart of a northerner. He shrugs, a fatalist, but a little more lonely than before, and returns to his nightmarish visions.

Anna, dressed in her *haik* and carrying a small overnight bag, makes straight for the Place des Martyrs. She is increasingly nervous. Her plan suddenly seems completely idiotic! How could she have given it a second thought?

The boy is there, firmly ensconced in his usual place. She proffers him a large note. The urchin sniffs, displeased:

"Hey, Yemma Laziza [Mother dear], since when does one buy five dinars' worth of peanuts with a 200 dinar note? With that much money, I could buy up the whole of Algeria!"

The Yemma answers, in French:

"Keep it. It's for the bag of peanuts I forgot to pay for this morning."

Flabbergasted, Jallal splutters indignantly, in a mixture of Arabic and French:

"Ah, so it's . . . it's you again . . . ! But what have I done that the Good Lord should send you to mock me from morning to night?"

The woman in the *haik* leans forward:

70

"Keep the money, my child. I'll give you more, if you'll do something for me."

Anna is a little ashamed of herself for adopting such wiles. She has a sudden vision of herself as a satyr trying to pick up a young boy. Blushing beneath her veil, she goes on hurriedly:

"I'm going to Batna and I need a guide. Take me to see your parents. If they say that you can come with me, you'll be well paid for your trouble."

Jallal can't believe his ears. He gazes uneasily at the stranger, only her blue eyes visible behind the veil. Anna panics, sensing that he is about to refuse. She takes out two more banknotes, discreetly folding them into four and putting them into the urchin's hand:

"Here, I'll buy your entire stock."

The boy quivers, hesitating between greed and disbelief. He glances to left and right, then closes his fist over the money.

"Old woman, you must be crazy. What I have to sell is hardly worth 30 dinars. And you've given me 600. No-one gives away that much for nothing . . ."

Jallal is on his feet, his body rigid with distrust, ready to flee at the first sign of trouble. Looking at her accusingly, he lashes out:

"I don't get it. I'm dirty, I stink, I don't have a roof over my head and I have nobody left in the world. What do you really want with me, *roumia*?"

5

It is a small hospital, not far from the Ravin de la Femme Sauvage. The entrance is cluttered with stalls selling merguez, kebabs, lemonade, cigarettes. Nassreddine storms out, beside himself with fury. Jaourden's wife had been admitted around ten o'clock the previous night, virtually comatose. The poor Targui, his half-conscious wife slumped on his shoulder, had waited for hours for the doctor on duty. When the latter finally turned up (a mere intern, in fact, heavy-eyed from much-interrupted sleep) he grumbled that he didn't want to go to prison and refused to take responsibility for treating a woman in her advanced state of deterioration. Faced with Jaourden's imploring gaze, he lost patience: "It's for the Assistant Registrar to decide on the treatment of difficult cases, not me! But, as usual, he's not here. He won't get into trouble, not him, he does as he likes . . ." In the end, to be rid of Jaourden, he ordered a nurse to put the old woman on a drip. By the time the intern left it was long after curfew, and Jaourden was obliged to spend the night on a chair in the emergency ward waiting-room, to the intense satisfaction of the hospital security guard, a dark-skinned Kabyle who muttered incessantly under his breath, fulminating against these near-pagan blacks from the Sahara who, just because they have discovered Islam, take themselves for whites and think they can do as they like in Algiers.

Nassreddine joined Jaourden the next day, having found out what had happened from the receptionist at the couple's hotel. This man had told him to inform the Targui that the proprietor was turning them out, he didn't want sick people in his hotel. The couple's belongings had been bundled into a plastic sack which the hotel would hand over on payment of their bill. The employee had remarked disdainfully:

"Come to that, it's only a load of junk which nobody would take even for nothing."

At the hospital, Nassreddine had found an exhausted Jaourden, ashen-faced with fear. He was sitting at his wife's side in a vast ward with two rows of beds lining the central aisle. All the beds were occupied, sometimes by two women lying side by side. Some of the women were breast-feeding, or trying to calm an infant bawling with all its new-found strength. People came and went, visitors, patients from other wards, amid a din that was astonishing in a hospital. Nassreddine cast a grim look at the bedclothes: grubby, if not downright filthy, stained with blood where a mother, turned away from the overflowing maternity ward, had recently given birth. Two cleaners were listlessly mopping the tiled floor, henna-dyed toenails protruding from plastic sandals. Every few metres, having moved their buckets, they stopped to lean on their mop-handles for a chat. Where a bedside table was covered in crumbs, or odds and ends of plastic, they would give it a quick swipe (with the floor cloth!) before continuing on their leisurely way.

Jaourden's wife, the drip connected to her arm, lay on a narrow trolley normally used for transporting patients. Although she was unconscious, her body appeared to be in pain. The face, its features made ugly by the ravages of age and illness, was swept by a series of faint contractions, not unlike grimaces of disgust. Jaourden sat, hunched up, unshaven, more crumpled than ever, watching his wife's lonely struggle against extinction. Standing there ill at ease, Nassreddine wondered at the depth of his friend's grief. On the sole occasion when he had visited them at their encampment near Tamanrasset, Jaourden and his wife Douja hadn't given him the impression, with their rather formal behaviour, of an overweening affection. He remembers how he was firmly snubbed when he had dared suggest that to be still living in a tent was, well, a little extreme. At their age, it might be time to exchange the austerity of open-air life among the scorpions and lizards of the dunes and *hamadas* for a stone-built house on the oasis. Amused, Jaourden had explained that a true Targui was an *avellemed*.

"And an *avellemed* is someone who refuses to learn. Because he who learns, surrenders! Whether we die of cold or drought, or both at once, it will be in a camel hair tent, Nassreddine, like our fathers, like our grandfathers! A song of the *tindé* says of us, the Touareg, that we are the gob of spittle in the eye of the epoch, the stone in the gullet of the epoch! So drink up your tea before it gets cold, townsman, and stop driving us crazy with your talk of dolls' houses . . ."

Now, instead of in a tent open to the four winds, the fastidious Jaourden finds himself a prisoner of hospital walls whose grey paint is flaking away like his wife's increasingly faltering grip on life. Now Nassreddine, too, is overcome by depression: he, too, is old, and should he fall ill, he would certainly end up in a bed like this one, manhandled like some useless object, at the mercy of the indifference and unwelcome proximity of others, without even the shield, ineffective but glorious, of the anxiety, the anguish, of somebody who loved him. "Love? love? Whatever next? I must be going mad, worrying myself sick about such things!" He rumbles on, barely intelligible, until a patient gives him a fixed stare: "Silly old fool, talking about love at your age, can't you find something better to do?"

Around midday, Jaourden panics: his wife seems to have stopped breathing:

"Doctor! Doctor! My brothers, my sisters, come quickly!"

A furious nurse turns on him, asking him who he thinks he is, "the President's son":

"Stop your din! Do you imagine that you only have to bark out orders for the doctors to come running like common soldiers? They're over-worked, the doctors in this place, they'll come when they can. Besides, your wife isn't the only one who is dying. It's nothing to make a song and dance about, at her age!"

Nassreddine is positive that, had the doctor not appeared at that moment, Jaourden would have slapped the nurse in the face. The doctor – in his forties, with prematurely receding hair and a disdainful, world-weary pout – listens with ill-disguised impatience as the man explains that his wife has almost stopped breathing and something must be done:

"Doctor, I implore you, in the Name of God . . ."

Grudgingly, the doctor applies a stethoscope to the Targui woman's chest.

". . . Diabetic coma . . . nothing to be done . . . don't teach me my job . . . it's a waste of time . . ."

He asks the nurse to administer a second injection, then turns on his heel. Jaourden grabs him by the sleeve and begs him to save her. He stammers that she is all he has, he loves her, he can't live without her, it would be like dying of thirst: "Doctor, how can I go back to the Deep South with a corpse when in Algiers there is nothing you cannot cure?" The doctor, irritated but also amused by the incongruity of such a declaration of love from this wizened, dark-skinned fellow, shrugs without replying. He hesitates, taking out a packet of cigarettes to save face. He looks curiously at the haggard man who is clinging to his sleeve, grinning like a whipped dog. The Targui's exaggerations, almost obscene, make the doctor want to laugh out loud, but the other patients are eagerly awaiting his reaction and he stifles his guffaw. A few chuckles escape him nevertheless. He lights a cigarette and, inhaling the first puff with intense pleasure, brusquely detaches himself and slips away.

It is this puff of cigarette smoke – a puff of mockery and contempt – that causes Nassreddine to flee the hospital, beside himself with rage. Back in his apartment, he has just collapsed into his armchair, drained by his anger and his powerlessness to help his friend, when he remembers what the receptionist at Jaourden's hotel had told him. Cursing himself for having a memory like a sieve, he puts on his shoes again and rushes out. He will invite Jaourden to stay with him for as long as necessary. He should have thought of it sooner: the blundering idiot can hardly be rolling in riches, yet nothing in the world would induce him to ask anybody for money! He is barely a dozen paces down the street when a neighbour hails him from his balcony:

"Hey, there's a letter for you! The postman couldn't find anywhere to put it so he left it with me . . ."

Under his breath, Nassreddine consigns to hell all those damned kids who systematically vandalise every letter-box in the district. He shouts up to his neighbour that he is in a hurry, he will collect the letter later.

Seeing the bus, Nassreddine breaks into a run, and he fails to hear his neighbour add that it might be as well to come and get his letter right away: ". . . the envelope is marked URGENT, I tell you . . ."

*

75

She rests her hand lightly on the urchin's head. Despite his patent distrust, and his efforts to stay awake, he has finally dropped off. Shrouded in the mystery of an abandoned child, he is like nothing so much as a poor wounded puppy, violent and gentle by turns, particularly when reduced to helpless laughter. She might be a grandmother cuddling her grandson. Tenderly, she ruffles his wiry curls, wondering if she is right to involve him in such an escapade. They have been travelling for at least two hours. The weather is magnificent. Once through the traffic jams at the exit from the capital, the orange SNTV bus has made good speed thanks to the motorway. Yet the passengers are far from happy about this. Already, between Algiers and Boudouaou, they have passed a dozen or so army roadblocks without the least difficulty. Each time, the bus had halted at a well-guarded barrier with soldiers crouching behind sandbags, vehicles bristling with machine-guns, sometimes even a tank. Then one or two heavily armed soldiers had boarded the bus and, guns pointed ahead of them, scrutinised its passengers, demanding identity papers at random. But so far this had worried nobody. The passengers know that the hardest part is still to come, for the stretch of motorway will soon give way to an ordinary road, narrower and thus more dangerous. Especially as they are approaching the endless Palestro gorge that cuts through the elephantine mass of the Monts Béni Khalfoun, and there, at fake roadblocks set up by the terrorists, armed attacks, including the assassination and kidnapping of passengers, are an everyday occurrence. The sector seethes with armed bands for whom the impenetrable vegetation of these highlands makes an ideal hide-out.

Anna is aware of all this, having discussed it, as it were casually, with Majid and the hotel receptionist. The way things are at the moment, Majid had confided, one has to be either broke or reckless to undertake a long journey by road unless one really has no alternative. In which case, he remarked, one should avoid taking a State bus at all costs, since the partisans wouldn't hesitate to set fire to it and then wreak their vengeance on its passengers for lining the pockets of the enemy.

"In fact," Majid had continued sardonically, "it's public knowledge that the owners of private bus companies are happy to pay the 'Islamic tax', the protection money demanded by the terrorists. A solution obviously denied to a State-run enterprise, which thus bears the brunt of the damage. From which one may conclude that certain private firms are financing the sabotage of their principal competitor . . ."

Anna remembers Majid's eloquent grimace. Whatever would he say if he knew that she was doing precisely what he advised her against: not only travelling by road, but by bus – and a State bus at that – there being no other seats available? She smiles, rubbing together palms damp with anxiety. She is hot; the air-conditioning isn't working. What's more, the kohl is stinging her eyes. She prays that the antimony doesn't run. The boy decided that her eyes were too blue, too "French" (his term!), and might attract unwelcome attention, and thinking that kohl on the eyelids would help "Arabise" her, he had bought her a phial and a wooden applicator from a store in the Lower Casbah.

"But whatever you do, don't look people in the eye! Keep the veil high up on your nose, never raise your head and don't utter a word. I tell you what, if there's time, put some henna on your cheeks, wear a few bits of local jewellery, and you'll be perfect. From now on, I'll address you as El Hadja, a woman who has made the pilgrimage to Mecca!"

The urchin was so enchanted with his idea that Anna hadn't the heart to refuse. She had merely made a face at him before going to put on her make-up in the bus station public lavatory:

"Are you sure, my little would-be muezzin, that you don't want to make me carry a copy of the Koran?"

The heat is truly unbearable. Drops of sweat are running down her back. Now Anna has a desperate urge to scratch. She rubs herself discreetly against the seat, not daring either to remove her *haik* or detach the veil from her face. Instead, stoical, half mesmerised by the passing landscape, she loses herself in contemplation of its austerity and magnificence. It is the second time in her life that she has made this journey. Between the first bus and the second, 40 years have passed. She recognises so little of her surroundings, everything is different, at times upside-down, as though the positions of remembered mountains and *oueds* were reversed. Yet Anna cannot shake off the impression that this second journey, taking place in warped time, a time already lived, is a sinister joke whereby the present is counterfeiting the past. For obvious reasons, there are no longer any Europeans to occupy the best seats, relegating the natives to the rear; the Arabs are less poor, less bowed, more dignified. But poisoning the air of the vehicle is the same extraordinary resignation in the face of unrelenting cruelty, without taboos, inflicted by army and partisans alike, the same fear of inviting a horrible death, the merest hint being enough to inhibit defiant stares and close talkative lips!

With difficulty, Anna unglues what little saliva the heat has left in her mouth. Drifts of poppies and ox-eye daisies brighten the wheat fields and the little plots of land hedged by cactus; dilapidated huts lean like tumours against unlovely four-storey villas planted in the middle of the landscape. The traffic is heavy, fast-moving and chaotic. The bus driver overtakes constantly, sounding his horn. Just as it was 40 years previously, the sun is inexorable, the soil fine and powdery, and dust rises whenever the bus mounts the verge. Anna, too, is afraid, more afraid than she thought possible, but she is also conscious of a strange, choking happiness. Since this morning, she has been on her way to a reunion with her two very young children who never had a chance to grow up, their laughter and tears frozen for ever. The old lady tries to hold in check the sadness which is now so familiar and which so closely resembles the joy that seizes her – pricking her gently like the claws of a friendly cat – whenever she succeeds in conjuring up her children's faces. An exercise to which she has disciplined herself regularly since their deaths, it consists in closing her eyes and slowly, precisely, reconstituting the features of her murdered babes: first, the little girl ("hazel eyes, funny little snub nose, pouting mouth"), then the little boy ("brown as a berry, dimples, eyebrows which had appeared early and promised to be bushy . . ."). At first, just after being deported from Algeria by the French authorities, she was even able to call up the cadences of her children's laughter. At which point she would start to laugh, then to cry, crying for hours on end. For years, she was dogged by remorse at not having had the twins photographed before it was too late. In those days they had had so many expenses, she and her husband, that anything they considered inessential was put off till tomorrow. So, no question of photographs! But how could they have foreseen, she and Nassreddine, that for those whom they had brought into the world only to long outlive them, there would be no tomorrow? On the darkest day of her despair, when they had been gone for ten years or more, she had visited an artist in Geneva and asked him to paint their portraits based on her memories of them. He replied briskly that her descriptions were so vague that they could apply to any two kids picked at random in the street, and he feared she would be disappointed by the lack of resemblance. He had the effrontery to joke about it: if she wanted identikit portraits, she should go to the police; they could worm anything out of anyone. She left, cursing him under her breath. The next day, she managed to persuade another artist. He listened to her attentively, noting everything down and making increasingly detailed sketches before handing her the portraits of two splendid-looking children who bore not the slightest resemblance to her own. She paid him, thanking him warmly for his trouble, and departed with the feeling that she had committed blasphemy. She burnt the portraits of the two unknown children as soon as she was home, then took to her bed with a raging fever, obstinately refusing to confront the question that tormented her: was she still able to remember her children, or was she cheating in order to fend off even greater unhappiness? Later, she had a recurring dream which left her covered in sweat and shivering with cold. In her dream it had begun to snow while she slept. She awoke full of foreboding. And this foreboding turned to joy: etched into the snowflakes that encrusted the windowpane were her children's smiling faces. But when she went to the window her children cried: "no, Mama, no Mama!" for she was melting the snow with her hot breath. And she woke up, in her own bed, devastated by grief and crying in her turn: "no, Mama!, no Mama!"

Anna sighs. She must have sighed rather too loudly, for the woman in the seat in front, a woman of her own age who had been squirming with boredom ever since the bus had left Algiers, turns round and flashes her a smile of complicity:

"Remove part of your *haik*, little sister. It's so hot! At our age, neither God nor anyone else will mind if we uncover ourselves. Then we can chat. They take so long, these bus journeys! Where are you taking your grandson, by the way? May God in His Mercy protect your family!"

Anna jumps, nearly surprised into replying in French, and the sudden movement wakes Jallal with a start. Blushing with confusion, he realises that he had fallen asleep and his head had slipped on to the foreign woman's lap! He snaps crossly at the inquisitive old woman:

"Leave her alone! Can't you tell that my grandmother is a deaf-mute?"

The passenger rolls her eyes in astonishment. Ruffled, she wedges herself against the window.

"Cheeky rascal, you might show a little more respect to a woman of my age! I haven't touched a hair of your precious grandma's head. Well, that'll teach me to be nice to people!"

Piqued, the old woman takes a rosary from her capacious bag. With half-closed eyes and set lips, she clears her throat ostentatiously and embarks on the recitation of the Blessed on High. Anna stifles a giggle. She tugs at the child's shirt and breathes very softly in his ear:

"While you were at it, you might have added congenital idiot to deaf-mute!"

She coughs, choking back her laughter. Jallal stares at her, alarmed and a little shocked. His lips slowly curve into a smile. Hiding his amusement, he reflects that the old *roumia* may be crazy, but with a sharp tongue like hers, she would be more than a match for "Fatima".

He too is both anxious and joyful. He considers his situation, still half incredulous: he is well-dressed, his hair is well-groomed, he has new shoes and he is travelling in a comfortable bus with a full stomach and four genuine 200 dinar notes in his pocket! The foreign lady certainly knew how to do things properly: the day before, she had taken him shopping in Bab El Oued and, without haggling over the cost, had bought him a complete new outfit. She had told him to go and find a bathhouse for the night ("Don't forget the ears and nails! . . .") and meet her first thing in the morning at the bus station.

With the money she had given him, he spent the night in a *hammam* where some 20 mattresses were laid side by side in the large hall that served as the bathers' rest-room during the day. All night long, deafened by the snores of the other guests, he mulled things over.

The *gaouria* had made a deal with him: he was to accompany her to a *douar* near Batna where she claimed to have relatives; he would be in charge of buying tickets and food and asking directions, in other words, anything that involved speaking Arabic. In return, she would reward him generously. So far, so good, but while he could understand why she needed to disguise herself in a *haik*, he found the story of the family near Batna far less convincing. For one thing, why couldn't those famous relatives have come to meet her in Algiers and taken her back with them to the Aurès?

Then it occurred to him that she might be a pervert, one of those women who abused children. Hardly likely though, she wasn't slimy like some of the people who had wanted to rape him. He thought disgustedly of Hadda, the rubbish-dump tramp who would show you her hairy pubis for a few dinars and, for 20, let you touch it and masturbate in front of her. But she was a poor madwoman, repulsively dirty, an unfortunate wretch who had been kicked out by her husband, and who, perpetually starving, would do anything for a crust of bread. In exchange for food, the gang at the dump would make her dance on an oil barrel, skirts lifted, and sing obscene ditties about the Ninjas. "Fatima" told him that he had gone farther with her, but Jallal was sceptical, it would take considerable determination to ignore the tramp's foul smell. Not to mention the utter repugnance which, in his opinion, any sane person must feel at the idea of mutual friction between the organs that produced piss and shit!

No, that couldn't be it; but on the other hand, he mused, perhaps she was a spy? Now that was more like it, and he wouldn't lift a finger to denounce her! After all, what did his native country mean to him these days: life on the street, hunger, fear, policemen who chased you and beat you up, respectable family men whose one idea was to stroke your buttocks and sodomise you, and now that stinking bitch of a dump which wanted nothing more to do with him! Oh no! They certainly need not count on him to sing the Kassaman every time the flag was raised!

By morning, heavy-eyed from lack of sleep, he decides that he has nothing to lose by giving it a try. And in fact, although he doesn't like to admit it, he longs to feel secure for once! Perhaps it's a true gift from the gods after all: to get away from Algiers for a time, from nights curled up in his cardboard box frightened half to death, and with a bit of luck, to be forgotten by those madmen who evidently couldn't wait to cut his throat for having "betrayed" his friend Saïd! He would rather not think about poor Saïd for the moment, the anguish is too great, and it brings back the taste of the absolute terror he experienced during those first bursts of gunfire.

*

"We'll be two or three hours late by the time we get to Batna," she calculates anxiously, contemplating the ludicrous sight of the bus driver, black with engine oil, perched on top of a mountain of melons. The bus has been held up outside Bordj Bou Arréridj, a town some 200 kilometres from Algiers, with a broken fan-belt. The furious driver has hitched a lift back to Bordj Bou Arréridj on a tractor, its trailer piled high with melons, to find a replacement fan-belt in the local bus company depot.

The passengers, at first no less annoyed than the driver, soon settle down to make the best of their mishap. It is getting on for two o'clock in the afternoon and as intolerably hot in the bus as it is outside. Everyone tries to find a shady spot beneath one of the few trees lining the road. Hunger prevailing, a gigantic picnic materialises. Provisions emerge from hampers and baskets and in no time all the passengers, or rather all except two of them, are tucking in. It might have been a scheduled stop, Anna observes, amused: some have even produced raffia mats from their baggage and are spreading themselves in comfort.

"I wouldn't mind having a siesta so that I don't have to watch those guzzlers. The sight of them tucking in is giving me hunger pangs. How about you?" Anna teases.

She and Jallal have installed themselves some distance from the others, beneath a nettle tree with, miraculously, a little spring gushing at its foot. Anna darts an ironic look at her little guide, who silently hangs his head. That morning, despite the Swiss woman's insistence, he had refused to buy food at the bus station on the grounds that those cheap stalls were not above using donkey or cat meat. When Anna appeared unconvinced, he retorted haughtily – lying through his teeth – that she could go on saying Ah! in that stupid way for 10,000 years, but he was an experienced traveller, he knew what he was doing and no foreigner was going to teach him about Algeria. He explained that since they would pass dozens of roadside cafés, there was no point in carrying food with them in this heat. The bus had indeed passed a great many roadside cafés. But, each time, the driver refused to stop, assuring his famished passengers, who protested that it was long past noon, that he knew an excellent restaurant "where the food, may Azraël strike me down if I lie, is just as good and wholesome as if your beloved mother had cooked it! I'm one to look after my passengers' health . . ." In fact, no-one was taken in by the driver's glib prevarications. It was customary for a company driver to have an arrangement with a restaurant proprietor whereby, in return for a good tip, he delivered him a daily cargo of famished, exhausted customers. But they were now stranded by this damned breakdown.

Sulking, Jallal tries as usual to forget the rumblings of his stomach when obliged to go hungry, by closing his eyes. With any luck, merciful sleep will soon blot out the intolerable sight of people gradually munching their way through roast meats, juicy olives and crisp galettes. Still, he curses himself for a fool. Thanks to his desire to sit at a table in a real restaurant for the first time in his life (and as the foreign lady would be paying, he was determined to eat till he was fit to burst!), he will probably have to go hungry until they reach Batna. Anna rubs it in:

"Well, you little wretch, speaking for myself, I would be perfectly happy with two or three cat meat brochettes on crusty fresh bread, served with mayonnaise, tomato sauce and a judicious seasoning of pimento . . ."

At the sight of Anna miming the gesture of stuffing food into her mouth, Jallal bursts out laughing.

"Ah, me too! The trouble is, though, being a respectable Hadja you could only consent . . ."

Anna can't wait to hear the rest of the sentence:

". . . to eat cat meat on two conditions: first, it must be a plump kitten with lots of fat on it, even on its whiskers, if possible; and it must be hallal: slaughtered like a good Muslim sheep. We're not pagans, you and me; we don't eat any old thing, do we?"

Giggling, they egg one another on, comparing the best ways of cooking cat, Anna opting for a tender stew with sauté potatoes, Jallal preferring a simple grill sprinkled with *harissa*.

"But what are you thinking of, Madame, everyone knows that a cat can't be cooked like a rabbit!" he yelps, trying to keep a straight face.

"Maybe, but your precious cat, Muslim or not, doesn't go baa baa like a common sheep!" Anna retorts, doubled up with laughter. Their delirium is only just beginning when a sour voice behind them says ironically:

"She may be dumb, your grandma, but she obviously has no trouble laughing!"

The old woman whom Jallal had insulted on the bus is only metres away. Has she overheard their conversation? Anna feels herself blushing with shame but cannot control her giggles. Glaring at her, the woman places two chunks of bread and cheese and some fruit beside them on the ground.

"Here," she says gruffly, embarrassed, "it's not right that you should be the only ones not eating. We all have our troubles, but if we can't help one another out a little . . ." (She pauses, attributing their silence to disappointment.) "Er . . . it's not much, I know, but I swear by Sidna Mohammed that it's all I've had myself. The cheese is nothing special, but the oranges are excellent . . ."

The old woman is bewildered. Abruptly, she turns and waddles off, perspiring and breathless, her gait threatening to topple her enormous bulk. Anna and Jallal pounce on the bread and cheese. Jallal remarks gaily:

"It's not quite the same as a cat meat cutlet, but it will fill the gap until this evening!"

"Hmm . . . our good neighbour has forgotten the coffee . . ."

"Ah, forgotten the coffee, has she? We'll soon see about that!" The urchin walks purposefully over to the passenger with the rosary. Seconds later, he is back, triumphant, carrying a mug of steaming hot coffee.

"Are you mad? How on earth did you manage it?"

"Simple. I just said that you didn't have any coffee. Isn't that what you wanted?"

"How did she react?"

"She was very surprised. She took a thermos out of her great basket and poured me a cup so quickly that I could swear she is scared of me. I bet she's got some cakes in that basket. Would you like one with your coffee? Because, if so . . ."

Anna grabs the young rascal by the shirt:

"Jallal, I'll box your ears if you start that again!"

"Let go of me, Hadja! Why shouldn't I have some nice honey cakes too?"

Anna is suddenly aware that the other passengers, their air of virtuous compassion unmistakable, have been watching them for some time. Doubtless they strongly disapprove of a child being left in the care of such a badly behaved old woman who is probably mentally ill. She adjusts her *haik* and veil, blows her nose loudly and struggles to regain her composure in the face of her little guide's disgraceful face-pulling and miaowing.

By the time the driver returns with the spare part, the Swiss woman and the Algiers street urchin are chatting like old friends, happily mixing Arabic and French and resorting to mime when at a loss for words. Anna tells Jallal that she used to be an acrobat in a circus. The boy only half believes her:

"You, an acrobat? But you're too old!"

"I wasn't born with white hair and wrinkles. It may not look like it now, but I too was young once. And I still have the muscles from that time. If there weren't so many people, I would show you that I can climb a tree quicker than you can, lazybones!"

"I bet . . ."

Jallal relates a few anecdotes about the dump, talking about it with ironic tenderness, as if it were a second mother ("At my worst moments, she always provided me with enough to keep me alive. She stinks, she's a real plague factory, but who cares if his mother smells!") In the course of conversation, he lets drop Saïd's name. In reply to Anna's questioning glance, he says defiantly: "he's . . . er . . . he's a friend . . . I mean, an uncle I lived with in Algiers." He blushes, looking shifty, and Anna changes the subject. Equally, she avoids asking him about his parents, waiting until he should mention them. The boy with the homely face chatters non-stop, at times boasting naïvely, and pausing only when, incredulous, she purses her lips and laughs unapologetically when he finally admits to exaggerating. On the whole, however, he expresses himself with an astuteness almost worrying in a child of his age. They discuss his business prospects.

"Sometimes it goes well, sometimes not. When it goes well, I eat, when it doesn't, I go without," is his philosophical comment. "Perhaps, one of these days, I'll come up with something better than peanuts. In the meantime . . ."

Grimacing, he tightens an imaginary belt. Then he breaks into strangely adult laughter:

"I suppose I'll just have to be very, very patient. Lady luck is perverse, it's well known that she hates the unlucky!"

It is late afternoon when they finally reach the bus station car park at Batna. Anna starts to collect her belongings, asking Jallal to go on ahead. Once he is out of sight, she leaves her seat and bends over her travelling companion who, half asleep, hasn't yet realised that they have arrived. Anna touches her on the shoulder. Gradually the obese woman emerges from her somnolent state, uneasy. Anna has carefully prepared a sentence in Arabic. She leans forward and articulates laboriously:

"Many thanks, little sister, for the food and the coffee . . . Er, please excuse a stupid old woman's bad manners . . . One day . . . er . . . God will reward you for your good deed. Goodbye, and take care of yourself . . ."

Anna places a kiss on the traveller's cheek. Wedged into her seat, the old woman puts a hand to her cheek as if she had been slapped:

"O my God, the deaf-mute, she can talk! . . ."

Anna, who has already reached the step, hears the sibilant voice:

"A dumb woman who has found her tongue. May the Good Lord preserve us from such devil's work!"

Unyielding, Anna refuses Jallal's demand to be allowed to stretch his legs in Batna's mean streets. If her memory serves her right, it is only about 30 or 40 kilometres to Hasnia, her first husband's *douar*. Less than three quarters of an hour by car, depending on the state of the road: in her day, it had turned into a steep, narrow track for the last few kilometres. Jallal is not pleased to be taking to the road again so soon, but the elderly lady is adamant. Given her promise that they will spend no longer than an hour at the *douar* and, on their return, regale themselves at the best restaurant in town, the boy, resigned, goes off to haggle with the group of unlicensed taxi drivers prowling round the bus stop. All refuse the job at first, protesting that the road to the *douar* in question is none too good, and that it will be dark before they are back. The owner of a red Peugeot 405, a young dandy in a dazzling green and yellow tie, joins in. He declares himself willing to be of service to the old lady and her grandson ("For the love of God, my brothers!") as long as they are prepared to pay. He mentions a sum so outrageous that Jallal and the other illegals think he must be joking. With an imperious gesture, Anna indicates her agreement to the disgusted boy, who is sickened by such waste. The youth is as surprised as anybody, but none the less demands payment in advance as soon as they are in the car. He insists that someone, the boy, for instance, should sit beside him. That way, he explains, if they are stopped by the police he can say that he is giving a lift to members of his family, free of charge, naturally. For the most part, the journey passes in silence. The youth, nervous, drives at top speed. With a heavy heart, Anna prepares herself for the event she has awaited for so long. Jallal is sulking, convinced that the little runt at the wheel must take them for complete imbeciles. Gradually, he allows himself to be lulled by the swaying of the car. He awakes, bad-tempered, to a shake from the driver. The youth gives him a mocking glance:

"Watch out, kiddo, or you'll fall on the gear lever!"

Jallal sits up straight, infuriated by the driver's condescending tone. Watch out for your tie, you scented camel! He is especially annoyed because the driver has interrupted his daydream at the best moment. He had just finished inventing a new family for himself: a grandmother (the elderly foreigner who listens to him so attentively, who is tough and has a sense of humour), an uncle, Saïd, naturally, quickly transformed into an elder brother, smiling, indulgent and very much alive, and, of course, the pick of the bunch, his sister, his poor sister as she was before the catastrophe, with her gentleness, her goodness ... In this dream, having made a great deal of money, he had assembled them all in a fine house endowed with a magnificent garden in which there was shade, sun, a creeper-covered arbour and, above all (but how is it possible, he wonders even as he dreams), an extraordinary scent of happiness. The driver had wrenched him out of his dream just as they were sitting down to breakfast around an enormous copper tray laden with doughnuts, butter and jam ...

He sighs, sad at heart. A few minutes ago, they had turned off the main road. The track is now climbing steeply. The surface is very bad and the driver has to keep changing gear to avoid the potholes, swearing nervously each time he does so. They haven't seen another car for at least 15 minutes. The youth turns his head from left to right at regular intervals, flashing anxious glances at the countryside, then in the rear mirror, as if searching for something. Bored by the silence, Jallal asks the Swiss woman:

"How much farther to your *douar*?"

Lost in her thoughts, Anna opens her eyes and replies vaguely, in French:

"I don't know, little one. It's such a long time since I've been there. Maybe 15 minutes, 20 at the most."

The driver's reaction could hardly have been more violent had he been bitten by a viper. He brakes so abruptly that the car nearly turns over. His face is white with fear and anger. Anna recoils from his outstretched arm, but he still manages to tear off her veil. He is stammering with rage:

"Filthy bitch, you're not Algerian! What am I to do, O my God, what am I to do! Why did you lie, you bastards?"

He is spitting with fury, and the saliva catches Anna full in the face. Nauseated, she explodes:

"You lout, what on earth has come over you? Nobody has lied. I don't see what business it is of yours whether I'm a foreigner or not. So drive on. We've paid you well and it's getting late . . ."

The effect on the driver of hearing her speak French for a second time is still more disastrous. He yells:

"Bugger off, go on, get out of my car before I use force. They'll kill me, they'll cut me to pieces if they see me with you!"

"But who are *they*?" Anna yells back, her voice shrill with fury.

"As if you didn't know! The emirs of the freedom fighters, that's who, you crazy old bitch! They've sworn to kill anyone who helps Jews or Christians like you. Go on, out with you, quick!"

As neither Anna nor Jallal seems disposed to obey, the fellow scrambles out and opens the rear door. He drags Anna from her seat and deposits her, like a sack, on the side of the road. Too late, Jallal gets out of the car only to see her collapse in a heap on the stones. Hearing her shriek, his blood runs cold. He runs round the car and jumps like a cat on to the man's back. Gripping him by the hair with all his might, he pushes him to the ground and, mad with rage, hammers kicks into his body.

"Swine, you hit my grandma!" Jallal yelps. "Shame on you, hitting a grandmother!"

But the driver easily gets the better of him. He grabs the skinny urchin round the waist and deals him a violent blow on the nape of the neck. Receiving a second punch on the nose, the boy, groggy, staggers. Anna, horrified, gets to her feet in spite of the agonising pain in her coccyx.

Swearing at the brute in German, she pelts him with anything that comes to hand: stones, twigs, even handfuls of earth. The youth gives Jallal's recumbent body a final kick, spits with disgust and climbs back into his car. After reversing with much crunching of gears, he drives off, tyres screeching on the stones, in the direction of Batna.

Anna is the first to make a move. She wipes the blood from the boy's face as best she can. He has two black eyes. A large purple bruise extends either side of his nose, which appears to be broken, with an abnormal dent on the bridge. Things could hardly have turned out worse. Anna feels like bursting into tears, especially as she has just realised that her handbag, with her passport and money, is still in the car. She grits her teeth instead. After all, it is thanks to her and her selfishness that the boy has suffered this nasty blow. He whimpers with pain every time Anna's handkerchief touches his face. She is swept by a wave of tenderness for this poor kid from Algiers who, hardly knowing her, has fought for her like a lion.

"Don't cry, son. Look, it's gone, it's all over."

"I'm not crying, I'm just sniffing," Jallal protests between sobs. "You can see that I'm not crying . . ."

And he begins to shed hot tears. Anna, heartbroken, takes the boy in her arms and, quite unselfconsciously, dissolves into tears herself. Hugging one another, each strives to comfort the other. Jallal hiccups: "But Grandma, crying won't help!", and Anna, her tears flowing more copiously than ever, responds: "I'm not crying . . . what gives you that idea? You're the one who's crying . . . I'm just blowing my nose!"

At last, the little guide's two black eyes focus on the Swiss woman's kohl-streaked face.

"Shit, what a sight! Your face . . . it's all black!"

"And what about yours, my little pirate, do you think you look any better?"

Suddenly, they burst out laughing. Jallal puts a hand to his nose:

"Ow, ow! That arsehole, that fucker of his mother's lover! Ow, ow, just wait till I catch him."

Anna, startled, says wickedly:

"I shouldn't say such things at my age, but . . . arsehole, fucker of . . . how did you put it?"

"... his mother's lover ..."

"That's it ... damn him, he has certainly taken us for a ride! What are we to do now?"

Once more, with Jallal's help, the elderly lady struggles to her feet.

"He's broken my back, the brute."

Contemplating the road, she scrubs her cheeks with a fold of her *haik*. With death in her soul, she looks for the last time in the direction of the *douar*:

"We'll walk back to Batna. Better luck, tomorrow, perhaps. But for now, no malingering. We'll make it in less than an hour. Let's hope we can get a lift."

They set off hobbling and then, as the precariousness of their remote situation dawns on them, they quicken their step. Funereal in the gathering twilight, the forms of immense cedars line one side of the road. The opposite side overhangs a ravine with, in its depths, a puny *oued*. There is nothing around them to indicate the presence of human life. Anna, dry-mouthed, can't decide whether or not this is a good sign. They cover several kilometres in silence. At first, the boy goes on ahead, zigzagging across the tarmac with apparent confidence. Eventually, he takes her hand. He too has his misgivings.

Anna is finding it harder and harder to walk, the pain in her back is agonising. She has taken off her *haik* and flung it around her shoulders. It is dark and, despite the faint light from a half moon, they trip over stones and stumble into potholes. Jallal tries to cheer them up:

"We would make a great circus act, you and I: the lame and the blind ..."

His joke falls flat. Anna is anxiously looking at a fork in the road. "Which way?" she wonders, close to panic. She is about to take the right fork when, from the left, twin beams of light leap out of the darkness. They disappear behind a bend and reappear almost at once.

"Headlights!" Jallal shouts joyfully.

Anna, appearing calmer but in fact equally excited, feels herself revive. As the car draws up in front of them, Jallal sounds disconcerted:

"It's a red 405! Do you think the swine has taken pity on us?"

"Hush!" Anna says crossly. "What matters is that he should take us back to Batna."

"Are you the Swiss woman?" a youthful voice calls from the car.

"Er, yes," Anna replies, shading her eyes from the glare of the head-lights. "But how did you know? I never said . . ."

She breaks off, for the head of the man facing her is covered in a black hood. She steps back, startled, but not yet frightened.

"Don't be alarmed, we're police officers," says the hooded head with a short laugh. "We've arrested this fellow" (he indicates the taxi driver with the gaudy tie). "He had a handbag in his car containing a passport and some currency" (again, the head laughs). "He attempted to deny everything at first, but he soon confessed once we showed him that lying is a sin. You agree with that, don't you, Grandma . . ."

Anna nods, bewildered by the policeman's familiarity. Still dazzled by the headlights, she can't make out the other occupants of the car. The policeman's laugh tails off in a sharp whinny:

"She agrees with us, the old nanny, she agrees that one should never tell lies!" he exclaims, slapping his thigh.

The other passengers follow suit. Even Jallal joins in the general hilarity, letting out a chuckle. He circles the car, flings open the rear door and joyfully prepares to deliver one of the ripest insults of his life:

"Son of a . . ."

A man with a rifle is propping up the youth in the green and yellow tie against the back seat. The illegal taxi driver stares back at Jallal so blankly that the boy's insult dies on his lips. Indeed (and Jallal's teeth begin to chatter), the man who so callously abandoned them on the mountain track is staring at nothing at all: a second mouth, a dribbling mouth which had no business to be there, stretches from one side of his throat to the other.

Anna has already understood. She is not surprised when the man in the driving seat points a long butcher's knife at her and says, in excellent French:

"It's your unlucky day, Madame, welcome to the forces of Allah!"

No, indeed, she is not surprised. So that's the face of the devil, who had crossed her children's path before hers. Not that recognition prevents terror from crushing the breath from her body like a great boulder that has rolled down the mountainside and felled her in a single blow.

Urinating helplessly, without even opening her legs, she has just enough strength to turn and look at the little peanut-seller.

Perched on a stepladder, Nassreddine sips his tea. Preoccupied, he feigns interest in the exuberant ramblings of his neighbour, a retired chef from the ground floor, who as he talks is energetically hoeing a patch where he intends to plant carrots.

"I would have liked to plant a banana tree, a real one," he sighs, "but I can't afford a greenhouse, not even in plastic. Perhaps it's just as well. Fancy having to keep watch over the bunches as they ripen. Every scallywag in town would be after them!"

The chef smoothes his moustache, his sparkling eyes pierced with regret for the fabulous bunches of bananas which would have greeted him every morning when he opened his ground-floor windows. Nassreddine chuckles, aware that the chef is not speaking lightly. Two years ago, the old rascal illegally appropriated the strip of ground that runs alongside the apartment building. Then, when the Town Hall and Public Housing department ignored his coup, he built a low brick wall behind the old wire fence and planted the 30 square metres or so he had annexed with a rich variety of vegetables.

"It's my hedge against inflation," he would joke. "No matter how many stupid tricks the government gets up to, I shan't starve!"

When the tenants complained of the smell of the manure that he boldly spread on "his" garden, the wily old boy, after railing against human envy, presented them with boxes of carrots and potatoes "grown, my dear friends, with the help of that excellent manure!" Battle-weary, the neighbours yielded, and thereafter to take a glass of tea with the chef while he lorded it over his thriving vegetables became an obligatory ritual among the building's tenants.

Today, Nassreddine has no stomach for his neighbour's tea, nor for his whispered confidences. The chef is telling him about his nephew, a humble clerk at the local town hall, who narrowly escaped assassination. A complicated story about a young terrorist who nearly shot him for having refused to falsify a birth certificate.

"Well, the bloody fool only positions himself behind my nephew, ready to draw his pistol, when he fumbles and pulls the trigger with the gun still in his belt. Bang! no more prick, no more balls, blood all over the place and howls like a ship's siren!"

The chef roars with laughter:

"And who should rush to the killer's aid but my wonder of a nephew, who hadn't a clue what was going on . . ."

Nassreddine abruptly makes his excuses, saying he has an urgent matter to attend to. He has just decided that he cannot leave Jaourden to cope on his own at the hospital. The poor Targui hasn't slept more than two hours a night for a week. The previous evening, he had agreed to come home with Nassreddine. But, in the middle of the night, the desperate man changed his mind. Despite the curfew, he managed to reach the hospital in order to stand vigil over Douja. The doctors said that she could die at any time, there was nothing to be done except to wait for the end, and let it be understood that it was time he took her home since, moribund, she was occupying a bed unnecessarily.

The chef blinks, put out by Nassreddine's haste. He mutters between gritted teeth that at their age nothing, but nothing, should be allowed to interrupt a good gossip over a glass of tea, and that no measures, however drastic, could prolong by a single second the life of old greybeards like them.

"Speaking of urgency, Mister Impatient, I nearly forgot. Here" (he holds out an envelope folded in half), "the postman left this for you with our neighbour on the first floor."

"Ah yes, I remember, the letter that came yesterday!" Nassreddine replies absently, stuffing the envelope into his inside pocket.

He sets off limping (his corn is troubling him again) towards the bus stop. There is already a queue. He has been standing there for 15 minutes, squashed by the crowd, before he remembers the letter. Freeing his hands with difficulty, he manages to extract the envelope. It is stamped URGENT in the top left-hand corner.

A brief note from Batna *wilaya* post office informs him that the enclosed telegram, addressed to him at the *douar* of Hasnia, could not be delivered due to his absence and, in accordance with the law pertaining to telegrams, they had obtained his present address from the police. It concludes with the curt advice to leave an address at Batna in future, to avoid the same thing happening again.

Nassreddine unfolds the telegram:

AM AT HOTEL ALETTI UNTIL 20TH
WILL THEN GO TO YOUR MOTHER'S HOUSE
IF YOU ARE STILL ALIVE COME TO ME ANNA.

He feels sick. People are jostling one another all around him. The bus has arrived, full to bursting as usual. The crowd presses forward. A woman at the back yells:

"What does that old man think he's doing? Can't he read his letters at home? Either get on the bus or leave the queue, don't just stand there!"

Another voice, equally furious, chimes in:

"That's right, shove him out of the way. The old fool is going to make us miss it!"

The bus moves off with its cargo of passengers, leaving Nassreddine at the bus stop. Blood rushes to his head, beating so hard at his temples that he fears he might vomit. In his agitation, his trembling hand crumples the blue paper. He re-reads the telegram. Perhaps it is a practical joke, a dirty trick? But who could have concocted such a thing? None of his friends and acquaintances from the city or his old job knew that he had married a foreigner and had had two children. They all treated him like an old eccentric who, for some reason, had remained a bachelor. It wasn't as if he had ever mentioned the subject to anyone since . . . how long ago was it? . . . He puts his head in his hands:

"Oh, Anna, Anna, it can't be true . . . Oh, Anna, Anna! . . . My love, why has it taken you so long? Oh, Anna, Anna . . ."

A teenager leaning quietly against a lamp-post, enjoying a quiet cigarette, grins at the sight of the dishevelled old man tearing down the middle of the road. He jeers:

"Hey, Granddad! Found a new lease of life, have we? If you can fuck as well as you run . . ."

The man with the painful corn doesn't hear the mindless taunt. Straining his bandy legs and bursting lungs, bumping into passers-by who turn in shock or amusement, the old man runs: away from the fast-declining years, away from the cruel fate that has robbed him of his family, towards his lost love, towards the infinite paradise of his youth . . .

II

6

Old Anna, terrified, wants to scream. But no sound comes. She stretches out her arms, as if begging the killers for help. The armed men laugh. Therefore she closes her eyes. Time, with its memories as sharp as knives, rises to her throat. As a last, desperate measure, she holds out a hand to her childhood. But no help is forthcoming from the four- or five-year-old girl that she was then, for she too is absorbed in her own suffering . . .

1928

The boat is drifting over the lake in the sunshine. A little girl is lying in the cockpit. Before long, she will die of sunstroke if nothing is done to bring her ashore. The child's ears are ringing. Her closed eyes are watching a huge red disc which, at intervals, turns black. It is the sun: for hour after hour, it has been gazing down upon the little girl with the wildly beating heart. Her internal respiration – that of the soul – had ceased three interminable days ago.

What happened? At dawn, the canton police had knocked at the door and taken her mother to the frontier. They told her that, as a German, she no longer had a permit to reside in Switzerland. Switzerland was neutral, and Switzerland didn't want to get into a quarrel with Germany when all Europe would soon be at war. The little girl hasn't really understood what the police meant by the word war. All she knows, peering through the morning mist, is that her mother is surrounded by policemen, her mother, who is shaking with fear and shouting, in a mixture of German and Swiss-German, that she is legally married to a Swiss. "Look, here's my marriage certificate!" "But this certificate isn't valid, Fräulein, it's a forgery." Unmoved, the policemen take pleasure in calling her Fräulein rather than Frau. Her husband stands there without a word, red in the face. "But Fräulein, even if this certificate were valid," ("which it isn't," mutters the second uniformed man) "the fact remains that you entered Switzerland illegally, seven and a half years ago, to be exact. In this country, we dislike illegal immigrants." The policeman's gaze holds no real malice, merely the faint contempt reserved for those unlucky enough not to be Swiss. The husband studiously avoids looking at his wife. "Tell them that we're legally married, Gunther, tell them!" Now she runs to him, multiplying her feeble protests. Then, appalled, she realises that he is not going to stand up for her. All right, so they had quarrelled a lot of late, their raised voices audible in the street . . . "But Gunther, I am still your wife, you are Anna's father, anyone can be forgiven for having a row!"

Her mother was taken to the German frontier and handed over to the Reich police. She had screamed, her Mama, but with such a strange scream that the little girl would never see or hear its like again for the rest of her life. The gaping mouth was hideous, the scream inaudible.

That same night, the little girl discovers that, if anything, her father is glad to see the back of his German wife. "All she had to do," he snaps at his daughter before downing his glass of beer, "was keep quiet and not talk politics."

She ran and ran, then fell asleep in the boat. Seeing the drifting boat and, in it, the little girl, still as a corpse, a part-time fisherman flings himself into the water. He rows the boat ashore with its burden, proud of his good deed. Her father, said to be "half dead with worry", welcomes her back with a monumental thrashing. The blows increase her hatred for the man to whom, henceforth, she will give a nickname: "The Dog". That same evening, she puts pebbles in his soup. In revenge. Her father breaks a tooth. Furious, he swears by the gods that it's the last time he buys bread from a bloody baker who puts earth in his flour. The little girl, feigning sleep, laughs silently till she wets the bed. Then she cries herself to sleep.

As for the fisherman, he contracts pneumonia after his charitable swim. Trembling, pierced by the fear of slipping into the velvet paws of the Great Unknown, he curses the child and his own sudden urge to make a "grand gesture". On the night of his funeral, his wife comes to the door. Crazed by grief, she spits on the little girl and accuses her of having killed her husband.

The little girl is thinking of her mother. She loves her mother, who used to call her "my darling little bantam" on account of the stiff-necked pose she would adopt when disobedient. But her love is becoming vaguer as her mother's image recedes. When she ran away from her father's house, she took refuge in a travelling circus, concealing herself in a caravan for the duration of an entire stage (100 kilometres or more, during which she grew weak from hunger and thirst). The circus was on the shabby side, alas, but for the child, it came as a revelation: a world where human beings flew like birds, oblivious to the weight of flesh and entrails, where wild beasts turned into tame lap dogs at the behest of their trainer. My God, it was beautiful!

What we call conversion or, better still "grace", must be something like that. It fell like a bolt of lightning: the child, open-mouthed, received the revelation of beauty. With a sharp pain clawing at her heart, she realised that not all men need be as wicked and brutish as her father, nor all women as badly treated as her mother. In a turmoil of bitterness, she wandered about the big top all day before burying herself – like a would-be suicide – in a wardrobe. There, the following morning, a woman discovered her wrapped up in a costume. She was fast asleep. Rina, alarmed at first, then touched, had woken her. Seeing the child's horrified expression, she burst out laughing and called in her comic accent:

"Hey sailors, come and look, we've got a stowaway! What shall we do with her, throw her overboard, or what?"

"How about the lion-cage?" a lad from the menagerie giggled nervously.

Somebody fetched the boss. Charles's immediate reaction was to say no. Business was bad, creditors were pressing, and the last thing he wanted was trouble with the local constabulary. He spoke angrily to the little girl:

"What do you think this is, a boarding school? Besides, you're holding up the show!"

He questioned her at length, eventually dragging her father's address out of her. She pleaded with him, repeating the same mulish words over and over again, almost aggressively,

"Please not, I hate him! . . . Please not, I hate him!"

Finally, he shrugged, disturbed by such hatred. And by its force in such a little body.

"But Anna – you did say that was your name, didn't you? – what do you know about the circus, after all? It's a hard life, you might find it hell!"

The child bent her head. Charles sighed:

"Little idiot . . ."

Then he grumbled:

"Idiot yourself, Charles, you'll always be a loser, you don't know how to say no."

He left first thing in the morning and succeeded in obtaining the consent of "The Dog", who was only too pleased to find somebody willing to relieve him of this wicked child who refused to call him Papa.

The circus band strikes up yet another waltz. It's time for the trapeze artists to perform their double somersault. On their respective platforms, Adrian and his wife Vera are caught in the crossbeams of the searchlights. The young girl stands at the ringside with others whose act is finished. She is shivering; she ought to go and change, her clothes are sticking to her body. Yet she cannot tear herself away. Tired as she is, she follows the couple's performance with intense concentration. Anna's heart is bursting with admiration. They are so beautiful up there and so in love down here, even though they fight like cat and dog . . . In the circus, their mutual love is the object of teasing and also envy. Anna vows that, one day, she will emulate them. And her immature mind doesn't know what she envies most, their amazing skill or the strength of their love . . .

A clown, one of the group at the ringside, grunts:

"Something's up. Why doesn't he jump?"

Perched on his platform, the trapeze artist seems to be taking his time. Slowly, he rubs powdered chalk on his hands, then seizes the bar. He pulls it towards him as if to launch himself, hesitates, inspects his hands and lets go of the bar. Once more, he dips his hands into the box of chalk.

In the darkness below, murmurs of impatience rise from the audience.

Anna senses that something has gone wrong with the turn, normally precisely timed to conclude with the third fanfare from the band. Once again, with added emphasis, the ringmaster announces the daring double somersault. Anna isn't yet anxious, merely uneasy.

At last, Adrian decides to jump. The magnificent body takes flight like an immense sequinned gull. Tracked by the searchlight beams, it reaches the half-way point between the two platforms. With the reverse swing of the pendulum Vera, his wife, is supposed to launch herself in her turn.

"O my God!"

Anna cries out, along with dozens of spectators. Adrian has lost hold of the bar. The searchlights fail to track his fall. For interminable seconds, they stay trained on the empty trapeze as it swings back and forth . . .

Anna finds Rodolphe waiting for her in the big top as arranged. A new horse is due to be schooled. There is a babble of voices outside but, by tacit agreement, she and the trainer avoid talking about Adrian. After his accident of the previous night, the trapeze artist has been given the sack and is forbidden by the doctor to work with the trapeze in future.

The young horse is nervous, and Rodolphe has to make frequent use of the lunging whip. He is annoyed, Anna's mind isn't on her job. He quickens the pace. The animal grows dizzy and stumbles. Anna only just has time to leap off her perch on its hindquarters. Its mouth is flecked with foam.

Rodolphe laughs:

"Eh, girlie, you've transferred your nerves to the horse!"

There is a deafening report.

"Sounds like a gunshot," the trainer mutters.

The groom Emiliano sticks his head through a flap in the heavy canvas of the tent:

"Anna, come at once. Vera and Adrian have had a fight."

People are running in all directions. The young girl's heart is in her mouth. It can't be serious: Vera and Adrian are protected by their love . . . Breathlessly, Emiliano explains that after getting the sack, Adrian tried to persuade Vera to leave the circus with him. She protested that they had nowhere to go. The argument became heated, Vera shouting that she didn't want to end up as a hotel chambermaid. She screamed at him and he shot her.

"You wouldn't believe it, Anna," Emiliano says, gasping, "it was all over in an hour! Vera was alive, then hup!, she was lying there like a piece of broken china."

The police arrive, followed by an ambulance. Everything becomes confused in Anna's mind: the dizzy horse, the screams from Adrian whom nobody has dared attempt to gag . . . She gazes at Vera's recumbent body half hidden by ambulance men. The toe of a slipper protrudes from the sheet. Foottit, a dwarf with the grotesque face of an aged child, pulls the sheet over it. There is a strange air about the scene. Even the police seem awed by these circus folk who have sprung from nowhere, some in leotards and full make-up, others, equally flamboyant, still in their street clothes.

The girl doesn't cry. She is simply a little paler than usual.

From all this, she was to retain an extraordinary notion of love. If she were ever to love, it would end in death. Vera loved Adrian. Adrian loved Vera. That should have been enough.

Love is death, two figures insanely reckless, flying between a pair of trapezes and ending in a fall, for no reason . . .

7

In this, the fifth year of the terror that reigns over his country, the elderly Algerian runs through the streets of Algiers. He is gasping for breath, his legs are failing. Worn out, he stops for a moment to recover. Yet again, he wants to scratch the black mark on his hand. It is unusually painful today. But he scorns such temporary discomfort, for he is drunk on a mixture of rapture and bitterness. He is about to have an extraordinary opportunity seldom granted to a human being: to revisit his past happiness, his lost Andalusia! Ah, Father, Father, he wants to cry out in jubilation, if you could see the old fool I am now! An old fool like you, when you fell head over heels in love with my beautiful young mother. Nassreddine explodes with laughter and sets off again, bumping into a passer-by. It is exhausting him, this race through time, and it had begun long before he was born: a year before, to be exact . . .

1928

In those days, Dahmane lived in a *douar* to the east of Batna, dividing his time between cultivating his plot of land and running a small wheat wholesale business that frequently obliged him to visit merchants elsewhere. Long married, he has recently decided to wed for a second time, but without divorcing his first wife.

Oh, it's not that his wife, Aldjia, displeases him! Quite the contrary: with the passing of the seasons, and the hard labour that was their common lot, his affection for her has turned into the sort of solid esteem that one has for a trusted partner. Naturally, there was the occasional kick, the odd slap in the face, followed by days of silence and sulks, nothing much really, considering the harshness of the land, the grinding toil, the cold, often accompanied by snow and, above all, the brutality of the French settlers. Peasant uprisings are a thing of the past, of course: the infantry battalions of the last century, by smoking out and massacring whole tribes, had successfully quenched the spirit of rebellion for a long time to come. For now, in Dahmane's *douar*, people are resigned to eking out a living from the soil and having as little as possible to do with the *gaouris*, those Arab "brothers" who often outdo the Christians themselves in ferocity.

Colonisation, nearly a century old, still has many a long, terrible year to run. That it would end one day never crosses Dahmane's mind. How was one to defeat by force of arms these strong, handsome people who grabbed all the best land and whose native country across the sea was reputedly a miracle of power and luxury? Dahmane's own grandfather was killed by Saint-Arnaud's troops, and his ears, together with hundreds of others, were thrown into a barrel and handed over to the battalion quartermaster in exchange for an equal number of 100 centime coins. So one can only sigh at the harshness of fate and condemn those pork-eating infidels to the Hell which God reserves for the unjust. Children who refuse to go quietly to bed at night are told the story of the ogre Boubrit, a corruption of Beauprêtre, an officer whose name was a byword for terror at the beginning of the French conquest, and whose motto it was that Arab heads could assimilate civilisation only when cut off at the neck.

Gradually, having been assured that a man not actually starving ought not to deprive himself of a second wife, Dahmane becomes convinced that he should take the plunge for the sake of his reputation. This might have remained no more than a mere temptation had he not just met Zehra, the daughter of Hadj Slimane, an hour ago. He had come to negotiate the sale of a few bushels of wheat with the Hadj in question, a merchant from a nearby village, wealthy enough to have treated himself to every Muslim's dream: a pilgrimage to the holy city of Mecca. The old man had talked of his visit to Mecca with the same exaltation as if it had taken place yesterday. Dahmane, his attention on the passing sacks, had listened vaguely with one ear. Hadj Slimane may have become a better Muslim, but it didn't follow that, given the chance, he was above hoodwinking a client as to the weight and quality of his merchandise.

A dealer in goods himself, Dahmane didn't hold it against him: a dealer cheats by nature, and always will, even in Paradise! At that moment, Zehra had entered the warehouse, her face unveiled, only to leave again at once on seeing a strange man with her father . . .

Impatient, Dahmane smacks his mule on the rump yet again. He is almost home. He has just let himself be conned into paying top prices for poor quality wheat. He had watched it happen, yet he hadn't protested. His throat tightens at the memory of that exquisite figure:

"This time, for good or ill, I've made up my mind. It's her or nobody!"

Some 18 years previously, Dahmane and Aldjia had had a son and a daughter. The boy, like so many children at that time, died of consumption. While his loss affected them both deeply, it also brought them closer together. Soon after reaching puberty, the girl married a cousin and went to live near the capital, too far away for her parents to visit her regularly. Once again, Dahmane and Aldjia found themselves alone. Until he met the wheat merchant's daughter, Dahmane had believed that no-one could be more important to him than the companion of his years of misfortune. He would unhesitatingly have given his life for her. Yet, from one day to the next, Aldjia ceased to count.

It was not that he started to beat her, or to deny her the rights of seniority. On the contrary, the wedding over, he enjoined Zehra to obey Aldjia in everything to do with the running of the house. To which Zehra, by nature carefree and without malice, cheerfully submitted. The trouble was that Aldjia loved her husband with a passion terrifying in a simple peasant. It was so strong, this love, so absolute, that it became part of her being; indeed to tell the truth, it was all she had. Year in, year out, she breathed, ate and slept this love. In consequence, the pain of her husband's wedding day was all the more agonising. Unable to speak her love, for she lacked the vocabulary to express such madness (what, an ignorant peasant woman in love!), she remained dumb. To begin with, all had seemed well. Never once did Aldjia speak out of turn to the young woman. The gentle Zehra did all that was asked of her; the house was well tended, the plot of land also. The two women laboured side by side with none of the usual recriminations in a household of cohabiting wives. Indeed, the entire village envied Dahmane his good fortune: not only a beautiful new bride, but an understanding first wife. But every time that Dahmane came home, ate his evening meal and retired with Zehra to the new room that he had built with his own hands, Aldjia felt her heart stand still. The bile rose to her mouth, she wanted to cry out that it was unjust, God was a liar, the only reward for good was evil.

It is snowing. Dahmane is not yet back. The night is pitch dark, and the heat from the little *kanoun* cannot penetrate the modest room at the centre of the house. Zehra may give birth at any time. Already she is groaning with each contraction, fearful but also radiant with the special joy of an expectant mother. Aldjia has never felt so despondent: it has been almost two months since Dahmane last shared her bed. She had hoped that, with Zehra pregnant, her husband would turn to her again, at least until the birth. The opposite had happened. Dahmane showered Zehra with little attentions and rebuked Aldjia sharply for allowing her to do too much.

Now Zehra's groans are louder than ever. Aldjia is seized by panic, she knows the birth can be only a matter of hours. She can't fetch the village midwife; it is snowing too hard and, in any case, the woman lives too far away, almost half an hour's walk, even in good weather. She thinks of summoning a neighbour, then decides against it. She builds up the fire, places a large basin of water on top, prepares the necessary strips of cloth and the herbs for rubbing into the belly to relieve the soreness after birth, then sits down to wait. Having had two children herself, she isn't unduly worried.

An hour passes, then two. She dozes off and has a nightmare. Someone is chasing her, panting. It is a man. Nevertheless, Aldjia recognises her son, the boy who was carried off by sickness, let me see, how long ago was it? . . . She starts to count on her fingers in spite of her fear. Just as the man is about to catch her up, she cries out, waking herself. It takes her a minute or two to realise that it wasn't she who had cried out, but Zehra, calling for help:

"Dahmane, are you there, Dahmane?"

Feeling as though her heart were caught in a vice, Aldjia jumps to her feet. She runs for the basin. The water is boiling. Holding the basin with the strips of cloth, she carries it over to Zehra's bed. The water is too hot, she will pour in a little from the large pitcher to cool it down. As she moves to do so, Zehra, her labour plainly over, starts to scream:

"O my God ... Aïe ... Dahmane, my love ... Dahmane, help me. Aïe ... I love you ... Dahmane, don't let me die!"

Now Aldjia, a woman who has never harmed a soul, whose life has been one long sacrifice, is overtaken by madness. It is too unjust: her own son dead, this whore bringing hers into the world to be the usurper in the household, stealing not only her husband's love but also the bitter memories of their joint suffering! She is still holding the basin of scalding hot water. As she tips it over the panting young woman, a black mist descends over her eyes ...

"You must be a barbarian, my God. Why did You let me do it?"

She runs, panting. The snow is coming down in flurries. The cold cuts like glass, yet she feels nothing. I have to die, she thinks, I have to die. It is not possible that I should live after that. Just after tipping up the basin, she had rushed out of the house. The mother's screams, and those of the baby, feebler, more terrifying, are still in her ears. She doesn't know their fate, the worst probably, but she is certain of one thing, that she must die.

She runs on. She is growing breathless. How could she have done such a thing? The demon Borgne ("blind") must have taken possession of her while she was in the grip of anger. No, that's not it. She alone is responsible. Even the frozen stones bear witness. She is the ogress from those stories which she heard as a child. The one who ate babies. She would give anything not to have been born. Now Aldjia has reached the foot of the hill which lies just beyond the village. And she wonders, stupidly: how does one set about dying?

She senses the full moon watching her, hateful with its prying glare. She retches from breathlessness. A thread of saliva runs down her chin, a drop of sweat down her forehead. The perspiration quickly freezes over. She is barefoot. Suddenly, she is aware that her feet are hurting abominably and, to her surprise, although determined to die, she finds herself wishing she could die with her feet in a pair of warm slippers. The wind has dropped. Soon the enveloping silence is like velvet in her ears. She knows that she deserves to be put down like a sick animal.

A rabid animal has no right to life. She tries to think objectively. Aldjia must kill Aldjia. It is the only service which she can render her. She examines her surroundings. There is nowhere from which to throw herself. There are stones, of course, but she hasn't the strength to beat herself about the head until she is dead. She has to admit, shameful though it is, that she is too soft for a peasant. Suddenly she feels very cold, colder than before. Perhaps it comes from standing still. It has stopped snowing. Aldjia has the answer: she will let herself die of cold. It is said to be a quick death. She remembers the day when the villagers brought back the body of a tramp who had died from cold in a ditch. He didn't appear to have suffered. They said that he must have fallen asleep and never woken up.

That's it. She sits on the ground. And she waits. Not for long. She shows no sign of dying. She stretches out, face down. There is earth in her mouth. She turns on to her back, it is much less uncomfortable. She remains like that, losing all sense of time. All of a sudden, she screams. From fear. And also from pain: a myriad needles of ice are pricking her body all over. To stop her screams, she slaps her face . . . She takes off her clothes, everything but a thin chemise. She is surprised not to feel colder. She smiles: perhaps death is creeping over her. With all her failing strength, she wills herself to die quickly. Thus far, she has managed not to think of all the rest, of her husband, of Zehra, of the baby. She knows that she will not be able to avoid seeing her life pass in front of her. The cold, burning at first, turns glacial.

The moon is suspended above her. It reminds her of a ceiling-lamp. She wants to switch it off. What she has to do should be done in the dark. A few snowflakes alight on her face. Her head is swimming. She must have been there for three hours.

There is a sudden noise. Terror rampages through the peasant woman's heart. Is it Death? Would She who is known as the Discreet One make so much noise? Aldjia turns her head towards the village. A dark figure is approaching. She can hear its rasping breath. Then she sees.

Zehra holds a knife, the long butcher's knife used to slaughter sheep. She is the personification of anger: dishevelled, eyes bulging. When she comes across the body lying on the hillside, she pounces on it, delivering kick after kick and yelling:

"I'll kill you, devil's spawn, I'll cut your throat!"

Aldjia, groaning beneath the kicks, makes no move to defend herself. The woman with the knife bends down and tugs violently at her hair:

"Filthy whore! What made you do it? I'll cut your throat, see if I don't!"

Aldjia, still lying on her back, murmurs to the woman who is holding a knife to her throat:

"What about the baby?"

Zehra, nonplussed, withdraws her hand. She answers surlily but in a lower voice:

"You missed him, you crazy bitch."

"Are you sure?"

Aldjia, wide-eyed, her throat ready for the knife, looks at her with longing.

Disconcerted, Zehra mutters angrily:

"His hand is scalded, that's all."

She adds, tugging harder than ever at Aldjia's hair:

"But you scalded my belly, and you'll pay for it!"

Aldjia has closed her eyes. Despite her grimaces as Zehra pulls her hair, her relief shows in her face. Zehra repeats:

"I'll cut your throat, see if I don't!"

But the timbre of her voice has changed. Anger has given way to resentment and fatigue. The left hand that holds the knife threatening Aldjia is growing increasingly hesitant.

Puffing like an old woman, Zehra, the young and pretty Zehra, clambers heavily to her feet. She has let go of her rival's hair. She takes a few steps in the direction of the village. Rubs her sore belly; down below is where it hurts most. She is shivering with exhaustion. Her anger – the source of her strength – drains away. Her one desire is to be reunited with her poor, wounded infant. Her heart melts with sadness at the memory of that minuscule bandage on the scalded hand. The buttocks had been splashed as well, but only needed a little oil. O my God, what is happening to us? What can You have in store for us if You let a life begin like this? She blasphemes: You are idiotic, my God, to vent Your anger on a newborn baby!

She is swept by a gust of fury. When the crazed woman tipped up the basin, Zehra had but one thought: the baby. Her body was crying out with pain, but she kept her head. She grabbed the infant and leapt for the end of the bed. Having dragged herself to a corner of the room, she bit through the umbilical cord, then washed and oiled the terror-stricken, bawling little body. It was some time before she could calm the baby down. Worn out at last, it took the breast, eyes tight shut, and then it slept. Gritting her teeth, she hastily washed and put on clean clothes. The huge blister on her belly was growing more and more painful. And suddenly she was consumed with fury. Arming herself with the knife, she rushed outside.

In the all-pervading bluish glimmer, a young woman walks away from an old woman who is dying of cold. The younger woman drops the knife. She continues on her way. Then, because good knives cost money, she retraces her steps to pick it up. As she does so, Zehra says in a calmer voice:

"Whatever made you do it? Were you really so jealous? Yet we got on well together, you and I."

The outstretched woman doesn't open her eyes. Zehra shouts, her voice bitter:

"May you be cursed for ever, Aldjia!"

She walks on, legs apart, waddling like a duck. With angry joy, she flings over her shoulder:

"It's a boy, you know, Aldjia. Now die!"

The silence of the countryside is muffled. The moon, threatened by an approaching cloud, is brighter than ever. Aldjia scrapes up snow and pebbles with her arms, covering her body. In so doing, she hopes to hasten things along. Only her face remains uncovered. The snow creaks, it is so cold.

Aldjia waits. She moves as little as possible now. Her arms feel like lead, making movement painful. She has no alternative but to look at the sky. The stars are bright, but the lunar disc is slowly disappearing, eaten into by the cloud. Intent on its progress, Aldjia has the horrifying impression that it is eating into her head . . .

"What you see in the north" (she cranes her neck to follow the point-ing finger) "is a herdsman. A dog gambols at his heels. They are taking their animals to pasture. It is a very peculiar herd . . ." Yes, of course, she knows that voice!

Beneath her carapace, Aldjia has become a little girl aged five or six. She is with her grandfather, sheltering beneath his burnous. In his inimitable voice, hoarse yet gentle, he is describing the map of the night sky. What was his name, this grandfather of hers who smelled of wheat? No matter, she never called him anything but Djeddi, Grandpa: "Naturally, there are sheep in this herd, and bullocks, and a few camels with a calf . . . Look, there are the camels, and that star which you can hardly see, that is the calf . . . And there is the billy-goat, together with his wives, making sure that the grass is no greener elsewhere. Do you see?"

The little girl beneath the burnous (and the old woman in her cocoon of snow) nods, fascinated. "But there are also enemies prowling around: jackals, and two female hyenas with their young, all of them eager to make a meal of the baby camel . . . On the opposite bank of the river, that cloud of white dust cutting across the sky, you can just see, if you open your eyes very wide . . ."

Aldjia and the little girl open their eyes wide: "Ostriches, guarding their chicks." The little Aldjia wants to draw her beloved Djeddi's attention to something special, but he has already vanished.

Aldjia knows that she is delirious, but she can't fight it. She has lost control of her mind. Little by little, the dam holding back her memories is giving way. She is immersed in the past, and its warmth is even more lethal than the cold. Now she understands what is meant by "to die": it is the sharp wrench of losing all those little things that one has lived through.

Something rises inside her. Like a knife-thrust from within. Dahmane, where are you? In the first days of their marriage, he had been, oh, so very amorous! At night he would caress her tenderly:

"Now we shall taste the new honey . . ."

He would say:

"I am your cloak . . ."

And she would reply, happy beyond belief:

"And I yours . . ."

". . . I'll be your cover all the rest of my life," he would add, "we'll keep each other warm."

And then he would kiss her, O my God, so clumsily!

Feeling a dampness on her cheeks, Aldjia realises that she is weeping. She should never have released the waters of the past. The snow has frozen hard. Aldjia no longer has the strength to move. Tears blur her vision. The stars are iridescent. To die like a rabid animal, that is what awaits her. And nobody mourns the death of a rabid animal. The thought that nobody will mourn her increases her yearning for death.

"O Redouane, how I would have loved you!" After her son, Redouane, was carried off by the sickness, she followed tradition step by step. She poured fresh water into an earthenware jar and put it out for the birds in order that they should fly her little Redouane's soul to Paradise. One day, the jar broke. She ought to have continued slaking the birds' thirst on behalf of all the other children who were dying like flies, but had neglected to do so.

Is she now paying the price of her negligence? "O Judge of Judges, ruler of our present and future life, forgive me ..." Suddenly, as she invokes the King of Kings, Aldjia senses the approach of Death. Now she no longer wants to die. She struggles, but finds that she is paralysed. Maybe the snow is too hard, maybe her body has already crossed to the "other side" ... She is seized by a nameless dread that further hampers her movements. Now all she can do is weep. And even that causes her unbearable pain.

She therefore ceases to weep. She is reduced to a ball of terror ...

... Into which she shrinks even farther on seeing fingers approach her face. She wants to scream with horror. The fingers touch her face, then her body. Slowly at first, then more and more frantically, they scrape away the snow. An exhausted voice mutters in her ear:

"Come on, Aldjia, get up!"

The voice repeats:

"Get up, you crazy bitch, nobody is dead, so there's no point in your dying for nothing!"

Zehra has put an arm under her co-wife's back and is trying to lift her up. Aldjia stares into her face, uncomprehending. Zehra looks away. She coughs, embarrassed:

"Hurry up, I've left the baby alone in the house."

She holds out a baby's bottle wrapped in a *couffin*.

112

"Here, it's still warm, drink it, and put on this burnous."

Now Aldjia is trembling in every limb, but not from the cold. Painfully, she swallows the milk while Zehra wraps her in the burnous and puts slippers on her feet. Aldjia's body is one enormous chilblain, the least movement is torture, but she still has that uncomprehending stare. Long seconds pass before she can murmur, choked by a gratitude as poignant as a long-drawn-out agony:

"Zehra, may my life serve as a ransom to yours one day . . ."

No-one ever knew the secret which, henceforth, was to bind Aldjia and Zehra together, the old wife and the young wife. At a word from Zehra, Aldjia could have been banished. As the mother of a male child, Zehra could demand anything of her husband. And Aldjia, still traumatised by the horror of her act, would have acquiesced without protest.

Yet Zehra said nothing, restraining herself each time the desire gnawed at her entrails. Naturally, Dahmane, on seeing the baby's tiny bandaged hand, was horrified. Zehra belittled the incident. She merely said that it had been splashed by hot water from the basin, and Dahmane, overjoyed at having fathered a male child, was content to leave it at that. Nor did Zehra have any difficulty in concealing the more serious burn that disfigured her belly, a new mother not being expected to submit to her husband's conjugal rights for a certain period after the birth.

That first week, Zehra's loathing of Aldjia was such that she fled with her baby at the sight of her. The following week, Dahmane decided to invite friends and neighbours to a celebration worthy of the arrival of a son and heir. Numerous guests were expected, and the preparation of all the dishes befitting such an occasion meant that the two women were obliged to work side by side all day. Aldjia could have managed on her own but Zehra, tired though she was, insisted on helping with the main dish: a couscous of dried meat and seven different vegetables.

In silence they rolled the semolina grains with butter, the baby suspended between them in its cradle from a beam. The two women kept their eyes obstinately fixed on the huge clay platters, their hands moving rhythmically back and forth over the grains. From time to time, they added a bowl of semolina to the mixture, sprinkling it with cold salted water. They had to hurry if they were to roll enough. Dahmane seemed to have invited too many people, and the reserves of rolled couscous had run out.

Next they lit the charcoal braziers to go under the two great couscous pots. Then, while Zehra cut up the vegetables, Aldjia seasoned the long strips of dried meat. Having sealed the upper and lower parts of each couscoussier with cloths dipped in a paste of flour and water to hold in the steam, Zehra went outside to pick the beans and chillies. Thus far, the two women had not exchanged a single word. Interspersed with the delicious smells now wafting through the ante-room to the little court-yard were puffs of a subtle, acrid scent, that of burning alum. Aldjia knew at once, with a sinking heart, that early in the morning her co-wife had burnt an alum stone in the kitchen to ward off evil. For Zehra on that precise occasion, Aldjia was the personification of evil. With each puff, Aldjia was reminded of her act of folly, and of her new humiliating situation in which she was at the mercy of a word from her co-wife.

The baby cried, and Aldjia reached out a hand to the cradle made of bay and plaited rope. Startled, the baby stopped crying and smiled. A wave of tenderness engulfed poor Aldjia's parched soul. A song which her mother used to sing to her came to her lips: "happy is he who has a mother and a cradle . . ."

The baby was gurgling when Zehra returned with the beans and chillies. Aldjia was leaning over the cradle and pulling faces to make it laugh. Choking with rage, Zehra pushed her violently out of the way. Snatching her child from the cradle, she shouted:

"Ah, don't you dare! You are never to touch him again, do you hear, never!"

Now the baby was howling, terrified by its mother's rough voice. Aldjia bowed her shoulders, as though under the lash of a whip. She started to make a gesture of protest. Then she let her arms drop. With infinite weariness, the old woman looked at the young woman:

"I see that I'm never to be forgiven. I was led astray by the devil, father of the Embittered. I no longer counted for anything in this house . . ."

She added:

"I tried to punish myself, Zehra, but I was as cowardly as a nanny-goat."

Zehra, contemplating her grey-faced co-wife, tried to hold on to her anger as she felt it drain away:

"Old fool, and how about the baby, what harm had he done you?"

Aldjia made a grimace of despair (and it occurred to Zehra that the comparison with a nanny-goat was not unjust):

"Oh Zehra, I swear on the soul of my poor dead baby son that, from this day on, no child could have a more loving second mother than me."

Taken aback by this vow, Zehra muttered something unintelligible. Furious at finding herself moved, she retreated to the kitchen, knocking over one of the couscous pots that lay in her path and spilling its contents on the ground.

"May the devil take your tongue, Aldjia. Now what shall we do?"

The young wife was kneeling, her baby in her arms: the couscous had spilled over the dirtiest patch of ground, just where she had piled up the charcoal ready for the braziers.

Aldjia straightened her back and set the couscoussier upright. The situation was serious, for the meal was supposed to be ready in half an hour at the latest. There was no question of their rolling an equal quantity of semolina in the time.

"Will you leave it to me?"

Aldjia's eyes were sparkling. Zehra sensed her co-wife literally coming to life. She nodded her agreement. Aldjia fetched a brush and a platter which she proceeded to use as a dustpan. In no time, all the dirty couscous had been swept up. Watched by the dumbfounded Zehra, she emptied it into the upper part of one of the great pots.

"We have two couscous pots: the one that wasn't upset we'll give to the family. The other will do perfectly well for all those so-called friends who are coming to fill their bellies at our expense."

And so it came to pass. That evening, Dahmane came to congratulate them with the condescending air of a husband proud of his two wives:

"I don't know what special spices you put in the couscous, but it was truly delicious. All my friends asked for a second helping. A real feast!"

"And how about you, did you like it?" Zehra asked, rather put out.

"Certainly I did. I don't mind saying that it's the best I've ever tasted! I hope that there will be some left for tomorrow . . ."

Dahmane never understood why, at that moment, the two women

115

should have dissolved into fits of giggles. They laughed and laughed and then, watched by the helpless Zehra, who would have liked to comfort her but didn't dare, Aldjia wept.

The boy, therefore, was brought up by two women who loved and loathed one another to the point where, in a moment of fury, each would have done anything to rid herself of the other, and then, afterwards, anything to save her life. The child called the younger one Ma and the elder one Yemma, both meaning mother. Throughout his childhood, he exploited their mutual jealousy: to get his way, all he had to do, when one said no, was to run to the other with an ostentatious display of affection. And the first, green with envy, would instantly reverse her ban.

So he was spoilt, but the term is relative: he was spoilt only so far as a child can be spoilt in a poor family. For the family sank farther and farther into poverty: a combination of successive droughts and unpaid loans from the money-lender eventually led to the expropriation of most of the land owned by father and son, such as it was. There remained only the revenue from the wheat business, but this too was dwindling fast.

Then came the year when there was no market for figs, the year when competition from French settlers with their powerful machines brought about a collapse in the price of Algerian oil. This was the Year of the Great Hunger, as it came to be known later, the terrible year when famine was rife among the Arab population, both in the countryside and the *medinas*. Dahmane's family was not spared. For days on end, Nassreddine, by then a boy of eleven, had but one thought in his head: food.

In time, the village boys came to incorporate the desperate search for food into their games: play consisted of finding something to eat. Every morning, they would spread out over the countryside, checking on rudimentary snares laid down the night before, catching grasshoppers which, when grilled, tasted of hazelnuts, gathering any plant that was remotely edible. Every evening they returned, as hungry as ever, dusty and a little scared, but at least proud to have held out until sunset. Sometimes they would struggle up to the rocky heights overlooking "the Valley of the French". In the distance, beyond hillsides planted with cypresses and pines, the settlers' farms, neat and well-tended, lay bathed in sunlight. The little brown-skinned boys, barefoot, often shaven-headed except for a lock of hair hanging down one side, would stand and stare, forlorn and bewildered: in that attainable beauty they scented food in abundance, milk, sweetmeats, and all the other delights of an incredible way of life, its injustice all the more terrible because it was no more than a dream. They descended with bellies still empty, heads buzzing with the chirring of cicadas and eyes dazzled by the glare from the bright yellows of sunlight and broom, feeling ill at ease and not a little inferior until, in tones of defiance, one of the boys would exclaim:

"Anyhow, they stuff themselves with pork, those sons of Ibis, so they'll all go to Hell . . ."

Without admitting it, Nassreddine felt that, personally, he wouldn't mind sampling the animal in question, however repugnant, if it would guarantee him everything else. Recovering their high spirits, the boys scrambled down the stony hillside, *djellabas* tucked up the better to run, ears blocked in case the breeze should carry the faint echo of church bells from a Christian settlement: they had all learnt that, to a good Muslim, the sound of bells was a pure abomination.

Nassreddine never strayed far from his playmates, for the district had become dangerous. Half-starved fanatics prowled the roads, and it was not uncommon to come across a dead tramp in a ditch, the victim of a mugging or, quite simply, of exhaustion. Once, when out scavenging with his companions, the boy had found one such at the foot of a fig tree.

Early one morning, five or six of the boys went to check their nets and snares. They came away discontented with themselves: the traps had been set so badly that not a single bird had been fooled. Their disappointment was short-lived, however, for one of them was lucky enough to put up a nice, plump weasel in a bush. Best of all, the animal proved easy to capture and kill. It certainly behaved strangely. Instead of bolting, it merely retreated 40 metres or so then stopped, as if waiting for the young hunters. It was visibly trembling, yet seemed to be challenging its pursuers.

"It's been smoking kif, it's been smoking kif!" Nassreddine shouted, laughing with excitement.

Once again, spitting and squealing like a mad thing, the weasel retreated, but no farther than before. The boys quickly caught up with it, putting an end to its desperate, enraged yelps with a rain of stones. They managed to light a fire and, the creature having been roughly skinned by the older boys, cooked and ate it. It provided no more than a mouthful of dry meat each, but no matter! Laughing, they fought over the heart. Wasn't it said to give you the power to foretell the future for a whole year!

Their squabbling, made more aggressive by the taste of meat in their mouths, grew noisier. Nassreddine was urinating in the bush where they had put up the weasel when he saw the four hairless balls. He said nothing to the others. One boy shouted:

"We're off to find some figs! What are you doing in there? Tossing yourself off?"

The better to hide the four baby weasels, still blind, their muzzles opening and closing in search of their mother's teats, Nassreddine had pushed them farther into the bush with his foot. His hand shook so that he could hardly finish urinating, for he had suddenly understood the tactics of the animal which they had put to death. Weighed down by the knowledge of the crime which he had helped commit, he rejoined the others, outdoing them in laughter and throwing his *chechia* in the air.

They nearly stumbled over the body. A corpse. The man, still young, had evidently eaten a poisonous plant. It was a common enough accident: when in a state of desperation, it is easy to confuse the roots and stems of some poisonous plants with those of a thistle or a *talrouda*, a bitter-tasting plant which, when boiled down, temporarily staves off the pangs of hunger. The wretched man's face was still screwed up in horrible pain. His chin was wet with green saliva. It was the first time that Nassreddine had seen a dead man close up. He took to his heels, terrified, yelling:

"M'ma, mother, Yemma!"

Back at the house, he had thrown up the contents of his stomach with the horrifying impression that the weasel, come to life, was avenging herself by eating his intestines.

That rag doll of a man, already putrefying in that superb landscape of lentisks and olives, that bloodstained weasel with her warm, smooth belly, defending her young at the cost of her life, made an indelible impression on Nassreddine.

For a long time afterwards, death for him wore the horrifying mask of a poisoned stranger around whom prowled the low-slung form of an animal endowed with a painful cunning . . .

This was the period when Nassreddine learnt to look at his surroundings, to love his country's violent colours, its dryness, even its harshness and the austerity of its brown soil that couldn't vanquish the green of fig or olive, the trees of life so cherished by its people, often more than their fellow men. He put his nose to the spikes of absinthe, inhaling the coating of grey dust and wishing that he were a bird, for birds always find something to eat. And he was amazed that nature, which he greatly loved, should be indifferent to his suffering, to the nagging hunger that gnawed at his whole body and never left him, any more than a tick will leave a mangy dog. His child's heart racing with fear, he discovered the strangeness of life's burden, infinitely weighty to him yet utterly insignificant to the world around him. He knew, with a disgust that filled him with resentment, that he could die unnoticed in this landscape exhausted by the sun.

Thanks to his two mothers, his perpetual hunger was a nuisance rather than life-threatening. Ma and Yemma always managed, surreptitiously, to give him their share of the food. The younger, Zehra, though the more robust, didn't survive this treatment for long. These privations, and a cough which racked her chest, forced her to take to her bed. The moment came when everybody knew for sure that she would die. This was no rare event during the great famine, when villagers were often reduced to begging, tramping the roads, aggressive, desperate and worn out by hunger, till they collapsed by the wayside, never to get up again.

The bone-setter, summoned to the house, pronounced that Zehra had entered her death agony. Whereupon Dahmane invited a few relatives to keep vigil. This show of respectability proved costly. Keeping up appearances in this case meant sacrificing the last of the tea and semolina. But since the bone-setter had predicted that she would die the next day, the expense was limited to a single meal for the guests.

Dahmane, though grief-stricken, appeared resigned to the inevitable. In the course of the vigil, he even managed to raise a smile at the jokes with which, mistakenly or not, certain guests tried to take his mind off his misfortune.

As for Nassreddine, he didn't even know that his mother was dying. Two weeks earlier, he had been sent to stay with an aunt who needed a shepherd. As an inducement, she promised his parents a lamb if his work was satisfactory. No-one was taken in, for the woman was notoriously mean. But at least they could economise on the boy's food. He hadn't really wanted to go, but the prospect of having a full belly for once had pre-empted the inclination to sob.

Aldjia, on the other hand, felt as though she had had both legs amputated. To know herself to be in rude health while her co-wife was slipping, little by little, into the dreadful void of death seemed like an offence against nature, or worse, to be a sin for which she was responsible. Filled with terror, she remembered the vow she had once made to the young woman who had saved her from a well-deserved death. "May my life serve as a ransom to yours one day!"

She went in and out of the room where Zehra lay, now holding her hand, now pressing an ear to her mouth to catch a murmur. It was not long before she had persuaded herself that she was the cause of Zehra's approaching death.

"I shall be damned," she thought. All of a sudden, a terrible need, far greater than the physical hunger that twisted her entrails, invaded her entire being: she must do something to save the young woman lying prostrate on the bed. When she thought that she had overheard Zehra say in her delirium: "I'm hungry, get me some meat, I'm so hungry . . .", she rushed out of the house. It was already morning. A leaden sun beat down on the village. The guests slept on and the dying woman was not yet dead.

Aldjia wrung her hands. The stupidest ideas came into her head: stealing a chicken or a young goat from a neighbour! But most people's livestock had already been eaten or sold. In any case, not knowing how to go about it, she would be caught and soundly beaten. For nothing.

She raised her eyes to the sky, dazzled by the sun, ready to curse God. Storks were flying over the distant marshes, swooping down at intervals. Storks were creatures beloved by the Prophet, and, all her life, Aldjia had believed that these birds were sacred, and that to kill them would be to offend the Messenger of God.

She began running towards the marshes, fighting for breath. After half an hour, she arrived at the wetland edge. The baking landscape shimmered before her eyes. The tall waders were dipping their yellow beaks in the water, taking a sip at a time. Dazed by the heat, their stomachs weighty with grasshoppers swallowed by the dozen, they had a heavy, clumsy gait. They flapped their great wings to cool down. Concealing herself behind a bush, still gasping for breath, Aldjia noticed a group of storks gathered on a bank some 20 metres from her hiding-place. When they get together like that, passionately clattering their beaks all day long, her grandmother told her, it's because they are telling stories of their travels. Each boasts of all the wonderful things she has seen and eaten. Since they never manage to agree, it can take hours. "Be quiet, Grandma," Aldjia grumbled, irritated. She wiped her forehead and decided that she could catch one if she ran fast enough. But she would have to take off her clothes, for they would only hamper her in this mire. Blushing with shame, she undressed, careful not to make a sound. Soon her wasted frame stood revealed, with its slightly protruding ribs, flaccid breasts and small brown tuft at the crotch. Contemplating her body, Aldjia sighed at its ugliness.

The first signs of unease disturbed the group. The storks seemed to be growing suspicious. Aldjia grabbed a stone and launched herself forward on tiptoe, crouching low. Sweat stung her eyes. Some of the storks flew off. Instantly, Aldjia straightened up and ran like a madwoman, her breasts flapping against her ribcage like sacks. With a noise like the rustling of leaves, dozens of frantic wings rose in a great white wave. A few storks remained on the ground, probably stupefied by drinking too much. Aldjia summoned up all her remaining strength and threw herself on the nearest bird. With her stone, she beat every part of its body. The stork struggled violently at first, clattering furiously. Aldjia, kneeling, had it by the neck and was hitting it on the head. By the time she had stopped, the wader's white plumage was stained with red blotches and patches of mud.

For a few seconds, Aldjia was incapable of reaction. She looked down in a daze, at her legs, splattered with drying mud, at the dead bird hugged close to her chest. Her breasts and face were cut all over where the stork had pecked her. A sob, quickly stifled, rose to her throat. There was no time to be lost, for Zehra might already have given up her soul. Filled with anxiety, she put on her clothes, then, as best she could, she bundled up the stork with its great bruised wings in her scarf. Only its long pink legs were still sticking out. Retracing her steps, she set off once more on her desperate race against time. She had almost reached the village, her bundle under her arm, when she felt a colossal blow on the head. She fell, face down: "O my God, is this how You avenge the weak . . ." A second blow on the nape of the neck cut her short, putting an end to her terror and her life.

The bearded face peering down at the inanimate woman stank. Dirt-encrusted hands quickly explored the body for a piece of jewellery. The tramp spat on the ground with disgust. He was sick of it, sick of wandering for days on end, his legs giving way under him, without so much as a crust to eat in this country full of shit! This bitch wasn't going to fill his belly, she was no better off than he himself. Scratching his face, he looked with interest at the stork half hidden by the woman's body. As he extricated it, the murderer's face broke into a smile:

"Peasant whore, no respect for anything!"

He gave the body a kick in the buttocks and soon, beneath the impassive gaze of the landscape, he had vanished for good.

The body was found almost immediately. A woman who had been gathering edible plants came screaming to Dahmane to tell him of her discovery. The women of the village, who were patiently awaiting Zehra's death, immediately lifted their voices in the usual lament. Tradition demanded that sympathy for a neighbour's recent bereavement be expressed as loudly as possible. Nevertheless, the women's eyes shone with curiosity: what, a man who loses both his wives on the same day? What sin can he have committed that Heaven should come down on him like that?

They carried the body into the room where Zehra lay, placing it on a thin blanket on the ground. Dahmane looked on helplessly, with an air of total incomprehension. There was deep silence when a person exclaimed, pointing to the wounds on the head and neck:

"Oh, my poor Dahmane, somebody has murdered your wife!"

Dahmane put a hand to his head. He was seized by a brief fit of coughing. A woman added:

"And the murderer can't have gone far because I saw Aldjia leave the house when I was at morning prayer!"

The men looked at each other and at Dahmane. Then, with loud mutterings of anger, each man rushed outside, picking up whatever came to hand, a stick, a broom handle . . .

Left alone, the women formed a circle around Aldjia. They gazed at the corpse in silence, with a sort of avidity, wavering between repulsion and pity. Each was thinking that she could have been in poor Aldjia's place, lying there, ugly and in the way, with people staring down at her. So this was the purpose of life, after all that hardship and suffering: to end up like some broken-down animal!

"Just look at that mud," sighed the bone-setter's wife after a while.

"Yes, she's really dirty," agreed her neighbour.

Pleased to have found a way of relieving their feelings, a mixture of fear and embarrassment, the women chattered on. As everyone knew that the second wife was as good as dead, they spoke loudly, without restraint. What could she have been up to, old Aldjia . . . And how about those damp patches on her dress . . . Look, she has even lost her scarf. You don't suppose that she was . . . And the lewd insinuation, coming from Aicha, the blacksmith's wife, still young and pretty, was greeted with scandalised giggles.

"Get out . . ."

The voice was so weak that they didn't hear it the first time. Aicha screamed. From her bed, Zehra turned her head towards them and repeated:

"Get out, you bitches . . ."

Offended, but also terrified by this voice that seemed to come from the grave, they almost knocked one another over in their haste to leave. The voice whispered hoarsely:

"Aicha, you stay."

Later, Aicha told them that it was like being present at a resurrection. May God the All-Powerful preserve her from witnessing such a thing again! Zehra told her to lift Aldjia on to the bed and undress her, and then to bring a bowl of water and a cloth. She said that she could remember Zehra muttering between her teeth:

"Whatever possessed you, you stupid old woman? Now I can't even die in peace!"

Aicha had offered to perform the rites of washing the dead, but Zehra refused. She managed to sit herself up. With a trembling hand, she began to wipe her co-wife's bruised body with the damp cloth. Aicha watched the operation, scared to death: it was though, in washing the body, Zehra was gaining strength. She heard her groan in anger:

"Aldjia, you had no right to die! What about Nassreddine, our little boy, as helpless as a toothless goat, who is to look after him?"

The dead woman's mouth was hanging half open, showing the yellow teeth which, all her life, the old co-wife had tried in vain to whiten with walnut bark. Carefully, the young peasant woman closed the mouth, but the teeth clattered none the less. Zehra's eyes watered, and a long tear ran down the once pretty face:

"Forgive me, Aldjia. We never stopped quarrelling, you and I, we were as jealous as hyenas, yet I loved you, oh so much, my dear sister."

And slowly, the regret at never having told her so welled up, bitter and heart-wrenching.

8

Anna looks out of the porthole. The sea is black, banal, indifferent to the destiny of the world. The sky, despite the odd twinkling star and an innocent moon, is equally bland. At intervals, an anxious sigh, irrepressible, escapes the girl. Of course she already knows that her Swiss passport isn't strictly legal, and that her adopted "mother" is Polish. But she has just discovered that Rina is also a Jew. Anna smiles weakly, but the fear, the sordid fear that makes you want to piss and defecate, won't go away.

Luck had been on their side today, otherwise they would have been in serious trouble! They were in the middle of embarking the menagerie at Port Vendres when the telegram arrived. It was an order: the circus manager was to be arrested for fraud, and the artistes taken in for questioning. In case of doubt, the telegram stipulated, all necessary steps should be taken immediately, including the verification of work permits and racial status. Anna, following Charles into the little office, saw him grow pale, then increasingly nervous. At first the Port Superintendent had hesitated when Charles, choosing his words carefully, offered him money to "mislay" the telegram in a drawer. The policeman threatened to call the guards and have him thrown in jail there and then, but Charles sensed that it was nothing but bluster, in order to raise the ante. After two hours of hard bargaining, and Charles, with iron in his soul, had handed over a considerable sum (nearly all the money that the circus had left), matters were resolved. The Superintendent also insisted on having a good half of the artists' reserves of food delivered to him on the quiet. The butter and the smoked ham in particular seemed to send him into ecstasy. He blurted out, his eyes sparkling:

"You ought be shot, you profiteering bastards!"

The boat left Port Vendres around two o'clock, amid general chaos. In the rush, a leopard-cage, insecurely fastened to the hook on the crane, fell into the harbour. The leopard, a young beast which happened to be the property of a juggler whom Charles had recently recruited, set up a demented howling. The howls quickly turned to plaintive yelps. Other animals took up the chorus: first the lions, then the elephants. This soon developed into an indescribable cacophony of roaring and trumpeting. Even the local dogs joined in this strange display of animal solidarity. Charles, red in the face with fury and anxiety (the elephants were still on the quay, secured by nothing but chains), tried to persuade the sailors to rescue the leopard while the juggler, an Albanian without a word of French, looked on with a mixture of despair and disbelief. He performed an extraordinary juggling act in which the leopard, dressed in a sort of tuxedo with an enormous bow tie, played a startling role: every time the juggler threw a ball into the air, the big cat, a veritable feline ballerina, vigorously headed it back, bounding with joy as it ran in circles around its master. Circus people said that the juggler had stolen the leopard from a Czechoslovakian zoo soon after it was born. The most malicious said that this was quite possible because the zoo had been bombed, and that instead of devouring his spoils like the other starving looters, he had fallen in love with it and taken it with him on his flight across Europe. The majority dismissed this theory however ("What, cross Europe with a wild animal, let alone find fresh meat for it in these times of shortage!"), claiming that a cool customer like the Albanian was more likely to be a spy, working for the English or the Germans!

The cage having fallen the right way up, it floated like a raft at first. With a little skilful manoeuvring, the animal might have been rescued. But the terrified leopard's assaults on the bars of the cage finally caused it to overturn. By the time the cage was dragged from the oily waters of the harbour, the splendid beast's life was extinct. It looked like a huge, sodden cat, and the bystanders gazing at its mortal remains, hushed but excited, were vaguely disappointed that all was over so quickly. The Albanian, kneeling down, drew one of the animal's paws through the bars of the cage and carried it to his lips. He leant towards the leopard's ear as if murmuring something. Then he stood up, white in the face.

His lips trembled, but he didn't weep. Anna overheard one bystander say to his girlfriend with a chuckle that if the trainer had been so fond of his leopard, he should have tried mouth-to-mouth resuscitation.

"How about me," the woman replied, aroused, "would you have given me mouth-to-mouth resuscitation if I were a great big pussy?"

The loading proceeded more carefully, but only once the animals had been fed to calm them down. Anna saw two lads from the circus carrying the leopard's corpse on board. Her heart missed a beat as she realised that the drowned leopard was going to be fed to the lions, his former companions in misfortune.

Anna and Rina succeeded in getting a cabin to themselves. In fact, this presented no great difficulty since, apart from the circus troupe, few passengers were prepared to brave the boat to Algiers. It was rumoured that, two days earlier, German Stukas had not hesitated to sink a ferry packed with passengers for North Africa, even though the vessel was flying a neutral ensign.

The passengers scanned the skies all afternoon, fearing the reappearance of these sinister fighter-planes that carried heavy bombs beneath their wings. Charles even had enormous Helvetic crosses painted on the cage roofs. But, in the end, optimism prevailed. That evening, beneath a huge portrait of Marshal Pétain, the vessel's saloon resounded to the songs and laughter of drunken passengers. As the evening wore on, a violent fight broke out, a man having claimed, to the approval of his companions, that the Nazis might be brutal, but there was a lot to be said for them when it came to restoring order and morale.

An enraged young man jumped on the speaker's back. Neither combatant, being drunk, could keep his feet. They exchanged furious blows and obscenities. The younger one shouted that he had no love for Jews either, nor for Communists, nor, come to that, for anyone remotely resembling a wog or a mongrel, but he wouldn't stand for people insulting France by defending her occupiers. They rolled on the round, each accusing the other of selling out to the Germans, and ending up, curiously enough, by insulting one another in identical terms: "Dirty Jew, English lackey, you're no better than an Arab!" and "You just wait till we get to Algiers, licker of Jewish cunts!"

*

Anna can't get to sleep, despite being worn out like everyone else by the crazy pace at which Charles has driven the Nee Circus for the past few days. She looks at Rina. The clown is tossing and turning on her bunk, tense and vulnerable in sleep. Overwhelmed by a deep pity, the girl longs to get out of bed and seek the comfort of her arms. She feels that she would gladly give her life for this apparently frivolous woman who hadn't hesitated to share her caravan and few possessions with her from the day she joined the circus. She reproaches herself for not being more sensitive to the Polish woman's changeable moods; she could have gained some inkling of the terrors that were paralysing her a little sooner. Certain things about Rina's behaviour are now crystal clear, such as her obstinate refusal to go for a stroll in town after a show, her dispro-portionate anxiety (it would wake her with a start in the night) whenever she had to go to a police station to renew her work permit.

Anna recalls a morning when the French police had surrounded the circus in force and ordered everybody to keep to their caravans for the rest of the day or risk imprisonment for disobedience. No-one ever knew precisely what went on inside the big top, for a line of police armed with machine-guns was stationed in front of the huddle of caravans to ensure compliance with the order. All day long, lorries could be heard coming and going. Some said that they carried saboteurs who had been rounded up by the authorities, others that they had heard women and children crying. Either way, the interior of the big top had needed hosing down, for those confined there had had to defecate where they stood. Anna, sickened, helped clear away hundreds of turds, some of which had clearly been produced by children. That evening, when she tried to talk about it, Rina had thrown such a tantrum that Anna shouted back. She had never raised her voice to Rina before. The Polish woman stopped her:

"Please don't shout. We might be overheard. Those people in the big top, they were probably . . . Jews . . ."

And lowering her voice to a whisper:

"They are arresting everybody. Parents, children . . ."

Anna still remembers her utter astonishment:

"That's horrible . . . But what . . . what has it got to do with you?"

Rina had said nothing. She was staring into space. A cowardly rage filled Anna. Her heart thumping, she stuttered:

"But you're not . . . you're not . . . ?"

Rina had opened her mouth as if to deny it and stayed like that, gaping like a fish out of water.

"But why decide to be Jewish all of a sudden? Haven't we got enough problems as it is?" Anna had protested stupidly, with tears in her eyes.

Anna's sleep always gets bogged down in the same places in her nightmare: Charles, the circus, the war . . . She dreams of Charles, Charles the boss, the circus manager who had accepted her into his troupe all those years ago. In her dream, she shares his worries. Things are going badly with the circus, with its troupe. It's the fault of this bloody war. The whole troupe knows that this trip to Africa is a gamble. Charles has spent the last of his savings on the ferry passage. To listen to him, the North Africans are short of entertainment and a circus is sure to make a fortune. It stands to reason . . . Anna remembers his making the same prediction before every journey abroad, without noticeable improvement. Somebody sneers that there may be some French there, but the fact remains that the place is full of penniless Arabs, and Arabs, unless he is mistaken, are not exactly famous for a love of circuses. Anna remembers too many evenings in the past two years (and in her dream, she is suddenly famished) when meals at their overnight stops have been anything but nourishing. You try being an acrobat on the back of a horse when your belly is crying out with hunger!

The boat is rolling from side to side and in her sleep, mixed up with the creaking, she can make out a deep-throated growl from an uneasy lion. Now and again, a seal barks, disturbed by the unaccustomed swaying of the deck, and also perhaps by the smell of the surrounding sea, invisible to her. The elephants, placid by nature, are sleeping deeply while, as usual, one of their number keeps watch.

In a way, Anna is like those elephants. Frightened by the war, unable to sleep unless there is somebody to watch over her. She knows that a solitary elephant always feels threatened. Without a sibling to protect it, it cannot bring itself to sleep and ends up going crazy from insomnia. When she moans with fear on the verge of sleep, confronting some invisible enemy, Rina is there to calm her down. The girl has not been unaware, during the long, featureless nights of this voyage, that Rina too has her fears. Yet Anna has a solution. She feigns ignorance, not wishing to deprive herself of the loving hand that is trying, as far as possible, to protect her from this waking nightmare . . .

". . . Wake up, come on, wake up, little squirrel! We've arrived!"

Anna, struggling to open her eyes, groans crossly:

"Do shut up, Rina! Arrived where?"

Rina, a wide grin on her face, shakes her more roughly still:

"Where do you think, with all this sun? In Algiers, idiot! Sultans await us with luxurious feasts!"

And Rina drops a curtsey before dancing round the little cabin. In spite of herself, Anna is infected by the Polish woman's cheerfulness. She jumps out of bed, startled by the screaming of the gulls. From the porthole, she can see a stretch of coastline, and some little white cubes that must be houses. Then her heart beats faster, for the boat is slowly turning to starboard, allowing her, as if tantalisingly unwrapping a precious gift, her first ever sight of the bay of Algiers . . .

9

Trembling from head to foot, the baby jackal creeps up to the tree-trunk on which the man is sitting. Nassreddine stretches out a hand. The jackal (five or six weeks old at most) shivers, baring its teeth. Its back is shuddering with fear, yet it allows itself to be stroked. Nassreddine can feel the bones sticking out beneath its already roughening coat. The animal must be famished, clearly too young to look after itself. Uttering little mews, it crouches at the man's feet, and he scratches its head affectionately.

"That's not a very clever thing to do, you foolish creature! How old are you? A month, six weeks? If you're as reckless as this at your age, putting your trust in the first man you see, I would be surprised if you grew up to sport a fine pair of balls like Grandpa Jackal!"

The tiny creature with the pointed teeth is now purring like a cat. The sun is about to drop below the horizon. Despite his keen eyesight, the man can hardly make out the sharp contours of the East Algerian massif, the Hauts Plateaux. Nassreddine smiles, in pensive mood:

"You're a long way from your mother, aren't you? And you do stupid things, like me ... That doesn't make us very intelligent, eh? Life isn't the best thing ever invented, little brother, as you'll soon find out ..."

He is still tormented by guilt. This morning, at dawn, his mother had taken him in her arms and then, suddenly losing her temper, berated him for his latest style of dressing:

"You may think that it makes you look like a *gaouri*, but people will only laugh at you!", and her lips had trembled with indignation. Nassreddine was about to retort that, truly, this wasn't the moment to argue, as he probably wouldn't see her again for four months, when, nonplussed, he noticed a tear in the corner of one eye. His mother, to prevent herself from crying, had resorted to shouting at him . . .

He put a hand on her shoulder. The teardrop swelled, making the pupil iridescent. The other eye, the angry one, remained dry.

"Mama . . ."

The poor woman stopped instantly. Nassreddine stroked the eyes of the peasant who had given him life: short, fragile, brittle as a piece of straw after the harvest, yet so alive, so full of love for her family, and so very fiery! The tear still refused to fall. Her eyes were misty, unfocused. She murmured gently, in a voice he barely recognised:

"Here in the mountains, son, without you and your father, I wither away."

She had turned her head away, as if to hide her face from him. And said, in the same hopeless voice:

"You've only been here two days . . ."

His mother had even essayed a jest:

"I haven't seen enough of you, my son. Come back to me soon from your accursed town, and beware of its bridges."

Nassreddine coughs. He wishes he could go back, take his mother in his arms and say that he would never leave her. But how could a poor peasant boy make a promise like that? He left her everything that he had earned in Constantine – and it was so little! He knew that it wouldn't even cover the interest on the debt to the money-lender. So he must take to the road once more, try and find something better than his wretched job in the tannery. Up to his knees in water from morning to night in the trench for treating the skins, he was wasting both time and health. Ah, those dreadful nights spent scratching legs that were raw and inflamed from the mixture of salt, tannin and alum!

Now the baby jackal is yapping, its tiny, sad eyes gazing up at him. It obviously wants something to eat. Nassreddine finds a piece of galette in his pocket and throws it to the jackal. The little animal sniffs it suspiciously, takes a cautious nibble, then ravenously gobbles down the rest. Nassreddine watches it, amused. He sighs:

"If you're as clever as they say, little chicken-killer, why can't you tell me where to find my father?"

He straightens up, anxiety flooding back:

"Poor Papa, what wasps' nest have you stirred up?"

They had had no news since his father left for Sétif, to where, in obedience to his mother, Nassreddine had promised to make a detour. Although they never spoke of it, their anxiety was the same: in these terrible times of unrest, anything might happen, even the worst . . .

Yet again, the animal drags the man out of his deep reverie. Nassreddine rubs his calf-muscles, groaning with cramp. He has walked all day since leaving the *douar*. The spring weather is glorious, but the going proved unexpectedly hard when, late in the afternoon, he was obliged to take to the forest. Coming down the road towards him was a police patrol that he wished to avoid. The men were heavily armed and accompanied by police-dogs. The dogs barked, but Nassreddine jumped over a cactus hedge just in time. Something serious must have happened locally and he knew, like every other highlander in these mountains, that in such circumstances it was best to put the maximum distance between oneself and the representatives of French justice. The latter were in the habit of beating up any poor wretch in their path and asking questions later. Softening him up, they called it. If the fellow were guilty, so the argument ran, he deserved it; if not, then it would serve as a salutary warning.

The baby jackal nips at his trousers, asking for more, and Nassreddine, in a gesture of impotence, turns out his empty pockets. The animal gives a feeble yap, then curls up at the traveller's feet. Touched by the animal's trust, Nassreddine smiles:

"And you, my little brother in poverty," he whispers, "is that your recipe for survival?"

Suddenly, the little carnivore raises its head, uneasy, then jumps to its feet, petrified. Nassreddine looks at it with amused curiosity:

"Hey, idiot, what did I say to put you in such a state? I take it back. Here, wait! Come back! Shit, what the hell . . ."

The dog, a large German shepherd, springing from the thicket without a sound, has cut off the jackal's desperate flight, knocking it over with one swipe of a paw. Stunned, the jackal does its best to get up, but the dog is already upon it, planting its teeth in the animal's tiny throat. Before Nassreddine, horrified, can make a move, a jovial laugh explodes behind him:

"So, my precious wog," a voice says in French, "you thought you had shaken us off, did you? No, no, no, my lad! You shouldn't have run off like that when you saw the forces of law and order. So now you can explain to us what was pricking your conscience because, as you can imagine, we're dying to know . . ."

Gun in hand, the policeman walks cautiously towards the young man. Prudently, Nassreddine has put up his hands. When faced with the French police, he was told, always pretend to be as stupid as a donkey (indeed, he knew from personal experience that Christians didn't like Muslims to be too intelligent), show them the utmost respect to tickle their vanity and, above all, never contradict them. It seems only too likely (to judge by the man's icy expression) that he is in for a beating. His one aim in appearing so docile is to reduce this to a minimum. Other uniformed men have emerged from the thicket. Now that advice will be put to the test, Nassreddine thinks, his throat tightening with fear. The first policeman seems more interested in watching the dog, its muzzle is still foraging in the jackal's bloodstained neck.

"The brute seems to be enjoying it. Tell me, boy, that other meal . . . was it the same for you?"

"Meal? What meal?" Nassreddine exclaims in Arabic, more in astonishment than fear.

"The lieutenant, you bastard! The big-bellied lieutenant with all that good, nourishing fat, not to mention his leather boots and cap!"

And a monumental slap connects with Nassreddine's nose. Staggering with pain, holding his hand to his face, the youth stumbles backwards and trips over a clump of brambles. He examines his bloodstained hand. Eyes bulging with indignation, he protests, this time in Chaouï.

"Sons of whores, are you mad or what? What stupid lie have you invented now?"

The policeman walks up to him, his face tense with anger:

"Stinking wog, I don't know what you're gabbling about in your filthy lingo, but one thing's for sure, you don't need a dictionary to understand me!"

And he gives the highlander a vicious kick in the balls. Turning to his comrades, the policeman, a chubby fellow with the jocular manner of a pétanque player, mutters with a grimace of disgust:

"These Arabs, they go in for cannibalism, yet they collapse at the first clip round the ears! I tell you, they're not real men . . ."

At last, after a terrifying week of interrogation, Nassreddine understands that the chubby policeman had not been speaking figuratively. He is literally accused of eating a man, a French soldier! Or more precisely, two men, a French lieutenant and a *bachagha*, but for the policemen who take it in turns to gape at Nassreddine before beating him up, the Arab official didn't really count: the "cannibal", in daring to assault, in the literal sense of the word, the very flesh of the glorious French Empire, had done the unthinkable!

Yet the young Chaouï would look back on the ensuing six months of prison as one of the most "interesting" periods of his life. Even the blows and the bullying, which had made his first days of imprisonment at the local police station a veritable hell, rapidly lost their intensity. His status as a cannibal, a criminal captured thanks to the doggedness of the French police and the co-operation of the native population, soon earns him some surprising marks of respect. The authorities decide to hold a full State trial, with an exemplary custodial sentence designed to nip in the bud any derisory signs of revolt among the Arabs, should the current rout of the French army in France have given them ideas. The overnight journey to the capital lasts eight interminable hours, the train stopping at every station and sometimes taking a loop line to allow oncoming trains to pass. "Here am I," Nassreddine thinks bitterly: "travelling across my own country for the first time in my life, only to do it in the pitch dark! My poor mother, if you could see how your son is disgraced. Your son, the son of Zehra and Dahmane, a man-eater! And goodness knows what people will come and tell you." For the young Chaouï, the idea that his mother might hear of his predicament through malicious gossip is a torture worse than any beating. The policemen travelling with him, more or less drunk, indulge in endless dubious jokes. When Nassreddine fails to join in, a few well-placed blows instantly remind him that his guards' relative bonhomie doesn't extend to the enemy. Giving up in despair, terrified lest he was letting himself in for a game which, if anything, would reinforce his supposed guilt, Nassreddine makes the obligatory time-honoured responses that trigger hilarity.

"What did the lieutenant taste like?"

"Sir, he tasted of pork."

"And the *bachagha*?"

"He tasted of lamb. He was a Muslim, you see."

"And their thingummies? What did you do with them, make sausages, one pork, one merguez?"

Luckily for Nassreddine, they soon find the real culprit, a wretched peasant from a *douar* on the Hauts Plateaux. The man makes his capture all the easier by giving himself up. Prison rumour, spreading like wildfire, quickly establishes the truth: the lieutenant and the *bachagha* had been kidnapped by the men of the *douar*. Working together, the pair had operated as particularly ruthless tax-collectors at a time when the village had been decimated by famine. Every villager who had lost a close relative was given permission to take his turn at torturing the prisoners. The two men were then burnt alive. To seal the pact of silence, the village headman had had the fat from the victims collected and spread on pieces of bread which every single inhabitant, man, woman or child, was then forced to eat. This was done. Next they drew lots to decide who would serve as the scapegoat should the French discover the remains. The fateful choice fell on the aforesaid Abdullah, a man in his thirties who, on reflection, agreed to take the sole blame on condition that the villagers swore by the Koran to feed his wife and young daughter for the rest of their lives. He was guillotined only a few days after his trial in the courtyard of Barbarossa prison. He had refused to talk, accepting his fate with stoicism. The condemned man being held in solitary confinement, Nassreddine only caught a glimpse of him. The ordinary face, a little bemused, hardly corresponded to his horrific image of a cannibal. The other prisoners report that he behaved with great courage, walking unaided to the guillotine, but put up a struggle at the last moment, shouting that he refused to go like that, he wasn't a bullock to be led to the slaughter, and he wanted to kiss his daughter goodbye first. The guards stunned him and he was half conscious when they cut off his head.

The examining magistrate does not free Nassreddine at once, partly out of negligence, partly to pay him back for having the impudence not to be the guilty party whose arrest was celebrated so prematurely. In order that the judgement should not be seen to be reversed too suddenly (and to justify the extra months of imprisonment, potentially the source of a claim for compensation) the nervous judges take three minutes to sentence him to six months for "defeatist talk". The prosecution claimed that fellow prisoners had overheard the accused criticise French justice, something which in times of unrest could be interpreted as aiding and abetting the enemy. The Chaouï's counsel very wisely advised him not to lodge an appeal, the results of which might be disastrous.

For good or ill, Nassreddine becomes adjusted to the merciless world of prison, where the least weakness can cost you dear. He quickly discovers that the first task of a new prisoner is to protect his anus. In other words, to be handsome, freckled and polite is enough to ensure that any unfortunate detainee is subjected to the brutal advances, more often than not crowned with success, of long-term inmates.

Equally, he has to adapt to a regime of apartheid worse than that outside. He learns that there are canteens for Europeans and canteens for natives. Europeans have two courses, Arabs only one. European detainees have "free use" of the two showers, with razors. Non-Europeans must make do with a single visit. The absurdity even extends to drinking mugs: the ones with handles are for Europeans, the ones without for natives ...

During the nights following the execution, the Chaouï's sleep is fitful: but for the merest chance, Abdullah's fate could have been his. Nassreddine, irritable, has frequent rows with the other inmates, unable to take his anger out on screws whose fearsome powers of retaliation make them invulnerable. In one of his recurring dreams during this period, he succeeds in getting hold of a revolver and blows out the brains of all those responsible for his predicament: policemen, Europeans of all sorts, prison rapists ...

Nassreddine is on latrine duty in the Spaniards' cell-block, a bucket of excrement in his hand; by chance, he finds himself standing behind the Boar, one of the most hated screws in Barbarossa. A veritable wardrobe of a man, the Boar is cursing an inmate, also on latrine duty, who has had the misfortune to knock into him with his bucket, splashing his trousers with the malodorous filth.

A dozen pairs of gypsy eyes watch the scene apprehensively. Everyone knows the prodigious strength of this particular screw; once, in a fit of rage, he killed a recalcitrant prisoner with a single blow to the face. Indeed, his fury appears undiminished, for he has seized the prisoner by the collar and is pinning him to the floor:

"Now you can eat your bucket of shit, you balls-aching dago!"

The young gypsy, asphyxiated by the mad brute's punch, tries to resist. But, inexorably, his head is pushed nearer the lip of the bucket. Nassreddine has the vision of a chicken struggling with its butcher. The prisoner sobs in desperation, but nobody in the block makes a move. As the head plunges into the excrement, the Boar bursts out laughing:

"Stuff your guts, my lad, cram it down! With what you've been eating in this dump, it's bound to be tasty!"

What induces Nassreddine to pick up his own bucket and throw its contents over the Boar's head? He has only a month left to serve, and he knows by now that in prison it's everyone for himself, that solidarity is not only dangerous but absurd in a world where the entire moral hierarchy is reversed. Simultaneously, he is overcome by the unbelievably nauseating stench and the appalling realisation of what he has done:

"Interfering swine, what's got into you?"

Through a curtain of excrement, the Boar's eyes regard the prisoner with stupefaction. Nassreddine stands rooted to the spot, too paralysed by fear to back away. The screw, mad with rage, roars:

"Answer me, wog!"

Nassreddine just manages to duck in time, thus probably saving his life, for the brute's fist was aimed at his skull. Suffocating with pain, the Chaouï puts a hand to his chest. He has felt his ribs crack. He falls to his knees, terrified, waiting for the coup de grâce.

"Touch him again, Boar, and I swear that I'll cut your throat!" The unthinkable has happened: an elderly prisoner has sprung out of nowhere and is clinging like a monkey to the warder's back. The Boar thrashes about with all his strength but fails to dislodge the old man. All of a sudden, he freezes into immobility, the point of an improvised blade pricking his throat. He grunts contemptuously:

"You wouldn't dare, vermin!"

"At my age, Boar, I've nothing to lose. I hacked at my whore of a wife with a knife, so an arsehole of a screw will bother me less than a cat's fart!"

The old man presses harder with his blade. The warder squints with fear, and a pearl of blood oozes from his Adam's apple.

"Don't forget that we're all gypsies here, Boar. And every one of us as hard as nails! Now I promise you this in the name of Christ. I know where you live, you scum: near the square, not a hundred metres from the Padovani bath-house. A member of my tribe will be there to disembowel you, your wife and all your offspring if you so much as touch a hair on Manuel's head, or this one . . ."

He jerks his chin at the man doubled up in pain, and murmurs softly:

"Understand, Boar? You don't lay a hand on anyone, the wog included!"

"OK," the warder says grudgingly.

"Thanks," Nassreddine grunts painfully as the Boar lumbers off, grumbling but visibly defeated.

"No-one needs your thanks!" the gypsy snaps.

The Chaouï, bewildered, stands up to retort, but the old man has already gone back to his cell.

"Who does he think he is, son of a . . ."

"Drop it, comrade! Camacho is only furious because it took the courage of a lousy Arab to set an example. Tomorrow, when he's in a better mood, he'll thank you!"

The gypsy whom the old man had called Manuel gives a wry grin. He clears his throat and spits with amused disgust:

"How am I to clean all this up?"

"You're the same as the rest," Nassreddine says with growing anger, "you think you can insult someone just because he's an Arab. I should have left you to drown in your bucket of shit!"

The pain in his chest is agonising. Unbearable. He coughs, and it is even worse. Manuel gives him an understanding glance:

"Apologies, Moor, but don't get on your high horse. Take a look at yourself, you're no better! But now we're even: if you're the king of lice, I'm the prince of turds!"

He leans towards Nassreddine with a conspiratorial air:

"Listen, Arab, I've made an amazing discovery: shit soup is definitely not my favourite dish! However, it's my humble opinion, based on recent experience, that the menu in Barbarossa could do with a change, it's a little too ... how shall I put it ... a little too runny, not rich enough ..."

Nassreddine's spontaneous laugh is immediately suppressed by the outcry from his ribs:

"Shut up, you beast," he chokes, tears in his eyes. "You're hurting me worse than the Boar. And kindly keep your distance, it's impossible that anybody could smell so horrible!"

Nassreddine is freed two weeks after Manuel, on a Tuesday morning around nine o'clock. Empty-handed, his stomach in knots, he leaves the prison via a side porch. Glad though he is to be free, he finds himself at a loss, without money, friends or plans ... The feel of smooth tarmac beneath his feet reminds him that he is barefoot. Those bastards of screws took back the shoes issued to him in prison, his own having disappeared in the early days of his incarceration by the Sétif police. His first impulse is to run like a madman so as to put the sinister prison building as far behind him as possible. After no more than 20 metres he stops, puffing, furious with himself: a running man is always suspect, especially when ragged and penniless. Feeling ashamed of his behaviour ("Look at me, I've turned into a positive coward, gutless as a chicken"), he emerges on to a large square.

After a second's incomprehension, he bursts out laughing: on the horizon, an immense, sparkling band separates the sky from the cascading terraces of the Casbah. It takes his breath away, and he has to lean against a tree for support. The blue-green, a colour unimaginable to anybody who has never seen the sea, enters his dazzled eyes and spreads through his body and veins like a healing balm, filling him with an extraordinary sensation of happiness.

So this is the sea, this sumptuous gift of colour! The simple highlander from the Hauts Plateaux of Sétif slaps his thighs with excitement at his first glimpse of the sea. He closes his eyes, then opens them again, delighted to find the incredible spectacle still there. He exclaims softly:

"Ah, Yemma, if you could only see it! It's unbelievable!"

"Are you daft or something, fathead? What's the idea? First you scuttle away from Barbarossa like a rabbit, now you're wriggling your hips all by yourself like a lunatic?"

The voice hailing him is hoarse. Manuel comes up, panting, carrying a *couffin*. His angular face looks thinner. He is wearing a labourer's clothes. Dumbfounded by the gypsy's sudden apparition, Nassreddine opens his mouth, and finding nothing to say, closes it again.

The gypsy sets down the *couffin* at the Chaouï's feet, doing his best not to laugh at Nassreddine's astonished face.

"I only heard yesterday that you were coming out this morning." He indicates the *couffin*. "I managed to find you an old pair of shoes and some clean clothes. Take off those . . . those filthy rags, Moor. You look like a mule that has started to moult!"

Manuel grins:

"Not in the street, idiot! There's a hut on an abandoned building site not a hundred metres from here. Nobody goes there, so you won't be disturbed."

They take the steep road down to the shacks on the building site, Nassreddine carrying the *couffin* and feeling rather foolish. He coughs before asking:

"Why are you doing all this?"

"Er . . . Let's say that I needed a dumb partner to beat at cards and I would rather he didn't disgrace me! OK, Nassreddine?"

To his astonishment, Nassreddine sees that the gypsy is blushing. Twisting the buttons of his jacket, Manuel mutters that it was the least he could do.

"You got me out of the shit in more ways than one, and you didn't think twice about it, what's more. Maybe it's my turn, no, Nassreddine? Anyway, the devil take your questions. Get a move on, I've got things to do. We must get busy on some sort of racket, my Moorish friend, or we'll die of hunger!"

To hide his embarrassment, Manuel pushes Nassreddine into the hut and closes the door. From outside, suddenly sounding more cheerful, he shouts:

"Hey, cousin, you should see the chick I've picked up! She's a smasher, an absolute smasher!"

"I bet! You're boasting. Any chick who fancies you must be as hump-backed as a camel!"

"You're jealous!" the gypsy protests. "What's more, she's a circus artist. A female clown, can you imagine that!"

Nassreddine roars with laughter. The hut smells of rot, but the Algerian's heart exults. His first day in Algiers has definitely got off to a good start, it having generously presented him with a friend, no less. Pulling on his trousers, his thoughts turn once more to his mother. Had she not said one day, during the great famine, that life tosses each one of us upon a bed of roses or thorns and that, naturally, in the case of people like them, it was more often a bed of thorns? But the Aurésian peasant had added with passion, taking him by the chin and gazing into his eyes:

"You'll see how strange life can be for all that, my son! Even at the worst of times, you'll find that you can never have enough of it, for life is like salt water: the more you drink, the thirstier you get!"

10

"He'll never do it will he, Rina? It's unthinkable!"

"And where's the money to come from to feed the other elephants and the rest of the menagerie?"

Anna, horrified, watches the mahout lead Orféa into the middle of the ring. The Polish woman looks on, stony-faced. The elephant sways from side to side, visibly uncertain about what she is doing here in the ring, long after the evening show. Her eyes seem to be demanding an explanation from the mahout wielding the familiar steel-tipped prod: why her alone when her fellow elephants were allowed to go on sleeping? She places a friendly trunk on her mahout's shoulder all the same, asking for the usual tid-bit.

The mahout, an Alsatian with a swaggering moustache, furtively wipes his eyes. Then, beneath Charles's imperious gaze, he guides the pachyderm with short, guttural, onomatopoeic commands:

"Daha, Orféa! Dacon, Orféa!"

Obediently, the elephant manoeuvres herself between four enormous pillars fixed in the ground, bows her head to her master and kneels, bending first one front leg, then the other. The mahout slips some carrots into her mouth and Orféa shakes her ears with pleasure.

"Has she swallowed enough?"

"Yes," the Alsatian replies, gloomily. "She'll drop off in a quarter of an hour at most."

"You're sure that she won't wake up?"

"Quite sure, Sir. It's the same stuff that the vet gives them before he makes a dental inspection."

Only a few lights are lit. Most of the circus artists are present. Charles

143

has ordered the staff to be ready to assist the knacker's men if necessary. Again, the mahout taps the elephant on the flank. Her trunk emits a disagreeable sound, a sort of squeal, as if in surprise that her master has not yet given her the command to rise.

Everyone is waiting for the animal to lose consciousness. An acrobat pats her eyes with a handkerchief. Bodu the dwarf only half succeeds in stifling a sudden fit of coughing. All are resigned, understanding that their livelihood depends in part upon the death of this animal which has served them faithfully for so long. The gigantic shadows on the walls of the big tent seem to be judging them in mute reproach. Anna shivers. She has always known Orféa. As a young elephant, she had a terrible temper, once causing a panic on a parade day by charging into a bistro, but she had settled down with age. Nowadays, all are agreed that she acquits herself well in the ring, doing a hilariously comic turn in which, balancing on a ball while uncorking a make-believe bottle of wine, she mimics a drunk. For some years, paradoxically, as the oldest elephant, she has been in charge of disciplining those who were too high-spirited. At a gesture from her master, Orféa would blow tempestuously through her trunk and push the recalcitrant elephant to the ground with her forehead. Only when she considered that it had been punished enough would she permit it to rise. Anna was always greatly impressed by this spectacle: Orféa seemed to be enjoying herself prodigiously, appreciating to the full the intoxicating pleasure granted her by her master of ordering others about for once!

Anna feels as though she is witnessing the murder of a sister creature. Worse: a sort of infanticide, for the gigantic beast with the brain of a child is being betrayed by the one person in whom she has complete trust. Soon, the movements of the trunk become jerky. The elephant, uneasy, does her best to get up, but her eyelids close. Suddenly, the body rolls over on its side. The head hits the floor of the ring and rebounds violently without awakening the elephant. A powerful smell of urine pervades the big top. Transfixed, the Alsatian stares at the growing pool between the feet of the pachyderm. He gives a gulp of pity, for he knows what it means from experience: poor Orféa, divining some plot against her in a final spark of consciousness, had been terrified!

"What are you waiting for, Albert?" Charles grumbles testily, pushing the Alsatian forward.

The mahout sighs, then goes to work. He claps iron shackles around Orféa's legs, checks the fastenings and signals that all is ready. Charles in his turn verifies that the massive chains are correctly fastened to the pillars.

The mahout's question, though spoken in a murmur, is audible to everybody in the silence of the big top:

"Is this really necessary, boss? Couldn't we do it some other way?'"

Charles, white-faced, ignores him. He takes a pair of pistols from a case and makes sure that they are loaded. Anna recognises the guns carried by the security guards during those acts that involve wild animals. The mahout takes one of the loaded pistols from the circus manager and examines it, whispering: "I can't do it." But he walks over to the shackled body none the less.

Charles places the gun-barrel to the elephant's right eye. After a moment's hesitation, the Alsatian does the same to the other eye.

"Right, start up the lorry!"

Anna doesn't see Charles's nod, but she has the impression that the twin detonations, deafening despite the roar of the engine, have awoken the massive beast. Orféa's head shudders with the shock. A little blood runs from the eyes to the mouth. The trunk makes a sudden movement and relaxes. A chain tautens with the jerk of a leg, then nothing more.

"Back to work! Everything has to be ready by dawn. Prepare two loads as specified, one for the animals, one for you. Then we will weigh them."

Charles's voice is firm, seemingly emotionless. Only his hand trembles a little. The butcher complains:

"It's not going to be easy. I haven't cut up an animal this size before. We'll start with the head. Pass us the saw, Jeannot, and be ready with the basins!"

The knacker's apprentice, grinning, hands him a large meat saw. While his boss sharpens the saw, he scatters sawdust round the body. Anna shudders. Overcome by anger and disgust, she rushes outside. A refrigerated lorry is parked beside the big top, its motor still running. An inscription in large letters covers one side: Habirous, Horse Butcher, 3, rue . . .

Anna bites her nails with anxiety. This circus seems to be falling apart. She returns to limbering up, exercising till her muscles ache. She is on in less than two hours. Sweat runs down her neck. Irritably, she wipes it away and continues with her flexing and stretching. She ought to stop, she is becoming overtired. But her anger, poignant and bitter, refuses to go away. She vents it upon her own body.

Ah, Rina and her new lover! The chap has come round nearly every evening for the past three days, and now he has taken to spending the night in the caravan. And, as if that wasn't enough, the day before yesterday Rina had to go and ask her Manuel to bring round some friend whom he had taken under his wing, a fellow called José who only turned out to be a young Arab dressed as a European!

The meal passed off in an icy atmosphere. The Arab was clearly mortified by the two women's reaction, a mixture of surprise and reserve, when he took off his absurd beret. He was dark-skinned, stocky and, for a native, rather well-dressed. "Black-market money, I suppose," Anna thought, with slight contempt. Improbably, Manuel introduced him as a distant cousin from Andalusia whose French wasn't very good. The young man blushed violently, and so visibly, his dark complexion notwithstanding, that Manuel was seized by a fit of the giggles. Anna herself no longer felt like laughing, for the Arab had put his hands over his ears, an unconscious gesture perhaps to hide their redness. He glared at his friend, then didn't open his mouth for the rest of the evening, barely touching the excellent meal which Rina had concocted from anything to hand. Manuel and Anna did their best to lighten the atmosphere, but it became so oppressive that the Arab stood up and made his excuses. As he was leaving, he looked across at Anna and said that of course he wasn't called José ("that was my friend Manuel's stupid idea, he often has stupid ideas"), his name was Nassreddine, which meant Victory of Faith, and he was a Chaouï ("But, naturally, that means nothing to you") from a remote mountain village in the Aurès, and what's more ("It goes without saying . . .") he was half Berber!

At which juncture, scarlet in the face once again, he bowed to the two women and departed without a word to his friend. Manuel rushed out after him. Anna thought the young man rather absurd, but felt that he had a certain panache. Suddenly, she wished that he hadn't left in such a hurry. This must have shown, for Rina, ever the tease, said mockingly:

"That Andalusian ex-con certainly has a temper! You fancied him, didn't you?"

"You don't know what you're talking about."

She and Rina heard shouts, then Manuel returned, abashed, saying that really, his friend should learn to take a joke:

"After all, I can't help it if he's an Arab! All I did was try and help him out, the imbecile . . ."

Yesterday evening, somebody had told Charles. He came straight round, furious, hurled abuse at Rina, saying that her behaviour would bring disgrace on his circus, and then forbade her to entertain guests in her caravan in future. Especially not gypsies, and still less Arabs! As a parting shot he added that one tart in a circus was enough, and he trusted that Anna would not follow Rina's example. Otherwise, he would throw them both out without the slightest hesitation! Rina blanched, but made no reply, merely pouring herself two large brandies in quick succession. Having turned out the oil-lamp, she went to bed. Anna heard her blow her nose once or twice discreetly, then silence fell on the caravan, broken from time to time by the trumpeting of an elephant. Anna spent a dreadful night worrying about what would happen if Charles were to carry out his threat. Rina would probably go off with Manuel, but where could she, Anna, go? This circus, with its ups and downs, was the only home she knew. And what other job could she do with her hands, apart from juggling? A barbarian, a semi-barbarian, that's what they would take her for, those smug bastards, clinging like mussels to their apartment blocks! Upset though she was, she repressed a smile: she had used almost the same words as that strange bad-tempered Arab who blushed so easily . . .

In the morning, when she runs into him during training, Charles greets her as usual. Apparently, he has forgotten all about last night's incident. Anna, shamefully relieved, doesn't like to mention this to Rina. She has felt painfully alone since the Polish woman's love-affair with her Romany, Manuel.

She sighs, displeased with her training. Feeling thirsty, she walks back to the caravan. Perhaps she should also grab a bite to eat before getting ready for tonight's show? With any luck, she tells herself in an effort to shake off the pessimism that is threatening to get her down, we'll have a few more spectators than usual!

"Ah, Anna, just a minute!"

A stage-hand grabs her by the shoulder. She is slightly annoyed, she is in a hurry, for one thing, and it has started to drizzle. The man is insistent:

"I've got something to tell you."

He lowers his voice. Anna listens, uninterested at first, then appalled. She stammers:

"But are you sure?"

"Every word of it is true, I promise you."

Anna puts a hand over her mouth. She is suddenly weary. Tonelessly, she murmurs:

"My God, that's all we need . . ."

Anna enters, and with her the cold from outside. An interminable drizzle is covering everything it touches with sadness. She takes off her coat and sits down beside Rina. The clown is gently removing her make-up. Her skin is tender from its oily application of grease-paint.

Rina smiles at her absently. She is preoccupied by her coming meeting with Manuel. How is she to tell him about that bastard Charles's interdiction? Anna murmurs:

"Do you know why the Colonas were late?"

"No, but you're going to tell me, is that it?"

Anna looks at her friend. Rina is carefully removing the last of the rouge from her ears. The clown adds:

"Those damned trapeze artists might at least have apologised. I had to do 15 minutes longer in the ring, thanks to them."

"Rina . . ."

"What is it?"

Rina turns towards Anna. The girl's face is pale and tense. Rina looks at her tenderly:

"You're working too hard, my pet, I must take better care of you."

Anna continues in a lower voice:

"They caught a burglar."

"A burglar, well I never! Where?"

"In their caravan."

Rina is now cleaning her neck. Patches of white are coming off on the towel. She is slightly vexed with the girl for interrupting her amorous daydream. Her legs feel weak, her sex throbs softly, like a heartbeat. She longs to be left in peace to savour the memory, as one sniffs a nosegay, of her lover's weight on her body.

"And what do you expect me to do about it, little one? They should have kept an eye on their belongings. In any case, they caught the burglar, didn't you say?"

"Rina, listen . . ."

Anna, close to anger, raises her voice:

"The burglar . . . he was your Manuel!"

11

It is pelting with rain. Streetlamps do their best to light the pavements and the rare pedestrians. Nassreddine crosses the road at a run. He just avoids being crushed beneath a tram, provoking a furious clanging from the driver's bell. He walks along the Rue d'Isly, his jacket collar turned up, hugging the wall. He is in a foul mood. Indeed, it occurs to him that he hasn't felt so sorry for himself for a long time. Manuel hasn't kept their appointment, even though they were supposed to meet a fence about disposing of some electric torches. Nassreddine sighs, trying to persuade himself that he is depressed only because he is afraid of going hungry. He is down to his last few francs, and they have to stretch as far as possible. This morning, when Manuel announced that it had been a week since he felt able to face another spiny cardoon, Nassreddine protested:

"But Arab cardoons are the cheapest vegetable there is. At least they're nourishing, which is more than you can say for stones, as you'll find out for yourself when the crate is finished!"

In front of the Milk Bar, a passing black-and-white police car splashes him from head to foot. But he is already so wet that it hardly matters. He gazes enviously at the interior of the Milk Bar. Lights float over the customers' heads, iridescent in the vapour of exhaled breath. He imagines the comforting warmth, the spotless counter, the welcoming, almost affectionate atmosphere associated with the sale of good quality wines and spirits. But Nassreddine is well aware that, should he take it into his head to enter, he would be shown the door. He is equally aware that it is getting late, and that if he doesn't change into some dry clothes soon he is in for a bad chest cold!

At this minute, soaked to the skin, Nassreddine dreams of having a big slice of *calentita*. His mouth waters at the thought of the floury chick-pea flan with its somewhat sickly warmth. He really ought to have returned to the hut at once. At this late hour, it is almost impossible to find a bus for Saint-Eugène.

"Bah! Why not go to the Casbah and spend the night in a *hammam*? There's bound to be a cheap one!"

He takes a narrow street that overhangs the Ali Bitchnine mosque and plunges into the maze of the old town more or less at random, turning his back on the sea and its modern Berbers. Occasional streetlamps struggle to illuminate the mute, hostile façades with their minuscule windows. A few pedestrians, exclusively Arab, scurry along. At last, the Chaouï discovers a *calentita* stall set in a corner alcove beside the Cemetery of the Princesses. But the flan is cold, and it is like swallowing sand. He even lacks the energy to complain to the itinerant vendor sheltering in a nearby doorway.

"Blessings on you, my brother!" he thanks him, finishing his flan. The man places a hand to his breast, disconcerted in spite of himself by the gravity of his customer's salute. Nassreddine enters the first Moorish café he comes to and orders a pot of scalding tea. But the warmth of the tea fails to ease the constriction round his heart. A humble pot of basil on a stand gives off the scent of childhood. Around him, men in *kachabias* are playing at cards or dominoes. Others are gossiping in undertones. A few, like himself, are locked up in their solitude. Lower lips resting slackly on their chins, they sit hunched up, lost perhaps in dreams. Two oil-lamps struggle to light the centre of the café, leaving the customers on the periphery in the gloom. Between gusts of rain, there is a faint echo of the toneless, melancholy chants of the Koran. Suddenly, Nassreddine wishes that he had never been born. Or else that he could kill all those frozen-faced Europeans, and then die.

Anna runs to the caravan. She has left behind something she needs for her act. The girl is depressed. For the last two days she seems to have been living in a nightmare. The story of the burglary is common knowledge. Now the rumour that Rina was an accomplice is spreading, and to such an extent that Charles has decided to terminate her contract. She risked becoming a jinx, he said, and what with all those unpaid taxes, he couldn't afford to attract the attention of the French police. Worse still, he added, the Maltese know that she is a Jew. She was a moron for not holding her tongue, he said, calling her every name under the sun. Rina swore in vain that she hadn't mentioned it to a soul. Charles went berserk. He shouted that the Maltese were vicious bastards who were well aware of the heavy penalties for employing Jews.

It is cold. An intermittent, sullen rain despoils everything in sight. She tries to cheer up: "Africa, Continent of the Sun, I don't think! Now if you said Newfoundland, OK!" Everything she sees these days, everything she touches, gives off an odour of weariness and defeat. And now she must decide her own fate, and that for her is quite impossible!

A man is sitting on the steps of the caravan. She doesn't recognise him at first. Her heart gives a leap of anger as he gets to his feet. Smiling foolishly at the sight of the girl in her gold-braided costume, he stammers:

"Er . . . hello, it's me . . . you know, Manuel's friend!"

Astonished, Anna stares at the young man blocking her path. He is visibly discomfited by his cool reception. He quavers (careful, in spite of everything, not to open his mouth too wide because of the gaps in his teeth):

"The thing is, I'm looking for . . . Could you possibly tell me . . ."

"Get out of my way, I'm in a hurry!"

Anna surprises herself by the violence of her tone. She is shivering with cold. Her voice rises:

"Come on, let me through, for God's sake!"

And without more ado, she gives him a violent push and sweeps past him into the caravan.

Nassreddine almost stumbles. He is scarlet in the face. Who does she think she is, the silly goose? He shouts through the door:

"Hey, calm down! I only wanted to ask you if you had seen Manuel. He hasn't turned up for three days. There's no need to get in such a state!"

Anna comes rushing out of the caravan, bag in hand. Slamming the door behind her, she goes up to this friend of the man who is responsible for their misfortune:

"Oh? Do you mean . . . are you really looking for that . . . that swine? You mean, you don't know what he has done to us, your crooked pal?"

Nassreddine, flabbergasted, looks into the eyes of the fury confronting him. The girl's jaws are so tightly clenched with resentment that Nassreddine smiles. No question, she is as pretty as a picture, this acrobat in her comic uniform!

"What are you grinning at, imbecile?"

A punch hits him on the nose. Nassreddine puts his hand to his nostrils. They are oozing blood. The pain is so unexpected that he stands there like a fool, paralysed, watching as the girl tears off towards the big top. The ludicrous encounter (and his resulting mortification) has thoroughly dampened the young man's spirits. He suddenly finds his tongue:

"Ape-woman! Cockroach!"

The figure has already vanished into the huddle of caravans. He is choking with indignation. Searching desperately for insults of the same order, the young man resorts to Arabic:

"Pisser on your own fat arse! Leather cow-pat!"

Unable to think of anything more outrageous, he fumes, examining his bloodstained fingers.

"Anyhow, you'll have to come back to your caravan sometime, you little pest!"

He settles down on the steps, determined to wait for as long as necessary. She will have some explaining to do, that one, he promises himself! He gives a sour grin: at least he could thank his lucky stars that Manuel hadn't been there to witness his discomfiture.

"Ah, he would have laughed till he cried, the moron!"

Tilting his head back, he carefully wipes his damaged nose. The fact that it had nearly been broken by a mere slip of a girl is so incredible that he laughs out loud:

"As a seducer, my old cock, you've got a lot to learn!"

But what on earth had she meant, that crazy girl, by what Manuel was supposed to have done?

The brassy music starts up again. With a sigh, Nassreddine looks towards the huge, illuminated mass of the big top: he has never been to the circus. And today won't be the day!

"In this country, a Muslim counts for no more than a melon rind! The only right he has is to die of hunger or typhus, rotting in his own shit!"

The highlander spits in disgust. Grim-faced, he watches the gob sink into a puddle. He would protest about it if he could, but adding to his sense of grievance is the certain knowledge that there is strictly nobody to whom he has the right to complain.

The circus is camped on a little plateau and, if he cranes his neck, Nassreddine can see the sea and part of the port. A ship's siren lets out a sudden hoot. Another replies in kind, like an invitation to a council of war. His heart still heavy, the young highlander thinks: "The sea belongs to everybody. One of these days, I'll travel like other men." He savours the phrase: "like other men". Gradually, as the last rays of the autumn sun sink below the horizon, calm descends on Nassreddine. His nose is still painful, he still has the taste of humiliation in his mouth but, philosophical, he resolves to look on the bright side. He is alive, he is young, and for once he isn't hungry: isn't that enough for one day?

The trapeze artists' number is in progress. Instead of the usual four, there are only three. Masud is missing. The act is brilliant none the less. A particularly daring double somersault brings the house down. Anna contemplates these artistes who have brought disaster upon Rina and herself. She knows that God won't intervene, won't cause one of them to fall. Even the reckless snatch which, to her trained eye, is left to the last possible moment, passes off without mishap.

With ice in her heart, she spits:

"God of shit, God of vomit, God of dirty tricks, You always take the side of the strong!"

She searches for insults worthy of the Master of the Universe and finds only stupid curses that might be uttered by an inarticulate stallholder. Her body is rigid with hate and impotence.

Just then, a hubbub breaks out in the audience, followed by shouts of laughter: near the barrier, two figures are fooling about in the shadows. A projectionist makes a sweep with his beam, hesitates, then, encouraged by the shouts, spotlights the pair, one dressed like his fellow trapeze artists, the other as a clown. The audience now has two spotlights to choose from: the first trained on the three Colonas, still going through their routine; the other tracking Masud as he drives the clown towards the rope ladder, waving a club and using a sort of pitchfork to prod him in the rear. Masud's expression is gleeful, but the clown's face is invisible, hidden by a mask in the shape of a bear's head. At his microphone, the ringmaster, halfway through a long harangue in praise of the Colonas, falters and begins to stutter with surprise. Unable to understand what is happening, he looks round desperately for Charles. Meanwhile, he resorts to stammering into the microphone:

"And now, to follow . . . the next . . . the next number! Music!"

The audience's laughter has redoubled, for the stumbling clown-bear, pursued by Masud with his pitchfork, no sooner gets to his feet than he falls down again. The trapeze artiste is behaving like an animal trainer:

"Lie down, boy, lie down . . . Hup! Forward! now . . . Hup! . . ."

Anna stands transfixed. Her first thought is that the clown ("Bad . . . could hardly be worse . . .") is Rina's replacement. But was that possible? Charles would never have dared engage someone so quickly!

White-faced, she whispers through clenched teeth:

"But . . . it looks as though he is really hitting his partner, the brute!"

The brass blares out louder than ever. The three trapeze artists have stopped in mid-act. Everybody in the big top is watching the pair's progress towards the rope ladder. The jabs with the pitchfork come thick and fast, but the "bear" doesn't utter a sound. Charles, furious, marches past Anna. From the barrier, out of sight of the audience, he tries to attract Masud's attention. Masud ostentatiously ignores him.

Anna, in common with most of the audience, senses that something untoward is happening. She stiffens: those jabs are no pretence, they are meant to harm. She is well accustomed to circus falls: these are involuntary, the clown appears to lack all technique, falling stiff-backed, almost flat on his face. But in that case, why does he comply?

The crowd is still laughing, especially the children. Yet the laughter has undergone a change. It is a joyless, sour gaiety, growing ever more raucous, like the laughter of mischievous urchins chasing some drunk or poor idiot down the street.

Now the "bear" is climbing the rope ladder, clumsily, nearly losing its grip with each jab from behind. Soon, it reaches the platform. As Masud scrambles up to join it with his fork, he drops his club in the ring at the foot of the ladder. He mimes pushing the "bear" off the platform. The "bear" clings comically to the struts, only to receive a volley of blows

155

from the handle of the pitchfork. The effect is instantaneous: the clapping spreads like wildfire. Even the other trapeze artists join in. The children stamp their feet and yell in chorus:

"Hit the bad bear, hit the bad bear!"

Under the big top, all is cheerful chaos. Masud is striving to prise the "bear" off the platform. The "bear", despite the kicks and jabs, is clinging on to the metal strut with all its might, refusing to let go.

Rina, her face flaming, goes to remonstrate with Charles. Anna, equally indignant, runs after her.

"Listen, Charles, you must put a stop to this spectacle, it's disgraceful! It's no joke. That idiot Masud is beating the poor wretch up. Who is the guy, by the way?"

Without looking at her, Charles says sarcastically, his voice cracking with rage:

"Aha, the guy, you mean you don't recognise him . . . ?"

Anna understands. She puts a hand over her mouth. The Polish woman seems to have been struck dumb. She looks from Charles to Anna. Then she makes a curious movement with her lips:

"Manuel!"

The scream makes a spectator jump. Rina flings her arms wide. Rina lets her arms drop. Rina resembles a frog, opening and closing its mouth without a sound. Anna, her throat dry, no longer recognises her tender Rina ("Rina, dear Rina, my shield of love") in this ugly, raving woman.

". . . Listen to me . . ."

Shaking off Anna's restraining hand, the Polish woman makes a dash for the centre of the ring, barking, yapping, yelping:

"Leave him alone, you bastard, you'll kill him, leave him alone!"

She is out of the spotlight. The ring is in almost total darkness. The music is very loud, drowning the woman's shouts. But he, Masud, has spotted her. Triumphant, gloating, he addresses himself to his victim:

"Do you hear her, your tart, you bloody thief? So, are you going to jump, or what, my fornicating Romeo?"

He attacks the cringing body with renewed viciousness. The audience is entranced by the extraordinary drama being played out before its very eyes: several metres above ground, one man lays into another while, to the roll of drums, a trio of trapeze artists perform miracles of flight;

in the ring below, a shadowy figure is clamouring for something, seemingly in vain.

Rina's cries have died in her throat. She will lose everything: the circus, Anna, Manuel.

She seizes the club, takes a step towards the ladder.

Her despair is an irresistible force, piercing as a dagger. It's as if the door to the world has been slammed in her face and she left outside, useless, disabled, stripped of her existence. If she could only breathe, simply breathe. A wild cat is struggling within her breast, clawing at the shreds of her will to live.

Fear entwines Anna like ivy, half suffocating her: this grotesquely painted woman is too tragic, too sinisterly comic in her rebellion. Anna stifles an impulse to shout rude things at her: come back, Rina, stop acting like a tragedy queen, it's only someone beating up a thief who doesn't give a damn for you! Her vision blurs, she is unable to stem the flood of salty tears.

Audible through the clashing of cymbals, a hysterical scream rises from the shadows. Panic-stricken, a projectionist sweeps his beam over its source. A woman is jumping up and down, shrieking:

"She's hitting herself over the head! She's like a madwoman, she'll kill herself!"

The beam swings round to the centre of the ring.

"Ooh!" The audience gasps as Rina is revealed, her forehead streaming with blood. She raises the club and brings it down on her head. She staggers, regains her balance and puts her free hand to her hair. The madwoman is staking her life on the only blackmail open to her: either they stop torturing Manuel or she kills herself, there and then, in front of all these spectators! Her executioner's arm is uplifted once more. It comes down on her nose. As her face turns crimson, gouts of blood drip on to her costume. One can imagine the red drops soaking into its gaudy colours, unnoticed.

The spectacle is unreal. The band comes to a ragged halt. Charles springs into action, Anna, fretting, behind him:

"My little Mama, my little Mama!"

The club lies harmlessly on the ground. The Polish woman protests feebly in Charles's arms. Hundreds of eyes look on. A few spectators stand on their chairs in order not to miss anything, but the rest remain seated, as though these goings-on were part of the programme.

Masud's high-pitched voice echoes through the big top:

"Ah well, she didn't go the whole hog after all, our precious vamp!"

The Maltese articulates carefully:

"It's a shame about . . . your pretty little head . . . Jewess . . . But it will teach you . . . not to deceive . . . decent people . . ."

He pirouettes:

"She's been . . . sleeping . . . with thieves!"

A dull rumble rises from the audience. Perched on the trapeze, the Maltese addresses the crowd in a dreamy voice: "Jewess, Jewess, that's a good joke . . . Tell me, what gave you the idea, in this day and age, that a Jew could make people laugh?"

12

Anna doesn't even look up when he enters the caravan. It smells of a mixture of eau de Cologne, grease-paint and onion soup. He looks at the woman on the bed. Still bearing traces of make-up clumsily removed, the clown lies unconscious on a flowered coverlet. Her right leg sticks out from her body at an awkward, almost obscene angle. She whimpers at intervals. Sobbing and sniffing, Anna is cleaning the blood from her face and matted hair. The light from an oil-lamp accentuates the unfathomable drama of the scene. The girl wrings out a blood-soaked handkerchief.

Anna seems shaken, defeated by grief:

"See what he has done, your Manuel! Is she going to ... please tell me, she's going to live, isn't she?"

Nassreddine stammers that, yes, of course, it's nothing ... er, it's obvious! He adds that he has seen people recover from far worse injuries in two or three days, with no ill effects.

"Why blame Manuel? He would never hit a woman ..."

"Do you really not know what's happened? Really and truly?"

"What should I really and truly know?"

Anna regards him without hostility. He looks rather ridiculous with that purple bruise on his nose.

"Are you good friends, you and Manuel?"

Embarrassed, Nassreddine replies that Manuel had come to his aid at a time when he was at rock bottom.

"He owed me nothing, and it was bound to get him into trouble. In fact, to tell you the truth, I was as surprised as anyone ..."

Grim-faced, he adds fiercely:

"I may not count for anything in this lousy country, but Manuel knows that I'll always stand up for him, no matter what he has done!"

Suddenly, the clown's body shakes from head to foot. Disturbingly, almost comically, her right hand trembles as it if has a life of its own. Anna strokes her face.

"She has head wounds. You'll hurt her, touching her like that . . ."

Nassreddine has come closer and is looking down with sympathy at the prostrate woman:

"Poor thing."

At this, Anna pours out everything, her voice overshadowed by anger and grief: the discovery of the theft, the Colonas' vengeance, its dreadful effect on Rina. Nassreddine listens to the girl's confused story.

"It can't be true! No, it's impossible!" he exclaims in Arabic. "The whole thing is a tissue of lies!"

The Chaouï goes on in French:

"You say that he stole something. You didn't catch him in the act, did you? In that case, why are you lying? Why? You are all in league against him. But I won't let you get away with it! No, I . . ."

And the louder his protests, the greater his feeling of impotence. How is it possible that he is so insignificant, as unimportant as a cockroach?

He is suffocating in this dainty caravan, he feels out of place, as if he has intruded upon some special feminine intimacy.

"Where is Manuel now? Please tell me. We can't leave him in the hands of those madmen!"

Rina's whimpers are becoming louder. The yelps of a puppy. Anna pats her hand in a futile gesture of protection. Then the clown stops whimpering altogether. Anna puts her ear to Rina's lips and screams, the bloodstained handkerchief in her hand:

"My God, she's dying! Quick, go and see if the doctor has arrived. Please hurry! She's going to die! Oh no . . ."

Nassreddine rushes outside. The big top is still brightly lit. Nearby, a small knot of people is holding up two vehicles which, despite their blazing headlights, the Chaouï immediately recognises as an ambulance and a police car. Approaching the group, he sees a man in handcuffs being pushed along by two policemen. The man's head is bent, and he is naked except for his underpants. He is hobbling, protesting weakly. A policeman thumps him in the back:

"Shut your mouth, you crook!"

The headlights catch the man's grimace of pain as his shoulders flinch under the blow. Nassreddine, stunned, as if by a punch over the heart, recognises his friend Manuel.

Early this morning, two detectives had come to interview Charles. He swore by all the gods that he hadn't known of his employee's Jewish origins. The two men called him a dirty liar and gave him 48 hours to get out of Algeria, him and his bunch of layabouts.

Anna is tidying the caravan. Her hands are trembling like two terrified animals.

There is a gentle knock at the door. Anna opens it and stares blankly at the Arab. Nassreddine forestalls the cutting remark:

"I've found out where she is, your friend!"

The Arab adds, half ironically, half defiantly:

"It was Manuel who told me . . ."

The two young people face one another, on the verge of quarrelling:

"Come in, instead of standing there like an idiot!"

Feeling that she shouldn't have called him an idiot, Anna blushes:

"Sorry, I'm so tired I don't know what I'm saying. Please come in."

She offers him tea. Nassreddine, abashed by the girl's change of tone, accepts without a word. She busies herself at the oil-stove. For once, the caravan is in a state of disorder.

"Tell me about Rina . . . and Manuel. How are they?"

Nassreddine can sense that this odd girl from the circus is genuinely distressed. He tells her the little he knows. Manuel is in Barbarossa prison, Rina in the prison hospital at El Harrach. He didn't add that he owed this information to a Spaniard whom he had met while in prison: a Spanish refugee from the Civil War who is a feared pimp in the Lower Casbah. Thanks to him, Nassreddine got a message to his friend Manuel. Amazingly enough, Manuel knew where Rina was imprisoned. The pimp mimicked Manuel's plea: never mind about me, get news of Rina, and be sure to see that she has some money and a *couffin* of food from time to time . . .

"So I came straight here. You can visit her more easily than I can. I don't see the prison governor at El Harrach giving an Arab permission to visit a woman who isn't even a relative. And with reason: the one a Chaouï, the other a Christian!"

But Anna pales: "She's not a Christian, you fool, she's Jewish!" She picks up her cup of tea and puts it down untouched. Some tea slops on to the table.

"*Ouachbik, ya Hamama*?"

Nassreddine has exclaimed in Arabic ("What's the matter, little dove?"). Anna is engrossed in wiping the table. She is fighting back tears.

Nassreddine repeats his question in French.

"What's the matter? You should be pleased to have news of your friend! She's alive and well, isn't she?"

Anna looks at him. He seems so gauche, so uncouth, with his rusty French, his crumpled jacket, his curly hair plastered down with brilliantine. She opens her mouth to make a sharp retort. Suddenly, she dissolves into tears.

Now she resembles a bedraggled goose, or rather (somewhat exasperated, he tries to tone down the unflattering images which spring to his mind), a big stork, were it capable of weeping.

"Anna, *oualach tbki*, why are you crying? It doesn't do any good, you know. *Oualach*. It will be all right . . ."

"The circus is leaving . . . And, you see, I can neither go nor stay!"

She repeats her phrase, as if it still surprises her:

"Neither go nor stay."

The troupe is to leave next day for Oujda and, "obviously, since I have no job and nowhere to live!" she is supposed to follow, but she can't, "because there's no question of my leaving Rina on her own in some awful African prison when I don't even know whether she'll come out alive or dead!"

Anna's voice falters.

"But why would an Arab from Algeria give a damn what I do, a crazy girl like me?"

Sometimes Nassreddine doesn't understand a word the Swiss girl says. He studies her. How can he be of help to her, a man who has nothing, who counts for nothing in this benighted country? In his bitterness, he wants to say: "And you, you poor stuck-up little thing, at this moment you are better off than a worthless Arab yourself!"

She takes down a suitcase, opens it.

Nassreddine clears his throat.

". . . Manuel and I, we have . . . well, a sort of shack. It's nothing, less than nothing in fact, but . . . er, you can stay there for as long you like, until your friend . . ."

Anna's cheeks flush scarlet. Already regretting his offer, he adds:

"I'll wait at the exit to the ground, near the cross-roads. If you're not there in ten minutes, well, God speed, and may He preserve you from the misfortune of setting foot in this land of hyenas again!"

Before closing the door behind him, he exclaims in Arabic: "With you or without you, little donkey, eh! I'll keep my promise to Manuel. No matter what happens, I'll take care of that stupid Rina of yours!"

Co-existence, with its suspicions and resentments, proves difficult at first. But very soon Nassreddine has the incredible feeling that, at long last, the white camel of good fortune has deigned to kneel at his door and take him to the distant land of happy days. Andalusia: that is his name for it, the country where towns and villages possess the precious substance essential to those "perfect" days which occur so rarely in the lives of human beings. When Anna wondered at his choosing that name, he explained that it must have come from Manuel and his Andalusian tales. The gypsy would often recount one in particular. He loved to talk about a certain caliph of Cordoba, Abderrahman III, who had the singular idea of keeping count of those days on which he was happy. Riches, honours, pleasures: Manuel's powerful caliph knew them all during the 50 years of his reign. His rivals the kings envied and feared him, Heaven granted him everything that a man could desire. Yet in the evening of his life, when this scrupulous caliph came to count up the days on which he had been happy, he found that they numbered only 14!

The time would come, much later on, when the highlander was to consider that this first day spent with Anna, though rainy and unpleasant in other respects, deserved the honour of being dubbed Andalusian.

So the Chaouï finds himself helping Anna load the donkey cart with her luggage: three large cardboard suitcases and a multitude of small bags. She mutters apologetically that some of it (most, in fact) consists of Rina's belongings. To Nassreddine's great surprise, nobody from the circus offers to give them a hand. Charles had thrown a fit of temper, pointing out sarcastically that she was leaving at the right moment, when his circus was short-staffed and he virtually ruined on account of that crazy Ekaterina. It was a fine way to thank him, he said, rubbing it in, for all the years when he had looked after her like his own daughter: to use Rina's imprisonment as an excuse for wallowing in debauchery with the first man who came along!

"If you had at least made a decent choice . . . but a darkie, an ape not yet out of the trees who wipes his arse with a stone!"

Anna retorted that she couldn't just abandon Rina on the roadside like a dog.

"You don't understand, Charles, she is like a mother to me!"

"Some mother: a half-wit and a tart! And what about me, haven't I been a father to you?"

"But Charles, Rina is helpless . . ."

Ignominiously, she even came round to Charles's point of view, stammering that she would try and find somewhere more suitable to live and that, once reassured about Rina, she would rejoin them in Morocco. In the meantime, she assured him, she was quite capable of putting the wog in his place if he forgot himself . . . and was instantly ashamed of having spoken, without thinking, the language of French Algeria. Charles, unimpressed by her shilly-shallying, sneered:

"You propose to live with an Arab for the sake of a Jewess who has ruined me! Ah, she had a bad influence on you, that madwoman! No, that's too easy: if you leave me, I never want to see you again!"

He had threatened anybody helping Anna to move her belongings out of the caravan with instant dismissal. Nassreddine, returning with the donkey cart, can't help noticing Anna's scarlet face, but attributes her tension to sadness at leaving the circus. He respects her silence, remembering his own feelings when poverty forced him to leave his *douar*. As the cart moves off, a dishevelled woman appears from nowhere: Charles's wife. Anna jumps down and runs to greet her. To her surprise, for they had never been close, the proprietor's wife embraces her, seeming as moved as Anna herself. She whispers:

"Good luck, my girl. We shall miss you, Charles and I. Promise me that you'll forgive him for the unkind things he said. He has always cared for you as if you were his own daughter. Things are going so badly for him just now that he takes it out on the people he loves. And whatever you think, he loves you very much . . ."

She presses some notes into Anna's hand and slips away like a thief in the night. With a lump in her throat, Anna climbs back on to the cart, seating herself on one of the bags, facing forward so as not to have to look at the big top which she is probably leaving for ever.

The rain has stopped, the wheels rumble over the stones. As they reach the main road, the driver cheerfully hails a friend. Anna sighs, the moment seems so ordinary and yet so final. Apparently it was decreed that today should see the death of her childhood, the second childhood so generously provided by Charles the Wonderful, Charles the Egoist, her first having been destroyed by "The Dog"!

The journey passes in silence under the scornful eye of the Kabyle driver. When they draw up at the hut, the girl's consternation, though unspoken, shows in her face. At the sight of his passenger's reaction, the Kabyle lets out a guffaw, remarking in his dialect:

"Hey, my son! You'll have a job convincing the . . . your . . . let's say, your wife, no? that she has come to live in a palace!"

Nassreddine, furious, ignores the driver's lecherous wink. He is fully conscious of the insult behind the man's pretence at hesitation. Stifling a desire to throw the money in his face, he pays him and unloads the luggage, dumping it unceremoniously in an empty corner of the shack.

Anna is pale and tight-lipped. At first, Nassreddine feels deeply humiliated by the girl's obvious disappointment as, frowning, she takes in the meagre furnishings. It dawns on the highlander that this hut, which to him had seemed a veritable gift from the gods, a haven beyond price for himself and his friend, is probably in the eyes of this silly goose with her affected ways nothing more than a hovel that smells of mustiness and damp!

He wishes that he could forget the whole thing, this girl who looks down on him, his solemn promise to Manuel, the unfamiliar confusion which he feels when Anna suddenly touches him on the arm: she appears embarrassed, as though ashamed of her disdain:

"Thank you for your hospitality. Er . . . it's very nice here . . ."

Seeing Nassreddine's defensive expression, she adds, with a forced smile:

"It's only that it's a little . . . a little too . . . that is, not quite . . ."

Losing the thread of her sentence, she falters piteously: "Surely you see what I mean," to which Nassreddine replies with an acid "No, I don't!"

It is probably the case that Nassreddine's nights, during this period of his life, were a great deal more troubled than Anna's. Until then, apart of course from his mother, he had never spent an entire night in the same room as a woman.

Women had always intimidated him, despite the occasional experiment. Before Nassreddine's arrest, Manuel had dragged him into two or three brothels in the Casbah from which he emerged shamefaced, vaguely revolted that the act should always be performed with such indifference.

The first night, he hardly sleeps; nor, for that matter, does Anna. She is lying fully dressed on the mattress he has put out for her. It annoys Nassreddine that she should be so suspicious when he has done all he can to make her feel safe. True, she had tucked into his barley broth with gusto, and even complimented him on his cooking. But once the meal was over, they were left face to face, embarrassed by each other's presence, their conversation reduced to a few banal phrases. Nassreddine had excused himself, saying that he had something to attend to outside. When he returned, she was already lying down, her blanket carefully rolled around her like a shell. Wishing her goodnight, he blew out the candle. After about an hour, Nassreddine is aware of something abnormal about the total silence engulfing the hut. When Manuel spends the night there, the room gradually fills with the sounds of his breathing and his movements as he tosses and turns in his sleep, trying to get comfortable. The Chaouï imagines the girl (and he laughs inwardly at the absurdity of the picture) lying there, on her guard, eyes wide open, no doubt wondering the same thing, but with greater anxiety: why can't she hear the regular breathing of a sleeper, that of her potential rapist? Nassreddine turns over and tries to sleep. He has a hard day ahead of him, for a builder has offered him a temporary job. It's absolutely essential that he should be in top form, especially as the ribs which the Boar had cracked are still giving him the odd twinge. But he finds the presence of this timorous sentinel, so anxiously waiting for him to fall asleep, deeply disturbing. To his irritation, he feels the warmth creep over his sex until, suddenly, it rears up like a horse . . .

It is dawn before he hears regular breathing, at last! The girl, worn out by her night's vigil, has finally dropped off. He gets up, knowing that there will be no more sleep for him tonight. Cautiously, he opens the door. Outside, the winter sun is busy sweeping aside the darkness with broad strokes of milky light. The air is damp and freezing cold. The sea, in sullen mood, flings its breakers upon the shore. From time to time, flecks of spume in the wind land like salt rain on the young man's face. Nassreddine gives a final glance inside the hut. It is already light enough to see the girl's face, her features still strained, even in the abandonment of sleep. She clutches part of the blanket to her body, but a corner of her dress has ridden up, exposing a hint of thigh. Nassreddine smiles: so much for her desire to cover everything up! To take his mind off his confusion, he muses:

"But she's as thin as an underfed turkey, this *roumia*!"

This then was his image of Anna that first morning, as the cold daylight crept up the beach: a little, stray animal, curled up around its fear, persuaded that nobody would come to its aid.

He mutters between clenched teeth:

"Well, little cousin, it looks as though I'm the only family you've got for the moment!"

And he feels inexplicably happy. Shivering, he hurries off to find a corner in which to urinate.

For days on end, Anna besieges the reception desk of El Harrach prison in vain. Each time, the same employee with the drink-sodden voice tells her that she can't have a visitor's pass because she isn't related to the woman Ekaterina Giroud. Nevertheless, he unbends enough to tell her that Rina has almost recovered and is now in the native cell-block.

"But why?" Anna asks indignantly, "Madame Giroud is a European. She's . . . she's . . ."

167

"She's white, you mean!" the official retorts crisply. "That may be so, but she's still a Jew, hence a native! Besides, it's for the prison governor to decide where a prisoner is to be kept, not for a foreigner like you!"

He smiles, amused:

"So your friend is European, but not European enough, given the way the law operates in Algeria, to avoid being classed as a native!"

Eventually, after the hours spent kicking her heels at the main gate, Anna gets into conversation with the wives and families of other detainees. On discovering that the young foreigner has been refused permission to visit her mother, most are sympathetic ("Ah, Sacred Mother of God, they're a heartless bunch in there," they hiss at the prison walls. "May God drown them in their own saliva!"). But they are noticeably cooler when Anna plucks up courage to ask if anybody knows what conditions are like in the native block.

"And why should you want to know something like that?"

So Anna admits that her mother is confined there . . . "Whatever for? That's impossible!" they ask, surprised, still friendly, but with awakening mistrust. It is predictable that, when Anna reluctantly says that Rina is Jewish ("But a European Jew, of course!"), someone should retort sourly that it makes no difference, they themselves are all good Christians! And if the young lady ("who would be Jewish too, of course, well, well!") insists on finding out that sort of thing, she has only to ask the fatmas . . . The Frenchwoman jerks her chin disdainfully at the women in *haiks*, huddled together in groups apart, some of them squatting on their haunches. Anna falls silent, cursing herself for having said anything. Suddenly, she longs for Nassreddine to be at her side; at least he could have questioned all those squabbling women who dispute their places in the queue at the top of their voices and, every now and then, when the prison authorities refuse them a visitor's permit, burst into tears and claw at their faces. Anna, shocked, soon makes sense of their wailing:

"*Matt Oulidi! Gatlou Rajli!* My boy is dead! They've killed my husband!"

She eavesdrops on the conversation of some nearby women in particular distress: the subject of typhoid fever crops up again and again. Several detainees have died of it, apparently. The seamstress who is there nearly every morning (taking the opportunity to pick up orders from the waiting women) relates that her husband had to bribe a screw to get him a clean mattress.

Anna rejoins the queue and when her turn comes has to use all her powers of persuasion before the mulish warder agrees to take the precious *couffin* with its scanty supply of food to her friend Rina. Then, worn out and despairing, the girl returns to the station to take the train for Algiers. For the rest of the day, she wanders the streets, pondering the futility of her morning. She counts and recounts her remaining money: it would be barely enough to keep her going for another two weeks, and not even that, if she is to go on sending Rina the *couffin*! And then what was to become of them? Anna closes her eyes, feeling faint. Everything that she sees around her and should have found attractive, the picturesque bustle of the port, the smooth, powerful sea, briefly ruffled by the winter wind, the dense, languid crowds thronging the streets, seem to give off an odour of decay. She enters the first park that she comes to and sits down, trembling, fighting an impulse to give the whole thing up. She is buffeted by gusts of cowardice accompanied abruptly by noises that start in her head and are so real as to be deafening: the fanfare of the circus, the whinnying of horses, the uninhibited roars of applause. By the time has pulled herself together, it is evening. She makes some hasty purchases and returns to the hut by the last bus.

Often, Nassreddine would be there before her. Mechanically, they would go through the motions of preparing a meal, hardly exchanging a word. At first, Nassreddine did his best to get her to talk about the circus, but the girl would cut the conversation short, claiming that the subject no longer interested her. The washing-up done, she immediately sought refuge in what the Chaouï contemptuously referred to as her burrow. The day after her arrival, the girl had piled up her belongings to form a barricade that shielded her from the eyes of her host. Thereafter she took herself to her makeshift bed, as suspicious and wary as she had been that first night. Left to brood on his irritation at her reserve, and deciding that it was an insult to him, Nassreddine would go outside to smoke, prey to the conflicting emotions of curiosity, exasperation and desire. Returning to bed calmer, his thoughts turned immediately, almost automatically, to Manuel.

Nothing encouraging there, either . . . According to the pimp, Manuel was to be transferred to a military prison. Rumour accused him of having avoided the call-up of North African Europeans at the outbreak of war by falsifying his identity papers. Nassreddine was eager to hear more, but the pimp, incensed, told him not to push his luck: "your pal is no patriot, and I have no love for yellow-bellies! In Spain, we didn't hesitate to do our duty!" he snapped at the bemused Nassreddine.

"We showed them, those Franco lovers, believe me! Ah, if only I could still fight . . ."

He stabbed his finger threateningly at Nassreddine:

"And what about you, are you legal? Why aren't you in the army, you balls-aching weakling?"

The pimp, who had spoken in the commanding voice of a European addressing a native, shoved the Chaouï in the chest. Nassreddine stammered that for Arabs, mobilisation was carried out by lottery, and that in his case, he had drawn a lucky number. The pimp gave him a suspicious look:

"You Arabs, you always try to wriggle out of everything. Now, get going!"

Nassreddine, sickened by the pimp's attitude, had already turned the corner of the street when the man caught up with him. Suddenly ingratiating, the Spaniard tapped him on the shoulder:

"That girl you've got living with you . . . when you're through with her . . . it can happen . . . when you want to be rid of her, I'll take her off you myself, and at a good price!"

Nassreddine stared at him, aghast. The pimp laughed:

"Hey, don't get so worked up! Ah, she must be a bit of all right, you old bugger!"

The refugee winked:

"You devil, you certainly know how to act the innocent! All the same, don't forget my proposition. Scratch my back and I'll scratch yours!"

The highlander watched the pimp walk away. He had a vaguely disgusting taste in his mouth. He muttered in Chaouï:

"Stinking vermin . . ."

The broad back was still within a stone's throw. Nassreddine, rigid with hatred, thought he could easily kill him without a second's remorse.

13

Ten days later, however, Nassreddine was to return from Barbarossa prison cock-a-hoop.

Despite the persistent rain, the day had definitely got off to a good start. That morning, the builder paid him off, even adding a small bonus, for Nassreddine had been particularly conscientious. The young man's disappointment at being once more out of work was tempered by the Mahommedan's promise to take him on again at the earliest opportunity. Nassreddine set about the customary partition of his wages there and then: two thirds for himself and Manuel, one third for his mother.

On the way home he passes a bakery. The smell of hot bread is so appetising that he buys two brioches, one for himself, one for his tiresome guest. Pushing open the door of the hut, he is surprised to find her there. As a rule, Anna comes home much later. The expression pleases him: comes home . . . Anna is leaning on the window-sill, gazing at the sea. She acknowledges his greeting with a nod. He holds out the brioche, hoping for a smile. But he can tell from her crumpled face that she has been crying. She bites into the brioche and, cheeks bulging, slowly masticates an over-large mouthful. Then, without warning, as she takes a second eager bite, the tears flow: noiselessly, flooding her cheeks and mingling with the pastry's sugary crust.

And, spontaneously, the whole story comes pouring out: her dealings with the authorities at El Harrach prison, the fact that she hasn't once succeeded in seeing her friend, her misery at finding herself penniless in a city which she detests, her job in the circus which she misses so much, the French, with their contempt for everything and everybody foreign . . .

Nassreddine stands there, feeling foolish. He doesn't like to start on his brioche, even though Anna, while becoming more and more embroiled in her tale punctuated by tears, is tucking into the rest of hers with remarkable appetite. The contrast between the girl's despair and the motions of her sugar-encrusted mouth as she munches greedily on the pastry, provokes him to irresistible laughter. Anna, taken aback, instantly stops crying. Scarlet in the face, Nassreddine struggles valiantly to stifle a further outburst.

Hideously embarrassed, he feels the stirrings of desire (as he fears must be obvious) for this woman who, despite her grief, is so full of life. Mucus is dripping from the girl's nose. Mechanically, she wipes it away with the back of her hand, at the same time smearing flour and sugar over her face. Nassreddine rushes to the box containing their toiletries. He takes out a fragment of mirror and hands it to Anna. "What's so funny, you idiot?" she exclaims, snatching the mirror.

". . . My God . . ."

Slyly, Nassreddine hands her a flannel. Anna, glaring, carefully wipes her face.

"How could you make fun of me when I was pouring out my woes?"

"God save you, cousin, it was just that I've never seen a woman in floods of tears tuck in with such an appetite!"

Then Anna bursts out laughing, as if weeping; and Nassreddine understands that, underlying this hysterical laughter, there is yet more pain . . .

"Anna . . . please . . . *Ya Hamama* . . . little dove, why didn't you tell me that you were unable to see your friend?"

"I didn't want to bother you with all that when you've been so good to me! Anyhow, you've got your own problems . . ."

Nassreddine looks at her tolerantly:

"In other words, little foreigner, an Arab has no business meddling in your affairs."

Anna opens her mouth to protest, but Nassreddine interrupts firmly:

"I made Manuel a promise. For now, your friend's problems are also mine. Tomorrow, we'll go to the prison together. It may be necessary to bribe a warder."

She murmurs:

"But I have no money left . . ."

Nassreddine curses silently. He looks at her, worried:

"I earned a little money this morning. I hope the screws aren't too greedy, otherwise . . ."

Seeing Anna's disconsolate face, Nassreddine starts again:

"Tomorrow will come soon enough. No point in worrying now. Meanwhile, let's go out for supper this evening, shall we?"

Anna shrinks back. Nassreddine shrugs bitterly:

"A *roumia* and . . . someone like me . . . they don't go out together in this country, is that it?"

The girl doesn't reply.

"But who do Europeans think they are? Made themselves at home, haven't they? There was really no need for you to travel so far!"

He feels like telling her his mother's favourite saying when mocking the arrogance of the French: "Just because their arses are whiter, it doesn't make their turds smell any sweeter!"

Even this girl, who is so fresh and pretty, gets filthy ideas into her head when she thinks of the Arabs! The Chaouï looks about him, his face stiff with disappointment: the primitive shack which he has come to love suddenly seems to him unbearably shabby. Inwardly, he curses himself for a fool. He flings the Swiss girl a hostile glance. She sees a not very prepossessing young man who is boiling with rage. She admires his anger:

"Forgive me, that isn't what I meant . . ."

Anna shakes her head:

"Well, it's more or less what I meant! Only . . ."

"Only . . ."

She comes closer. Nassreddine steps back. Defiantly, she looks him straight in the eye:

"Only, I have a right to be stupid now and then, haven't I?"

Taking him by the arm, she leads him to the door:

"OK, where shall we go? Blubbing like a kid has given me an appetite!"

Nassreddine hesitates, troubled. For the first time he notices how beautiful she is. Anna's eyes, iridescent from her tears, watch for the Chaouï's reaction. He has the disconcerting impression that one of innumerable doors separating them has just opened. His heart is hammering: iridescence like that is a poignant reminder of the rainbows of his childhood, of his mother folding him in her arms and whispering in his ear: "See, little frog, there are times when the world makes up for its wickedness!"

For want of anything to say, he grunts:

"Let go of my sleeve, or you'll tear it!"

He immediately feels like a perfect brute, a stubborn mountain mule, as his mother would say in one of her scolding moods. Anna withdraws her hand. For a few seconds, they study one another surreptitiously. His voice hoarse, Nassreddine says:

"We can go for a walk, there is just enough money for a bite to eat at a cheap restaurant in the old town. But first . . ."

Nassreddine is rummaging through a box. He pulls out a heavy brown cloak.

"Here, my mother wove it herself."

Anna weighs the *kachabia* in her hand, amazed.

"It has a big hood. Tuck in your hair, wear trousers and boots (look under the little chest, there's a pair belonging to Manuel) and the disguise will be perfect! It's raining, so no one will be surprised if you don't throw back your hood . . ."

"And in the restaurant?"

"Bah, if anyone asks, I'll say you've caught a cold in the head!"

The young woman, partly shocked, partly intrigued, exclaims:

"So I'm not supposed to talk?"

"You know perfectly well that gobbling down that brioche has given you such a sore throat that you've lost your voice!"

"And what about you, are you going to wear your turban?"

Nassreddine doesn't answer. The girl slips the *kachabia* over her head. Bending down, she hums to herself, her sorrows almost forgotten. So how is it, then, that he sees her as a fragile dragonfly?

The two young people embark on the long trek to the Casbah. Luckily, the rain has stopped and a small, cheerful sun has decided to brighten up the late afternoon. In silence, they follow the endless pavements along the seafront. Along the promenade at Bab El Oued men are fishing with rod and line. Their backs to the stone parapet, staring into the distance, they seem lost in contemplation, oblivious to all activity bar that of the waves. Nassreddine envies their serenity: they might be contented mussels on their rock . . .

Anna observes, in a tone of disillusion:

"Yours is a peculiar country I must say, my friend!"

"Tell me a country that isn't peculiar, a person who isn't peculiar, an act of violence that isn't peculiar!"

On a wave of exasperation:

"To begin with, this country isn't peculiar. It's monstrous!"

The Chaouï hangs his head. Anna catches the end of a sentence:

". . . You're all the same . . ."

"Why say that? I've done you no harm, for one!"

Nassreddine is almost hostile:

"Let me tell you a story: a few kilometres from our hut, at Zeralda, there is a superb beach. Last summer, the mayor put up a notice: 'No admittance for dogs, Jews or Arabs.' A good joke, eh?"

If he isn't careful, Nassreddine rolls his "r"s, making his accent almost incomprehensible, it is so guttural. Anna smirks, embarrassed:

"Don't be cross! True, the notice was absurd, but one can live without going to the beach . . ."

"You don't know the end of the story. About 50 poor bloody Arabs went to the beach nevertheless. The idea of taking a notice like that seriously! The mayor had them arrested and thrown into a municipal cell so minute that 27 of them suffocated to death! And if you think there was ever any idea of prosecuting the mayor . . ."

He sighs:

"Since the beginning of the war, the meanest *gaouri* thinks he can ride roughshod over the Arabs. Oh yes! Over here, they love their misguided Pétain for that! You could even say that they welcomed defeat in a way, because they believe that, as compensation, it has finally ensured their God-given right to consider themselves the all-powerful masters of this benighted country! Not that they have the slightest justification: after all, the French who treat us so arrogantly lost the war within a few days, and in what a manner! Now it's as though they are trying to make us pay for their cowardice in the face of the Germans . . ."

Anna protests:

"Listen, I'm just me, I've got nothing to do with your bloody stupid French! And don't have any illusions about the Germans!"

"As if I could, Anna! I'm sure that they would trample over us without a second's hesitation! They had no mercy on Europe, so why should they have mercy on us, especially as we have forgotten how to build guns? Have you seen the face of their leader, Hitler?"

She is tying her shoelaces. All Nassreddine can see of her is the shapeless *kachabia*. He has never really known a European woman till now. At first, he was flattered to have her sleep in the same room, almost within arm's reach. Now he wants to shake her, pull her hair, slap her, spit the crudest insults he can think of in her face. "Damn it all, you are no different from us, you and your kind, neither better nor worse! Just because your skins are as white as a corpse, or pink as a pig rather, it doesn't make you our superiors!" Anna straightens up.

"These damned boots, if you knew how they hurt!"

A wave of tenderness takes the Chaouï by surprise. All anger spent, he has a sudden urge to kneel down, take off her boots and slowly massage her poor feet. She murmurs wearily:

"At present, I admit, one can't say that intelligence rules the world. But what can we do about it, you and I?"

Smiling:

"Your disguise works brilliantly, on the other hand!"

And, giving him a comradely slap on the back:

"Come on, peasant, show your country bumpkin of a cousin some Casbah night-life!"

Anna's first impression of the ancient city-fortress is that it seethes with life. The Chaouï and his companion have penetrated the maze of streets that, following the logic of the labyrinth, bore their way into the rock of the Casbah. The timber-framed houses, practically windowless, crowd so closely together that their upper storeys sometimes meet, as if, tottering, they had no alternative but to seek mutual support, at the same time forming an arch over the public way for some considerable distance.

Yet very soon (was it when climbing the flight of steps that overlooks the synagogue, or the street that narrows till you wonder if you will be able to squeeze through it?) she has the strange certainty of having crossed an impalpable frontier: not a single European to be seen, only brown faces of every description, dark, lean, chubby, smiling, frowning, imperturbable, liberated from the wariness, almost servile, which they adopt for their protection in that other city, the French one. With a feeling of unreality she thinks stupidly: "I am truly among the Berbers here, on this spur of rock. It only needs a few pashas and turbaned corsairs . . ." Amid the din of coppersmiths, and the hoarse shouts of porters, trotting at top speed despite their incredible loads, people stand about in front of the innumerable small shops, endlessly gossiping and hardly bothering to move aside when, menacing everybody with urgent cries of *"Balek! Balek!"*, a donkey driver emerges from a narrow passage with his puffing, blowing animal. In this jumble of alleyways, stairways and dead ends, a minute glassware workshop, or a vegetable stall stand cheek by jowl with butchers' counters on which exposed in the middle of the street, lie bloody carcasses of meat and huge bullock heads with parsley in their nostrils. Everywhere, the beggars, some of them revoltingly dirty, a few almost naked except for rags and sacking, shake their bowls (but Anna notices that most people in the street seem poor enough themselves) urging their claim to compassion with weary stubbornness.

Then, as they approach the Upper Casbah, the streets empty, enlivened now and then by a group of urchins shouting with laughter and splashing barefoot in the icy puddles left by the rain. From time to time Anna spots a half-open door, a dark passage which, she guesses, leads to a patio. There are decayed remnants, faded *azulejos*, a few twisted marble columns of unexpected elegance, a pair of niches (for sentries?) on either side of the entrance of what must have been, in another vocation, a palace, or else the splendid residence of a *bey* . . .

A veiled woman with a bulging *couffin* on her head passes just as Nassreddine has stopped in front of a *kouba*. He is explaining to Anna that the tiny mausoleum is supposed to be haunted by a lovesick muezzin who was murdered by a jealous husband. The startled woman turns to look at them. As their eyes meet, Anna sees that she is horrified. The stranger hurries away in alarm. Anna smiles uneasily, a little alarmed herself, and moves closer to her companion. Nassreddine is stroking the worn enamel on the lintel as if he has found an old friend.

"You see, I hardly know the Casbah. I'm a highlander myself. It intimidated me at first, I had heard so many stories of its glorious past: the early warriors, the Sanhadji, the Andalusians and the Turkish *beys*, the splendour of its former palaces . . . Now, when I'm feeling sad, I spend an hour or two there to raise my spirits. I explore the narrow streets, come to a dead end, retrace my steps, arrive in a little square. When I'm tired, I stop for a doughnut or a glass of tea, whatever I can afford. I never stay very long because in the Casbah people are quick to notice anyone wandering around for no apparent reason. But, like a visit paid to a fond grandmother who has become a little shrewish because no-one remembers or cares that she was once beautiful, I'm always glad to have done it."

He glances with amusement at his companion's hooded head. When she looks up it is with unconcealed surprise at Nassreddine's emotion and his outburst of lyricism.

"You notice only the filth, the peeling walls, the crumbling houses. To you, it represents the height of ignorance, typically Arab, no doubt! You'll see, perhaps, in time, you'll learn to respect and even to love the historic Casbah."

He adds, on a note of caustic melancholy:

"Even so, to the inhabitants of the Casbah, I'm merely a poor ignorant shepherd boy fresh from his mountainside who still has much to learn before he deserves to breathe the same air as they do!"

Anna giggles:

"Come on, you're not as stupid as all that, shepherd boy!"

"Ah, I still am up to a point, you mean? You're right, I'm talking my head off when we're dying of hunger."

They descend the stairways of the Casbah and enter one of the seven restaurants built into the outer wall of the Ali Bitchnine mosque. They seat themselves at the far end of the dining-room, Anna, as a precaution, with her back to the other customers. Nassreddine, striving to make himself heard over the racket from the nearby tables, shouts in Arabic:

"Chick-pea soup for two, patron, good and spicy!"

"What did you order?" the girl murmurs suspiciously.

Nassreddine doesn't answer. Irritated, Anna makes a face. Shifting her chair, she becomes absorbed in watching the customers in the packed dining-room: Arabs, Kabyles, Mozarabs, their breath mingling with the steam from the plates to form a mist that adds to the impression of twilight. A pair of hanging oil-lamps light a row of cooking-pots standing on braziers. The overworked proprietor ceaselessly dips his ladle into the pots and fills plates to order before handing them to the waiter. The whole place has an acrid smell, a mixture of food, sweat and damp wool. The indescribable din makes conversation difficult. Anna supposes that she ought to feel uneasy at being there, but finds instead that she feels safe, as though swaddled in the warmth of these people. The waiter brings them two large bowls of steaming soup.

"This smells good," Anna says, bending cautiously over her bowl.

"It doesn't just smell good, it is good!"

Anna hesitates, wary, then makes up her mind, encouraged by the Chaouï's blissful expression as he swallows spoonful after spoonful.

"This soup is foul! It's an absolute furnace!"

Half choking, she glares at Nassreddine. The Chaouï, tears in his eyes (as much from laughter as from the chilli), places his finger on the girl's lips:

"Hey, not so loud!" he murmurs. "Or else speak Arabic . . ."

Anna, her cheeks flaming, discreetly brushes away the impertinent finger and protests:

"There are more chillies than chick-peas in this bowl! Do you want to kill me?"

"Smell it, cousin, inhale the cumin, the coriander, the celery. Take a proper mouthful: it's just the thing for keeping out the cold!"

"A potion for anaesthetising the mouth and stomach, you mean!"

Hunger wins. She picks up a spoonful of chick-peas. Nassreddine encourages her:

"Forget that the sauce burns. Concentrate instead on its warmth and above all its taste. Yes, that's the way . . . There now, give it a month and you'll have the cast-iron stomach of an Arab!"

Her forehead beaded with sweat, the girl remarks:

"It's delicious, this stuff, but my tongue seems to have gone numb. As soon as the feeling comes back I'm sure to scream!"

"Don't, whatever you do!" The Chaouï is alarmed.

He brings out a large checked handkerchief ("Don't worry, it's clean") and, before she can stop him, wipes the Swiss girl's forehead. Taken by surprise, Anna awkwardly mutters her thanks. Nassreddine ignores his companion's reticence. He eats another spoonful:

"It's true, that cook must have used a spade!"

"You'll laugh on the other side of your face if I pass out before I've finished this bowl! You'll have to get me to hospital, to the emergency burns unit . . ."

The two young people leave the restaurant with flushed faces. They rinse their hands in the drinking-fountain beside the mosque. Nassreddine proposes finishing off their expedition at a café on the Rue de la Lyre.

The big, blue-washed room contains few customers. The café is sparsely furnished with wooden benches and plain tables and chairs. Anna, seated on a chair that wobbles on the uneven floor, thankfully seizes a glass of tea with sprigs of mint. Taken in small sips, the hot liquid gradually soothes her fiery mouth. Beneath her hood, she murmurs, making a clucking sound:

"I've got the use of my tongue back, thank God. And you?"

Nassreddine is leaning against the wall, carefully rolling a cigarette.

He lights up, inhaling voluptuously:

"It's nice here, like this, don't you think, juggler? I could easily fall asleep. How about you?"

Anna agrees, but her companion hasn't noticed her shake of the head. She wanted to explain that she isn't a juggler, she is a talented equestrienne who doubles as an acrobat, and even, on occasion, as a trapeze artist valued by her circus. She makes an effort to mock her vanity but is suddenly overcome by sadness, as if she has been tripped up. Nassreddine closes his eyes and slowly exhales smoke through his nostrils. A cat winds itself round Anna's legs. She shrugs in resignation and bends down to stroke it.

"And which are you," she murmurs, "a French cat or an Arab cat?"

The cat purrs an answer intelligible only to itself. Anna smiles: "Why go into all that, you mean? You have your own cat problems, you don't want us butting in with ours!" Succumbing in her turn, little by little, to this peaceful place, she stretches out her legs and puts her feet up on a stool. Nassreddine counts his money and orders more tea. They sip it slowly, taking their time, making it last. They chat casually, keeping to everyday subjects, careful to avoid any inadvertent hurt. It is almost dark when Nassreddine stretches himself:

"It's time we started back, cousin."

The noise from the street has noticeably abated. Anna removes the cat from her lap, reluctant to forgo its warmth. They get to their feet, exchanging a look of gratitude for the shared moment of serenity. Nassreddine places some coins on the counter. As they turn to leave, the proprietor, an old man wearing a scarlet fez, remarks in French:

"I trust that the young lady has enjoyed her tea . . ."

Anna reddens under the man's impenetrable gaze, but she replies evenly:

"It was excellent. My friend and I will certainly come again."

She half uncovers her face. Her hand on her heart, she salutes the owner, bowing slightly. Flattered, the man in the fez returns her formal salute. Nassreddine is pleased by the old boy's benevolence which, he eagerly concludes, implies tacit approval. His heart leaps, for he believes that he has read the same interpretation in the girl's eyes.

Anna takes the bucket of water which she has put to heat on the *kanoun*, shivers as she undresses, and squats over a tin basin. She tips the warm water over her body, soaping herself energetically. Outside, it has started to rain again, enveloping the hut's one room in a sadness that brings a lump to her throat. She rinses herself slowly, examining her body with disfavour: her skin is a mass of freckles, her breasts are too small and the nipples almost invisible. Her hips are too boyish . . . The water runs over her pubis. The Mount of Venus emerges from the suds, delicate and shameless. "Even here," she thinks, "there is room for improvement!"

She sponges the soap from her pubic hair. The soap slides between the lips of her vagina. She directs the stream of water into the opening. Little more than tepid, it insinuates itself like a living hand. She is deliciously breathless. With her finger, Anna presses harder on the root of the vulva . . .

She dresses, exasperated: all the time she was caressing herself she was thinking of Nassreddine. Then, seized with a sudden joy, she laughs.

14

Nassreddine is leaning against the window of the hut. The sea stretches before him, magnificent, intimidating. A slight swell is licking the piles. The young man can't swim. It sometimes occurs to him that the piles might founder, sending the rickety hut and its occupants to the bottom of the creek. Perhaps, he thinks, that would solve all their problems in one go ... He throws out a fishing-line to take his mind off the scene that he witnessed that morning at the port. If he doesn't catch anything soon, he will take his bucket and collect some mussels from the rocks at the mouth of the creek. He is apprehensive. The swell is considerably bigger out there, and he hopes that his courage won't fail him. Perhaps Anna likes mussels. Before the smile has had time to fade from his lips, this unaccustomed resentment sweeps over him again: why isn't she here? At least she could share this bitterness with him, which is polluting the depths of his soul. He tells himself that he is a fool: the girl obviously sees his hospitality as a simple act of charity, so why should she do anything of the kind?

And yet, this morning had begun radiantly. They both awoke at the same moment, in equally good mood. Lately, he had sensed that she was less guarded; when they ate together, she lingered over her meal, chatting about this and that with none of that wariness which he had found so gauche, so humiliating. While he shaved, he even managed to make her laugh at his first efforts as a small-time black marketeer. On the doorstep, about to leave her, he succumbed to an impulse: stammering, he tried to say something to the effect that it was nice having her there. He blushed, she blushed. Then she muttered "Good luck!" before pushing him outside and slamming the door.

His heart rejoicing, mocking himself for his lack of sexual experience and glorying in it nevertheless, he took the bus to Algiers. He was to meet a chap who had promised him a few sacks of cement. Nassreddine waited for a good hour at the rendezvous before admitting, with a sinking heart, that the man wasn't coming. The cash from the resale of the cement would have been more than welcome, his funds being at lowest ebb. His good mood began to wane. To ward off his chagrin (and above all prolong the delightful lightheartedness which he had felt since his conversation with the girl) he decided to go for a stroll in the port. It was there, near the steps, that he had come upon the scene: a bunch of Arab urchins rummaging for vegetable peelings in the dustbins of a restaurant; the enraged French proprietor yelling and cursing; the famished urchins ignoring him; the proprietor bursting out of his restaurant and spraying the bins with disinfectant. The ragged kids, resigned, had quietly dispersed, leaving the proprietor to crow over his clever trick . . .

Anna has still not returned. She must have had some shopping to do. Nassreddine takes his bucket and goes outside. He is barefoot, in an old pair of jeans with the legs cut short. The sea is cold. He wades out to the rocks, fills his bucket with mussels and, water streaming off him, returns to the hut. Gently, he pushes the door ajar. Anna is singing to herself. He listens, the melancholy words bringing a lump to his throat. They tell the story of a mulberry tree whose fruit has turned crimson with the blood of lovers murdered beneath its branches. Brushing a hand over his wet hair, Nassreddine thinks with tender irony:

"Well, well, they have mulberry trees in Switzerland, do they?"

Filled with curiosity he enters the room, intending to announce his presence with a cough . . .

Anna is standing with her back not quite fully turned to him. She is holding up a dress, examining it carefully. He can just see the profile of her face in the gloom, and her long, tangled hair. He determines to keep his eyes fixed on this profile come what may, for it is the only part of the young woman's body that he can look at and still breathe. All the rest of her, naked, is gloriously revealed: back, hips, thighs; even (O Archangel Gabriel . . .) the tuft of hair, that which should never be seen, protruding from her crotch!

Anna hasn't changed position. She is still considering the possibilities of the dress, singing her sad little refrain with the same unforced gaiety. She looks so vulnerable in her dazzling nakedness that Nassreddine murmurs:

"Anna, how beautiful you are . . ."

The young woman spins round and gives a cry of alarm at the sight of this man, flushed in the face and soaking wet, a bucket in his hand. Hurriedly, she slips the dress over her head, shrieking: "Get out, you idiot, please get out!" But in her haste her arms become tangled in the sleeves. She can't pull the dress down over her body. Nassreddine hasn't moved a muscle. Crimson with despair, he gazes at Anna's half-naked body while, inside his wet trousers, his sex grows erect as a young tree.

He repeats in a trembling voice:

"Anna . . ."

Anna stops struggling with the folds of her dress and contemplates him gravely. He is still holding his bucket of mussels, his damp hair curling more fiercely than ever. As for the rest . . . she has never found him more ridiculous.

Dry-mouthed, breathless with panic, she smiles. A fine rain falls on Nassreddine's heart, awakening his soul to the unbearable happiness of a possible miracle.

He takes a step forward, icy with desire. All resentment is forgotten, there is only gratitude for being alive. He touches Anna on the shoulder and, without a word, without the slightest resistance on her part, undresses her again.

Going without food, Anna and Nassreddine pass the whole of the rest of the day and evening in an insatiable exploration of their bodies. Anna is no longer a virgin. She feels pain at the moment of deflowering. But the pain is so strange, so irradiated with pleasure, that she lets out an exclamation of surprise. She opens her eyes. Nassreddine is looking at her apprehensively, conscious of his clumsiness. He starts to say something. She puts her hand over the mouth of the man who is penetrating her with such exquisite brutality. She feels half suffocated by this forced entry which is both with and without her consent. She tastes her partner's sweat, her own sweat. She strokes the hair covering the Arab's chest and surrounding his penis. She puts her hand on his testicles, then on his buttocks. She is bewildered by her own body's rapture. A drop of saliva gleams at the corner of her mouth and the man, with the utmost delicacy, leans over and touches it with the tip of his tongue. Anna has the impression of coming back to life like parched earth after a miraculous (and dreaded) torrent. The young woman's heart, swelling with desire and, already, bitter nostalgia for what must end, shatters piece by piece into fragments of stone. She closes her eyes, assailed by a dull anguish, promising herself never to forget the least particle of this moment when, for the first time in her life, her flesh touched the shore of an unknown island: the body of a man.

Nassreddine declares his love for her (in Arabic at first, the too facile phrases offending his sense of propriety). Anna, unnerved, doesn't know how to respond to this sweet-natured man with skin the colour of cinnamon bark; but that same evening she dismantles what Nassreddine calls her "burrow" and places her mattress next to the man who is now her lover.

All his life, with an emotion that never failed to make him tremble, Nassreddine was to remember that sublime first morning: Anna waking to find an enormous bunch of flowers beside her bed; he, feigning indifference, pouring coffee spiced with a sprig of artemisia into two chipped cups; the bread and butter on an upturned crate. How had he managed to get hold of flowers, let alone butter and coffee, all so terribly expensive in wartime? He refuses to say. Shyly, he mutters that she is worth more than twice as much, that she is his magic bird. Anna isn't sure that she has heard correctly. She looks at him and, suddenly, her blossoming joy resembles the roses in the bouquet.

That day he takes her on a tour of the hills above Algiers, by the Path of the Seven Marvels. They walk all morning, jumping on a bus here and there. Nassreddine is in a frenzy, determined to show off his country at its most beautiful.

He shows her the bay of Algiers from the heights of Saint Raphael. "It's so blue, so incredibly blue," he murmurs. "And those houses, they make me think of a pine cone, they're so tightly packed. One feels that it's undeserved, that it can't last, all this beauty in a city so full of wickedness . . ."

Anna detects a tinge of bitterness to his joy. He continues, not explaining the transition:

"Listen, I'll tell you everything that I have learnt. And you must tell me everything that you have learnt. Perhaps then we'll understand one another. One is so alone in this country . . ."

"I understand you? There simply isn't time, and I wouldn't know where to begin. Yours is a multifaceted world, my dearest Nassreddine," she thinks, close to despairing of this man who dares not take her arm in public. She draws nearer to him, ignoring the disapproving glances of other strollers in the park. He is wearing his only jacket and has parted his hair in the middle, something which Anna finds comical. She muses with irony and disquiet: a fine honeymoon it's turning out to be, this forced march in the dust!

Nassreddine laughs, for no reason. They seek the shade of a tall cypress. Discreetly, he strokes the woman's hand:

"Look at the waves. They've come from God knows what quarter of the globe. When they fetch up on these rocks, I bet they wish they didn't have to leave!"

Anna's eyes light up at the clumsy allusion. Touched, she asks her blushing companion:

"What do you mean, Nassreddine?"

The gangling young man avoids the question:

"Are you hungry, explorer?"

And without waiting for a reply, he hails a passing vendor of prickly pears. Anna has never eaten this green, fig-like fruit covered in spines. She makes a face:

"Surely you're not suggesting that I swallow bits of cactus?"

Her eyebrows raised in distrust, she watches as the man takes an oval fruit between two cautious fingers, skilfully peels away the skin with a knife and, with an authoritative gesture, presents the fleshy interior in the palm of his hand. She nibbles at it, grudgingly at first.

"It's not bad, your funny cactus orange, Nassreddine. In fact, I wouldn't mind another!" she exclaims, the corners of her mouth reddened by the juice.

When with growing appetite she has swallowed a fourth, Nassreddine, embarrassed, whispers to her that these delicious figs have one disadvantage:

"Er . . . um . . . more than four or five . . . make you constipated, and it's very, very uncomfortable!"

Anna feels the blood rush to her cheeks with anger:

"No . . . really? But why didn't you warn me?"

"Er . . . well . . ."

She is convulsed with giggles. She holds up her hand, spreading her fingers:

"What's that saying of yours? The hand of Fatima to ward off evil!* Come on, we'll stuff ourselves: honey cakes, beans with cumin, whatever we happen to come across on our walk. As for the consequences, we'll wait and see! Aren't you hungry?"

Happily, the young woman tugs Nassreddine by the sleeve. He looks helplessly at this foreigner who is dragging him towards the gate. He knows himself to be a captive of this laughter, and his heart thumps. He murmurs, but so quietly that the raucous voice of the fig-seller calling his wares drowns his words:

"Anna, I don't think I could live without you now."

On the ninth of November 1942, Anna and Nassreddine are woken at daybreak by the deafening noise of caterpillar-tracks and the engines of heavy lorries. They hurry to the coast road: the Americans have landed in their thousands in North Africa! The powerful armoured columns rolling past have just disembarked at Sidi Ferruch: ("Like us in 1830!" an onlooker exclaims with a guffaw, "I say, we must have forgotten to lock the front door!" Another retorts, giggling: "Will you look at those apes! At least we had a bit more class! We didn't bring along a bunch of niggers . . ."). They are now lumbering towards the capital, ostensibly hostile: light machine-guns, combat uniforms, soot-smeared faces, camouflaged helmets.

Anna is incredulous with joy. Nassreddine, doubtful, asks her why.

"But it's obvious: Rina will be freed. The Americans are here, the race laws will be abolished!"

The young man doesn't know what to think. Moreover, it takes him a

---

* A literal translation of an Arabic expression referring to the hand of Fatima (the daughter of the Prophet). The symbolic five fingers of the hand are believed to protect one from evil, covetous eyes.

minute to realise that she meant the laws applying to Algerian Jews. "Ah!" he replies with a shrug. It will change nothing for the Arabs. But he is pleased for his Anna. Only a few people among the dense crowds now massed on either side of the road are applauding the Americans. The majority are more reserved. It transpires later that, at Oran and Casablanca, where French troops opposed the landings, the human cost was nearly one and a half thousand dead. The children, on the other hand, run confidently up to the trucks while the GIs, with much dumb-show, hand out chocolate, chewing-gum and packs of Lucky Strike . . .

The American landings in Algeria are not what is uppermost in Nassreddine's mind at the moment. Anna's friendship with the wife of one of the shore fishermen had turned out to be extremely useful when it came to obtaining cheap fish. Quickly discovering that Anna was penniless, the woman contrived to reserve her the occasional fish for which, on the grounds that her husband would only throw it away, she charged almost nothing. Anna wasn't fooled, and if her pride was a little bruised, she grew fond of this garrulous, fat woman with her Italian-studded dialect whose generosity even extended to ingenious recipes for cooking stale fish. Yesterday Anna returned from the village grim-faced. At first, she refused to say what had upset her. It took Nassreddine a long time to drag it out of her. Apparently the fisherman had forbidden his wife to see Anna again. The couple were questioned by the police, who had received anonymous letters from the neighbours about Anna and her companion. The letters even accused Nassreddine of being the girl's pimp, claiming that a constant stream of men visited the hut at night. The fisherman's wife said that, for her part, she didn't believe a word of it, "but still, my little signorina, if one is so foolish as to take up with an Arab, one shouldn't complain of the consequences . . ."

Nassreddine listened, incredulous, rendered speechless by a seething-hot anger that choked him like a stone in his gullet. Having nothing on which to vent itself, this anger frightened even him. Anna, still pale, busied herself preparing a meal. She tried to conceal her distress, but her shoulders shook. He didn't stay to comfort her. Instead, to calm down, he left the hut and walked, spitting, swearing and blaspheming, until he was exhausted. He returned with his mind made up: they must find somewhere else to live at all costs, possibly in the Casbah. He could easily find a room for rent once he had the money. He need only work a little harder, even if it killed him! He went straight up to Anna (who had clearly been crying), took her in his arms and swore that nobody should insult her with impunity, that he was quite capable of looking after her, that he wouldn't let them get away with it, those police thugs with their informers, and a great many other things which she pretended to believe.

Then they made love, as they do every day now, morning and evening. It always begins in the same way. Having unbuttoned Anna's blouse, he touches her breasts, furtively at first, then lingeringly. He kisses them, she closes her eyes, he murmurs that he can never have his fill of them. Slowly, his hands descend, caressing each curve with a sculptor's concentration. He gently parts the hairs and rubs his forefinger back and forth over the root of her sex. He says with a nervous laugh (but he isn't joking) that these hands are voyaging to Hufaidh, the legendary island that no human being can see without losing his mind . . .

Anna, surprised at her moistness, feels pleasure invade her body stealthily, like a wolf in a fold. Alive to a rising tide of voluptuousness and yearning for it with every fibre of her being, she parts her thighs, then closes them as tightly as if her life depended on it. Anna has abandoned all modesty: clumsily she tears off her remaining clothes, grabs Nassreddine's penis, first squeezing it between her fingers till her partner grimaces with pain, and guides it to the opening between her legs. Half fainting with joy, she awaits the moment when she can detect the peppery scent of sperm flowing from her vagina. In delicious agony, she wilts against Nassreddine: she has the impression that the entire hut is eavesdropping on her piercing shrieks.

Clasped to the Arab, she returns, little by little, to the consciousness of time and matter. She shivers, for the sole source of warmth is an inadequate oil-stove. Is this love, then? she wonders, almost fearfully, since at that precise moment she can imagine no greater pain than to be torn away from this stranger. And if it is . . . my God, what is she to do about it? How can she remain in this country without a job, her acrobat's muscles wasting away in this miserable hut? For whom? For him? But when all is said and done, what does she really know about this person, about his cruel country, about his strange tongue, when she can't even decide if he is good-looking, if his nose is too big or not big enough?

And what about Rina, her poor crazy Rina, what would she think?

Pressing her ear to Nassreddine's chest, she can hear his heart beating like a frantic animal, then reluctantly subside, vanquished. The Chaouï tells her that he sometimes thinks that his heart is trying to escape from his body at that moment as if, even at the risk of its life, it wanted something more than Nassreddine could offer.

"My heart is more intelligent than I am, and it probably feels cramped inside the carcass of an ignorant highlander!"

Such ironies apart, Nassreddine talks little. He says that he has so much to tell her, he doesn't know where to begin. Or rather, he corrects himself, he cannot bring himself to do so in French:

"In French, I would feel that I was lying to you, juggler. I'll teach you Arabic and Chaouï: perhaps then, with your soul, you'll understand all the impossible words that go through my head?"

He smiles shyly, crooning a melancholy little song in his harsh tongue, holding her tenderly in his arms as if covering her against the cold . . .

That evening they stay in, listening to the soughing of the sea, trying to quiet their respective fears. Anna has put on a leotard and is doing her exercises. She has been working out seriously for a week. She confessed to Nassreddine that she had inquired at the Algiers Opera, where someone said that there might be something for her in a music hall number towards the end of the month. It was only for two weeks, filling in for an acrobat who had been engaged somewhere in Tlemcen, and, furthermore, not very well paid. But if it came off, she sighed, full of longing, it would mean making a start in Algiers.

Nassreddine is fascinated to discover how arduous such training can be. The girl thinks nothing of repeating the same movements for hours on end, contorting her body like a rag doll, leaping into the air and crashing to earth in splits so brutal that, unable to bear it, Nassreddine has to go outside for a cigarette. She teases him for his squeamishness.

That night, on the door of the hut, Nassreddine, even though not superstitious, paints a minute, barely visible eye: the same "protective eye" which his prudent mother would draw on the walls of their house in the *douar*. Anna is already asleep. He strokes the wood around the painted symbol and laughs shortly:

"Watch over us, eye of happiness!"

A little ashamed of his childishness, but with a lighter heart, he closes the door.

At first, Nassreddine is indifferent to the presence of American soldiers in Algiers. The shady political manoeuvrings between Roosevelt and Churchill over their respective pawns, Giraud and De Gaulle (Darlan, meanwhile, has been assassinated) which are the talk of the Arab cafés, don't interest him in the least. As his mother would say, it doesn't profit an ant to meddle in the affairs of an elephant. Besides, whether France were liberated or not, would the misery and humiliation suffered by the Arabs in her colonies be any the less? The French, once rid of the Germans at home, would certainly have no cause to relinquish their hold over Algeria voluntarily. All those fine phrases about the nation's future gratitude to anybody prepared to fight for her freedom were merely the usual salesman's patter. True, the tens of thousands of Arabs who died in the first war are no longer around to remember France's magnificent promises of equality. The dead have no memories, they don't protest, they simply lie and rot! But their widows are still to be found in every village, bent with age and sorrow ... The young highlander knows instinctively that those with power always lie, it is one of their privileges. Every mustachioed concierge or loud-mouthed docker of dubious European origin expects to have an Arab slut at his beck and call! Does a wolf file his teeth for the sheep's benefit? they say in the *douars*, shrugging. If some fools want to believe the opposite, that is their privilege, but he, Nassreddine, has every intention of keeping well out of it. He can't forget the sight of turbaned Arabs emerging from the crowd at a Foreign Legion rally, eager to swear eternal allegiance to Pétain!

It was shortly after he had been freed from prison. Those dolts of peasants, applauded by an almost exclusively European crowd, had declared themselves ready to die for the Marshal's "National Revolution". To prove it, they demonstrated their willingness to enlist, there and then, as volunteers in the Foreign Legion, a service whose contempt for Arabs, well-attested what's more, is second only to their intense hatred of the Jews!

That day, Nassreddine was trying to sell lemonade to the crowd of curious onlookers. For the past week, he and Manuel had been completely broke. Reduced to pilfering lemons from an orchard, they filled some bottles with the juice on the spot and went their separate ways to try their luck. Nassreddine was accosted by a legionnaire, a tall, blond fellow, corseted into his uniform and carrying a truncheon, who, with elaborate sarcasm much appreciated by the crowd, told him to clear off. The "wog", he said, was annoying people with his crate and his filthy lemonade. Nassreddine, furious but prudent, hid behind a lorry, reappearing only when the fellow with the truncheon had gone. But the insults and the sneers of the onlookers stuck in his gullet to such a degree that, in a fit of rage, he topped up the bottles with his own urine. It took all his powers of persuasion to unload this questionable mixture of lemon and piss, at a much reduced price, to the Europeans in the crowd who, racist or not, were still not averse to a bargain. Spotting one of the Arab volunteers, Nassreddine offered him a free glass of lemonade. The man accepted, surprised at such generosity. He gulped it down, wiped his moustache and said appreciatively: "Hm, a trifle on the acid side, your lemonade, but damn good! My thanks, brother, may God reward you!" Nassreddine had laughed so much when telling this story to Manuel that he nearly pissed himself.

Nassreddine's chief worry, in fact, is Rina's impending release. He has never wished anybody ill, but he has gradually come to realise that with Rina free, Anna will have little reason to remain in Algiers. In any case, he has so little to offer her!

One day, as if casually, though Anna can see that he is serious, he says:

"To be honest, I wish the war would go on for ever, because I expect you'll be leaving when it's over, won't you?"

They are huddled under the blankets, curled up together for warmth, for reassurance. Messerschmitts are launching their bombs on the bay of Algiers, and they can hear the explosions, far off but distinct, closely followed by anti-aircraft fire from the batteries and gun emplacements surrounding the port. The raids, an almost daily occurrence, do little damage to the town, for the enemy planes seldom succeed in penetrating the bay. Caught in the searchlight beams and the terrifying swarms of tracer bullets, they usually explode in mid-air before reaching the coast.

Plunging into the sea, wings aflame, they look oddly comical, like gigantic broken toys.

He repeats his question, with the same feigned indifference:

"You'll be leaving, won't you?"

He bites Anna's neck, his hands playing with the tips of her breasts, but his whole body is tense with apprehension. She remains silent, merely seeming surprised. The bombardment is fiercer than ever, and she clings to him.

"You are my swallow," she murmurs, her voice strained. "And when I'm with you, I feel I can rise above everything, you are everywhere . . ."

She prevents him from replying by pressing her lips to his. Her nipples have hardened. Joyfully, she kisses him again and again: "As for me, I'm like a farmer, I till the ground, then I harvest your kisses." She bestrides him, rearing up and then crashing down upon him with her full weight. Nassreddine, exultant, dares not move a muscle for fear she should realise that she is hurting him and change her position. Their clothes lie in a heap on the floor beside their narrow mattress. Little by little the hut, notwithstanding its gloom and the distant din of war, becomes filled with the sights and sounds of an afternoon remembered from his childhood. He is lying in a sweet-smelling copse and there is a taste of peaches in his mouth. It is as though, by her very presence, the young woman has scattered drops of happiness over the shabby room.

"Take me," Anna mumbles.

Thus, his question unanswered, he embarks on the long voyage that leads from his body to his lover's. On emerging from his ecstasy, he wants to question her again and, not daring to do so, is left with an unease that keeps him awake half the night. True, the girl seems fond of him, but he doesn't delude himself. She hasn't known him long, and her passion for her work outweighs the value of their brief time together. Moreover – or so he supposes – Rina's intention would be to quit this country where she had known only imprisonment and humiliation, and she would doubtless refuse to go without the friend who had sacrificed so much for her. Cravenly, he begins to hope for Rina's release to be delayed ("O God! two or three months, that's all I ask. I'll see to it that she has all the *couffins* she could desire!"). Was it not possible that, in the meantime, he would succeed in binding Anna closer to him, thus making her departure less inevitable?

Meanwhile, Nassreddine had promptly revised his ideas about the presence of Anglo-Saxon troops in Algiers. As well as their spectacular armament, the tens of thousands of soldiers had brought with them from across the Atlantic a staggering quantity of foodstuffs and consumer goods. The French Algerians (the others had no money) were discovering or rediscovering corned beef, Coca-Cola, chocolate, blue jeans and stockings. A frenzy of consumerism gripped French Algiers, bringing with it as a matter of course an elaborate black market to regulate the exchange of goods between the GIs, avid for pleasure before being sent to the terrible battlefields of Europe, and a frustrated populace eager to renew its acquaintance with pre-war abundance.

Like most young men of his age, Nassreddine launched himself headlong into this new "business". With the help of a few tentative words of English picked up here and there, he managed to "come to terms" with the quartermaster of the American army camp on the heights of Algiers, at Ben Aknoun. This man, a loud-mouthed barber from the suburbs of Cleveland, declared only half jokingly that Nassreddine seemed to him more trustworthy and less wily than your average Muslim; and, since his French go-betweens had proved too greedy, he resigned himself to the indignity of dealing with an Arab, a "brown nigger".

"Heard of Al Capone, have you? Try fucking me about, boy, and I'll blow your brains out . . ."

The sergeant had drawn his revolver and pointed it at Nassreddine's head. But Nassreddine, despite the American's offensiveness, hasn't the slightest intention of cheating him; the terms are good, and he is making far too much money from the sale of cigarettes, stockings, chocolate, even whisky, to wish to spoil so profitable an arrangement. Especially as in other respects his situation has worsened: two days ago the owner of the hut (he had forgotten about him!) turned up, demanding his property back at the earliest opportunity. He looked with undisguised contempt at the young woman standing at the Arab's side. "That wasn't part of the bargain!" he barked out, jerking his chin at Anna who, having been surprised in bed, was in her dressing-gown.

"Out with you, my girl, and look sharp! You can tell your boyfriend that I'm not putting up with having my cabin turned into a brothel!"

Grabbing a piece of wood, Nassreddine advanced on him, swearing in Chaouï (when really angry, he felt tongue-tied in French or Arabic) that he would break it over his head if the bastard didn't get out. The fellow beat a hasty retreat, for the young man's face was livid with rage. He departed, belching threats: we shall see what we shall see, an Arab needn't think that he could threaten a Frenchman with impunity. To avoid confronting Anna's distraught face, Nassreddine departed in his turn, saying that he had urgent business to settle with the barber. Only the wind lashing his face with icy drops prevented him from vomiting out of impotence. He went straight to Ben Aknoun, intending to persuade his American to let him have still more goods to sell, never mind the risks involved. In fact, Nassreddine had found lodgings in a collectively owned house in the Upper Casbah, but the landlady, a spiteful, impecunious widow, demanded four months' rent in advance.

Within four months, he had earned enough to pay her, having sold a vast quantity of sneakers, blue jeans (ah! that tough cotton so prized by the gilded youth from the heights of Algiers!), tinned jam, spirits and all manner of other desirables. Nervous about Nassreddine's imprudence in visiting him several times a day, the quartermaster began to be less amenable. But the money was rolling in, and the barber's greed got the better of him. He complied, while deciding that the current transaction should be the last. His superiors, he complained to Nassreddine, who was barely listening, were beginning to examine the accounts a little too closely for comfort.

Proudly, the Chaouï shows off the money he has accumulated: they can move out tomorrow! But Anna isn't as pleased as he had hoped. That morning, she had tried in vain to see her friend. Faced with her persistence, a warder finally told her that Rina was in hospital, no, nothing serious, but he couldn't say when she would be discharged. He refused to say more. Anna, wringing her hands, explains that she is very worried because the warder wouldn't look her in the eyes.

Nassreddine is ashamed of his unworthy joy. If Rina were seriously ill, it was less likely that the two women would leave together once the Pole was released! Every morning, his poor Anna scrutinises the newspaper in the hope of discovering that the powerful Americans were at last going to force the Algerian authorities to repeal the race laws. In vain, of course: it later transpired (at the time, neither Anna nor Nassreddine would have believed that it could take so long!) that the laws were not to be abolished until a year after the American landings at Sidi Ferruch . . .

They move their belongings in glum silence. The house is in the Street of the Saracens. Only Anna notices the irony of the name. The building, in a state of advanced decay, must once have been magnificent. Now it is squeezed between a *hammam* and a traditional pastry shop. The room allotted to them, dimly lit by a single minuscule window, is on the top floor. Its entrance overlooks a tiled interior courtyard in one corner of which is the only water tap. A flaming bougainvillea, scrambling up to the first floor, and tubs of gerbera and jasmine attempt to restore the ancient house to a modicum of its former glory. The other two rooms on the floor are occupied by the widow and her family, twins aged about ten and a very old lady, her mother-in-law. The children, inquisitive, come to watch the *gaouria* move in. From the faces they pull, Anna can tell that they are disappointed: with so few belongings, the newcomers must be poor people. Like themselves . . .

In his excitement at moving in, Nassreddine embraces Anna in front of the children, causing them to flee, squawking like frightened chickens. He counts his savings and hands the major part to Anna ("I'm not very good with money. Anyhow, when it comes to banking, you're the one who's Swiss!"), saying that he has to meet his American at Ben Aknoun. Anna tries to detain him, more touched than she cares to admit by her companion's gesture:

"Couldn't you rest today? You've been running about from morning to night for days . . ."

She doesn't feel up to facing the first day in such unfamiliar surroundings without Nassreddine's help. She clings to his arm. The Chaouï, misunderstanding, smiles. Ready to yield, he caresses his lover's nose with amorous fingers. How pretty she is, so pretty that he promises himself that he will have her photographed. He will have himself photographed at the same time, and put both pictures in a frame to hang on the wall. But he must first paint the wall, a nice cheerful yellow, perhaps. Before being photographed, maybe he should buy a handsome new suit, with a waisted jacket and wide lapels, and trousers that break over the shoes? "I'm being silly, but perhaps silly thoughts like these are a sign that I'm entering Paradise!" The girl's hand is gripping his arm.

"I can't, gazelle of my heart. The American will think I've been scared off, given up for good. But we'll go to a restaurant at the Fish Market tonight, to celebrate. You won't have to wear a disguise, and we'll treat ourselves to a cream tart for dessert. Now that we have a little money at last, let's make the most of it! OK?"

"No . . ."

Anna pulls him gently into the room.

"Stay here, just for today, please . . ."

She stops his protests with a kiss. The scent of Anna's hair against his face prompts the long groan of desire, that glorious pain, to stir within him. He inhales deeply, steeling himself to resist the flood of pleasure. The woman presses herself closer to him. He takes her in his arms. He fondles her ear, her neck. His other hand descends to the base of her spine. He and Anna are still kissing. His saliva mingles with the saliva of the woman whom he is crushing against a wardrobe. From here, he has a view of a patch of sky through the little window. But he sees nothing. He is almost tipsy, like a bee drunk from sipping too much honey.

Anna's dress has ridden up. She thrusts her belly forward. She takes Nassreddine's hand and squeezes it between her thighs. She moans gently. Nassreddine imagines the readiness of her sex beneath the cotton slip, a fount of life in a thirsty land. He starts unbuttoning his fly. With a tremendous effort, he pulls himself together:

"No, Anna, it's impossible, I must go!"

He pushes her away, almost roughly. Both of them are panting. Anna is still leaning against the wardrobe. Eyes lowered, she smoothes down her dress with exaggerated care. Her movements are confused, meaningless.

"Go on, you're right, it's only sensible!"

The sharp note of rebuke makes her voice sound harsh.

"Anna . . ."

"No, it's all right . . . It's OK."

She has raised her head. She is tidying her hair. She essays a smile. But the smile crumples, she is trying not to cry.

"Nassreddine, listen, don't be long. I . . . I need you."

The Chaouï is at the door. He is not very proud of his behaviour. He murmurs, touched:

"Anna, you are the best thing that has ever happened to me. You . . ."

"Be quiet, before you say something silly . . ."

Anna has recovered a semblance of good humour. They are standing in the doorway. Nassreddine goes to kiss her (is already bending over her, inhaling the odour of moistness arising from his lover's belly) when he notices the landlady's mother-in-law avidly watching them, holding her bucket beneath the courtyard tap. He jerks back as if he had been bitten. In a thoroughly bad temper, still filled with desire, he takes the flights of stairs at a run and goes out, slamming the massive wooden door behind him. He makes his way down through the steep streets of the Casbah, then ascends the avenue of magnificent orange trees. He walks fast, humming to himself, intoxicated with a mixture of joy and guilt.

On reaching the Ben Aknoun barracks, Nassreddine hails the GI on guard duty, making a joke in his broken English. He knows most of the sentries by now. The man, who has recognised him, greets him with surprising joviality. Hustling Nassreddine into a small room, he says that the sergeant will be along in ten minutes. Nassreddine has just begun to worry about the barber's absence and the GI's over-friendly welcome when three Military Police burst into the room and grab him. They give him a good going over and, a few days later, hand him over to the French police. They in turn get rid of him by throwing him into a foul cell in the temporary detention centre below the Tafourah steps. There he passes a dreadful week fighting the rats, the fleas, and the fear of contracting a fatal dose of typhus. One morning he is dragged out and formally inducted into the 7th Algerian Regiment, which is about to take ship for the great butchery in Europe.

For a long time, he was to suffer more from the memory of his lover's scent and, intimately linked to it, of their unfinished embrace, than from his own misfortune.

15

May 1945

Still incredulous, he turns his army card over and over between his fingers, contemplating the word "demobilised" stamped across his photograph.

"My God, it's not possible! Not on the very day of victory! Surely they can't hate us that much . . ."

It takes Nassreddine nearly two weeks to reach his *douar*. Anger and bitterness are eating him up, like acid on a wound:

"A thousand times we risked our necks to free their country from the Nazis. And no sooner are they victorious than those French snakes massacre our people village by village!"

Several times he has narrowly escaped being picked up, either by the army or by the settlers' militia. He had started his journey by bus until alerted by Arabs returning from Constantine: the Europeans were erecting roadblocks, taking off the Arab passengers and, at the slightest hint of collaboration with the freedom fighters, executing them on the spot. Somebody says that militiamen accompanied by legionnaires had stopped a lorry-load of Arab labourers on their daily journey to work on a settler's estate. The French bound the wretched fellows hand and foot with wire, doused them with petrol and burnt them alive in the middle of the road. Nassreddine resorts to travelling by night on foot, cutting across fields and frequently getting lost. It is like living through a nightmare in which the powers of some buffoonish genie ("God is having fun!") have transported him several months back in time to Italy and Corsica, to confront the brutality of the German troops. The war on the Old Continent has been over for two weeks. Europe for him means two interminable years during which the fear of being killed never left him for an instant. And now that he has been demobilised, it is starting all over again, in Algeria!

At dawn on the last day but one, preceded as usual by the barking of Chaouï farm dogs, he comes to a village boundary. Having spotted a tank column on the far bank of the *oued*, he doesn't want to take unnecessary risks. Anyway, it wouldn't be the first time he had sought the hospitality of a *mechta*. He is therefore careful to walk in the open, so that those keeping watch can see him in time and not mistake his intentions. He shouts, but receives no answer. Turning into the first narrow street, he understands why. Even before he sees the bodies, his nostrils are assailed by the revolting stench. The corpses are bloated by the heat. While most of the victims are still in their night-clothes, others are naked, as if stripped before meeting their death. Now and then, a swollen body bursts with a whistling noise that resembles a fart. The dogs roam from one corpse to another, taking a bite and then, as if repelled, moving on. One is gnawing at a little girl's belly, and Nassreddine, horrified, pelts it with stones. The dog growls, raising its muzzle stained with blood. Reassured, it plunges once more into the viscera. For the next two days, Nassreddine hides in the long grass, or in a field of wheat, his teeth chattering at the least sound, feeding on roots and vomiting repeatedly at the memory of that pestilential stench.

His mother welcomes him without reproach, for all that she hasn't seen him for three years. She stoops a little more, and her eyes have dimmed.

"How is Ba?" he asks on a single intake of breath. She raises her eyebrows, nodding towards the back of the room. His father is in a delirium, his forehead bandaged, red bubbles bursting from his nose and mouth.

"Is that blood?"

"Yes, my son. From his lungs."

Blinking back tears, Nassreddine sits beside his father and takes his hand. The old peasant stares at him with a look of horror, then struggles, terrified:

"Who are you, stranger? Go away, leave me alone, I've done you no harm . . ."

"Ba, Ba dear, it's me, your son, you used to carry me on your shoulders!" Nassreddine protests, bursting into sobs.

"He has been like that from the first," Zehra sighs. "He recognises no one. And all for the sake of a few damned potatoes!"

She tells her son that Dahmane had gone to the local town to sell some vegetables. It was the day after the Sétif riots. With the end of the war, many Arabs believed that the day of independence had arrived. The police reacted by firing on demonstrators and distributing guns to Europeans, who then proceeded to take their revenge on every Arab in sight. Dahmane, knowing nothing of these events, was unaware that local French farmers had been killed that same morning by villagers come down from the hills. Finding the market surrounded, he tried to get through the cordon and was struck in the head by a bullet.

"When he first regained consciousness, he didn't realise that he was in a mass grave with dozens of corpses piled on top of him. Luckily, the killers hadn't filled in the grave, and in spite of his wound, your father managed to get out and make his way back to the *douar*. But it was already too late. His lungs had burst under the weight of all those bodies . . ."

For two days, the dying man calls incessantly on his mother. To the end, Nassreddine does his best to calm this father who is so terrified of being cared for by a stranger . . .

"Your poor father, he was like a child, he was so frightened!" Zehra mutters as they are on their way back from the cemetery.

The day after the burial he leaves for Algiers, despite his mother's wails of grief. The landlady at the house on the Street of the Saracens pretends not to know him at first. In any case, she says defiantly, the top-floor room is let. When the widow realises that the young man who is questioning her so urgently doesn't expect to be reimbursed, she unbends enough to tell him that the *gaouria* left three months after they moved in.

"She was always crying. In the end, we made friends. That girl broke my heart, she was so sad and lonely. She told me that her Mama . . . well, the person she called her Mama, had died of typhus."

Seeing her questioner's stunned expression, the widow adds, her pity mixed with reproach:

"She waited for you for two months after her Mama's death. She seemed very fond of you. You shouldn't have stayed away so long, my son. Life is seldom so generous a second time, you know."

He wanders aimlessly round Algiers, shattered by this series of disasters. He wants to howl, yet cannot. Now and then he shrugs, as if confronting an invisible interlocutor, his heart empty, unable to accept this ultimate blow dealt him by the war: his father's death and now the disappearance of the one woman who could, who would (of that he was certain during all those months in the vomit of the trenches . . .) purify him of the blood and vileness of which he was both victim and accessory!

He then sets out to look for his friend Manuel, with no more success. Eventually, he runs into Camacho, released from prison with the post-war amnesty. To his surprise, the old man greets him with open arms and insists that he spend the night at his place. He has no news of Manuel, other than vague rumours gleaned here and there. Some say that he was killed during the Italian campaign, at Monte Cassino, others that he was taken prisoner by the Germans immediately after the landings in Provence.

When it finally dawns on Nassreddine that he has lost everything that once made Algiers so dear to his heart, he starts drinking, little by little using up his meagre gratuity. He ought to go back to the village and comfort his mother, but he lacks the courage to return, poorer than before, stripped to the depths of his being. As if some merciless thief had spirited away all hope . . .

That evening Camacho the gypsy, formerly so irascible, treats him like a sick child. He takes charge, cooking a dish of lentils, not uttering a word of reproach over his young friend's behaviour.

"Drink up, my boy, drink till it makes you sick. The one thing we can be certain of, you and I, is that we'll always be flat broke. Drink and cry all you want."

The ex-convict clears his throat:

"I killed my wife because I couldn't forgive her. Yet, God knows, I worshipped her. I've always refused to let myself cry over her because I didn't believe that she was worthy of my tears, because a man, a real man, is nothing deprived of his honour."

The aged murderer smiles painfully:

"Listen, my son, real pain is to be unable to feel it because you think it beneath you!" He taps himself on the chest. "And if you don't sob your

202

heart out at the time, you never will. The pain becomes a ball of hate that hardens with age and turns you sour."

He reflects for a moment, as if ashamed of what he is about to say:

"You know, Moor, my wife turned out to be a real tart. Yet I truly believe that, given a second chance, I would throw myself at her feet and ask her forgiveness for what I did and, above all, for not having wept over the waste of both our lives . . ."

"What are you rambling on about, Camacho? It's different with my wife, she is somewhere out there . . . Anna is . . . she is . . ."

He breaks off, a sob dying in his throat. "My wife," he had said. "My wife!" Absurdly, he is suddenly convinced that were he to let fall a single tear, then nothing, not even a stork (a bird to which his mother attributes such power), could stem the ensuing flow. His very pain, he realises, has become his worst enemy. It would tear him limb from limb, like an ogress . . .

Slowly he comes to detest Algiers. Not the town itself, magnificent beneath its blazing sun, but its indifference, its cruelty, its servility and above all its French who, the war over and with it their dread of losing everything, have once again adopted the airs and boundless arrogance of avaricious landowners. Whenever a European looks straight through him, Nassreddine can almost hear him think aloud: "Ah, you thought your turn had come! You were taken in by those jokes: freedom, independence, equality. You poor fools, we are back with a vengeance, ready to reign over you for another hundred years!"

He dreams of leaving Algiers for another place. A place where he will at last be judged for what he is: a man, neither better nor worse than other men, valued for his worth, little though it be, not condemned out of hand by a dismissive glance like some talking dog!

His chance comes early one Sunday morning in the form of a suggestion from his foreman at work. Having found a temporary job in the docks, Nassreddine is now lodging with other Arab dockers in an empty property a dozen kilometres outside Algiers. It is still dark as he leaves the crumbling building. At the docks a yawning watchman directs him to quay 2, between two huge cranes.

The quayside is cluttered with caravans, crates and cages. From this one or that come sounds of growling, whinnying and yapping. There is a sour, choking smell of urine, faeces and damp fur.

A circus! Nassreddine has a lump in his throat. Greeted by a fellow docker, he hears himself reply, stupidly:

"Well, of all unexpected things . . ."

His voice trembles slightly. The docker laughs:

"Scared of lions, are we?"

"You could say that," Nassreddine replies with a painful smile. The first tentative rays of the sun reveal an extraordinary spectacle. Each caravan proclaims on its side in huge red and green letters: "Amar's Great International Circus". The menagerie is extraordinarily varied: troops of horses and ponies, lions, tigers, a hippopotamus, a family of elephants parked beside a dozen dromedaries. A vast cage of monkeys is surrounded by smaller cages of panthers and hyenas. Bears sleep on, ignoring the hobbled llamas placidly ruminating and eyeing all this human activity with suspicion.

"A real Noah's Ark," Nassreddine mutters nervously. The foreman gives his orders, putting Nassreddine in charge of heavy crates containing equipment. Jokes fly, the dockers as excited as children by the presence of the circus troupe and their animals.

Nassreddine fights down a treacherous feeling of happiness. Soon his lightheartedness will turn to rage and everything will hit him at once: Anna, the searing pain of not finding her on his return from the war, the months of desperate effort it has cost him to lock away the girl's memory and commit it to the depths of the pit of sorrows . . .

By the end of the morning, he acknowledges bitterly:

"My God, it might be yesterday! How is it possible that I should have to go through all that again?"

The sensation that everything is falling apart is familiar, it was the very same as had overtaken him when the widow told him that the woman he loved had disappeared. All around him, those he had loved, his father, Manuel, had died or disappeared! Only his poor dear mother is left, and he has let her down shamefully. Wandering round Algiers like a tramp, scraping a living as and when some miserable job presented itself: has his life really been reduced to this?

At the midday break, he can eat nothing. He tries chewing a few olives with a little biscuit, but his constricted throat won't let him swallow so much as a morsel. For the remainder of the day, an insane idea gradually takes root in Nassreddine's head. Until nightfall, dealing with the animals strains every nerve and sinew. By the time the moon has risen and the foreman has paid off the crew, Nassreddine's mind is made up. His stomach in knots, shivering as if it were midwinter, he stations himself at the entrance to the quay. Spotting the elder of the two Amar brothers, he takes a deep breath and, muttering "Help me, Yemma!" between his teeth, walks towards the massive silhouette.

Was God smiling when the owner agreed to engage Nassreddine as a circus hand for the remainder of the tour? At all events, Amar senior seems quite happy to hire this stammering, pleading fellow on the spot. He badly needs extra hands for the long, arduous voyage ahead, and they are hard to come by. He merely inquires brusquely if the applicant is liable for national service.

"Good, you have papers, then. See that you're here by six o'clock tomorrow morning, with all your paperwork. And don't be late!"

He adds, perplexed:

"You're very keen, I must say. Killed somebody, have you, and need to get out of the country pronto, is that it? That's your business, I won't interfere, but I warn you: it's not much fun, mucking out animal cages morning and night. And once the tour is over, you'll be discharged somewhere in Europe. You'll be on your own. I shan't be paying your return fare . . ."

Amar senior had not exaggerated. So far, Nassreddine has found this interminable voyage, with stops at Cairo and other towns along the Mediterranean coast, a veritable nightmare. The highlander was seasick from the moment they left port and this, combined with the smell of engine oil, the stink of the cages, the heat in the hold, made his first days at sea well nigh unbearable. He couldn't clean out the cages without vomiting.

They have been sailing along the Tripoli coast for hours. Although they stop at Benghazi for engine repairs, Nassreddine, not having a visa, is not permitted to land. During this day of forced inaction, he gets into conversation with an English juggler who has spent the past year with the Circus Nee. The Englishman has declined to stretch his legs ashore, doubtless being persona non grata with the Libyan police. Certainly he remembers Charles, he heard that the manager had to sacrifice his best elephant to feed the lions. Vigorously massaging his forearms, he talks of his former employer with a mixture of admiration and disapproval:

"Ah, he is a proper devil, there's nothing he won't do for the sake of his circus!"

Nassreddine mentions Anna:

"The equestrienne who is also a trapeze artist . . . Yes, a lovely girl . . . His daughter, no, or his adopted daughter, something of the sort . . . Anna Stressner . . ."

The Englishman explains that circus people are usually known by their stage names, not hesitating to change them from one act to the next.

"Anyway, I had a blinding row with that idiot Charles. I even left before my contract was up . . ."

Then, intrigued by the young man's persistence:

"How come that you, an Arab, are so interested in a Swiss girl, and a circus artist at that?"

Nassreddine mumbles something unintelligible. The waves lap against the ship's hull. On the cramped deck, the artistes exercise limply, flattened by the heat. Incongruously, a tight-rope walker knits herself a garment for the winter. At intervals, a languid growl punctuates the dromedaries' more persistent groans. A horse whinnies at the top of its voice, as though calling for help.

"The animals can smell the desert," the juggler remarks, tossing his cigarette overboard. "I hear that madman Charles intends taking the circus to Madagascar. Apparently the French army has agreed to pay the costs of the voyage and underwrite every performance, something like that. But not out of the goodness of their hearts. Part of the island is in revolt against the Europeans . . ."

He laughs:

"Ah, those French! First they give the blacks a good hiding, then they pacify them with a circus! You can hardly credit it: keeping savages quiet with acrobats, and clowns kicking one another up the backside!"

Disgusted, he lights another cigarette:

"Business is bad for everyone these days, and that's a fact. But still, fancy going all the way to Madagascar to earn one's bread!"

Across the harbour, the outlines of Benghazi Customs House shimmer and dissolve in the heat haze rising from the sea. The occasional gust brings with it puffs of even more scorching air from the nearby desert. Nassreddine contemplates the Englishman's scowling profile. It has been so long since anybody has given him news of Anna. But it is so unreliable ... He brushes the flies off his brow: supposing the whole thing were merely idle talk?

"O God, You kick me around like a football!"

His lips are dry. He feels the will draining out of him. Abruptly, he gets to his feet and makes his way forward. He has work to do. Before he is swallowed up in the foul-smelling darkness of the hold, he cries out:

"Please God, only give me a chance!"

16

He dreams incessantly that night and the following nights: a mish-mash of dreams, nightmares, lamentations and abrupt awakenings which leave him for hours afterwards with the distressing sensation that one half of himself is accusing the other, reproaching him for having done at every important stage of his life the very opposite of what he should have done.

Frequent apparitions in his dreams are the faces of the two women he loves most in the world: Anna and his mother. Each face dearer to him than life itself . . . Anna and Zehra implore him to come to them. Sometimes they dissolve into prolonged fits of giggles, inexplicable, despairing, infecting the sleeper entangled in his dream.

Once, a few hours before they are due to dock at Alexandria, he dreams that he is making love to Anna. The memory of his organ penetrating the young woman's cleft, firm and yet so silky, of those miraculous seconds when he holds her tight in his arms, comes back to him with such force that he can feel the weight of her breasts, her belly, her legs, against his body. At the moment when, as if suffocating, the young woman abandons herself to her joy, his frenzied hands grope avidly for his member and wake him up. The dream leaves him with an impression so exquisite and at the same time so poignant for being nothing but an illusion that Nassreddine has tears in his eyes.

The ship stays only a week in Alexandria before sailing for Port Saïd. The circus is to tour Palestine, calling at Jaffa, Beirut and Damascus before returning via Turkey and Europe. If he means to get to Madagascar, Nassreddine realises that he must quit the Amar brothers at Port Saïd. According to one of the sailors, his cheapest route would be to go via Kenya and take a banana boat to Madagascar from there.

"Anna, my sweet Anna . . ."

Is destiny really about to make restitution for having so viciously robbed him? Should he act on the basis of such a fantastic notion, and risk finding himself thousands of kilometres from home, with little or no money, all because an unreliable Englishman had suggested that Charles's circus might have gone there?

"Ah, my Andalusian, the things you make me do! As for You, God, You do nothing for free! You play cat-and-mouse with me!"

Amar senior shrugs with contempt when Nassreddine approaches him after the show and asks to be paid off because he finds the working conditions too hard. The circus owner pays up, grumbling that if there's one thing he can't stand it's a wimp. Nassreddine winces at the insult, wanting to explain but resigned to saying nothing, convinced that the hard-faced man wouldn't understand or, worse still, would laugh at him.

Before leaving the boat, Nassreddine takes a last look at "his" animals. He has become fond of them, especially since discovering that they too can suffer from seasickness. The big cats, for instance, would regularly vomit over their bedding during a storm. Afterwards, disgusted by the filth and stench of the straw, they would pace up and down their narrow cages. As soon as he began to fork out the straw through the bars, the lions would give little growls of pleasure. The Algerian could swear that the captive beasts were thanking him for removing what was an insult to them and to what remained of their majesty.

"There is no limit to the humiliations they inflict on you, my big cats. When all's said and done, they have fucked you up even worse than they have us," he mutters before locking the menagerie gate behind him, more moved than he cares to admit.

He was to spend an entire month combing Tananarive, doggedly asking for news of a circus said to be touring under the aegis of the French army. Eventually he learns that the Circus Nee was made bankrupt and its animals and equipment seized. The tour was a disaster because, half the island being steeped in blood by the troubles, the army had reneged on its promise to underwrite the day-to-day expenses. One of the principal creditors, a Hindu merchant, takes Nassreddine round a vast warehouse piled higgledy-piggledy with cages containing monkeys and seals.

"Here you are, this is what they left behind before making their get-away! What am I supposed to do with these useless creatures? No-one will buy them! They shit with fright when you go near them, they stink, they won't eat . . . I'll end up by killing them myself!"

Nassreddine, keeping his eyes lowered and his hands behind his back to hide their trembling, asks the question uppermost in his mind. Spitefully, the Hindu retorts that he has no means of knowing whether any of the artists had stayed behind.

"All I can tell you is that they didn't seem to get on very well, the misbegotten vagabonds, they even had rows in public. Most of them must have left Madagascar by now, with all this unrest."

However, he did hear that a foreign woman was killed at Antsirabé, he tells Nassreddine.

"I'm almost sure she was a dancer or a juggler or something," he adds in a tone of voice that implies "something of no interest".

His stomach knotted with fear, Nassreddine rushes off to buy a bus ticket. He goes into a hotel bar opposite the bus stop to pass the time. The sordid interior is afloat with puddles of sour wine and gobs of phlegm. He sits sipping his beer. A customer rather the worse for drink has made a grab at the waitress, who is roundly rebuking him. The man departs, letting fly with an insult of such rare obscenity that it provokes an outburst of laughter from the other customers. Lost in his gloomy thoughts, Nassreddine settles up without paying attention to the ensuing drama: the waitress walking past him, her face set, her head held high, trying to avoid the wandering hands of men guffawing at their own lewd hints, her "Oh!" of surprise as a glass slides off her tray and shatters on the floor.

He catches his bus, hands over his ticket and sits down beside a sad-faced old woman. The hen stuffed into her basket, its feet tied, shares its owner's melancholy expression. Worn out, he prepares to doze. Sleeping rough has taken its toll, but he is determined to make his money last.

What makes Nassreddine think of the incident in the bar at that particular moment? He hadn't even seen the waitress's face, merely heard her exclamation. Yet five minutes later he jumps up and yells at the driver to stop at once.

Back at the hotel, the young man finds her hiding in the kitchen, her head in her hands, sobbing bitterly. He bites his lip and lights a cigarette in order to regain self-control. The room is dark, cluttered with cooking-pots. Through the window there is a distant view of the hillside with its red, iron-rich soil, and the sea walls built to protect the town from floods.

He has done it. His lover is there before him, intimidating like a sheer, dark mountain slope, and yet fragile. She is unchanged. As pretty as ever. But, yes: her hair is different. From daisy to poppy, he thinks. The gaiety lurking somewhere within him smiles at the pointless comparison. Nassreddine puts out a hand to stroke the hair of the woman for whose sake he has travelled half way around the world. He arrests his gesture, amazed at the extent of his love for her. Could life have lost its venom? Could life have gifts to offer? A peculiar pain, like being pricked by needles of happiness, steals over him.

"Anna, Anna, don't cry, look, it's only me, Nassreddine! You can't have forgotten me?" is all he manages to say before he too breaks down in tears.

The woman sobs:

"What took you so long, Nassreddine? I waited and waited . . . you can't imagine how long I waited for you!"

"I couldn't help it, Anna, neither of us could help it."

The young man takes his juggler's delicately veined hand. Putting his mouth to the open palm, he brushes it lightly with his lips. And it is as though he is caressing the memory of high noon in the cabin at Algiers, the memory of a time, unbroken, dense, as fragrant as the hot sand on the fringe of the boundless ocean.

Anna was never to confess to Nassreddine that, on first recognising him, she had felt something akin to hatred: he had caught her in a situation of the utmost degradation. Long afterwards she was to be haunted by regret ("Regret is just like a fox! It takes hold and never lets go!" Rina used to say) that their miraculous reunion should have been thus tainted by humiliation.

That same day she quit the hotel. At first they rented a shack in the poorest quarter of Tananarive and then, by luck, found a Madagascan farmer in the neighbourhood willing to employ them on condition that Anna taught French to his numerous offspring.

For both of them, those five years in Madagascar were probably the most serene of their existence. Soon a boy and a girl, twins, arrived in the roomy shanty-house allotted them by the farmer. By tacit agreement, neither spoke of their lives during the period of separation. They "took up" their love where they had left it, in the doorway of the top-floor room in the old Casbah. Nassreddine merely said:

"For years all we have known is loss. I lost my father. You lost Rina. I refuse to speak of a past in which there is only misery. Words are like eggs: when they hatch, who is to say that they won't bring forth vultures?"

Anna therefore kept silent about everything that had happened to her since leaving Algeria and of which she would have liked to unburden herself, her despair at losing her lover (convinced that Nassreddine had abandoned her), her grief at Rina's death, her flight to Morocco, her increasingly violent relationship with Charles. Then, the succession of sordid events: her brief affairs, leading nowhere, the voyage to France, paid for out of the profits of one of Charles's rackets, the circus's slow descent into bankruptcy, leaving her stuck in Madagascar . . .

Nassreddine has never wanted to know all this and Anna, for her part, resigns herself to not questioning him about the war ("A squalid business" is his only comment) and the manner of his father's death.

They take their attachment more seriously, as though perpetually monitoring themselves. Not that their delight in one another is any the less. On the contrary, their love-making is full of laughter. Stroking his partner's long hair, Nassreddine pretends to bite her neck:

"Oh, oh, Anna, you're so lovely! It's worth crossing two seas and an ocean, and being nearly eaten by sharks. Oh, oh, it's like biting a croissant warm from the oven!"

He places his hand on her breast and, pinching the nipple beneath her blouse between his thumb and forefinger, then starts to undress her; as if (he tells her) he were peeling a mandarin.

"Yes, Madame," he likes to say, panting slightly, "an ice-cold mandarin."

"Ice-cold, in Madagascar, that's going a bit far," she protests, flushing with desire.

Taking Anna's hand, he places it on his member, whispering in her ear:

"Hush, no-one will know. This bandit here (he nods his chin at his erect penis) is our only witness, and I dare say he is easily bought."

He penetrates Anna, keeping his eyes open.

"Like this, I'm less frightened of losing you. If I close my eyes, how do I know that you won't take the chance to run away?"

Then, smiling, he resumes his tender explorations. Anna is submerged in laughter and sensual delight at his bawdiness. Her climax comes quickly, like a deliciously savage bird, hatching between her thighs and taking wing. Anna grips Nassreddine till he is spent. She loves to feel those last drops pumping into her, the pearls of desire, of her man's desire for her.

All the same, even after the children are born, she never feels entirely reassured. One day, he confesses to her:

"Sometimes I know for a fact that I'm too happy, that I have been dicing with God . . . and won. But can it be true that the Almighty lets Himself be beaten so easily?"

As Anna knows, Nassreddine regularly sends his mother money. He had told her so from the first, for they earned so little that he wanted her approval. Later their situation improved, the farmer having put his Algerian employee in part charge of his rice production, at the same time considerably increasing his wages. Nassreddine seldom talks about his mother, but Anna can tell that he misses her. She is therefore unsurprised when, on one oppressively hot day, he puts down his spoon and murmurs in tones full of guilt:

"Anna, it's time we went back to Algeria, I can no longer bear to be so far away from my country."

His voice is husky with nervousness:

"And I would like us to be married there. It's important for the children . . ."

He tries to smile:

". . . And for us, too! You'll see, we'll soon get used to it. We'll have a house, I'll teach you Arabic . . ."

Heavy-hearted, defeated in advance, Anna goes on with her meal. The sun is beating down, there are hordes of importunate insects to be brushed away with movements repeated a thousand times daily; the man she loves, his face burnt, beads of sweat on his upper lip, has his eyes fixed obstinately on his plate; the twins bounce joyously on their chairs . . . That day, when malign fate succeeds in getting its iron hooks into the twins' lives, is also the day when the half-blind storyteller comes to the door, begging for alms. To judge by his querulous, grandiloquent speech, he has either been drinking or smoking too much hashish. Farm workers gather, attracted by his antics as he squats in their small back yard. Anna, at first amused, asks one of the onlookers to translate the storyteller's exalted utterances. Awkwardly, he explains that the old man is speaking of Cain and Abel and their parents, and especially of their mother's grief, insulting the Creator to the point of blasphemy. Two of the watchers, outraged, order the drunken storyteller to stop. When they beat him for persisting, the audience, scandalised by the offence to Holy Writ, applauds.

That evening, as Anna lies down beside Nassreddine, her heart is full of apprehension for the future. She is fearful for themselves and their beloved children in Algeria, fearful of the settlers' ready contempt. Here in Madagascar they have found equilibrium, serenity almost. The neighbours are friendly; the farmer has even talked of taking Nassreddine into partnership. True, racism exists, but here they are not its chosen victims. They love one another, the children are growing up. Why bring Algeria into it? True, Algeria is the country where she met the love of her life. But it's also the country where stupidity and the will to humiliate others brought about the death of her gentle Rina, her surrogate mother.

The room smells of wisteria, which is odd, considering that it grows nowhere on the property. Nassreddine jokes, saying that it's the intimate smell of the sea when it abandons itself to desire. Anna closes her eyes, lamenting to herself:

"Oh, Nassreddine, you expect too much from this world. You want both the happiness of yesterday and the happiness of tomorrow. Why not be content with what we have built together, at such cost to ourselves?"

And at that moment, the woman lying beside the man whom she loves more than anyone in the world feels a bitterness so fierce that it is akin to hatred.

The man, doubtless aware of this, takes her hand in the darkness.

"I love you, Anna."

He giggles self-consciously:

"In our mountains, the villagers say that you can tell a man loves a woman because he leaves no footprints when he runs to her through the snow."

Stroking her hair:

"You know, I love you and the children so much that I'm sure I could do the same, and not disturb a single snowflake."

His voice has grown hoarse:

"Forgive me, Anna, I know that I'm putting you in an impossible position, but time is running out and I'm afraid that I might never see my country again."

III

17

1996

The smell is acrid, a musty odour of urine, bad breath, the sweat of unwashed bodies and mouldy earth. The old woman shudders. With the passage of time, her nightmare has presented her with ever sharper images. First the twins appear, Meriem and Mehdi, gifts of gentleness in the dark. She thinks they are at home, in Madagascar, thus safe and sound ... Then they cry for help: they are already here, in Algeria. So she struggles to wake up. In vain. The scenario never varies: one way or another, the twins must leave for Algeria, there to die! They go wild, they jabber, they laugh, then suddenly understand what awaits them ... The long years have taught her to decipher the amazement in her children's eyes. Why couldn't their mother – our Mama – protect them? How we loved you, Mama, yet what good did it do, our loving you? Maybe our love was small, like us, but how could we help that? O dear little Mother, please save us!

The old woman, still caught in the toils of her sleep, is aware of something more terrifying than this nightmare with its familiar duplicities. A shadow falls over her. A foot nudges her. She stifles a cry, for suddenly it has all come back to her: the driver with his throat cut, the two men in the Peugeot, their brutality, the little guide who had only just escaped death at their hands ... Even in her terror she had instantly realised that they would hardly cut the throat of a foreigner, just like that. She swore that Jallal was her grandson, that his mother was her daughter, married to an Algerian. Jallal gulped that it was true, begging them in the Name of God to spare him. The driver's body, dragged from the back seat of the car, toppled out on to the road. His head, almost severed from his body, bounced off Jallal's shoe. The boy, too petrified to move, made no attempt to get out of the way. Neither terrorist seemed convinced by their story. The man with the rifle was making a grab for the boy when the other in the black hood stopped him:

"Leave it! Who knows, she might be telling the truth. It's too complicated for us to deal with, this business of foreigners, it's for the emir to decide. In any case, it won't hurt them to wait!"

What followed was total confusion. Blindfolded, she and Jallal were bundled unceremoniously into the boot of the car. They drove for a good half hour, Jallal vomiting with fear. Then someone lifted them on to the back of a mule, threatening to slit their throats if they shouted for help. Riding up and down the precipitous mountain paths while Jallal clung to her for dear life, Anna lost all track of time. At one point, when the path grew so narrow that the captives were torn by briars, Anna gave an involuntary exclamation of pain. Punishment was instantaneous: a blow from a rifle-butt that knocked her unconscious.

She opens her eyes. The pain is still there. She puts a hand to her head: a lump has formed, encrusted with blood.

"Jallal . . ."

The bad smell is coming partly from herself. Her dress stinks of urine. When the hooded man laughed and saluted her in the name of the forces of Allah, her fear was so great that she could equally well have defecated . . .

"My God!"

Momentarily, she is filled with shame, then fear takes over again. A hand grips hers, and she jumps as if bitten.

"It's me, Grandma, it's Jallal! Don't be frightened . . ."

Her heart beating wildly, she reaches out to touch her companion in misfortune. It is dark, apart from a glimmer at the far end of some sort of corridor. An ineffectual oil-lamp flickers on the walls of a cave. Shadowy figures come and go. Jallal huddles close to the old woman.

"Were you knocked out too?"

"No, but I could have been: I tumbled into a ditch. My body is scratched to pieces. It hurts all over. Will they kill us, do you think, Grandma?"

Anna surveys the figures uneasily. Jallal whispers:

"They're women. They're cooking a meal!"

She feels him shiver and, trembling herself, puts her arms round him. With an effort, she stops her teeth chattering. One of the figures approaches. It is a very young girl, dressed in her indoor clothes. Holding out a piece of galette, she says simply:

"Eat . . ."

She is pretty, but when she opens her mouth Anna sees that she has several front teeth missing.

"Hurry, before the others come back," she adds in Arabic, lisping slightly.

"Thank you," Anna murmurs in French.

The girl lowers her voice to match Anna's:

"Ah, I knew it, I told the women you were foreign. That's why the . . . the others were so excited!"

Anna puts a hand on her sleeve to detain her:

"Where are we?"

"I don't know. The women here don't know either. They move us around all the time! Now let go of me, we're not allowed to chat. I should stay where you are if I were you, or you'll make them very angry!"

The waiting lasts all day. Gradually, for the captives, unendurable suspense turns to blind panic: are they really to be killed? And if so, how? And might they be tortured first?

Several women, a dozen at least, are scurrying about the cave, evidently expecting a large number for the meal. Jallal, exhausted, finally falls asleep. His head in Anna's lap, he is purring like a cat. After an hour, Anna gets to her feet; she is stiff, and she also needs to find somewhere to relieve herself. Taking care not to wake Jallal, she makes her way towards the patch of daylight.

"Oh, my God!"

A violent kick in the belly is followed by a string of insults ("*Ya Kalba*, bitch, pig, who gave you permission to go outside?"). A bearded youth with long hair threatens her with an automatic pistol. He is dressed, Afghan-style, in a short jacket and baggy trousers. His angry eyes are ringed with kohl.

"Next time, I'll flay you alive, you old turd," he adds, in French. "You stay where you are, or else . . ." (he passes a finger across his throat).

Groaning with pain, Anna turns to go back. The sentry, having assured himself that the prisoner is doing as she is told, returns to his post beneath the olive tree overhanging the cave mouth. The raised voices has petrified the women. Jallal comes running, his face contorted with dismay. Anna collapses at his feet. He tries to help her up, but she is too heavy.

"Leave her, child, we'll see to her."

A woman of about 50 calls to the girl with the missing teeth to help her. They carry Anna over to a foam mattress. The woman wipes the foreigner's face with a flannel. She touches Anna's belly. Anna lets out a yelp of pain. The woman, hard-eyed, says:

"May God help you in the days to come, my sister! It will be better for you and the boy if you do everything they want, and avoid doing anything they don't want!"

Then, turning to the young girl, she orders:

"Translate what I've just said, Khedidja!"

"Yes, Khalti."

The girl does as she is told. Anna hugs her belly, unable to think for the pain. The woman whom the girl has addressed as Khalti (my aunt) returns with a bucket. "Beat it!" she snaps at Jallal, who reluctantly moves away. Anna smiles tentatively at Khedidja, who bends down whispering:

"She brought you the bucket so that you can relieve yourself . . ."

"Thank you, I understand," the Swiss woman nods, blushing.

That evening their captors turn up in force. The sentries' coarse exclamations and the exchange of greetings, punctuated by many an "Allah Ou Akbar" and expressions of mutual congratulation, are audible inside the cave. Two men in balaclavas enter, pushing before them three prisoners whose hands are tied. The youngest is scarcely more than a boy. Anna's heart goes out to him. To judge by their bruised faces, the prisoners have been beaten up. The oldest is dressed in some kind of uniform, vaguely military, tattered and stained with blood from the wound in his arm. One of their captors orders:

"On the floor face down, you filthy hypocrites, and freeze!"

Turning to the women, he barks:

"Food, at once!"

There is triumph in his voice. Passing Khedidja, he mutters in her ear. The girl, busy filling a *gassaa* with couscous, hangs her head. But when she turns round, Anna sees that she is crying. Puzzled, she darts a questioning glance at Khalti. The woman sighs and says nothing.

Soon the murmur of prayer rises from the men. Then the women stand to pray in their turn. "What about the ablutions?" Anna suddenly wonders. She is struck by the contrast between the calm that comes over the captive women's faces with the Koranic litany, and the violence of their situation. But their calm is short-lived and panic reigns again with the terrorists' imperious demands for food.

An hour later, the man who had spoken to Khedidja returns. She follows him mutely, head bowed. A second bearded man, then a third, come in to beckon a woman. They are obeyed with the same terrified docility.

A woman aged about 40 addresses Anna curtly in French:

"You have eaten nothing. Take a little couscous. You will need all your strength . . ."

Anna shakes her head. The woman adds, more kindly:

"Well, then, think of the boy. He is frightened to death."

Jallal has hardly said a word all day. He clings to Anna, alternating between bouts of lassitude and convulsive trembling. Anna takes the plate from the woman and forces him to swallow a little of the semolina. Jallal breathes:

"Do you think they're going to . . . do something to us? *Ya Rabi,* I've never been so scared in my life . . ."

"Of course not, little idiot, what will you think of next? Come on, eat, or I'll be cross!"

"Do you mean it, they're not going to cut our throats?"

Anna, tense (and chilled by the precision of his question) whispers in a voice grown hoarse with terror:

"Certainly not! They saw my passport, and I explained that you are Swiss! They have nothing against the Swiss . . . Everyone knows that, for goodness' sake!"

The boy's lips curl in a hopeful smile:

"Did they believe you? Are you sure?"

"Stop nagging and eat!"

Soon the only sound is the boy's jerky breathing as he hungrily gulps down the rest of the couscous. He has almost recovered his spirits. Anna envies him the glimmer of hope which she has succeeded in communicating to him. She hates herself for dragging him into this terrible business. "Can it really be that I am to end up like my children? Forty years on?" Her belly goes into another spasm. She doubles over, jaws clenched: "O God, don't let my insides fail me! I don't want to die unclean!" Sickened, she remembers that there had been nothing on which to wipe her behind but stones.

The woman who had offered her food returns with two more plates. She hands one to Anna. In the half-light, Anna can see a look of determination in the tired eyes.

"Come, we are going to feed the prisoners."

As they approach the pinioned men, the woman whispers:

"My name is Saliha. I heard what you said to the boy. Take care, it's each for herself in here. The women in this hell-hole are so terrified that any one of them might turn informer to save her skin. You know, in this place . . ."

She breaks off, another captive woman has walked by, carrying the bucket of excrement. The prisoners are in a bad way. The man with the wounded arm is delirious. Anna and the woman roll the couscous into balls and poke them into the mouths of the prone men. The adolescent boy looks up at them, half crazy, whimpering between mouthfuls:

"*A Yemma, A Baba*, I want to go home . . . I want my mother and father . . . *A Yemma, A Baba* . . ."

"Be quiet, sissy!" Saliha slaps him lightly over the mouth.

There is something like hatred in the woman's whisper:

"If you anger them, it will be the worse for you and for us!"

The adolescent licks his lips where the woman tending him has stung them. For an instant he is quiet, then resumes his whimpering, but less noisily. Saliha shrugs and, despite her vexation, pokes another ball into the captive's mouth. Only the man in the middle seems resigned to his fate. He masticates the women's offerings obediently, asks for a little water, and mutters "Thank you" without emotion. Then he lets his head drop back and, turning his cheek to the ground, closes his eyes.

An hour later, the women who had accompanied the terrorists return, heads still bowed. Saliha responds to her companion's unspoken question:

224

"We have all been through it, from the youngest to the oldest. Even Khalti, who is over 50 (may God give her a long life, poor thing!) wasn't spared. When they return from battle, or from one of their killing sprees, we know that we're in for a bad hour. Did you notice their boots? All red! They must have waded in blood tonight. I suppose it is that which drives them mad with lust, the smell of death . . ."

She spits in disgust:

"There is no point in resisting. Have you seen our little schoolgirl's teeth? They kidnapped Khedidja two weeks ago, at the school gate. The first night she refused to go with them. They beat her, then raped her one by one. She spent three whole nights in the men's quarters. She couldn't sit down for a week, she was in such pain!"

She passes a shaky hand through her hair, without replacing her scarf:

"And you had better not get pregnant! A baby means noise, and another mouth to feed. Not only that, nobody knows who the father is . . . And so, either they kick you out and dump you on the roadside, in which case you can't go home. Nobody, not even your parents, wants to have anything to do with you, you have brought dishonour on the family. Or else . . ."

She lowers her voice, terrified by her own words:

". . . Or else, they . . . kill you, and leave your head beside an army post or a police station, to show them who are the masters!"

She scratches her cheek in perplexity:

"Of the two, I can't decide which is worse."

Laughing, with a sudden burst of spite:

"In fact, you can thank your lucky stars that you're old!"

The Swiss woman laughs with her, but her heart is beating so hard that she feels she must suffocate. She thinks: "If I go on being terrified like this, my heart will stop . . ." She forces herself to breathe, but the terror persists, like an interminable toothache.

Around midnight, a man enters the cave to check on the prisoners' bonds. He kicks the man in the middle, the calmest of the three, and proclaims:

"You are to hear your fate tomorrow, evil-doers! The emir is coming specially to pass judgement on you."

He turns to Anna and Jallal. With his beardless face, his checked shirt and jeans, he might have been a harmless student. He yells:

"The same goes for you, *gaouria*! Be prepared to explain what you were doing, wandering about the hills disguised as a Muslim. And don't kid yourself: it's pointless to lie! As for your little bastard, his fate will be no better than yours if we find that you've been telling us fibs!"

All night long, Anna curses Algeria, its killers, Islam, the Arabs, Nassreddine, the folly which had brought her back to this country. With such strength as she has left after her repeated spasms, she prays that her life will not end, like an animal's, at the stroke of a knife, without her having had a chance to see her dear Hans again, the only one of her children whom a malign fate has deigned to let live.

And such is her terror that she hardly gives a thought to Jallal, the little vagabond from Algiers who lies curled up against her, and who has finally decided (no child can believe in its own death for long) to stick by this crazy old woman that he might protect her.

Not much further now, Nassreddine tells himself. The old man is worn out by the events of the past few days. He had insisted that Jaourden come with him; left to fend for himself in Algiers, he would have starved. The Targui's wife had died the day after the doctor's visit. Burial was hasty. Dead in the morning, Douja was interred two hours later, immediately after midday prayers. The hospital staff pleaded lack of space in the mortuary; what with terrorist attacks and army massacres, they had more bodies than they could cope with. A doctor commented ironically:

"Corpses are the only things not in short supply in this hospital!"

His agitation over Anna's telegram notwithstanding, Nassreddine took charge of the formalities. A handful of regulars at the mosque joined the meagre cortège. One asked anxiously if the deceased had died of natural causes. When Nassreddine nodded, he appeared relieved. An imam gabbled a short prayer, the grave-digger rapidly heaped on the earth, and a few people came up to offer the conventional condolences: it was all over in less than 20 minutes, leaving Jaourden in a state of utter bewilderment.

Since the funeral, the Targui seems to have lost the power of speech. Unprotesting, he does everything his friend tells him, like a docile child. But Nassreddine knows that the moment he stops ordering him about Jaourden will crumple like an empty sack.

They bypass the market town and take the country road leading to Nassreddine's *douar*. It is full of potholes: he estimates that the journey will take them another two hours at least. Almost immediately, they find their way barred by armoured cars. Nassreddine tries to talk his way through, but the soldiers are in a highly excitable state; brandishing their Kalashnikovs and yelling insults.

"But I'm going to my own house," Nassreddine pleads, "my wife is there, waiting for me. Please . . ."

"Shut your trap, *sheik*, or your old lady won't have anyone to wait for! This area is a military zone. Clear off!"

One soldier, seeing the man at the wheel hesitate, cocks his gun and gives the car a furious kick:

"Go and fuck your mothers, filth! Come to spy on us, have you? One never knows whose side anyone is on in these stinking mountains! You smile at us in the daytime and help those terrorist sons of whores at night. Turn back, quick, before I change my mind!"

An eerie atmosphere reigns as they drive into the market town. The whole place swarms with soldiers, keyed-up, wary, some of them hooded. The car is repeatedly stopped for their papers to be checked. Each time Nassreddine explains that he is on the way to his native *douar*, where his wife is expecting him. State and local police examine them suspiciously before waving them on. The main square is thronged with haggard-looking refugees, camping in the roadway amid indescribable chaos. Each group is surrounded by its heap of foam mattresses, bundles, *couffins*. A cart and two battered lorries are piled high with shabby furniture. At the back of one lorry, an ancient crone sits perched on a table. Nobody has thought to lift her down. She gazes at the scene with the blank stare of the old when they have lost their bearings. Dishevelled women weep, dry their tears and resume their sobbing. Nassreddine is immediately struck by the silence of the crowd, many of whom are still in their indoor clothes, as if they had been surprised on rising from their beds. Now and again, a baby wails. A man whose clothes are spattered with blood comes up to Nassreddine . . .

The old man learns that they are peasants from a *douar* not 30 kilometres from Hasnia, Sidi Sghir. This hamlet, which, of late, had been unwilling to send its sons to fight alongside the terrorists, had been invaded the night before by "Afghans" armed with axes and machetes, sawn-off shotguns and chain-saws. They entered every house in the village, picking two or three people at random and executing them. They beheaded three young children from the same family in front of their parents, then cut the throat of the father, Hadj Kadour. They let the mother live; the killers' leader had ordered her hands to be cut off, so that she could testify to the ruthlessness with which "the forces of *jihad*" treated traitors who served the impious Pharaoh. Although in truth the killers were punishing the family for having married their daughter to a local policeman.

The man describing the scene is trembling:

"The din was terrible. The cries for mercy, the screams of the dying. Those who tried to run away were caught, drenched in petrol and burnt alive. Yet worse was to come. When it was over, they herded us into a barn and forced us to join them in a service for the dead. The emir led the prayers in person. One villager, a man in his forties whose eldest son had been executed with a chain-saw, had a seizure which the 'beards' took for a refusal to pray. This rekindled their rage. They made the man kneel in front of a bucket. They cut his throat and collected the blood. Then one of the killers forced the villagers, from the youngest to the oldest, to plunge their hands into the bucket . . ."

He weeps hot tears:

"I was visiting a relative. I thought it was safe to make the journey. I had seen the army trucks the night before, no more than two kilometres from the village! I told myself that there couldn't be any danger with the army so close to Sidi Sghir. I was wrong. The army didn't give a damn for us! Yet the soldiers must have seen the fires! They deliberately allowed the butchers to do their work, practically under their noses . . . O my God, how is such a thing possible? I was hiding in the wardrobe when they cut the throats of my host and his father, an old man so blind and deaf that he couldn't have known what happened to him. They broke down the wardrobe door and found me crouching behind the clothes. I yelled at the top of my voice . . . I said the first things that came into my head, that I was on their side, they were equal to God's angels, the embodiment of Mercy, I would lick their boots if they wished. I hopped from one foot to the other like a rat on a white-hot slate. My host's murderer laughed at my panic. He wiped his knife on his victim's hair, gave me a kick and ordered me to the mosque. I was one of those who had to dip their hands into the bucket. I was terrified, my brother, there was no act of cowardice I wouldn't have committed. I didn't know it was possible to be so afraid!"

He groans to himself:

"May God forgive me! May God forgive me!"

"And now the townsfolk want us to leave! And up there, the bodies of our dead are rotting without graves, abandoned to the dogs. Even the police are scared to go there alone. They say they are waiting for reinforcements! They don't trust us, they say the village is well known for its partisans. Also that it serves us right, why should policemen risk their lives for people who have supported the FLN fanatics from the beginning? But . . . And our children, my brother, what is their crime? O my God, what a country of jackals!"

The man plucks Nassreddine by the sleeve and tells him that, a few hours after their arrival, an army captain had come to see them. He suggested arming the men of the village and sending them back. The men refused point blank: they wouldn't return without the army. "Even armed with machine-guns what could we do, on our own, against trained and ruthless fighters? Anyone who hadn't already had his throat cut wouldn't be spared a second time!" The captain spat in contempt and called them weaklings, too cowardly to defend their honour, their children's honour. He ordered them to start leaving the town immediately, they were sapping the morale of the inhabitants. If not, he threatened with a sneer, his soldiers would send them back to their hovels with a kick up the arse! "And without guns, what's more! You aided, fed and clothed those crazy dogs. You got what you deserved! You had better learn to live with them. You liked them well enough when it was our heads that they were cutting off, and the heads of our families!"

During the man's recital Jaourden has kept his distance. Nassreddine decides to go to the police station and looks round for his friend. He thinks he spots him in a group of refugees, but his figure vanishes in the crowd. Nassreddine shrugs: the Targui has become more taciturn than ever since his wife's death. With difficulty, he detaches himself from his interlocutor (who addresses him oddly as "my brother, my father"). The police station is round the corner. Nassreddine hesitates. He is suddenly aware of an exhaustion that is draining his strength. It recognises his fatigue: as if his soul had been whipped for hours on end and the body which had so far sustained it were slowly disintegrating. The man continues to bludgeon him with his tale of horrors:

"My brother, if you could have heard the children scream! Ah, you can't imagine how piercing they were, those screams! They begged: 'My uncle, don't kill me, my uncle, I swear I won't tell . . .' And those men ran after them and caught them like rabbits . . . Ah, if you could imagine . . ."

The old man holds his head in his hands, suddenly dizzy. It is too much, too much! Will this barbarity never end? Harshly, he protests:

"Leave me in peace! Who do you think you are, taking that tone with me? Go back to the others!"

The survivor stares at him, dumbstruck. Nassreddine hurries on, almost fleeing, abandoning the man to his hideous distress. Of course he can imagine it, all of it! Nausea overwhelms him. For decades he has been unable to stop himself imagining his family's last moments as they faced their executioners, his children's screams as the killers finished off their grandmother and advanced on them . . .

Nassreddine senses the sobs mounting and swallows. No wavering, so near his goal. A dozen Land Rovers and two armoured cars block the side street leading to the police station. Bollards line the walls to prevent parking. A local policeman who has been watching him brusquely asks his business. Nassreddine stammers that he wants to see an officer by the name of Khaled. Looking him up and down, the policeman mutters gruffly: "Why? Is he a friend of yours?"

"Show him in!"

Nassreddine recognises a colleague of the officer whom he has come to see. The small building, transformed into a bunker, is a hive of activity. Ninjas with their hoods up are running up and down the stairs. More police in riot gear are standing about in the hall. Orders are shouted over raised voices, adding to the general tension. The officer opens the door to a kitchen, and waves the old man to a chair. Pouring himself a cup of coffee, he says:

"It's a long time since you were in these parts, isn't it, *sheik*?"

Nassreddine nods. The man hands him a cup of coffee.

"You're still living in Algiers, then?"

"Yes," Nassreddine replies, puzzled.

The officer sips his coffee, making a face. He must be in his early forties. A short moustache bristles across the embittered face.

"Some people have all the luck. Five years I've been here, mouldering away in this rotten hole."

Nassreddine interrupts, not disguising his impatience.

"And our friend Khaled, the brigadier?"

The man facing him smiles sourly:

"Dead as a doornail, believe me. They killed him five or six months ago. He was sure that his life wasn't in danger. He would be retiring any minute, he said, and didn't have an enemy in the world. It was his neighbour's son who betrayed him to the terrorists. They didn't kill him outright, *sheik* . . ."

Nassreddine bows his head. His interlocutor clears his throat and hisses through his teeth at the taste of the coffee:

"He liked everybody, did old Khaled. A bit of an operator, but no more than anybody else . . . People only had to come and cry on his shoulder and he let them off everything, fines, reports. He left the poachers alone, turning a blind eye whenever he could . . . An old fraud, all right, but popular with all his colleagues . . . Those terrorist bastards ambushed him . . ."

The policeman fiddles with his moustache. Nassreddine senses that he is deeply moved.

"It was too easy: he was as fat as a barrel and the least effort puffed him out. Not what you would call the ideal recruit for the anti-terrorist brigade! He let himself be kidnapped in broad daylight, like a novice. There were dozens of them. They tied him to the back of a four-wheel drive and dragged him round the streets for several kilometres. Then they castrated him and hanged him from a lamp-post, poor old Khaled!"

"My God!" Nassreddine sighs.

The wretched Khaled had been no more than a vague acquaintance, but the old man's hand trembles as he puts down his cup. The officer sips his coffee, turning his back.

"And we, his four colleagues, were stuck here, in the station. The army didn't come to retrieve the body till the next day. And no witnesses came forward. People saw the terrorists all right, but they were scared stiff, like us!"

A pregnant silence. The officer turns round at Nassreddine's embarrassed cough.

"Well, *sheik*, what can I do for you?"

"Nothing . . . that is," the old man stutters, "I wanted to ask him if the Hasnia road is safe, after what happened last night . . ."

The man gives a hollow laugh, pointing to the mountainside visible from the window:

"You must be crazy to think of going up there alone! There are more terrorists than grasshoppers! Have you seen what they did at Sidi Sghir? It's less then 30 kilometres from where you live. They would chop you to pieces!"

A man in civilian clothes bursts into the kitchen. He asks sourly:

"Any coffee left?"

"Yes, if you call this filthy brew coffee . . ."

The man washes his hands, drinks from the tap and pours himself a coffee. He hasn't noticed Nassreddine behind the open door. With a grim smile of satisfaction, he says:

"That bastard finally came clean. He may have been a 'beard', but he was tough! He held out for two days. We had to pull out his fingernails."

The man tuts:

"This coffee is revolting! I can't wait to get home, see my children again, get away from this filthy business . . ."

He hesitates, then finally drains his cup.

"He let the cat out of the bag. He killed the chauffeur, all right. And he confirmed the story about a foreign woman, perhaps the one who disappeared in Algiers. The chief said to finish him off . . ."

Nassreddine utters an involuntary groan. The newcomer spins round as if bitten by a snake. His face is bloated, like someone who has missed a night's sleep.

"Who's this? Look here, Ammar, you know it's forbidden to bring civilians into the station!"

He advances threateningly on the visitor. His colleague grabs him.

"Hey, calm down, he's an old friend of Khaled's! No need to get excited!"

"Ah, and you yourself, you still have friends these days, I suppose?"

Angrily, the man shakes himself free. Before leaving the room, he grumbles:

"If he knows what's good for him he had better leave town at once and, above all, keep his trap shut! Otherwise, he might well regret it . . ."

The officer closes the door, a little embarrassed:

"Finish your coffee, *sheik*, and go back to Algiers. Forget about going to Hasnia. The special forces are there. They'll be in action any minute now. They'll take the whole mountain apart. Even the airforce is involved. Those terrorist sons of whores won't know what has hit them. They'll be roasted alive in their holes, like rats!"

Nassreddine is fighting despair. If it was true, then anybody with the terrorists would suffer the same fate. He manages to articulate:

"What's all this about a foreign woman? She wouldn't be Swiss, by any chance?"

"A local group kidnapped an elderly tourist a few days ago. She had the stupid idea . . ."

The officer stops short. He stares with growing anger at the man slumped in his chair.

"Perhaps my colleague was right to be worried. What makes you so inquisitive all of a sudden?"

Leaving the police station, Nassreddine nearly groans out loud:

"Why can't I die and be done with this whore of a life once and for all? Were the children not enough? And now Anna?"

He wants to weep, but doubts if his body will grant him that solace. Absurdly, it occurs to the old man that, were his mother there, he wouldn't hesitate to bury his head in her lap and sob his heart out! He sets off to look for Jaourden. The Targui is seated on the ground, surrounded by children. He is telling them a story and, of all unexpected things, smiling. Seeing Nassreddine, he stops in mid sentence. The children protest:

"Go on, Uncle! Tell us what happened to your antelope? Uncle, please . . ."

Jaourden stands up. He murmurs, a little embarrassed:

"Later . . . I'll tell you later . . ."

His smile has vanished. The children slowly disperse. Absently, the

Targui caresses the head of the little boy clinging to his leg. Trying to detach himself from the child's grasp, he points to the villagers from Sidi Sghir:

"Go and find your parents, little one. Off you go . . ."

The child sobs. He wipes his running nose on his sleeve with a furious gesture:

"But Uncle, you know they killed them, my father and my mother and my two sisters! The people over there" (he points to the crowd) "are only neighbours, Uncle!"

He looks worriedly at his sleeve. He hiccups:

"Just neighbours, Uncle . . . Don't you understand?"

"They're very tense this morning. Their emir is late . . ."

Anna answers Saliha with a nod. Her palms are damp with apprehension. The emir in question, they had told her, would decide their fate, hers and the boy's. According to Saliha, who has been eavesdropping on the sentries, it seems that he is only a local emir.

"But they're the worst," she adds. "To be promoted, they have to demonstrate their ruthlessness."

Anna tries not to let her fear overwhelm her. It is lucky that she has a friend in Saliha. She is beginning her fourth day of captivity and is grateful for the woman's calm. Unlike the other enslaved women, who no doubt fear brutal reprisals if they fraternise with a Christian, Saliha sought her company. The night before, she had confided that she taught French in a secondary school, something which she took care to keep quiet about: if her captors found out, they would certainly kill her on the spot!

"They snatched me in the street at midday, not 500 metres from my house. When they asked my occupation, I said housewife. It was just as well that I didn't have my books with me! I happened to leave them at school that day because they were too heavy to carry."

She sighs:

"They slapped me in the face anyway, because of my make-up! They said I was wearing too much for a housewife. It was lucky that they didn't kidnap me at home. Otherwise my father and my husband would have put up a fight and been killed. My God, what has this country come to!"

234

Anna had squeezed her friend's hand, receiving a look of gratitude in return. Since then, they had passed the time whispering together, and it seemed to Anna that her fear had become more bearable. Saliha has just told her to be on her guard against old Khalti. Anna is surprised, for the old woman has been kind to her. Saliha glances cautiously at the other women: they are out of earshot.

"Kind, yes. She would give you her last piece of bread, but she is mad for all that!"

Their foreheads meet:

"She went crazy . . . She had four sons. The two eldest took to the hills and joined rival groups: GIA and AIS, or something. I suppose the poor fools each dreamed of becoming a power in the villages. It's very seductive, the *jihad*, given that it offers you a life of Moses and Al Capone rolled into one: cash from the rackets, girls to rape with impunity and Paradise at the end of your days . . . The two groups wiped each other out and the would-be terrorists lost their lives. The police arrested Khalti's other two sons as accomplices in terrorism: they didn't dishonour their brothers! Next day, their mother found their bodies, horribly mutilated, on a rubbish dump."

After a long silence, Saliha continues:

"The old woman turned bloodthirsty! Straight after burying her sons she came here of her own accord. I don't know how she managed to find the cave, she must have walked for days in the mountains . . . The . . . well, this group, decided to keep her because she was a good cook and they thought she was on their side. But one of these thugs, high on hashish, raped her anyway: they had made a bet, and it was the loser's forfeit . . . Afterwards she beat her head against the walls of the cave till it bled, but she made no attempt to run away. Personally, I'm sure she is mad . . . stark, raving mad, believe me! I sleep near her, and I hear her muttering . . . Sometimes she talks about her sons as if they were still alive. It makes your flesh creep . . ."

"Quiet!" a voice complains abruptly. "We're trying to listen!"

The women have gathered near the mouth of the cave. They can't be seen from outside but, stretching their necks, they can glimpse the tent which has been erected for the "court". The three prisoners, still bound hand and foot, are kneeling obediently near the entrance.

235

"They're here!" announces a voice, immediately followed by a flurry among the sentries.

"May the Blessing be upon you! May the Blessing be upon you! . . . May the Blessing be upon you!"

The man who has thus thrice repeated *Essalam Aleikhoum* is surprisingly young, barely 25 years old. He is wearing a large turban, a *gandoura* and desert boots, and is accompanied by three men in combat gear, armed to the teeth. Ignoring the group's respectful greetings, he goes straight up to their leader. Anna can't hear what they are saying, but the young emir's gestures speak for themselves: his face furious, he points first at the sky, then at the tent. Rushing to obey, the men take down the tent. Saliha murmurs:

"They're afraid of army helicopters."

Jallal pokes his head between the two women. He has forgotten his earlier fear. Finding himself still alive, he has decided that the danger is probably over. His voice is full of hope:

"Is it true, will the army attack?"

A violent blow sends him flying. Saliha whispers:

"Little fool, if they hear you talk like that they'll joint you like a chicken!"

The boy scrambles to his feet and clings to an indignant Anna. Saliha adds in an unsteady voice:

"Please God, not the army: if they bomb the camp we've all had it!"

Old Khalti screws up her eyes:

"You talk too much, Saliha. Far too much . . ."

Saliha pales and bows her head:

"Forgive me, Khalti, it was the devil speaking through my mouth."

The emir orders the three prisoners to be moved to a place beneath a tree. He himself sits opposite them, motioning to his companions to do likewise. In their turn, they too point uneasily at the sky, then to the valley. The emir, annoyed, holds a hasty council of war and approaches the three prisoners. He shouts something, his words inaudible to the women from their position at the cave mouth, then spits on the ground and signs to his men to go back the way they came. One man alone stays behind.

Anna takes a deep breath, inhaling the bitter scent of olive and lentisk.

It seems incredible that nature could be so beautiful on a day such as this! The man has grabbed hold of the prisoner with the wounded arm and is pushing him towards a flat rock. With a kick from behind, he forces him to lie face down. Jamming a knee into the small of the prisoner's back, he seizes his head by the hair and jerks it upright, at the same time pulling out a dagger with his free hand.

"My God, it's the butcher!"

The schoolgirl shuts her eyes just as the blood spurts out.

"*Ya Yemma*, I want my mother, *ya Yemma*! . . ."

Saliha claps a hand over the bawling mouth, firmly holding it there in spite of the girl's convulsive struggles.

"Hush, my darling. Pray to God, take comfort in Him. They'll kill you if you cry out like that . . ."

Jallal has watched the execution open-mouthed. The rock is now red. The second prisoner, before he has his throat cut, just has time to spit on his executioner. The butcher is beside himself with rage. Panting hard he gives the corpse, which is still bound hand and foot, a vicious kick. The adolescent, quiet till now, starts to scream and beg for mercy. He makes a futile attempt to escape but, his ankles being tied, falls flat on his face. The butcher, exasperated, pulls up a tuft of grass and stuffs it into his victim's mouth. He drags the jerking body towards the rock with one hand and, with the other, cuts the throat as swiftly as before. Then, having carefully wiped his dagger, he rubs his bloodstained hands against the bark of a tree. Appearing dissatisfied with the result, he recommences his cleaning operations, this time with leaves torn from a branch. Now that the wind has changed direction, the women can hear the man with the knife grousing to his companions in a jocular tone:

"It's usually the adults who give me the most trouble, not the kids . . ."

Jallal has fled to the back of the cave. Anna, frozen with terror, watches the executioner advance towards her. He addresses her in French, his sneering laugh tinged with regret:

"As for you, old woman, the emir has decided to discuss your case later. It's too serious to be rushed, apparently, you being a foreigner, but don't raise your hopes. In the meantime behave yourself or else . . . tchak!"

Anna is flabbergasted that a man who had just committed such vile acts should look so ordinary. Slowly she tries to work the saliva back into her mouth. Her heart is thumping as if it will burst. She has never known such pain in her chest.

"Don't look at me like that, you old whore! We're executioners, not murderers. And don't feel sorry for those three. All of them, even the youngest, belonged to the State militia! At least they had the benefit of the knife. It is clean, quick and merciful, the knife! The army tortured my father with a blowtorch. I used to be a wealthy butcher, I could buy anything I wanted, but I had had enough of the *hogra*, the contempt, the favouritism, the corruption of women, the way those in power insult our religion. So I followed my brothers into the path of the *jihad*. The special forces arrested my father. He had done nothing wrong, but they wanted to know where to find me. He took hours to die. But thanks be to God, he didn't talk. He was a true believer, may God rest his soul! We are not barbarians, *gaouria*, the barbarians are those who respect nothing any more, not God, not mankind, those dogs who serve the tyrant Taghout!"

The others applaud him warmly. The executioner is red in the face with anger. Anna lowers her eyes, awaiting the blows.

"We, the *moudjahidine*, are merely instruments of the Will of God. That's all. Betray God, and you will pay the penalty. Serve Him, and you will go to Paradise. It's as simple as that! If it is God's wish, all evil-doers and their accomplices, all those who suck the people's blood and refuse to join in the fight against the impious, will end up beneath the soil of this country."

Exalted, he repeats with tears in his eyes:

"*Inch Allah*, we shall succeed!"

"*Inch Allah*," chorus the others. The butcher wipes his eyes on his sleeve and embraces each member of the group in turn. He points once again to the sky and the valley, indicating that they should be on the alert, and takes himself off.

18

The attack takes place at dawn. It starts with planes making low-level passes and releasing their bombs just before pulling out and climbing at full throttle into the sky. At first it seems that the aircraft are scattering their bombs at random. Immediately after their passage, tall flames blossom among the trees. Visible from the cave, more and more red and orange patches appear on the mountainside, midway between summit and foot. A billowing cloud of smoke now hides most of the valley. The peculiar smell of burning oil is everywhere, catching at the throat.

"It's napalm, I tell you," one of the men repeats nervously. "The whole forest will go up!"

"Shut up, you arseholes, they're only incendiaries! Watch the sky instead of blubbing. They'll be sending over choppers next. They may not have spotted us ... Take cover, and don't fire until I give the order!"

Now the leader of the group turns to the women who have rushed out of the cave. He brandishes his Uzi rifle:

"Get inside, right to the back of the cave!" he yells, using his rifle-butt on those who have ventured too far.

In spite of the blows, the women retreat a few steps only. In her desperation, one woman blurts out:

"But we'll be burnt alive if we stay here! In the Name of God: use your eyes, the smoke is coming over here! Let us go, and . . ."

She hasn't time to finish her sentence. A sentry has grabbed her by the clothes and buried his knife in her chest. She collapses, face down. Her limbs are still twitching when the helicopter surges into view, almost clipping the tops of the olive trees. Anna just catches a glimpse of the pilot's face before the aircraft disappears, swallowed up by the forest. One of the terrorists yells:

"They've spotted us! We can't stay here."

"Quiet, son of a whore! The emir has ordered us to hold out here as long as possible. Otherwise all the other brothers will perish!"

Jallal is gripping Anna's hand so tightly that she whispers he is hurting her. The boy, trembling, doesn't hear. The women have retreated towards the cave mouth. Khedidja is crying, sniffing noisily.

"We shall all die," Saliha observes morosely. "If they don't kill us, the shelling will do the job for them . . ."

As if to prove her right, there is a muffled explosion as a shell explodes some way off. Then a second falls, closer, shaking the cave.

"My God, they are getting our range! They don't give a damn for us prisoners . . . We'll be blown to pieces!"

The voice wails:

"Will nobody take pity on us? What have we done to deserve this?"

There are sounds of a furious altercation outside. A man shouts that they must pull out before they burn to death. Another (Anna recognises the leader's voice) curses him for a coward and orders him to stay at his post, or he personally will liquidate him on the spot. The rest of his imprecations are lost in the terrifying din of an explosion. Fragments of loosened rock rain down from the cave roof. It is the signal for a stampede. A panic-stricken hand pushes Anna, knocking her to the ground. She feels herself being trampled, then momentarily blacks out. Trying to regain her breath, she inhales dust and is seized by a violent fit of coughing. Someone is whimpering in her ear:

"Get up, Grandma, or we'll be buried alive! Come on, get up, you stupid old woman!"

In his panic, Jallal is trying with all his might to pull Anna up by the arms. In vain.

"Get up, *gaouria*, the boy is right, if not you will die!"

What with the conflagration, and the prolonged bursts of gunfire, the din is so intense that the Swiss woman feels as if her head must explode. At first she fails to recognise this woman who is bullying her in Arabic. Every movement is horribly painful. With Jallal's help, old Khalti manages to get Anna to her feet. She grunts, still in Arabic:

"You, boy, tell her that she must run. Follow me, we'll try and make for the *oued*. I know a path."

Outside the cave Anna trips over a corpse. She stifles a cry: it is Saliha's shattered body. The face grimaces hideously without its lower jaw. The ground is strewn with the bodies of women and terrorists. The surviving terrorists are still firing in the direction of the valley. The fumes, a mixture of smoke and chemicals, make the air unbreathable.

Khalti, Anna and Jallal in tow, slips behind the cactus hedge leading away from the cave. Anna, heart in mouth, wonders if she is right to put her trust in this woman whom poor Saliha had described as raving mad. They scramble down a path for a few hundred metres, nearly losing their footing on the loose stones. Yet Khalti must know where she is going: the first oleanders appear, a sign that they are nearing the *oued*. There is a shout, followed by sounds of pursuit. Khalti pushes them into the bushes. A figure comes tearing past, then another close behind, yelling with rage:

"Thought you had escaped us, did you, worthless bitch? But you'll die like the rest! I'll cut off your head myself, sow's cunt!"

A terrified protest, a muted "Huh!", then nothing. On his way back the killer passes so close that Jallal gives a start and wriggles further into the bushes. The man stands stock still, staring in his direction. With a sudden burst of laughter, he stretches out an arm and grasps Jallal's foot. Swinging the boy from side to side, he fumbles for his dagger:

"Well, well, my little turkey cock," he grunts, "where do you think you're going?"

The exchanges of gunfire have redoubled in intensity. The wind is blowing the smoke towards the cave, further endangering those trapped inside. The young terrorist seems oblivious to their fate. Giggling uncontrollably, he sniggers:

"How about a game of football first, my little bastard . . ."

He aims two kicks in quick succession at the boy's head. Jallal, unable to catch his breath, his hands flailing the air, is helpless to fend off the blows.

"Why?"

Anna has appeared close by. Stretching out her arms to the terrorist in supplication, she implores him:

"Why him? He's only a child . . . Spare him . . . Think of his mother . . . He's so young . . ."

The man stops laughing. Still swinging his captive from one hand, he advances on Anna. His face is twisted with an ungovernable rage:

"Foreign bitch! Thought being a *gaouria* would save you, did you, while the rest of us die one by one? If the army is so powerful, it's your fault, the fucking Christians! Now it's your turn to feel the kiss of the knife . . . after this little worm, naturally!"

And without looking at Jallal, almost absentmindedly, he draws the blade of the knife across the boy's throat. Anna just has time to see a thin red line spring up in its wake before the terrorist knocks her flying.

"No, you shan't kill me, no!" she yells, as he seizes her by the hair. She falls over backwards, her heels drumming furiously on the ground. The terrorist, thrown off balance by the old woman's unexpected resistance, is attempting to hold her down with one hand while trying to find her throat with the other.

When the man topples forward, Anna thinks she has felt the stroke of the knife. She is amazed to find that she can still breathe, can distinctly hear Khalti curse. The Arab woman is sitting astride the killer's back, beating his head with a stone. As he struggles feebly beneath her, she shrieks at the top of her voice:

"*Mouss . . . mouss . . . Darbih*, she-ass, *darbih*!"

It takes Anna a few seconds to understand "knife . . . stab him . . ." The stone is too small, and the killer is still conscious. She sees the knife on the ground, close to the terrorist's hand. Then, without a moment's hesitation, uplifted by an extraordinary hatred, she snatches it up and plunges it into the man's back, withdraws it, and plants it once again in the same place . . .

Anna gets to her feet. There, the deed is done: for the first time in her life she has killed someone. She feels nothing except perhaps an immense fatigue. So it was as easy as that, to take the life of another human being!

Her frenzy undiminished, Khalti continues to hammer the dead man's skull. At intervals, splinters of bone fly off, smeared with a sort of greyish pink, gelatinous substance. When Anna touches her on the shoulder, she draws back reluctantly. The old woman is crying. She says, in Arabic:

"He was the one who raped me. Ah, if only I could kill him all over again!"

She spits on the corpse and stamps viciously on the face which is now safely in the Beyond. The body's immobility seems to aggravate her rage. She lifts her skirts, squats over the terrorist's head and, still crying, releases a long jet of urine.

Anna looks away. Jallal is lying on his side, quite still. She turns him over, ready to howl with grief, her fear of the approaching gunfire temporarily forgotten. She cradles the urchin's head in her arms. His eyes are closed, his lips twisted with a grimace of pain. A thread of blood trickles from the wound in his neck.

"O God, forgive me! It's my fault, I was the one who dragged him into all this . . ."

"*Ya Baghla,* don't shake him like that, he's still alive! The knife has only scratched the skin!"

She hasn't taken it in, hearing only the insult ("mule"). Impatiently shoving Anna out of the way, Khalti removes her scarf and winds it round Jallal's neck.

"*Hai, goultlek . . .*" (He lives, I tell you)

The old woman seems to have recovered her sanity. Anna puts an ear to the little guide's mouth. Her heart leaps: he is breathing, but only just! It's true, the child isn't dead! There might be a chance of saving him, if only he doesn't lose too much blood! . . . A hospital, they must get him to a hospital! Her companion scolds her: she is handling the boy too roughly. She shows Anna how to lift the little body so that his head doesn't loll. She herself tenderly takes the little peanut-seller's legs.

Their progress along the river bed is painful, the pebbles bruising her bare feet. Jallal is hardly breathing. Pink bubbles form at the corners of his lips. Khalti points to a concrete bunker in the rock face and motions to the Swiss woman to shelter there and wait for her. After an hour, just as Anna was beginning to lose hope, she sees Khalti's lean figure approach, driving a donkey. Having settled the child across the animal's back as best they can, they set off again. Helicopters can still be heard in the distance, but the guns are quiet. The battle must be over. A gigantic plume of smoke rises to the east of the mountain. The flames are attacking the groves of cork-oaks and olive, creating a glowing halo around its summit. Anna thinks with horror of the women who have escaped terrorist bullets and army shells only to find themselves, in all likelihood, trapped by fire . . .

They reach the market town around midday. Khalti leads them straight to a minuscule pharmacy that stands apart from the outlying houses. The pharmacist shakes his head doubtfully, but says nevertheless:

"We'll see if we can't patch him up."

He murmurs, more to himself, perhaps:

"The little chap would have been better off dead . . ."

He raises his head:

"Was he up there?"

Without waiting for a reply, he snaps in alarm:

"Hey, officer, what's all the racket? What's going on?"

Along with everybody else in the waiting-room, the two women are hustled out at gunpoint by some extremely nervous policemen. Army ambulances are bringing in the first casualties of the battle. There are no women among them . . .

Anna has instinctively covered her head. But nobody pays any attention to the two women, their clothes in rags, their faces grimy and blackened with smoke. Khalti climbs astride her little donkey. Her bony frame seems to be a human extension of her mount. Anna, her heart full, whispers in Arabic:

"Thank you, my sister."

"You speak Arabic, now?"

Khalti stares at the foreigner, her expression troubled, then sticks out her hands abruptly, like a child. Anna strokes the rough hands, deformed by age and toil.

"My country is so cruel to its children," the Aurésien peasant sighs. "They are eaten up with rage, and they go crazy, like wild beasts. And I have gone crazy with them. No, don't deny it, I've seen it in your face!"

Anna bows her head. She is afraid that, meeting her companion's dark eyes, she will be unable to hold back the tears.

"My country is slowly drowning in years of blood. And no-one takes pity on us . . ."

Khalti snatches away her hands. She makes a sign of farewell and with a grunted "Hup!" gives the weary animal a smack with her stick. Anna catches her up, trotting alongside:

"You are going back to the mountain? Why?"

"Where else can I go? I'll go to ground and bury my carcass in some vixen's lair!"

One hand on her mount's withers, she turns to the elderly European who is panting with the effort of keeping up with her, and mutters:

"I curse them all, those up there and those down here. I had four sons, my sister. They were fine, upstanding young men, they were my life! The 'beards' took the first two prisoner and the soldiers killed the others."

Her eyes are filled with an intense bewilderment. She adds (but by now the foreigner, out of breath, is too far behind to hear):

"My sister, I loved them so, my children . . . Now not even the heart of God is big enough to contain my hatred!"

The woman wanders the streets of this large East Algerian market town, anonymous. She is dirty, barefoot, clothed in rags. A black scarf covers her hair. She finds a fountain and washes her feet and hands, but not her face. It is her best protection: who would suspect a European tourist beneath this beggar's guise? For she is aware that people take her for a beggar (or a madwoman!). She can tell from the indifferent glances that slide over her, unwilling to linger for fear of the discomfort engendered by the sight of ugliness and poverty. Never straying far from the pharmacy, she turns from time to time to gaze at the mountain, reflecting that, up there, she had grown stupid, her mind destroyed by having witnessed so much blood and horror. Studying those rocky peaks, so near, so inaccessible, where her twins lay imprisoned for ever in their last terrible moments, she is reminded of Hans, her sole living child, and a little joy creeps back into her heart. She returns to the pharmacy, not daring to go in. And her breast swells with grief ("O God, let him hold out!") at the thought of the little vagabond from Algiers whom she has dragged all this way in order that he should have his throat cut.

"We'll try and stitch that up," the pharmacist had said, "but you'll have to take him away with you. We can't keep him here. Unless you can pull strings and have him evacuated to the hospital at Constantine . . ."

"What makes you think that?" she had protested.

He had shrugged, pretending not to have noticed that she was a foreigner.

*

245

He has been in the town for two days now. He and Jaourden have been sleeping in the car. The hotel-keeper refused them a bed on the pretext that all available rooms were under repair. The day before, the whole town had followed the course of the battle, the ballet of the helicopters, the bombing, the burning of the forest. Afterwards there was an army parade. Several dead terrorists were also paraded and tied upright to the back of a lorry. Certain corpses had been arranged in obscene poses. One, naked, had his hand twisted and tied in such a way that one finger was stuck in his anus. The townsfolk gazed in silence at these men who, as their masters, had reigned without mercy over the entire region. Yet, despite the encouragement and laughter of the soldiers who were driving the lorries with their macabre cargo, they showed no sign of emotion. Everyone suspected his neighbour. Furthermore, the spectators knew that, in two or three days at the most, this proud, powerful army would leave, taking their armoured trucks, their mortars and their special forces with them. And then, as usual, they would be left to confront alone the prospect of endlessly reinforced armed groups, of being led, bound hand and foot, to a slaughterhouse death, of rackets and the kidnapping of women in the name of the holy war ... Of the Sidi Sghir survivors still gathered on the square, only a few had the heart to come and stare into the waxen faces of their torturers. Some spat. The children threw stones. One woman, mad with grief, tore out a tuft of hair as they passed. A little girl wet herself with terror.

Both he and she, neither noticing the other, attended the funeral of the Sidi Sghir victims, the families having resigned themselves to taking their dead back to the village without any form of escort, military or otherwise.

She was present at the start of the procession only. The trembling fits that had so humiliated her in the cave having returned, she kept apart from the crowd. He stayed to watch as the five lorries drove past at a snail's pace. Shrouds of every size, brown with dried blood, were laid out in serried ranks on the tail-boards. Already, the corpses were giving off a smell of decaying flesh. A voice exclaimed:

"God have mercy on us, those lorries are from the rubbish dump!"

Another retorted, bitterly:

"Dump trucks are all that our dead have a right to in this country. The army wouldn't allow us use of their lorries. The corpses stank, they said. And there wasn't enough water to wash the lorries down!"

Nassreddine put his handkerchief to his mouth to stop himself from vomiting. He thought: "I have lived too long. What's the point of living if it is to see this?"

The same voice repeated:

"We are nothing but peasants. We count for less than a dog's turd in this country. Look: the mayor hasn't even bothered to come!"

The voice was soon drowned in the women's lamentations. A child cried and wouldn't stop, not even when the imam began the prayer for the dead. Somebody slapped it, and the imam continued, his voice breaking.

Hours later, more or less in secret, the army buried more corpses, transporting them in their own lorries. Nassreddine was to hear of this only afterwards, there having been no religious ceremony. An opportunistic street vendor told him that the dead were women, killed during the attack on the terrorists' hide-out. The army, suspecting that some may have joined terrorist lovers of their own free will, hadn't wanted to risk according the women a last religious tribute. He rushed to the cemetery, but the grave-diggers had finished their work. There were at least a dozen of them, drafted in by the police. Mounds of freshly turned earth were dotted around the cemetery; it was as if the entire area had been under the plough.

"We've never been so busy," a smiling grave-digger told him. "There are more bodies than blades of wheat, this year."

Nassreddine hesitated before shaking the man's earth-stained hand.

"No," the grave-digger replied to the visitor's question. "Naturally, we're not allowed to look in the body-bags. But these weren't properly done up. I retied them and, every now and then, I took a peek. No, my brother, there wasn't a European among them. They were all our countrywomen. But most of them had dreadful injuries!"

He laughed sourly:

"And they weren't old, not by a long chalk! It's a shame, some must have been real lookers. You could tell from their figures, even through the sheet . . ."

Nassreddine persisted.

"Perhaps there could have been a *gaouria* after all," the grave-digger admitted, "but if so, I didn't see one. It's possible . . . I wouldn't swear to it, either way."

"Were there any wounded, any survivors?"

The grave-digger's face darkened. The old man's insistence made him uncomfortable; perhaps he was a spy. Not bothering to disguise his impatience, he grumbled:

"I don't know and I don't care. Go and ask at the pharmacy. They might be able to tell you."

He picked up his spade to end the conversation:

"Excuse my rudeness, but we're really busy today. They don't have a morgue at the pharmacy. So they deliver the dead straight here. And what with this sun, there's no time to be lost!"

She has finished her baguette. She had passed a dreadful night in the shelter of a stone wall. Today she must make up her mind. She can still go to the police, put herself under their protection. But that, she knows, would mean instant deportation. And she can't abandon Jallal. True, her life would be saved. She gives a wry smile. She didn't have much longer to live. That much was certain, she had felt it in her bones ever since she was kidnapped. Her heart was like an old motor car. She sensed that, very soon, the old banger would give up the ghost. The fear that she had experienced on the mountain (greater than any human being could bear) had doubtless accelerated its decay. Such was the pain in her chest during the night that she had awoken half asphyxiated, wanting to scream.

So what would she gain by running away? A few more days of life, two months, perhaps? And shame in exchange. Jallal? She felt a kind of nausea. There was a time when she had trusted in fate. And fate had taken advantage of her trust by murdering her children. The little peanut-seller had called her Grandma; he had dozed with his head in her lap while she told him stories of her childhood. And it kept their spirits up. When they were in the cave after the butcher had done his work, Jallal was terrified. Yet, that same evening, he was laughing. He refused to believe the extraordinary story of the circus pony that fell in love with a seal. She promised him it was true; the ponies always came on after the seals, and so were accustomed to meeting the seals behind the scenes. One day a pony, having done its turn, refused to leave one particular seal. From then on, it would whinny for hours on end whenever they were separated. Jallal had protested:

"That's impossible, Grandma. You're making it up!"

He had stifled his laughter, but she could tell that he longed to believe her.

Anna returns to the pharmacy. She has yet to find a solution. The dusty waiting-room is empty except for an old man absorbed in his own thoughts. She will have to wait for the pharmacist with the disillusioned face, the man who told her that he would "try and patch the little chap up". She sits down. She is weary, oh, so weary. She is also hot. She removes her scarf. The old man is looking at her. Suddenly ashamed of her dirty face, her torn clothes, she puts her scarf on again.

He stands up. He has had a good look at her hair, her face. And then he tells himself no. He knows fate's little jokes only too well by now. He sits down again, then decides not to wait any longer for his informant.

He gets to his feet. He is short of breath. There is no mimosa in this squalid dispensary. And yet the old man has the heady scent of mimosa in his nostrils. He looks about him. There is only that poor woman with the haggard face, her hands folded in her lap.

It dawns on him that this waft of scent comes from his memory. His mind is like a dried flower which has been rubbed between the palms. The man approaches the woman. His voice trembles a little. He tries to smile, but cannot:

"Anna . . ."

The woman looks up, not recognising at first this person who seems to know her name. She closes her eyes tight, fighting down fear.

Now the man is smiling. The old woman's heart inflates. She dreads the pain that will soon follow. But she too tries to smile. She says, with a sigh:

"Is it you, at last?"

She still can't quite believe it. And the man realises that this exotic mimosa perfuming his skull is the smile of the woman who was once his wife.

19

At first they look at one another in silence. In turn, the man and the woman seek to distinguish, behind the furrows and wrinkles, the features of the person each had once been. These looks, intended to be direct, cannot help but be oblique, a little voyeuristic.

They both smile simultaneously, suddenly calmer. Like returning exiles who find that the country they have in common has undergone a metamorphosis, is a little uglier perhaps, but still reassuringly familiar. Anna blushes, conscious of her dirty appearance. Nassreddine remarks tenderly:

"You have grown old, Anna."

"So have you, Nassreddine."

Nassreddine laughs, filled with a sense of mischief that he hasn't felt since . . . since goodness knows when! He wants to explain this to the woman. But he can't find the words. So he remains silent. There is so much he wants to say, yet he is struck dumb. He takes Anna's hand. It is thin, the back is scratched with thorns and the fingernails are black. His heart turns over, the hand seems so fragile.

"Were you up there, Anna?"

She nods. He sees her eyes cloud over.

"Was it bad?" (He knows at once that he shouldn't have asked such a stupid question.)

"Yes. I would never have believed . . ."

Her voice grows faint, then falters. Anna is on the point of weeping with the injustice of it all: death, time, cruelty, opportunities wasted. Nassreddine bows his head, not knowing what to say. He whispers, his voice hoarse from the lump in his throat:

"Don't worry, Anna, everything seems like yesterday to me."

It is Anna's turn to laugh. The scrawny old man is like a child. She laughs and with an impatient gesture brushes away the two rivulets coursing down her face.

"No, Nassreddine, nothing is like yesterday. But . . . but you're here!"

The man has watched the fingers wipe away the tears. And he has seen the crumpled face clear. Suddenly his soul flutters with joy, like a sparrow trying to escape. Just then, the pharmacist comes rushing in. He halts in his tracks on seeing the couple: he, tall and bony in his worn suit; she, begrimed, trying to pass herself off as an Algerian. The pharmacist doesn't know which way to turn. He has just heard (by chance, a conversation between two military doctors) that the army is to leave town that afternoon. He has also received a telephone call. The voice on the line murmured: "Have everything ready. Don't stint on the quantities, cousin. Give the brothers all they want or it will be the worse for you . . ." and then hung up. He is very frightened: the same voice always telephones when there is to be a new delivery of medicines. But he receives hardly any medicines from the capital these days. At least . . . not those which interest the "brothers": anaesthetics, drugs for treating wounds, for preventing gangrene . . . The pharmacist sighs: that morning, he had filched several tubes from the army stores. The army took along its own medical services on its campaigns. During its "cleansing" operations against the local terrorists, several boxes of medical stores had been left at the dispensary. But the military trusted nobody. They had doubtless counted every syringe, every bandage. If they noticed something missing, they would first arrest the doctors responsible for the dispensary, then the pharmacists. Four individuals in all. If he were arrested, he would confess at once. He couldn't stand up to a beating. Who knows what would follow: would they kill him, or merely take him to court or, instead, torture him, suspecting him of a closer involvement with the terrorists?

On the other hand the others would take their revenge if he didn't obey them. And they probably wouldn't even bother to warn him by sending him the usual parcel containing a white rag and a bar of soap. "Considering the slowness of the post in this hole, I shall be dead and buried long before it arrives," he laughs sourly to himself.

He looks at the two old people, thinking them ridiculous. He calls the woman. She rushes forward, followed by the man. The pharmacist, annoyed, jerks his chin to dismiss this person whose name he hasn't called. The old woman hesitates, then stammers in French:

"This is . . . this is . . ."

The old man interposes without hesitation, but speaking too loudly, in Arabic:

"She is my wife!"

The pharmacist sees both faces blush simultaneously. He screws up his eyes in disbelief:

"And the boy? Is he your son?"

He has addressed his question to Anna. She lowers her eyes, raises them, and says, taking the plunge:

"No . . . he is my grandson!"

"And what is he to you?" He looks ironically at the old man who, taken aback, answers stupidly: "What? Er . . . er . . ."

The pharmacist, indulgent, gives a thin smile: the two old people have the air of children caught out in a bare-faced lie. Then exhaustion (and apprehension) overwhelm him. He says curtly:

"You're lying, why I don't know. In any case, it's no business of mine. But the boy . . . your grandson, must leave with you today."

Anna stares at him, not understanding.

"But why? Is he out of danger?"

The pharmacist hesitates.

"Almost: he must continue with the treatment. But you can't leave him here, I tell you! I repeat, he can't stay here!"

His face is tense. Nassreddine, to his astonishment, detects panic behind the anger. The pharmacist gives a quick glance round the waiting-room: it is empty. Suddenly trembling, he lowers his voice:

"The army leaves town this afternoon. The others will be here tomorrow . . . if not tonight. If they find the boy, they'll finish him off. Do you understand?"

Anna, white-faced, whispers:

"In that case, we should ask the army to transfer him to another hospital . . ."

The pharmacist makes a wry face:

"The military don't give a damn. They wouldn't evacuate the boy. He is of no importance. A street urchin counts for nothing these days."

And more aggressively:

"It's obvious that you're a foreigner – you are, aren't you? Let me tell you that in this region alone, dozens of peasants have their throats cut every day, and it makes not a blind bit of difference to those who govern this benighted country! Imagine if our best hospitals had to treat every unwashed son of a bitch stupid enough to get himself cut to pieces by . . ."

He breaks off. Somebody has entered the waiting-room. The pharmacist mops his forehead. He is sweating profusely. His tone becomes more impersonal:

"Do you have a car?"

Anna seems to have gone deaf suddenly; she turns to Nassreddine. The old man coughs and replies in the affirmative.

"In that case, we'll get your . . . your grandson ready."

Barely 20 minutes later the pharmacist, breathless with panic, lifts the unconscious boy into the back of the rickety car. Jaourden, in front, looks on in astonishment as an old woman in foul-smelling rags opens the rear door and scrambles in. She cradles the boy's head in her lap. Stroking his hair, she murmurs:

"They've knocked him out with tranquillisers, poor little chap . . ."

The Targui, dry-mouthed, stares transfixed at the huge bandage round the little boy's neck. The child's face twitches as if, despite his drugged state, he is in pain. Nassreddine, looking strained, asks Anna to conceal the boy under a blanket.

"Make sure his neck doesn't show," he insists. He turns on the ignition. He swears, then swears again. His foot slips on the accelerator. The engine stalls. At last, it fires. Nassreddine starts to reverse. The pharmacist taps on the window.

"Come with me," he orders harshly.

Anna gives a moan of fear. Nassreddine looks at her, swallows, then decides to get out of the car. The pharmacist leads him into a small office. He is sweating as much as ever. He hands the old man a plastic bag, explaining that it contains medicines and dressings for treating the boy. He shows Nassreddine a blue box.

"Don't forget this, or the neck will become infected. Change the dressings daily. Boil them afterwards, don't throw them away or you might not have enough. I've marked the dosage on each packet. I'm no doctor, but I'm only too familiar with . . . accidents of this type. Hide the bag under your jacket and get going. Don't turn back!"

He pushes Nassreddine towards the door, adding impatiently:

"Whatever you do, don't tell anybody that I've given you all this."

Nassreddine hesitates, his hand on the doorknob:

"You are obviously very frightened, yet you are helping us. Why?"

The pharmacist scratches his chin. He explains wearily:

"I'm not doing this for you. It's for the boy. I can't bear to see another dead child. Have you ever seen a child's corpse? And have you had to face one of our countrywomen, a mother, ignorant, illiterate, obstinate as a mule, pulling out her hair and howling non-stop because she can't understand why anyone should cut off a child's head?"

Nassreddine, ashen-faced, makes no reply.

"I hope for your sake that you never have to. This is a country of cannibals . . ."

Nassreddine swallows back a sob. He hears the engine start up.

"And what about you, your own safety?"

"Me? Like everyone else around here, I live between the rock and the hard place. If it's not one thing, it's another."

He forces himself to smile:

"I can't afford to move away. To be perfectly honest with you, most of the time I'm pissing myself with fear."

In the car, no-one speaks. The passengers stare straight ahead, deliberately putting off the moment for explanations. Nassreddine is thinking: "What now? What is to be done about Anna and, above all, about the child?" Jaourden is thinking: "So this is Nassreddine's wife, but why is she so dirty? And what has happened to that poor wounded boy? It's a hospital he needs, not a car journey!" Anna's mind is blank. She is so tired that she longs to sleep. Her heart is pumping, pumping, and its desperate striving is giving her pain. If only it were possible to stop it beating for a minute or two! Yet she feels almost safe, now that Nassreddine is there and she has retrieved her "grandson".

Before driving out of town, Nassreddine pulls up in a shopping street.

He returns with two large carrier bags, giving one to Anna and putting the other in the boot. He mutters something to Jaourden, who gets out of the car and follows him. They reappear with two cans of water and a plastic basin. Nassreddine gives a small smile of satisfaction as he starts the engine:

"There, now we're all set for a long journey!"

He meets Anna's eyes in the rear mirror. She is flushed, for in the bag which he gave her, she has found, along with two robes in the regional style, a scarf, veil, shoes and washing-things, a set of fancy underwear of the spicier sort.

Nassreddine chuckles, a little embarrassed:

"The robes and shoes are not exactly fashionable, and the others, well ... a little too much so, perhaps? I had no choice. It was the only shop that would take a cheque ..."

They pass the last army roadblocks without attracting attention. Nassreddine spots a cactus hedge. Taking the basin and one of the cans out of the boot, he whispers something to Anna. Blushing furiously, she gets out of the car. While she is washing behind the hedge, Nassreddine and Jaourden discuss their route. The boy wakes up. He stares at the two men, terrified. Jaourden, noticing, says:

"Of course! When he was put in the car at the dispensary, he was unconscious ..."

He opens the rear door. The child shrinks back, holding his hands before his face. When Jaourden prepares to climb in, the child crouches in the corner, whimpering with terror.

"Tell your ... your wife to show herself. The boy is scared to death of me!"

The Targui is upset. He has a nervous tic at the corner of one eye. He spits on the ground.

"What a filthy world!"

And he doesn't calm down until the boy relaxes and drops his defensive posture. For Anna has yelled at the top of her voice:

"Don't be frightened, little one, they're friends! Don't be frightened, I'm coming!"

Anna appears, her hair dripping. Nassreddine gives a wolf whistle:

"Well, we're a proper Aurésienne in our smart town shoes!"

The high heels are comically unsuitable with the Chaouï robes and Jallal, sticking his head out of the window, gives a curious sort of silent laugh. He puts a hand to his throat:

"It hurts when I laugh!"

Anna rushes to him, but the boy reassures her:

"It's nothing, Grandma!"

The old woman is very distressed. She hasn't seen him conscious since the terrorist had attacked him, and now he is almost voiceless. The pharmacist had warned her that the vocal cords were damaged, saying that it was difficult to tell if he would ever recover his voice. She is so upset that it is Jallal, in his strange, dead voice, who has to do the comforting:

"Hey, we're alive, Grandma! That's the main thing, no?"

She looks at him: at the rings round his eyes, the bruises on his thin face left by the boots of his torturer. She returns to the basin and her ablutions. As she passes him, Nassreddine whispers:

"And the other clothes . . . did you like them?"

"Idiot," she mutters in return, flicking him with the damp towel. She knows that he only wanted to make her laugh, but she feels more like crying.

They have been driving for an hour. They are making slow progress because of the state of the road. Anna has explained rapidly that there is no question of her abandoning Jallal. If they went to Algiers, the police would soon discover that her visa had expired and deport her on the spot. Nassreddine points out that the same will apply wherever they go, that if there is anything that is fairly distributed throughout Algeria, it is the police. In Algiers, she had only to wear a *haik* to pass as an Algerian. Anna won't hear of it: anywhere but Algiers! In any case, not for the moment, otherwise how could they be together?

"You haven't changed, Anna," he says with a smile, much moved.

She smiles back:

"No, the goods haven't improved with age! What was it you used to say: stubborn as a . . ."

Nassreddine laughs:

". . . As a nanny that thinks it is a billy-goat!"

The boy swallows his medicine and dozes off, his head in the Swiss woman's lap, she sleeping beside him. The old man's eyes sparkle with amusement as she begins to snore. He doesn't know how it will all end, but the old highlander is happy. He hasn't yet had a proper talk with Anna, but he is prepared to believe that for once, fate is on their side. Calm down, idiot! he admonishes himself, she hasn't come back to live with you. But why not, in fact? the voice remarks, you might be lucky. After all, she was your wife once, the mother of your twins . . .

He restrains himself from dwelling on the memory of those two magnificent children of whom he has only a few keepsakes: toys, like the miniature circus which had so delighted Anna, and their underclothes which, never washed, remain caked in blood. This blood, now so old and brown that it seems dyed in the cloth, is his sole proof (through their deaths . . .) of his children's existence. All these objects are preserved in a casket that he opens only rarely. Each time it took weeks, months, for him to recover from this plunge into pain, the pain of hell relived and the pain of knowing that he can never escape it. On the other hand, he had decided, a few years after the event, to eliminate all trace of the killings in the house. Every year, with the coming of spring, he toiled, making good the depredations of winter, migrant shepherds and marauders, repairing the roof, plastering the walls, weeding what was once his mother's vegetable patch. Why does he do all this for a house in which he never lives? Perhaps (but has he ever really admitted this to himself?) it is in order to preserve another sort of proof, different from the first, the proof that his life has not consisted wholly of misfortunes and that, long, long ago, he had had the good fortune to be a carefree lad, loved by two extraordinary mothers . . .

Tapping the steering-wheel, Nassreddine sighs:

"My God, how time flies!"

He is vexed at having said anything so trite, but he is incapable of expressing what he feels about the passage of time, that cowardly creature that kills you by degrees. Jaourden gives him a sideways glance, amazed. He too has been thinking that very thing, that life passes quicker than a heartbeat. Only yesterday (40 years ago?) Douja was a young bride on the first night of her honeymoon, paralysed with shyness, waiting for him to undress her while he, clumsy as ever, tangled himself up in his own clothes . . . Now she lies under the earth of some gloomy cemetery in a suburb of Algiers, she who had so wanted to be buried in the desert, good

Targuie that she was. The airline company had refused to take the coffin, saying that transporting coffins wasn't a priority and pleading pressure on space.

"Not a priority, my wife wasn't a priority . . ." His eyes fill with tears. He forces himself to plan the menu for the service for the dead which was to take place on his return to Tamanrasset. She had chosen it herself, this menu, in anticipation of her death . . .

Nassreddine clears his throat. His voice has grown hoarse. He says slowly:

"Jaourden, look . . ."

Men in civilian clothes are barring the road. They are armed. Energetically, they wave down the car. A guard cocks his rifle. Nassreddine glances in the rear mirror. Other men have appeared, making it impossible to reverse.

He brakes gently.

"O God, don't let Anna and the child wake up," he groans. Luckily, before going to sleep, the old woman had wrapped her head in the scarf. The boy too is covered up to the chin. The guard, whose rifle has a sawn-off barrel, asks to see his papers. He is young, with an enormous bushy beard that takes up the lower half of his face. While he examines the documents, he interrogates Nassreddine:

"Where do you think you're going, in this heap of old iron?"

"To . . . to Sétif to my parents' house."

"Who is the woman asleep in the back?"

"My wife. And the boy is . . . my grandson . . ."

Nassreddine tries to control his racing heart. He has heard too many stories about horrifying murders at roadblocks such as this! Despite the heat, his feet are as cold as ice.

"And him, the nigger?"

"A cousin by marriage . . ."

"Do you work for the State?"

"No, I'm retired. And he is unemployed . . ."

"And you weren't afraid to make the journey, Granddad? Don't you know that you need our permission to travel in these parts?"

"No . . . er . . . that is, we have done nothing to be ashamed of."

The man appears dissatisfied with this reply. He grunts:

"Are you making fun of me, *sheik*?"

He shuffles the papers and goes to open the car door. But he is undecided; indeed, he seems bored stiff. The barrel of his rifle, horizontal, brushes against Nassreddine's cheek. The bearded man turns towards his companions. One calls him. Before walking over to them, he says threateningly:

"Don't leave before I give you permission. This", he pats his gun, "has a long range. We shall have to see what to do with you . . ."

Nassreddine and Jaourden await the verdict. Drops of sweat blur their vision. They dare not speak. When the man returns, he has a mocking smile on his face. He hands Nassreddine his papers:

"Don't be so scared, Granddad, you're not dead yet. Go on, get out of here!"

They drive for ten minutes before Nassreddine takes a look at the papers. His identity card and driving licence have been removed from their plastic holders. Both documents have been stamped, in French and in Arabic:

"Islamic Army of Salvation, Brigade of the faithful unto death."

Nassreddine, seized by a fit of trembling, drops the papers. Jaourden bends down. The Targui needs all his famous impassiveness to mask the sensation hitherto inconceivable, that is crushing the breath from his body. He never expected to feel such an overpowering mixture of terror combined with disgust. He gathers up the papers, breathing an "Ah!" at the sight of the stamps. He is the picture of distress:

"Let us get away of this place as fast as possible!"

The speeding car lurches round a corner, waking Anna:

"What are you doing? You'll kill us, idiots!"

Nassreddine interrupts her. Fear is clawing at his throat, but his tone is reassuring:

"It's nothing, Anna. Go to sleep. We still have a long way to go!"

Jaourden suggests a change of plan: they would be better off going to Biskra, where one of his relatives will put them up till they can find some means of getting to the Hoggar, and from there, to Tamanrasset.

"But the distance from Biskra to Tam is enormous," Nassreddine objects. "The car will never make it . . ."

"Who said anything about taking your old banger? We leave it at Biskra. You can pick it up on the way back . . . that is, if you are still determined to return to the North! It's simple, we go by bus."

"It means several days' journey. Anna and the boy are exhausted . . ."

"We do it in stages. So what if we get tired, we stop! We have all the time in the world, isn't that so? And that way, we avoid . . . all the troubles in the North . . ."

Nassreddine looks doubtful, but Anna, to his great surprise, warmly approves the plan. Even Jallal joins in, saying in his odd toneless voice that he has always wanted to see a camel. Jaourden nods, with a thoughtful smile:

"Would you like to ride on one?"

The boy darts a look of surprise at the passenger with whom, so far, he has not exchanged a single word.

"Very much," he answers, a trifle coolly.

Jaourden turns to look at the boy, who averts his gaze. The Targui thinks bitterly: "That's right, make me the scapegoat, little Northerner. It wouldn't be the first time. I've had a long life, too long perhaps, whereas yours is just beginning . . ."

They decide to drive on for another two hours at least, so as to put the maximum distance between them and their bad experience. Nassreddine has chosen to take the Oued El Abiod valley, a much less direct route, but in his opinion one that offers fewer chances of encountering "unofficial" roadblocks. None of his passengers dares question the logic of this conviction.

The landscape is impressive: high peaks of reddish rock clad in cedar forests, succeeded by vertiginous gorges carved into the body of the mountain like wounds in a titan's flesh. The steep flanks are dotted with poverty-stricken hamlets, some near the *oued*, others keeping a distrustful distance as though to protect themselves from possible marauders.

Once through the gorges, the atmosphere in the car becomes more relaxed. Jallal exclaims:

"Oh look, palm trees!"

He lets out an "Ow!" He has forgotten his wound. He holds his neck, grimacing at the sharp pain. Jaourden is the first to notice. Alarmed, he touches Nassreddine on the hand:

"Stop the car. The child is in pain."

"No, it's nothing," the boy protests, penitent, "it's just that I forgot about the . . . the thing on my neck."

"Are you sure, Jallal?" Anna, worried, examines the edges of the bandage.

"Yes. Let's keep going. The further away we are the better, Grandma."

They drive on. Jallal gives the Targui a grateful look. Jaourden, more moved than he cares to show, nods in sympathy. Anna, noticing the exchange, is unable to suppress a twinge of jealousy.

The heat is clammy. The landscape has broadened into a grandiose succession of canyons and oases. Jaourden suggests stopping to picnic in a palm grove. Nassreddine drives on for a few kilometres before pulling up beside the *oued*. To Jaourden's gratification, his companions marvel at the scene: shaded from the sun by towering palms, lush orchards of figs, pomegranates and apricots crowd the banks of the *oued*. A rivulet of precious water at the base of the trees, like a friendly hand tickling their roots.

"Oh, it's like a different world!" the boy whispers eagerly.

For a second or two, Jallal's face darkens with resentment. Anna touches him on the shoulder ("Don't talk so much, Jallal, you'll tire your throat . . ."). She too is filled with a sense of injustice at the sight of all this serenity. Nassreddine takes the provisions out of the boot. They settle themselves down beside a patch of ground planted with tomatoes and pimentos. Jaourden, meanwhile, has taken his bag and retreated behind a clump of trees. Nassreddine cuts bread while Anna lays out the cheese. Jallal frolics around them, throwing stones and even attempting to climb a tree. Nassreddine murmurs with a smile:

"Your little protégé seems to be improving by the minute . . ."

Anna nods. The silence is almost total, broken only by the plop of stones into the water and the warbling of birds scattered among the palms. From time to time, briefly, there is a distant bark, or a child's cry. There is evidence of the inhabitants' ceaseless toil in their struggle for survival in the contrast between the tender green of the plantations and the aridity of the sandstone mountains that bar the horizon. Anna sighs, about to say something, then changes her mind and smiles at Nassreddine. She thinks: "My husband, my husband." Nassreddine smiles back. She knows that their smiles are more than mere smiles. They signify: "What's past is past. There's nothing we can do about it. Now we are together again. And that is already a miracle in itself." The sheer cliffs dominating the palm grove accentuate this feeling of extraordinary benediction. Nassreddine puts down his baguette. He too has something to say. Anna interrupts his intake of breath:

"There's no need . . ."

The old man picks up his bread and knife. He is sad, and his sadness has the depth of 40 years of separation. But at the same time he has never felt happier.

"Jallal, whatever are you staring at?" the Swiss woman suddenly exclaims.

Speechless, the boy points to the clump of trees into which Jaourden had disappeared. A man comes striding out, his face concealed behind a blue-black veil, a *cheche* over his head. He is robed in a superb indigo *gandoura* and shod in leather sandals. He advances towards them. It lacks only the traditional sword to complete the picture of a warrior. Jallal stares open-mouthed at the stranger.

"Hey, little one, close your mouth, or the great desert lizard will jump in and build himself a burrow!"

"But it's . . ."

"Yes, it's me, young man! Who did you think it was? From now on, I'm in my own country. With the desert watching me. I couldn't go on wearing a Northerner's ugly garb, no disrespect to you, naturally . . ."

He gazes back at them, preening himself. Anna has to admit that the transformation is startling: the little man, wizened, ungainly, has turned back into a Targui noble and, with the blue-black veil masking his face, a man of mystery. Just now, as he looks at the foreign woman and the boy, his dark eyes glitter with amusement at their surprise. Nassreddine gives his friend a knowing wink:

"You've certainly made an entrance! It will bring us luck to have a real Hoggar warrior as our escort."

Lost in admiration, the boy approaches the Targui. He points to the leather pouches suspended from the man's neck. Visibly pleased, Jaourden explains:

"This one is for tobacco, kohl, and money . . . when there is any! And this is for talismans. But we don't talk about them much, in case they lose their magic. I'll give you one if you like, the most powerful . . ."

"Ah!" the boy breathes, half curious, half fearful. The Targui, suddenly grave, takes out an amulet, shortens its leather thong and places it around Jallal's neck. The boy, flushed with emotion, looks down at his amulet.

"May I touch it?"

"Yes, but don't overdo it."

Jallal strokes the little leather square. He asks (and his face reflects an inordinate hope):

"What will it protect me against?"

"Against misfortune, my son."

"Any misfortune?"

"Almost. All except those which are inevitable . . ."

Jaourden ruffles the boy's hair. Jallal listens, his eyes shining with gratitude.

" . . . and it will help you endure even those. At least, in most cases . . ."

Anna doesn't see the bitter twist to the Targui's lips. She merely hears his voice grow duller. But Jaourden, recovering himself, continues with forced jollity:

"Come, child, help me build a fire for the tea! What am I thinking of, welcoming you to the gates of our desert without offering you our own special tea? Go and find me some twigs . . . and mind the wood is dry!"

"Grandma, do you believe in his amulet?"

Jallal is gripping Anna's hand, whispering in her ear. She is changing his dressing. The wound, bad as it is, appears to be healing. The child hasn't once complained. Anna isn't fooled; when changing the dressing, she had read the worsening pain in his eyes. She knows that the boy doesn't want to cry in front of Jaourden and Nassreddine. The Targui spoons first sugar, then tea into the battered teapot. He blows on the twigs, bringing the fire to life. The others are silenced by the look of concentration on his face, even Jallal, who is still waiting for an answer to his question.

A breeze gets up, so light that it hardly stirs the tops of the palms. From its channel, the water runs along the irrigation ditch in a melancholy trickle. Smiling her thanks, Anna accepts a glass of tea from the masked man.

"In the desert, we have a saying that the first glass has the bitterness of life, the second, the strength of love, and the third, the blandness of death!"

He gives a short laugh:

"If you ask me, that third judgement is too severe on the tea and much too lenient on death!"

Jallal too is allowed his glass of tea. He makes a face; it isn't sweet enough.

"Don't you like the tea of the Sahara?"

"No, it's not that . . . But I was wondering . . . Do you have children, Uncle?"

The Targui shakes his head, surprised. The others pretend not to have heard. He clears his throat and refills Anna's glass.

"I'll tell you a story. Would you like that?"

"Yes, yes!" the little peanut-seller exclaims.

"I shouldn't really be doing this," Jaourden grumbles. "It's said that children who have been told stories in broad daylight go bald in later life. I hope the thought of that doesn't alarm you?"

"Of course not, I'm not that stupid," the boy protests.

"Nassreddine, you translate when I stumble."

"We were camping near the Sudanese frontier. The drought had chased us out of the Hoggar, and we were on the verge of starvation on these poorer pastures. The dromedary herd had suffered badly, but we were preparing to return home, nevertheless, for our soothsayer, the *amenokhal's* nephew, had predicted that the following year would be a good one. I was 36 or 37 at the time, quite old for a Targui. I hadn't yet troubled to marry, enjoying my bachelor state to the full. The elders of my encampment disapproved, but the fact that I was discreet, and a good worker, tempered their disapproval. One day, a member of my tribe, a fellow called Ikhenouk, came by just as a Sudanese merchant was trying to sell me a magnificent camel saddle, a *rahla* of exceptional quality. That I admired the saddle was obvious to this man from Thlis, but his price far exceeded my meagre purse. Ikhenouk butted in: 'My friend will take the *rahla*. Here,' and he handed over the sum demanded. Flushed with rage, I rebuked him: 'What do you think you're doing?

I'll never be able to repay you.' Ikhenouk grinned, saying that I would owe him nothing if I would only agree to do him a small favour. I was wary, for Ikhenouk had a reputation for deceit. What he proposed was literally breathtaking: on his behalf, I was to ask for the hand of a Targuie whose encampment lay three days' journey away by camel! He said that being so old, I would be acceptable to the girl's parents as an intermediary. Nobody in his own family was prepared to undertake the role, for our tribe was uniquely Kel Rela. We consider ourselves to be aristocrats, whereas Ikhenouk's girl came from a vassal tribe which, being virtually sedentary, is despised by the rest of the Touareg. I hesitated for some days. It was a task for a marriage broker, unworthy of a warrior. Moreover, I was unsure of the way. But covetousness won the day and I set off, taking the famous *rahla* with me. All went well until I was held up by a violent sandstorm that lasted for five whole days. Huddled up against my poor kneeling dromedary, I went through hell during that storm; it seemed as though all the demons of the desert were in league against me, punishing me for my greed . . ."

Jaourden coughs and pours himself a third glass of tea, thoroughly enjoying the interest his story has aroused. His friend's eyebrows are raised in astonishment at his loquaciousness. Seated on the ground beside Anna, Nassreddine does his best to translate whenever the Targui falls into Tamachak. The old Chaouï's own childhood dialect has never deserted him, something which perplexes him to this day. Jallal, panting with excitement, is all ears:

"Go on, Uncle!"

"All right, all right . . . So I knew that I was in for a bad time, that I might even die. I had taken provisions for three days' journey. Yet, due to the storm, I had covered only a third of the way to the young woman's camp. I thought of turning back, but the prospect of losing the *rahla* dissuaded me. In any case, I knew I would never find my way back in the sandstorm, even though it had considerably abated. I took the only possible decision: to go forward at random, trusting to my lucky star. On the brink of exhaustion, I came to an outcrop of rock where (miracle of miracles!) I found the remains of a camp fire. It had obviously been abandoned in a hurry because, buried in the dead embers, I found bread, a *taguella* reduced to charcoal. Then I found a basket containing dried meat, dates and even a little water in a flask. I was saved but only, I was convinced, thanks to a tragedy. The following morning, the wind having died down, I set out to look for the bodies. I found two a few kilometres apart. It was easy to reconstruct the travellers' last moments: for some reason, one man must have made the fatal error of leaving the shelter of the rock, perhaps to hobble their mounts. Then, unable to find his way back in the storm, he had wandered in circles like a madman till death overtook him. His companion had gone to look for him, thus signing his own death warrant. I buried them as deeply as I could, setting a stone to mark the place and repeating a few words of such prayers as I could remember. I even ended up (may God forgive me!) by improvising phrases from the Koran. I couldn't wait to leave that accursed place, and was about to go when I heard the sound of bleating. For a moment I was terrified. My mind was in such a whirl that I was prepared to believe it was the cry of the *djinns*, the 'solitaries' who wander the Sahara, condemned for eternity to expiate the crimes they had committed during their lifetime. I'm easily scared by such things. You too, I see . . ."

Jaourden bursts out laughing, but his laughter fails to reassure the boy, who gives a tense little smile.

"Do you want me to stop, child?" Jaourden asks, with a teasing expression that astonishes Nassreddine in this normally gruff man.

"No, please go on, but . . . just not too fast!" Jallal gasps imploringly.

"Hmm . . . So, I walked towards the rock where the sound was coming from. And what do you think I found, my brave fellow?"

"It was a . . . How do I know?"

Although he tries to conceal his fear with a scornful laugh, Jallal is genuinely scared. His puffy face is white. He is poised for flight, ready to run for the safety of the Swiss woman's bosom, or for the boot of the car. Enthralled, none the less, he whispers:

"What was it?"

"It was . . . a mouflon, a magnificent adult male! It was lying on the rock, bleating at intervals. At first I thought it was injured, having perhaps fallen from a great height. But there wasn't a scratch on it. Its eyes were glazed and it was trembling from head to foot. Green mucus ran from its muzzle. It was my dromedary that discovered the saddle-bag. Luckily, whatever it was munching tasted so good that it had begun to roar. I ran to drag the bag from between its teeth. The bag was in a wretched state, chewed to bits by the mouflon and the dromedary, but what do you think it contained?"

Jallal is wide-eyed. Anna and Nassreddine, amused, have the same reaction as the child. In all the years that he has known him, Nassreddine has never seen Jaourden so animated. He is glad to see that his friend seems to have thrown off his despair.

"It was kif! There were only a few grams left, caught up in the jute fibres from the saddle-bag. All was clear: the two dead men were traffickers in hashish, probably on their way from the Sudan to Tamanrasset. The starving mouflon, having swallowed huge quantities of this peculiar mixture, was quite simply drugged! The poor beast was 'high', at the mercy of the first jackal to come along. I decided to take the mouflon with me, either to eat or to sell. I hobbled it, threw it across the back of my mount and went on my way. Luck was with me. I fell in with a caravan with the same destination as my own. And there you are . . ."

Jallal protests vehemently:

"Is that all? What happened next?"

Jaourden gives a joyous chuckle, the first Nassreddine has heard from him since their meeting in Algiers.

"What happened next is no business of yours!"

"Uncle, please . . ."

Jaourden hesitates, but is plainly happy to continue with his story:

"At the encampment, I was received with every attention, especially when I said that I had nearly met my death in the storm. They nursed me, made much of me. I didn't pursue my goal at once. I first wanted to see the girl for whose hand I was to ask on Ikhenouk's behalf. She was beautiful, truly beautiful. And her playing on the little violin of the nomads was exquisite. Her name was Douja. I could quite see why Ikhenouk had fallen in love with her! When I was back on my feet, I presented myself to the girl's family. They offered me tea, and we talked of this and that without alluding to the obvious purpose of my visit. Then, in the course of conversation, I let it be known that I was there on 'serious' business. I offered them the *rahla* and the mouflon, and I asked for Douja's hand . . . for myself!"

"You did that, Uncle? You broke your word?"

Jallal wants to laugh, but he is so shocked that his laugh sticks in his throat. Jaourden, on the other hand, is openly cheerful:

"I couldn't help myself, little one! She was so beautiful! She was consulted, she accepted. Later, she told me that she had seen me arrive, and had liked what she saw. Let's say that, in those days, I wasn't . . . er . . . bad-looking. Two weeks later, I took her back with me to my encampment."

Jallal interrupts:

"But your friend Ikhenouk, what did he say?"

"Oh, nothing really, except that over the next months, he did his best to kill me. I was obliged to flee with Douja. We went into hiding till he calmed down. Naturally I couldn't give him the *rahla*, but I sent him a dromedary instead. All the same, I've been on my guard all these years!"

Nassreddine is touched: the old Targui seems rejuvenated.

"And . . . what about the mouflon?" Jallal asks thoughtfully.

"Douja grew fond of that mouflon. She nursed it like a child. But the poor beast bleated day and night, refusing to eat. We had to face facts: rather than remain a prisoner, it preferred to starve to death! Douja and I led it to the foot of a plateau near the camp. Douja set it free. The mouflon hesitated, then took off in leaps and bounds for the summit. Douja was truly sad, but she was sure that it stopped several times to salute us with its splendid horns. I didn't disillusion her, but it seemed to me that its terror of being kept hobbled by human beings was so great that, each time it turned round, the animal decided that it still hadn't put enough distance between itself and us . . . My wife's thoughts dwelt on that mouflon for years, to the point where I even became jealous!"

"What a pity . . ." the child sighs.

"Why? What would you have done with the mouflon?"

"I would have tamed it, I would have given it anything it wanted. I'm sure that we would have made friends. It would have followed me everywhere, like a brother . . ."

The Targui looks sceptical. He makes a dismissive gesture, but Jallal goes on eagerly:

"So, do you have children?"

"No."

"Didn't you say that you were married?"

"I was, my boy, but we never had children. It's my one regret. And now . . . and now, Douja is dead."

The boy gives a sorrowful "Ah!". He is at a loss how to respond, but the Targui says gently:

"If you like, I'll do my best to find you a young mouflon, and you can try and teach it to follow you like a puppy."

"Would you, really?"

Jaourden nods. Nassreddine casts a furtive glance at his friend: the Saharan has lost his habitual impassiveness. He might have been just another old gentleman whose heart is touched by his grandson's whims.

"Did you hear that, Grandma?" Jallal exclaims. "A real live mouflon! He promised, you're my witness!"

Anna coughs to disguise the emotions which the Targui's recital has stirred within her: anybody, anywhere, can fall in love, but it always ends badly . . . She nods without speaking. The child is wild with joy.

"Hey, look out for the teapot!" Anna cries. "Stop galloping about like that or you'll damage your throat again."

"OK, Grandma, but only if you tell us some circus stories. No, no, wait! Do one of your circus tricks for us instead."

"Don't be silly, I'm much too old! My muscles aren't like muscles any longer, they are mere cords!"

"Please, Grandma: just once! A single handstand, that's all."

Anna, appalled, looks at Nassreddine for help. But he is watching her with mocking eyes.

"Come on, Nassreddine! Help me! The boy is crazy!"

But Nassreddine is speechless with laughter. Anna, half angry, half laughing, stands up, knots her dress between her legs and grumbles:

"You asked for it. You'll have your puppet show!"

In one bound, she lands on her hands, feet above her head. Her dress falls back, revealing her thin legs. Scarlet in the face with effort, Anna manages a few steps on her hands before collapsing. Jallal applauds furiously, followed by Nassreddine and Jaourden.

"Ah . . . do you want to kill me! You're all in it together," she moans, rubbing her back. "I was a fool to listen to you. Ah, my ribs!"

Nassreddine rushes to help her up, but he is laughing so much that she throws her shoe at him . . .

Their hilarity gradually subsides. The sun, low on the horizon, emblazons the cliffs in purple light. Jaourden digs a hole and buries the tea leaves, then meticulously cleans teapot and glasses before putting them away. Nassreddine announces that it is time to go. Jallal, sitting on the bank of the *oued*, has been silent for a while. Suddenly, he gives a deep sigh:

"You know, I wish you were all my family!"

He picks up a big stone and throws it into the water. A bird flies up with a violent flapping of wings. The child, his neck deformed by the fat bandage, groans:

"Yes, that is what I would like best, if only I could choose . . ."

20

Nassreddine contemplates his sleeping wife. Her breath comes in staccato gasps.

It had been an arduous journey. They stayed no more than a day or two in Biskra. At first, Jaourden's friend had welcomed them warmly, putting them up in his maisonnette overlooking a palm grove on the outskirts of town. But then there was a terrorist attack on a police station in which two policemen died, and he took fright. It was rumoured that some of the assassins lived in the palm grove district. Jaourden's friend, blushing with embarrassment, said that he could no longer shelter a foreigner. If the armed groups were to learn of her presence under his roof, they would kill her, and afterwards vent their anger on the house-holder and his family.

The journey to Tamanrasset, via Ghardaïa and Aïn Salah, was long and tiring. To everyone's surprise, the boy survives it reasonably well. His neck has healed. He still wears the bandage, but only to hide the horri-fying scar left by the terrorist's knife. Yet his voice is much the same, still sounding as if it is on the verge of extinction. He would clear his throat in an effort to improve his speech, and then, when that didn't work, retreat into sullen silence.

Anna, too, suffers in silence, but the heat is too much for her. Nassreddine would see her put a hand to her heart and turn pale, opening her mouth as if, suddenly, she lacked the air to breathe.

At Aïn Salah, they almost quarrelled. Nassreddine insisted that she return to Algiers, then to Switzerland. He feared for her life, it was obvious that she couldn't last much longer out here: the interminable hours spent waiting in the sun for a hypothetical bus, the jostling at ticket windows to book seats, the nights spent under the stars because they couldn't register at a hotel, Anna no longer possessing the means of identification, all that would soon finish her off as efficiently as any assassin sent by the GIA!

She looked at him steadily:

"Once I leave, I'll never be able to return to Algeria!"

"Well then, I'll come to you!"

"They would never give you a visa. What you really mean is that you don't want to be burdened with a crazy old woman like me!"

She flew into a sudden rage.

"I'm sick of running away. This is my home too! Two of my children are buried in this country. That gives me certain rights, wouldn't you say? And what about Jallal, who is to look after him, tell me that?"

Anna's voice trembled with grief and indignation. Nassreddine was ashamed of his own anger. He embraced the woman who was once his wife:

"Calm down, Anna. I'm worried about you, that's all."

And, from the depths of his heart:

"I love you, Anna. I'm losing my teeth, I'm as wrinkled as an old monkey, but I love you as much as . . . as I ever did. There are moments when for me the past is like yesterday. Everything is fresh in my mind, you see! Algiers, Madagascar, the hut at Saint Eugène, those half-dead chickens we tried to sell in Bab El Oued market . . . By staying with me, you offer me a wonderful gift. I'm afraid that by accepting it, by ignoring the risks, I'm simply being selfish."

Her eyes swimming, Anna lowered her long veil to hide her tears. Fumbling for Nassreddine's hand, she held it tight, not saying a word.

Nassreddine is preparing coffee. He is careful not to make a noise. Anna is talking in her sleep, muttering incomprehensible words which, in spite of himself, Nassreddine tries to catch. Outside the sun is warming up. The house (one room and a kitchen built of breeze blocks) belongs to Jaourden. But he hardly ever uses it.

The side street is noisy. Jaourden has explained that the quarter is the haunt of illegal immigrants from black Africa, Malians and Ghanaians, fleeing from starvation and drought. It is also the local red-light district, he added, shamefaced. He advised them to go out as little as possible: police raids are not uncommon.

Anna and Nassreddine have talked at length. She has explained why she wears two wedding rings: the first is the one he gave her in Algiers, after their return from Madagascar; the second is from Johann, her Swiss husband. She has told him that she had Johann's child, Hans, who is now in his twenties, and who doesn't even know that she is in Algeria.

"He thinks that I'm in Egypt," she smiled contritely. "He won't understand why I lied to him. I never told him about Algeria, about you and our children . . ."

Suppressing a sob:

". . . his brother and sister, in fact."

In turn, Nassreddine has described his last 40 years. Haltingly. He has told her that at first he thought he would go mad, but was denied that luxury . . .

"To my own people I was a traitor. And no-one pities a traitor, for he isn't a human being . . ."

Then came the famous day of Independence.

"Never have I seen people so deliriously happy. I was living in the Casbah. The day before, the inhabitants hosed down the pavements, scrubbed the walls, framed the doorways with palm fronds and branches. Everyone was in the street next morning. I, too, joined the processions with their thousands of waving flags. I, too, wanted to laugh, to shout at the top of my lungs with the rest: 'May God have pity on our martyrs!' My country was gaining its freedom. It was . . . unbelievable. From now on, no-one could spit on us with impunity. We were human beings at last, and our greatest treasure had been restored to us: our dignity! All my life, I had waited for this moment. But such intoxicating joy was for others, not for me. And yet I longed for it with all my heart. But the highlanders (my own people!) had killed my mother and children . . . So what could freedom and joy now mean to me? That my mother and children were among the martyrs? All day, I wandered from one procession to another. Sometimes a hand would stretch out to pull me into a car or a lorry. People were singing, dancing . . . But I was neither singing nor dancing. I came across an old woman sitting on a bench. Her face was covered in tattoos and she wore a *haik*. She was weeping.

I sat beside her and asked her what was the matter. Her two sons had taken to the hills and died fighting the French army. Her husband and daughter had died in an air-raid only days before the cease-fire. She looked at me, her eyes brimming with tears: 'All day, I've been marching, throwing streamers; by now, I know the national anthem by heart. I know that my husband and children are in Paradise, and that they would have shared my joy. But I cry my heart out whenever I think of them. It is too cruel.' She took my hand: 'You have no idea of the pain, my son. May God spare you such unhappiness!'"

Nassreddine said that he had put the old woman up for a few days.

"She was destitute, having walked from her refugee camp solely to celebrate independence. On leaving my house, she asked me a question – and her voice trembled with anxiety: 'My son, you are an educated man. You understand the ways of the world. You will tell me the truth. All these deaths, have they served a purpose?' I answered her firmly, with all the conviction I could muster: 'Certainly, Yemma, certainly their sacrifice has served a purpose! Their country will never forget them! Thanks to their sacrifice, it will be a better place.' She thanked me, comforted, and called down the blessings of God upon me. I wept all day after she left."

Nassreddine shook his head:

"I have been waiting ever since. Not for you, I had no such pretension. Simply waiting. A few years later, I, too, got married, but one day she left me, almost without my noticing."

He said thoughtfully:

"Since making that discovery at the *douar*, I have spoken only twice about the things that happened to us. The first time was to Jaourden, and that was 15 years ago. The second is today, to you. Only twice in 40 years . . . All that time I was waiting for I didn't know what. For fate to make amends, perhaps. Little by little, I was suffocating . . ."

He groaned, suddenly overcome by weariness:

"And my country with me . . ."

Anna opens her eyes. Her husband (nowadays, to herself, she calls him husband) brings the coffee pot to the table. He is preoccupied. She knows that he worries about her, her health, her safety and the possibility that she will be deported. She calls to him softly:

"Nassreddine . . ."

The Algerian screws up his eyes. The room is dark and his sight isn't what it was. He comes over and sits on the edge of the bed. She knows him so well, her man. He hasn't changed: attentive and wary, tender and brusque.

The old woman takes his hand: speckled, rough, criss-crossed by innumerable small veins, with its black spot whose origin has always remained a mystery. She kisses this hand, wanting to fight against this inconsolable nostalgia, wanting to tell him how happy she is at this moment.

Nassreddine murmurs:

"Do you remember *Assafi Ala Diar El Andalous* . . . ?"

"Of course: 'Great is my longing for our past in Andalusia'. You taught it to me, and you made fun of my accent!"

"We have ended up in a funny sort of Andalusia, you and I."

She tries to smile:

"Nassreddine, where did we go wrong?"

"I don't know. We were always being shipwrecked. And we were not the only ones . . ."

Both think of those whom they had loved, the twins, Aldjia, Zehra, Dahmane, Manuel, Rina. And neither confides in the other, for grief has overwhelmed them with a sudden flood of pain.

"I've been against violence all my life, Anna. To live, that was all I asked. You too, my Andalusian. And it was probably too much to ask . . . We dreamed the wrong dreams, we took the wrong turnings. But were we entirely to blame?"

Anna whispers:

"And if we had to do it all over again, Nassreddine, would we take the same road?"

Nassreddine bends over her. She guesses that he has already asked the question of himself. And because of the twins (so dead and so alive in their parents' grief) there is no answer. The man takes a grey curl from the head of this woman whom he once loved so dearly, whom he still loves, and twines it round his finger:

"We can't live in the past, my Andalusian."

He repeats, like a prayer:

"My Andalusian . . ."

He is undoing the buttons on her dress. He sees the sagging skin, then the nipples. Anna has closed her eyes. A faint blush colours her cheeks. Her husband gently strokes her belly . . .

They can hear the sound of men on their way to work in the street outside. Two women are gossiping near the window. One is telling a joke, the other laughs aloud.

Jaourden's big day has arrived. The two dromedaries are saddled and bridled. The boy is doing well now. In his heart of hearts, the old Targui thinks: "My son." Jallal calls him "Uncle". The child is always laughing. He is proud of the clothes which his "Uncle" has bought him: *cheche*, *seroual*, leather sandals. He is still a little scared of his mount, but he will soon learn to ride . . .

The Targui and the boy have long conversations, broken by painful silences whenever Jallal is suddenly reminded of certain events. He talks at length about Saïd, his terrorist friend, saying that he bears him no ill will because he didn't believe he had meant to kill.

"He wasn't like those butchers in the cave, he took me in and treated me like a brother. It's true that he was always in a bad temper, but he was a brother all the same."

The first of these conversations took place in the palm grove at Biskra. Jaourden had turned the discussion to the subject of Jallal's parents. Perhaps he should try and visit them, he suggested.

"No," shouted the boy. "I never want to see them again!"

His face taut, Jallal looked like a trapped fox. He was choking. Jaourden dropped the subject at once. It was only when they reached Tamanrasset that the boy had confided in him. They had spent all day on camel-back, the Targui having wanted to teach the little Northerner to ride before the long journey to his wife's tribe, and they hadn't exchanged a word until nightfall, when they were seated by their camp fire. Jallal began to speak of the earthquake, of the day when the family house collapsed on top of them. Him and his sister. They weren't killed, because a wall had fallen to form a sort of roof over their heads. On that fateful day, his parents had gone into town. He was seven years old at the time, his sister almost 20. The army appeared on the scene. The soldiers helped the rescue workers to search the rubble. But so many houses had been flattened that the soldiers were divided into small groups of two or three, most of which operated more or less at random, without proper direction.

"When we heard the soldiers' voices, my sister and I knew that we were saved. We had been scared that they might overlook us, for our house stood apart from the others. We shouted. They started to clear away the rubble. We soon saw them: three young soldiers about my sister's age. And my sister was very pretty . . ."

The boy stopped drawing in the sand. Jaourden didn't break the silence.

"The three soldiers raped her in front of me. I screamed for help, and they beat me with their gunbelts. When my parents returned, my sister told them everything. Her tears gushed out like water from a tap. She was half crazy. My father and mother kicked her out of the house, yelling at her that she should have defended her honour. At dawn, she left and I never saw her again."

Jallal fingered the scarf that concealed his scar.

"I worshipped my sister, Uncle. And she wasn't to blame for what happened. I was never so angry in my life. I spat on my parents and ran away. I looked for her everywhere, but couldn't find her. So the idea of going back to my parents' house . . ."

Jaourden said nothing more, and Jallal was grateful for his silence. Jaourden told himself briskly: first let him learn the ways of the desert. The rest can wait till later . . .

Jaourden has checked the saddle-bags, then the water-skins. All is ready. Jallal, excited, is seated astride his mount. The beast had stood up rather abruptly. Even though the dromedary still scares him a little, Jallal is in a particularly happy mood. Jaourden hesitates, wondering what he could have forgotten. He had settled everything with Anna and Nassreddine: the boy's schooling, money for his keep . . . Anna had said to him:

"The three of us could have brought him up together, only we haven't long to live. So, Jaourden, think of the future!"

Jallal is impatient.

"What are we waiting for, Uncle?"

The Targui, a lump in his throat, urges his dromedary forward.

"Ah, Douja, how I miss you!" he murmurs, in Tamachak.

The old, bitter anger grips him, doubling him up on the saddle. The service for the dead would take place without his wife's body. All his family would be there, the elders and the younger generation; as well as friends from every quarter of the Sahara, and their prayers would be addressed to the empty air, to the stones and the sand. Not a single tear, not a single lament, would come to comfort his wife's body in her irremediable solitude.

He kicks the dromedary into a trot to catch up with the boy, who already considers himself an accomplished rider. Jaourden's heart is heavy but, little by little, he recovers his spirits. He manages a smile beneath his blue-black veil:

"Gallop on, child! It's high time that you made friends with all your new cousins!"

Paris, Algiers, Rennes.
September, 1997.

GLOSSARY

A Baba	oh father
A Yemma	oh mother
AIS	Armée Islamique du Salut (Islamic Army of Salvation)
amenokhal	Turkish term for a local dignitary, analogous to councillor
avellemed	Berber term for someone who refuses to learn
azulejos	ornamental tiles
bachagha	French term for a Muslim dignitary (often from an elite family) acting as a go-between for the French administration and the indigenous people. *Bachaghas* were considered as traitors and collaborators by the FLN
Balek!	get out of my way/look out!
bey	Turkish title for governor
calentita	a chick-pea flan
chador	a large veil, covering head and body
Chaouï	Berber dialect of Chaouï, in the Aurès mountains
cheche	a turban
chechia	a small cap worn by Muslim men
chetaba	a broom
couffin	a shopping basket made with jute or hemp
djebels	mountains
djellaba	a cloak with a hood and wide sleeves
djinn	an evil spirit
djoundi	a soldier
douar	a small village
fellagha	Algerian partisan, committed to ridding the country of the French
FLN	Front de Libération Nationale (the Algerian Liberation Front)

gandoura	a large sleeveless tunic
gaouri/gaouria	slang for a white man/white woman
gassaa	large wooden or earthen dish for serving couscous
GIA	Groupe Islamique Armé (the Armed Islamic Group)
gomina	lotion for the hair
haik	an oblong length of cloth, worn on the head and the body
hamada	flat areas of the Sahara desert (as opposed to dunes)
hammam	a steam bath/Turkish bath
harissa	a hot chilli sauce
hogra	contempt
Inch Allah	Arabic expression meaning "God willing"
jihad	resistance/struggle; often understood to denote a holy war
kachabia	long capacious blouse
kanoun	clay or terracotta brazier
katibas	a constituency; sub-division of *wilaya*
kouba	a dome built over a marabout's, or hermit's, tomb
mahboula	a madwoman
mechta	an Algerian hamlet
meddah	(masculine)/*meddaha* (feminine) originally someone who chants verses of the Koran. Also used to refer to a troubadour
medina	the ancient, native quarter of a North African city
moudjahid	(singular)/*moudjahidine* (plural) a resistance fighter
oued	a river
rahla	an ornamental camel saddle
roumia	a white woman, a European (originally meaning a Roman)
seroual	large Arab trousers
sheik	old man
taguella	a bread baked in the sand under a camp fire
talrouda	wormwood, a bitter plant with medicinal properties, often found in arid and rocky areas
tindé	song and dance of the Touaregs
wilaya	an administrative prefecture
Ya Rabi	O God